Praise for The Captain's Witch

"Jarman's long acclaimed and award-winning skill in the field of historical fiction has here created a terrifyingly believable historical novel of another world, shot through with harsh action and lush tenderness, and a remorseless evil beyond the wildest nightmares."

—**Tanith Lee**

Praise for Rosemary Hawley Jarman

Winner of the Authors' Club Best First Novel Award

". . . a magical writer . . . her prose glows with all the vividness of a stained glass window."

—**Eastern Daily Press**

". . . a rare talent."

—**Sunday Express**

"Her characters are real and three dimensional, with dreams and feelings . . ."

—**The Anniston Star**, U.S.A.

"[Rosemary Hawley Jarman] blends the artistry of the novelist and the skills of the researcher with the magic touch of the poet."

—**Kansas City Star**, U.S.A.

"The quality of her writing lifts her books far above others of the same genre."

—**Grimsby Evening Telegraph**

"Miss Jarman has at her command a colourful style and a feeling for drama . . ."

—**Journal**, U.S.A.

This book is a work of fiction. All characters, names, locations, and events portrayed in this book are fictional or used in an imaginary manner to entertain, and any resemblance to any real people, situations, or incidents is purely coincidental.

THE CAPTAIN'S WITCH

Rosemary Hawley Jarman

Copyright © 2009 by Rosemary Hawley Jarman

All Rights Reserved.

Cover Art (details):
"Perdita" by Anthony Frederick Sandys (1829-1904); "Madame de Loynes" by Eugène-Emmanuel Amaury-Duval, 1862; "General Desaix" by Andrea I Appiani, 1800-1801; "Nova et accuratissima totius terrarum orbis tabula" by Joan Blaeu, c. 1664; "The Knight with His Hand on His Breast" by El Greco, 1577-1584.

Interior Map Copyright © 2005 by Jon Parsons

Author Photograph Copyright © by Peter Pritchard

Cover Design Copyright © 2009 by Vera Nazarian

ISBN-13: 978-1-60762-046-4
ISBN-10: 1-60762-046-4

Trade Paperback Newly Revised Edition

November 5, 2009

A Publication of
Norilana Books
P. O. Box 2188
Winnetka, CA 91396
www.norilana.com

Printed in the United States of America

The Captain's Witch

Norilana Books
Fantasy

www.norilana.com

Her kiss can maim you
Her eyes can blind you
Her bed is shadows . . .

She is the dark of the moon
She is all that is dear
And she is death

Can you trust her?
Where will her lantern lead you?
To the bliss of death
Or the death of bliss

Know the most dangerous of all . . .

The Captain's Witch

Rosemary Hawley Jarman

The Lions of Taratamia

THE LION OF DAY
Wears Sun-globe on head, protects during daylight

THE LION OF NIGHT
Wears horned crescent, protects by night

THE LION OF POWER
Symbol of rulers and protection

THE LION OF WAR
Rampant with raised tail

THE LION OF CHIVALRY
Diplomatic lion rampant with raised paw

THE LION OF GRACE
Variable stance, for festive occasions

THE LION OF STONE
Couchant, effigy, for desperate times

THE CRYSTAL LION
Occult lion, most powerful, seldom seen

For Tanith Lee
who lit my way to fantasy
with love

Foreword
by Rosemary Hawley Jarman

First let me express my delight in being introduced to Norilana Books and its illustrious director, Vera Nazarian. This novel was written at the suggestion of Tanith Lee, mistress of sublime classic fantasy, to whom the book is dedicated.

Until now I have dealt only with painstakingly researched European historical fiction. *The Captain's Witch* proved to be a surprising refreshment—I was totally in charge. Some of the characters had their being in facets of people who once lived. Small liberties were taken with armour and fashion. The Taratamian and Karenian armies do not behave in the exact manner of modern troops, although there is a strong element of discipline from their high command. Neither, for plot's sake, do they yet have explosives.

I have always been drawn to the grandiose splendour of the 19th Century Austro-Hungarian empire. Those who may recall the novels of Anthony Hope (*The Prisoner of Zenda, et al.*), will be familiar with Ruritania, that fictional kingdom seething with glamour and intrigue. I believe that a similar atmosphere inhabits the climate of my Captain and his cohorts—beautiful men in glittering uniforms, luscious ladies, war and honour.

Anthony Hope's mythical kingdom became the setting for Ivor Novello's stage musicals in the 1930s and '40s; my world exists in an emotional verisimilitude. So, although a *bona fide* historian, it gives great satisfaction to shape my own courts, citizens and customs, religions, feuds, politics and alliances. Sometimes these reveal parallels to the real world, but they are still tailored to my libertine specifications.

Fantasy writing, I discover, is serious. True *gravitas* must obtain. These people are real, and all this narrative is as telling as a history which never happened—(and as someone said recently—"but which should have done"). In my historical world, the black arts run in tandem with acts of great heroism, love, cruelty, terror, murder and passion. The right *may* triumph, eventually, in this world within a world.

Immense thanks are due to Linda Reynertson, a most professional and very dear friend, for her tireless and immaculate work on the presentation of this enhanced, new version.

Long live Taratamia!

ROSEMARY HAWLEY JARMAN
2009

The Captain's Witch

Prologue

The child, a girl, had been born. After loudly protesting at this event, it now slept soundly in the royal cradle. A winter storm grumbled outside, but within the thick walls of the queen's birth-bower there was calm, and a great log fire casting light and shadow and warmth.

The palace at Karlinkis had settled for the night. King Enial had retired after surveying his new daughter, while the young mother lay exhausted in a bed carved with the royal arms of Karenia.

Queen Doro's eyes searched for her favourite chamberwoman, who bent tenderly over the cradle.

"Malkar, how is she?"

"The little Honyia is tranquil, highness. All's well. The name you chose suits her, madam. Honyia—honour. It befits such a sweet princess."

Malkar left the cradle. She was so beautiful that even the weary Doro found comfort in the sight of her. She stretched out her hand.

"Stay by me, Malkar. I am so tired."

"I'll not leave you, highness darling."

She crossed the chamber, soundless, fluent. She wore black, and her going about was like the soft dark curve of a sea wave.

"Sleep a little now, my love. I am near."

Doro closed her eyes. She was childlike, frail. A little frown lay between her soft dark brows. Malkar had given her an opiate, and it soon began to take effect.

Malkar waited. Then delicately she took the covers from the queen, drawing away stained cloths. It had been a difficult birth. Doro lay naked from the waist down. Malkar bent and tongued the queen's vulva lightly. After a moment, a thin bright thread of fresh blood appeared.

Malkar moved away, to stand by the blazing hearth. Firelight limned her, gilding her darkness, and the flames seemed to fold themselves inward, abashed.

She looked down briefly at the child. Seas froze in her eyes. Her gaze, dispassionate, moved again to the queen. The thread of blood had thickened, emerging in strong jets, one for each heartbeat. The bedlinen was darkening.

A change came upon Malkar. What stood in her place was unwitnessed. It was as well that the queen's eyes were closed. The change was momentary, almost subliminal.

She left the chamber and went out into the quiet passage, down a stone spiral into a labyrinth, to a door subtly set into the wall. A merman's face, with seaweed hair and long protruding tongue was carved into the lintel. She touched the tongue; the door opened. Thus she entered into her sanctum.

No one came here. Lanterns in the form of spire shells burned amber. The air seemed to have almost the density of water. The ghost of a jellyfish, tentacles trailing, drifted by and vanished, ephemeral as the mote in an eye. In a tall black mirror, Malkar gleamed like a spirit. Her beauty declared itself. She could have been an actress, adored by multitudes; a paltry destiny she would have held in contempt.

The sea, with its eternal energy, was her familiar. The deeps were within her, and without. In silence, she addressed them.

"Malkar is ready."

There came the rush of thousand-year-old seas, as if she stood within a conch. What had been assimilated over the eons had attained a balance. This was woman; its form suited the darkness well for the present. Malkar, the Subtle One, the waiter on change and chance. Her latent power was a hunger; she trembled from it.

Enough time had passed. She quit her sanctum. In the passage the night guard were drowsy, lulled by her distant oceans. It was time to rouse King Enial with news of Doro's collapse. Many times had Malkar been to the king's chamber; his son already grew within her.

II

So began the age of the enchantresses.

Poor Doro laid to rest in a pearl-encrusted mausoleum guarded by carved sea serpents and merpeople. Little Doro, face and body white as if sculpted in chalk and no sign that she had ever been a bride, woman, mother. King Enial wept, slightly bewildered, his tears salty with a guilt that faded soon.

Baby Honyia hustled away with a nurse to the farthest chambers of the palace, thereafter seldom seen.

A season or two of ripening.

The royal heir, Crown Prince Vergon—a disappointment. A grizzling, spindly toddler with a talent for cruelty—insects, small animals, mutely suffering servants.

The pearl and crystal diadem on Malkar's head. Long live Queen Malkar of Karenia.

The besotted King imprisoned by love of this powerful undine—bound by her tides, pouring his lust into her, so that now the beautiful Queen Malkar was with child again.

A daughter. The inheritrix, the hope of Malkar's mysteries. The heir to immortality and strength unimaginable. Labour was imminent.

The child's name had already been decided by Enial, doting father. Lilene. The holy lily symbol, pure as a white wave, deceitful as a straight horizon over an uncertain sea.

Now.

The lily-maid coming, and coming slow.

Night. Black satin drapes, coloured candles in bowls of pearl, and barely a sound, only something unseen outside on the sill, biting the glass, clawing to come in.

The Queen supine on her bed. No midwives, no chamberers, or nurse of any sort.

"I will birth my daughter alone."

And she had smiled, a shimmering smile that blinded with beauty the throng who waited on her, a smile to make them tremble and back away, feeling as if they had all been washed by a black salt wave and cast up, exhausted, on shingle.

This was a birth of rare reluctance, of a creature unwilling to venture through the dark silken loins.

A time of unforseen pain, suffered with resentment. The Queen strained. Allowed the tiniest moan.

King Enial stood outside the door, biting his fingers. He turned to the tall slim woman at his side.

"Andine, I am so afraid. It is not nature to deliver unattended. She could die!"

"Highness, be easy. She will not die."

Andine folded her arms inside the white habit she wore. She was training to become a nun. Her hair, the colour of sunlight through clear honey, was braided round her brow. She somewhat resembled the King, although race and religion divided them; the bright hair, blue eyes, the same strong beauty. No, Malkar will not die, she thought. The gods are sleeping.

"You are a comfort, Andine," said the King. "Your visit came at the right time. You will be able to bless the child."

"Then I must return to the House of Brides."

"It is sad that our faiths divide us."

Andine shook her head, smiling. "It need not be so. You were once husband of my poor sister. You have the Pearl. I have the Lion, and we are at peace . . ."

"Hush!" he said. "I thought I heard Malkar cry. Oh, gods! we must send for the midwife . . ."

Andine said steadily. "No. Let me go in."

She stood on tiptoe and touched the King's cheek with her own, which was unflawed as a peach, and the next moment had slipped through into the Queen's chamber. All the candles in the corridor suddenly dipped and died, leaving Enial in darkness.

In the chamber light was undiminished. Andine went steadily to the bed, praying under her breath.

"O Lion of Night, protect us. O Lion of Grace, defend us. Be on our right hand and our left . . ."

What lay on the bed was Malkar and not Malkar. It was not pleasant to look upon. It was unconscious. The child was out. It lay couched against its mother's thigh; a tiny, perfect babe, snuffling contentedly, moving its limbs in an oddly sensual way, exposing its sex like a miniature courtesan. There was only a little birth-blood, and its head was covered with a thick gleaming cap of golden hair.

As Andine watched, the child turned its head and curling into a ball, chumbled and bit at its umbilical cord until it parted. And then the beautiful babe looked straight at Andine with the bluest eyes she had ever seen, bluer even than her father's, and smiling very knowingly. And Andine said very softly: "Lilene." The smile was replaced by fear.

"Lilene," said Andine even more softly. "You are a witch, born of a witch, but now you are mine, and I have come to release you."

A moan, from the bed, a moan more like a growl.

One swift glance showed Andine the figure on the bed. Deeply unconscious, Malkar's beauty was returning, her eyelids flickered: she was fighting to awaken.

Andine whispered: "O Lion, great and merciful Lion, assist me . . .She held out her arms. *Go from her, witch.*"

"Come to me, Lilene."

There was a smear of blood from the natal string at the corner of the baby's mouth, and an unnatural glitter in the blue eyes. Andine's heart thudded painfully against her ribs. Help me, she whispered.

It was the first time in her novitiate that she had used the Lion-power. She had been drawn to Karenia from her homeland by a dream of demons. She stared at the child, holding out her arms. She called aloud on the Lion of Power, the Lion of Grace, the Lion of War, the Lion of Stone. A turbulence arose in the chamber. The air swirled, an invisible tornado, battering all within, and Andine felt her strength begin to wane, just as Malkar came out of sleep.

She had been warned against summoning the most powerful of the gods. Yet now, as the baby turned away and started to crawl up the bed into the mother's orbit, Andine was desperate. She called, she screamed on the Crystal Lion.

It formed a mist like a million shivering diamonds, a weightless net filling the chamber. Its image was immense yet ephemeral. Its outline shifted and shimmered, enveloping the child in a crystal caul, and lifting her in the air.

Malkar, fully awake, screamed curses at Andine, rising from the bed. Each word felt like a blow to the head; even then Andine held fast, to her purpose. She called Malkar by her known name, her secret, sea-demon name.

"Back, Maelikali! Release the child!"

Malkar spat venom into the mist. It dissipated, sucked away to the four corners of the room. The babe hung for a moment in the ether, then dropped on the bed like a bomb. Malkar clutched her to her breast.

"My beautiful one!" she cried. "Look! Look at the new witch!"

Lilene was crying and screaming. The last of Andine's power was ebbing away. A frisson seized her face and head, as if from a douche of iced water. And Malkar was laughing, clutching her weeping daughter. Laughing, mocking, pointing to a large mirror.

Andine turned and saw. Her hair was white as frost, and the flesh of her face was corrugated, lined as a rainless desert. Gaunt, gaunt and old. Even then she managed to say, weakly: "Lilene. You are mine!"

Malkar's reply, stinging with contempt:

"Leave our palace, old woman. And send a wetnurse. Malkar does not give suck."

Andine crawled sobbing from the chamber. Enial passed her without a second glance, hurrying to his Queen.

There had been one last flash from the tearfilled blue eyes of the child. Sorrow? Regret?

Oh, Lion. One last hope?

PART ONE

Sources

Almost twenty years later, a company was crossing the harsh northern border from Taratamia into Karenia. They came at last over Singstar Pass in a blistering wind that stretched their skin like fire. One hundred men, half mounted, half on foot, they crossed the Tiranian mountains by the safer of two passes. To the west lay Knife Pass with its easier terrain, yet closer to the coast and what might lie out to sea beyond. Hooves and feet sliding on hard shale, they went through rock canyons and saw their destination beyond steep green foothills. Karenia.

Two men on beautiful horses headed the column. They rode before the standard bearer who held high the snapping flapping banner of the northern kingdom whence they had come. Its device was a lion rampant with raised paw, snarling at the wind, opals worked into the brocade at its eyes.

The younger of the two leaders stood in his stirrups to look over the slope at the valley and the expanse of yellow-green flatland stretching to the horizon. Closer than that were two fortresses, one built on either side of the mouth of the pass. As the party came nearer, the bristle of spears could be seen, and men with loaded ballistas behind the walls.

"They're taking no chances." Lieutenant Narzet was gazing high over his mount's head. "They surely know our mission. Don't they, Captain?"

The Captain gave him a neutral sideways look. He sounds nervous, he thought, not answering. Well, he is only eighteen. This is the first time he's been across the frontier. I recall the first time I came to Karenia. Ten years ago—I was twenty-two. And I too was uneasy even though our countries had signed the peace. There is something about Karenia that sits ill with the heart. Too much blood hangs round it.

"Captain?" said Lieutenant Narzet, a little louder. He had a pretty baby-face which looked as if it rarely needed shaving, and large blue eyes. Long ago his ancestors had migrated from south to north, and he was a throwback to his Karenian forbears.

"Captain Tallis?"

The Captain looked at him, fully this time. What has he to be frightened of? he thought. He's never even seen action. His commission stems from his being the son of one of the king's favourites. He should have been in at our last battle against the Despran invaders, when we slogged it out, our backs to Avatal Bay on the treacherous western peninsular of Kardespra, when the blood ran down the rocks, and those barbarians kept coming . . . he'll see action soon enough. When we, the men of Taratamia and our dubious Karenian allies have to arm against another invasion. For it's said, kill a Despran and two spring up, like the monsters in legend. It's not his fault. All the same, I wish they'd sent me someone with a few scars.

"Indeed they know our mission, lieutenant," he said calmly. "You carry our credentials at your saddle, so I trust. A party like us coming over the Tiranians without good reason might raise a few eyebrows."

He glanced back to see that the column marched in order. Cavalry and footsoldiers were all armed, ceremonial tabards over their mail, their red and silver device catching the light. This was a detachment of the Red Royals, the active arm of the Household guard at the capital, Tam, in the far northwest. The company travelled well despite their fatigue after the long miles to the frontier.

The lieutenant readied his scroll of despatches, signed and sealed by the chamberlain of King Valm the Seventh in the great palace of Tam.

"Frontier guards first," said the Captain. "Then through customs. And you can be sure those bastards will try to hold us up."

There's still enmity, he thought, gently easing his mare round some fallen boulders. It's mutual. There, my beauty. He stroked her neck. She was the colour of old gold, her bridle dagged with silver weaving, bells jingling at her martingale, music to match the diplomacy of their coming. He leaned out of the saddle to watch her deftly lifting her feet around the obstruction, then straightened to survey the armed men strung out across the road.

The sergeant who stepped forward was tall, a short angry fringe of the white-blond Karenian hair visible under his round helmet. He wore wolfskin over his mail. His unfriendly eyes were prussian blue, his complexion the peach-tan of the Karenians, raddled from months of high frontier duty.

"Papers."

Lieutenant Narzet handed over his leather scroll. The guard drew out the contents and read, frowning as if seeking some hint of treason, magic or chicanery.

"These seem in order." He glanced over the column. "There's a lot of steel back in your ranks."

Nasty, suspicious cretin, thought the Captain. He's acting as if we were still at war. Doubtless he wishes we were. He kneed his mare forward.

"I am Captain Tallis, of the Taratamian Red Royals," he said frigidly. "And yes, sergeant, we are as stated—escort detail for the Duchess of Mayt. We're to fetch her Grace from the House of Brides down south and bring her back over the mountains to Tam. There's my reason for our full arms. Don't tell me, sergeant, there are no bandits left in the high Tiranians."

This brought grunted respect. "Ah. Oh. As you say, sir." Then: "Is it a fact, Captain, that the duchess is to marry your Crown Prince?"

"It's no secret," said Tallis. A gust of wind flapped the lieutenant's cloak against the face of Tallis's mare and she started. Tallis gentled her, staring at the sergeant with his deepset eyes. They were cold, brilliant eyes, a clear, blacklashed grey. The sergeant studied him while Tallis in turn assessed the sergeant. He's old enough, he thought. He could have been there when they killed my father. I wonder.

And the sergeant saw a slender, taut man, not tall, dressed in the scarlet tunic of the Red Royals, silver frogging across the chest, silver buttons and epaulettes, tight breeches and thigh-boots. A black and silver cloak lay spread out behind over his mount's quarters. Beneath a peaked cap with a short plume the Captain's pitch-black hair hung to his shoulders. His pale face was stern, spare. A thin white scar, almost invisible, ran diagonally across his lips. He had strong, beautifully shaped hands. He was at first illusory glance, inconspicuous. He could be part of the landscape, of a crowd. And he had killed his first man when he was seven years old.

Behind the fortress ramparts the slingmen relaxed their tension on the ballistas primed with great stones. The company moved forward where they were met at the further end of the pass by another party, brandishing parchments and tallysticks and all the paraphernalia of the customs office.

"Do you bring silver?"

"Only what we wear."

The lieutenant did the answering.

"You are aware of the new import tax on silver."

"No imported silver."

And no gold either, or fine horses, or black beer to sell, or weaving. Nor rare birds from the mountains, nor any of the prime opals from the Taratamian mine, opals for which the Karenian royalty and their multitude of sycophants paid high prices. The chief customs officer cast an eye over the line of fidgeting horsemen and footsoldiers.

"What's in the baggage?" He pointed at coffers tied on to pack mules.

Tallis's patience was shortening. He said brusquely: "Gifts. Tribute for the Abbess Andine at the House of Brides, and somewhat for her to pass on in homage to King Enial."

The latter gifts were placatory. The young Duchess of Mayt's betrothal to the Taratamian Crown Prince Rost had displeased Karenia, for her heir, Prince Vergon, fancied himself for her suitor. The Duchy of Mayt was fabulously rich from time immemorial, and there were no male heirs.

"Pass on," said the customs officer. The party gathered itself together and crunched forward over shale and rock, moving through a giant stone arch to begin the easy descent of the foothills.

Lieutenant Narzet stared excitedly ahead.

"The plain of Tirkar."

The greenish-yellow span lay like a lion before them. Tallis also regarded it, without relish.

Down there my father died. Shamefully. Not killed in fair fight over that coveted, arid terrain, nub of the long wars ended finally by the Treaty of Braf. He died shamefully. Horribly. In despair.

"Yes. Bloody Tirkar. Ceded to Karenia through necessity, lieutenant. You wouldn't remember all that."

"Oh, I do, Captain," Narzet said eagerly. "The original boundary was the River Takk. The plague forced the ceding of the land. That, and the mountains."

Tallis nursed his mount down a steepish bit of path, saying, "it was the transportation of arms and men and supplies down over the mountains. Especially under snow. The Tamian plague was only the final cut. That, and the failure of our wheat crop."

They had reached level ground. The horses pricked forward, renewed. Behind them, the infantry trudged stoutly. To the east they saw an enormous outcrop of high rock. From its hollow maw a stream of burdened people went in and out. On the wind came the faint sounds of a mine being worked: the heavy scraping of metal on stone, the clang and whine of pulleys and tackle. The richest gold mine of north or south, the reason for the boundary war which had cost so many lives.

The company veered eastward over the plain. They passed close enough for a view of the miners hacking at the grey rockface and trundling carts out of the dark gape of the mine under the eye of an overseer.

"They look poor," Narzet was staring. "And some are very young."

A stream ran beside the mouth of the mine and there, panning gold on flat rocks were women, their hair hidden under cotton rags, their bodies thin and threadbare. Some had babies in slings on their backs. There were children employed too, some no older than six, barefoot, dirt-streaked. One was crying; its thin, exhausted keening echoed the chilly wind.

The overseer's whip had a long lash. He made it sing on the air, as if he liked its rough music. A big blond man, he strolled among the decrepit pack, their lord and king. The whip pointed to a small bundle lying beside one of the women. The overseer's mouth moved in a command, and the woman argued weakly, spreading her hands.

"He wants her to open it," said Lieutenant Narzet.

Tallis was not staring like Narzet, but one glance had shown him wickedness.

The overseer flicked his whip in an arc round the woman's neck and shoulders and she staggered. The tail of the blow caught her child across the face. It let out a birdlike scream. The overseer kicked the bundle; a little round of bread and cheese rolled from it. "By the gods," said Narzet. "Look at that."

"He suspected she was stealing gold dust," Tallis said. He clamped his mouth shut.

"Gods," said Narzet again. "We don't treat our people like that."

"Ride on," said Tallis, turning his face away. In profile it was hawklike, hard and for the moment, merciless with anger. This bloody country. No, indeed, lieutenant, Taratamia does not use her people like beasts. We are proud of our firm compassionate laws. They are part of our honour. He shook off his fury and applied himself again to the mission in hand. The column moved steadily across the plain.

Soon enough, they had put days between themselves and the gold workers. They camped as evenings fell. Even the dusk had a subtle difference in Karenia; the sunset, a crystalline orange in the west, seemed to have a cloying decadence, a promise of wickedness when the sun had gone. Away from the mountains, it was almost possible to imagine warmth on the breeze from the far south, the coast where they were bound.

At the small villages through which they passed, people, mute, dull-eyed, came from their shanties to watch the procession. The first small town appeared on the edge of a pine forest, far north of the River Takk, site of the old boundary, when plain and mine belonged to Taratamia. Low grey buildings lined cobbled streets. Garbage heaps smoked in derelict squares. Dogs and crows scavenged in the choked gutters. Shabby folk went unsmiling about their business.

"And this is Karenia," muttered the lieutenant. "I thought they were rich."

"You'll see a difference when we get to the coast," said Tallis. "And down there," he pointed south-west, "on the banks of Lake Sigillan, there are villas. Full of vermin."

"Rats?" cried Lieutenant Narzet. Tallis laughed joylessly.

"Karenian lords," he said. "As I say. Vermin. Here's an inn. Big enough for us all, I hope." He turned in the saddle and called to a sergeant. "Keep the party in line, Delvas."

The inn was huge, its grim facade of dirty brown stones visible through a crumbling arch. There were rows of stables on the perimeter of the courtyard. As the party came under the arch, the fat landlord, wearing a grimy apron, came to the door. Tallis dismounted. The standard-bearer furled his banner, cancelling formality.

The Captain walked, stretching his limbs, towards the innkeeper. He glanced up at the swinging sign beneath the ale-bush. Great grey lips, half-open, and above them a pearl diadem. The Oyster and Crown.

The landlord bulked in the doorway.

"We're full up."

Tallis smiled coldly. "Travellers keeping you busy?" He waved a hand towards the row of empty stables. "All on foot, then, out here?"

He looked deep and hard into the landlord's puffy eyes, which shifted at once. "One hundred men," said Tallis. "Drinking. Make you rich for a moonspan."

"Quarter karin per man," muttered the landlord.

"Split that, and we'll do business. Most of my men will sleep with the horses. And no charge for the horses."

"You Tamian robber" said the landlord under his breath, but he was mostly wind. "Done, then. And no brawling. And leave my women be."

Tallis smiled faintly. He turned to his officers. "See to the mounts, Sergeant Delvas. Then join us in this louse-house. Come, lieutenants. By the Lion, I need my boots off."

They entered quietly, the Captain, Narzet, two other lieutenants, Pinpol and Recansky, the standard-bearer Kal, and after a time, Sergeant Delvas and his companion, Sergeant Mollane. Narzet made for one of the long tables in the centre, but Tallis steered him to the wall, sitting down with his back to it. The heavy oak table where they sat was scarred with knives and bleached in circles from spilled drink.

Carpeted with grubby straw the barnlike room was hazy with smoke from the hearth. A turnspit tended huge meats. A bird was flying back and forth in the rafters. The windows were opaque with grime. A merchant and his family were dining and two men played bugle dice at a board in the corner. But at the longest table by the door sat a dozen Karenian soldiers. Already they had cast whispering glances towards Tallis's party, and had vented a few uncompliments. Now they were shouting for more drink, groping the girls who came to serve them, and pounding the board in time to a dirty song.

One of the wenches pranced over to the Captain's table.

"Let's have some Karenian wine," said Narzet eagerly. "They say it's strong."

"Wine for my company," Tallis told the girl. And quietly to Narzet: "Go easy with it." Narzet was eyeing up the woman, a luscious blonde with great tan breasts. She winked at Narzet.

"I've never had a Karenian woman," said Narzet as the girl went off.

Nor any sort of woman, thought Tallis accurately.

The wine arrived in an enormous tin jug which looked as if it had been used in a kicking game.

"A health to King Valm," said Tallis formally, raising his cup.

"Long life," they answered. "Salute the Lion. Health to Capashenet. Royal House forever."

The toast, and the silence in which it was drunk, alerted the Karenian soldiers. Bleary looks targeted the little company. An elephantine witticism was followed by a roar of mirth. Tallis watched them, moodily, swallowing a little wine, his knife poised over untasted food. Fatigue gripped him, and he shook it off. The others were shovelling down roast pork and the wine-jug was emptying fast.

"There's no wine like Karenian wine. Makes you forgive them almost anything," said Lieutenant Recansky.

No, thought Tallis. Not so. Never. His eyes were working over the soldiers, minutely assessing them. White-blond hair, typical of the country. Sound legs, to a man. No deformity of hands. The one he sought, day after day, was not among them. And they were all far too young, anyway.

"He had at some time taken a leg wound," General Camlot had told him, all those years ago. "And he drank a lot. His hair was the colour of fire embers. And he had a sixth finger on the one hand."

Not today, thought Tallis. But one day I will find him. Before my life is done. My father's murderer.

The gang at the far table was singing. Their song had become political.

> *"There was a fierce old kitty cat,*
> *Its paw upon a golden mat,*
> *There came a pearly wind one day*
> *And snatched the kitty's rug away.*
> *Poor old cat, yo, ho, yo!"*

One of the drunks got down in the straw. He rolled over and over, rose, essayed a slinking gait, mocking a feline, yowling, sitting up and, with a clenched fist, pretended to wash behind his fair-fringed ears.

His friends guffawed and howled.

Lieutenant Pinpol half rose. His sword blade lisped, emerging from its scabbard.

"Sit down," said Tallis quietly.

Very slowly Pinpol sat, breathing out long and hard.

"Filth," he said. "Whoresons. Offal."

"Just so," said Tallis.

He pushed his plate away for the woman to clear. "And we're across their border, emissaries for Capashenet. Just because they lack manners, we needn't debase ourselves."

The fat innkeeper was plying the soldiers with more drink, sending girls over to cosset them. They grew noisier. The clown made miaowing sounds.

"How in the Lion's name, do you keep your temper?" Lieutenant Pinpol was still in a rage.

"With considerable difficulty," said Tallis. "Time we slept. We've a long road tomorrow."

Narzet shook the empty wine-jug, cast a last look of lust at the blonde bargirl, and, with the others, rose. To reach the sleeping quarters they had to cross the room, passing the drinkers' table.

Kal, the standard-bearer, loosely holding the pole with its draped colours, brought up the rear. He was nearly past the soldiers' table when the pantomime cat spat in his direction. "Good night, kitties," he cried inanely. A drift of spittle landed on the hanging fringe of the Taratamian banner, and Tallis, half-turning, saw this.

One moment he was an almost insubstantial shape, a passing shadow. The next he was a thing of flame and movement, of action so swift that its lunge startled everyone within reach. One instant the soldier was reeling and mocking on his bench; the next he was flat on his back in the straw, with Tallis's booted legs astride him, and Tallis's sword-point lodged at the base of his throat, where one bead of blood sprang, with a heavy silence falling on the room like snow.

The Karenian sergeant-at-arms emitted an obscenity. A couple of his company unsteadily half-rose, but most remained, asprawl yet rigid, their eyes transfixed by the tableau. Tallis's glance flicked upward. His ice-grey eyes had changed; the pupils were large, black with fury.

Without looking down, he said softly: "Beg the pardon of my country. Loud, so all can hear."

He pressed a fraction on the sword-tip. The bead of blood became a cherry.

"Pardon," gargled the man. "Pardon, Taratamia."

"Louder," said Tallis. His sword held the man, his eyes held the company. Behind him the room was emptying; the family had vanished and the players were abandoning their game.

"I beg pardon!" A choking shout. "Pardon, Capashenet."

"Kal, bring the flag." The youth came, unfurling the standard.

"Kiss our colours," said the Captain. With difficulty, the man twisted his head and pathetically mouthed the fringe. Slowly Tallis withdrew his weapon and the man heaved upright. Tallis surveyed the company. Almost twice our number. Angry now, like bees rattled in a honey hive. Then he heard the steel-shift behind him and knew that Narzet stood close, and felt the ready presence of the others. Thank the gods I rationed our wine enough to keep our edge. These drunks are slow. They're on furlough, possibly from Fort Nial in the far west, without backup. We have nearly a hundred men outside. This could become an incident.

And even now, with his comrades gathered close, the old feeling of aloneness came upon him. He felt as if he had always, would always, remain alone in the universe. He had felt its unexpected creeping presence even in the middle of roistering midnight company. A cold, unvarying aloneness, inexorable as death.

In the silence he heard Narzet's hard breathing, and saw from the tail of his eye the firelight shimmer on his half-raised blade. None of the Karenian party had yet drawn a weapon. They sat gazing at Tallis, or at their lightly bleeding companion.

The Karenian sergeant-at-arms was coming slowly to his feet.

"You . . ." he began aggressively. Suddenly, the trapped swallow, who had been flying distractedly in the rafters all evening, darted down across the table. As it dived away, it lifted its wings and excreted precisely on the sweaty brow of the man Tallis had wounded. And the one next to him said, with a guffaw: "It's just not your day, Carel!"

The awful tension was shattered beyond repair. All the Karenians were laughing like fools, banging the table and one anothers' shoulders.

"Our apologies, Captain," drawled the sergeant unexpectedly. "Our friend stepped over the line. It's his birthday . . ." This last evoked a further howl of mirth from the others.

"Your apology is accepted." Tallis sheathed his sword contemptuously. He gave the sergeant a cursory salute and marched from the room, past the cross landlord, who glowered in silence. The Karenians had started a new song, filthy but inoffensive.

The last light was bleeding from the sky over the ponderous gable of the inn. Torches set into the courtyard walls burned smokily. A staircase to the sleeping quarters rose on the outside of the building.

"Early road tomorrow," said Tallis. "Pinpol. Recansky." The others saluted goodnight and began the climb to bed. Narzet lingered.

"Aren't you coming, Captain?"

"I'll look in on the animals."

Narzet fell into step beside him, going to where the barnlike stables were warm with hay and the breath of horses, beside which scores of men were bedded down. Tallis observed that guards had been posted at his orders on the coffers of tribute. He found his mare, her head in a nosebag, one dark pool of eye visible. Gently he buried his fingers in the coarse, slightly oily roots of her mane, running his hand down the warm damask muscle of her neck. She shivered and munched her feed. Tallis and Narzet left the stable and moved on the perimeter of the yard.

It was quiet now. The Karenian party had succumbed to wine. A white owl drifted over the housetop. A quarter-moon had risen, almost obscured by cloud.

"Rain tomorrow, d'you think?" asked Narzet just as the quietness was sliced apart. A cry not unlike that of the owl; a frightened, angry human protest followed by a swish and a thud. The noise was repeated. Tallis began to walk towards its source, a group of buildings adjacent to the landlord's living quarters.

"We'll take a look."

They tracked the dim glow of a lantern to a stable door. Inside, a fat man was trying to wrest a whip from the hands of a young boy. Behind them a wild-eyed horse reared and lashed out at the wooden stall.

"Let go, damn your soul. You'll be next!"

The man rocked and wrestled. The whip was held fast.

"You-will-not-hit-him!"

The boy lowered his head and charged the man's belly, losing his hold on the whip. It rose and came down hard on the flank of the shivering horse. Tallis burst through the doorway, knocking the fat man to the ground. The boy sprang past them both, flinging his arms protectively round the horse's neck.

Another Karenian in the straw, thought Narzet. We're making few friends tonight.

"Up," said Tallis, and the fat man struggled to his feet. He was quite young, with an ale-paunchy face. The Captain seized the whip and began methodically beating the man about his lardy shoulders. He howled like a dog.

"How do you like it?" asked Tallis, laying on hard.

"Ow, it hurts, it hurts. Mercy."

"Yes, it hurts." Tallis flung the whip as far as possible through the door across the courtyard. "You son of a whore. Is this animal your property?"

"My father's," said the fat man, in tears. "Keeper of this inn."

The angry voice of the youth came from the shadows. "You bully. Swine. There, Brushwood. He'll not hurt you again."

"He needs discipline," sulked the fat young man. "Brute beasts need beating."

Tallis hit him again, this time with his fist, and the man cannoned off the stall with the sound of a thrown ale-bag.

"Come on. Hit me," said Tallis. "I'm only a brute beast."

Unwisely, the young man squared up and poked the air near Tallis's head. And found himself down again among the nervous horse's dung.

"I'll tell your dad!" shrieked the boy from the shadows. "I'll tell him you thrashed Brushwood!" The fat man crawled up. Plastered and reeking, he escaped across the yard. The youth—short, thin, dirty-faced, stared up at Tallis with big blue hollow eyes.

Tallis briefly sucked his knuckles and stared back. The lanternlight glazed his face, the cold eyes, the sharp cheekbones, the scarred mouth. The dirty-faced boy's glance never faltered.

"Why didn't you kill him?" he demanded. "You've a weapon. He was beating Brushwood just because he threw him today. His father thinks he's no good anyway. You ought to have killed him."

Lieutenant Narzet said brusquely, "Mind your manners, child. You're talking to a Tamian Captain of the Red Royals." Beside a pair of tattered breeches and tunic the boy wore a big slouch cap, tightly fitting and pulled down over his ears. "Show respect," said Narzet, and snatched the cap from the boy's head. Skeins and swathes of hair, which had it not been so dirty would have shone mint-gold, descended thick and free, waist-long and falling about the pale grimy face.

She looked older than in her male masquerade. She brushed back the hair impatiently and stared on at Tallis, who registered faint surprise, unlike Narzet, whose mouth was agape.

"You should have killed him," she repeated, but softer, her voice now recognisably feminine.

"Perhaps I should," said Tallis.

Narzet said: "Why, in the name of the gods, do you dress as a knave?"

"I'm the groom of the stable," she said. Her big eyes in their shadowy sockets travelled over Tallis in his smart uniform. "And I dress like this so I shan't go the way my mother did, with men."

"Your mother?" asked Narzet.

"Dead, of me. She used to serve the ale. No one knows my father. This crew"—she jerked her thumb towards the landlord's lodging, "brought me up. I work for my food. Soon, I shall shear all this"—she tugged at her hair—"and join the army."

Narzet laughed out loud. Tallis smiled faintly.

"I love horses," said the boy-girl. "Better than cursed people. I could tend the army's horses. No one would know the truth."

"Go on with you," said Narzet. He laughed again, and yawned, glancing at the Captain.

"Take me with you," the girl demanded, looking hard at Tallis. "I could fight."

"Are you crazy? This is a mans' army. Anyway, we're not afield. This is a Court mission."

As Tallis moved from the stable, the girl stayed on his heels for a moment. "Take me with you," she whispered. The whisper followed him like a ghost; the shadows swallowed her. "Take me away!" The hunting owl screamed.

"Strange child," said Tallis, aloft in his quarters at last. "Gods, I need a bath. Turn in, Narzet." He came with him briefly into the rickety gallery, along which the snores of the sergeants resounded. "Thanks for your sword-arm tonight. I knew you were right behind me." Gratified, the lieutenant left him.

Alone, Tallis stripped his uniform and hung it on a broken chair. He lowered himself into a tin tub of warm water and lay there, letting the tension go from his bones. He closed his eyes, and thought over the day. The Karenians have not improved since the signing of the Treaty of Braf. Still aggressive, still contemptuous of the House of Capashenet. We've not done with them. It's only the threat of Despra, our common enemy, that keeps them reasonably sweet. And King Enial isn't what he once was. Rumour tells how it isn't mere old age either. The power, if one can believe it, lies in daintier hands. The Queen. Malkar. Suddenly chill, he reached for more hot water. He had never seen Malkar, but had heard of her legendary beauty. He had no particular curiosity to verify the legend and would probably, he thought, never do so. Certainly not on this expedition. He thought: get down southeast as fast as possible, pay our respects to the Abbess Andine at the House of Brides, then gather up the duchess and bear her quickly and safely back north to the arms of her betrothed. No need to venture westward, anywhere near Karlinkis and the Royal Court... he opened his eyes, suddenly alert. A faint rustling noise was coming from beneath the rickety bed against the wall. Rats.

Dripping, he came from the tub, and with a broom poked under the bed. A small cry issued forth.

"Show yourself."

Out crawled the girl, rubbing her bruised bottom, and filthier than ever from the floor.

"And I only left the room for a second," said Tallis. "I should have known. I ought to throw you down the stairs."

"But you won't," said the girl, her eyes fixed, as before, on Tallis's. Tallis realised he was naked, and restored his dignity with a towel. He was greatly irritated.

"Before you ask, no, and again, no," he said crossly. "Women don't march with armies, only camp-followers. And you say you want to keep yourself chaste. Gods! You're an infant."

"I'm thirteen. Cadets join the army much earlier."

"And no parents," he said almost to himself. "Does the landlord abuse you?" "No. But I want to be away from here.

Seeing a new sky. Marching in step. Singing. In at the victory. I could tend the wounded," she said, bright with this new idea.

"Child, we're not even at war," said Tallis impatiently. "Just go away."

Chilly and cross, he rubbed himself hard with the towel. She stood gazing at him thoughtfully. Then with a couple of flashing movements, she stripped her tunic and grubby breeches, dragged off her toilworn boots and stood unclothed before him.

"That's no good either," said Tallis firmly. "I don't fancy boys. Dress yourself."

"You can have me," she said, with such abasement that he felt uncomfortable. "I'll do anything, but you'll have to show me how. Only let me come with you tomorrow."

Under the dirt her skin was lint-white, her breasts tiny flat buds. A spangle of transparent gold lay between her thighs. She was very thin. She shook out her long hair. The Captain felt a faint prickle of lust, which angered him even more.

He picked her up and threw her into the bath, splashing the floor. "Get clean," he said curtly.

"Then I can stay?"—eagerly.

"You may not. Here's the soap. Wash your hair. You're a disgrace."

She sank beneath the water for an instant, then rose, her face streaming. She sat in the tub and sobbed. He threw her the towel and turned away. He let her cry, disliking the sound of his responsibility. Sobbing, she washed herself. He got into bed while she dried herself and ran her fingers through her mane of hair. Still she was not done with him. Tears over, she fixed him with her tired eyes.

"You called me an infant. The Duchess Mayla isn't much older than me, and you're fetching her to be married."

"How impertinent you are," he remarked. "Is nothing private? Where do you come from anyway? You're very pale-skinned for a Karenian."

"I was born here. They thought my father might be a mountain man, from your border."

"So you've Tamian blood."

"I suppose so. My name's Barbel."

"It suits you." He looked at her, clean and pallid. "You're like a spiky little fish. You get your spines locked into an idea and won't let go. Here"—she was beginning to shiver. "Wear my shirt."

Eagerly she put it on, clasping its folds tightly round her.

"Can I at least stay with you tonight? It's so long since I slept in a real bed. I could sleep at your feet. I'll not move, I promise."

"What of your reputation?" He smiled not unkindly. "And what of mine?"

"No one will know or care."

He recalled suddenly how passionately she had cared for the horse, and knew himself beaten. Fatigued, he said: "Get in then. Take those blankets," and shifted his legs. She squeezed herself against the wall at his feet, made a foetus of her body and, with a happy sigh, slept immediately.

Tallis kept the lamp burning for a while. He lay with closed eyes, feeling the slight pressure against his ankles, like the weight of his wolfhound, Palbo, far away at Tam. Against the yellow darkness, he saw the arid plain of Tirkar, and scenes from the past, the fragmented hauntings of his nights. Then, oddly comforted by the presence of Barbel, he gradually relaxed.

He hoped tonight he would not dream, and slept soon, in a dark still void.

In the early dawn he found Barbel had somehow tucked herself within his sleeping arm, and her head was on his shoulder.

Her body was a white lantern. Naked, she lay in the secret chamber. Her flawless form and skin and face sapped light from the spire-shell lamps. Perfect, almost unearthly white skin clothed the body of a girl, pristine yet flourishing like a day-old rose.

The bed was covered by a fine smooth hide and by the drape of her long tar-black hair. Cascades of it reached the tiles on either side of the bed, and at its crown the blackness was bisected by a startling white streak, as if she had been struck by lightning. The black bush couched at the join of her luminous thighs was the only other contrast.

On her fragile ribcage the breasts stood high and round, with small shelly nipples. Her heavy-lidded eyes were a sparkling amber, like that seen in some cats. Her mouth was a split cherry, a ripe cherry, plentiful with juice. Her hands and feet were scarcely larger than a child's. Her belly had the smooth curve of a wavelet, and deep in her navel lay a shimmering pearl.

She was forty-five years old, and looked twenty.

She lay making love to herself, unhurried and gentle, shaken now and again by light spasms of pleasure. She touched the pearl in her navel with reverence; its incandescence travelled in filaments deep inside her, to the core where her womb should lie. She had drawn out her womb by herself after the birth of her second child, had coaxed it out on a fine occult thread. The dwarf had taken it to the river and thrown it in, to be carried back to the sea.

There was no need for her to bear more children. The inheritrix to darkness had been born. Gentle, beautiful, and completely unaware that she bore the stamp of darkness, of the thing that was Malkar.

Her hands stopped moving. The time for pleasure was over. The pearl's glow was strong today; it had been feasting on all that was contained within her. She rose, white cloaked in black, and withdrew the pearl from its cave of flesh. She laid it on a velvet salver and placed it before the black mirror, where its lucent globe hung as if on air.

It began to grow, swelling to the size of a full moon, enhanced by its mirror image. It became fully dimensional, and its glow assumed the quality of clear glass.

Malkar gazed deep into its silvery eye.

Show me the House of Brides. Find me the Duchess Mayla.

The picture appeared, shining clear as a landscape after rain.

Mayla, feeding birds in the cloister, quiet, a little excited at the prospect of her journey. Passing from the cloister, smiling, waving to someone. A light breeze tickling her hem, her sleeves. An orange and silver butterfly alighted for an instant on her head. The Abbey bell tolled. Through the pearl's dimension it sounded like a chime from some drowned city under the sea. Mayla ran, skipping, further away. The pearl tracked her, but Malkar let her go.

Find me the Princess Royal.

Instantly, another view of the Abbey. A chapel, with the ambience of prayer, demonstrated by a slight fuzzing of the pearl's vision. The princess was standing at a lectern, writing, with a hard rapid pressure, words too small to see in the distance. Her head was bent, furtive. She rolled what she had written and sealed it with her seal.

A young novice nun, one of the Brides of the Lion, entered the picture. The letter changed hands. The novice departed and the princess turned and entered an inner sanctum, closing a great oak door behind her. The pearl could not follow, although it tried.

My daughter. Born of darkness and my blood. The inheritrix. It is what is decreed, but why do I dislike her? Would it have been so were she ugly? But then, her inheritance would be void. I am uneasy. She has secrets. Is she writing to Enial, her father? Or is it a love letter? Has she begun, without my knowledge? Has she begun to *take*?

I will have her back here, at Karlinkis.

Show me my husband.

King Enial in his chamber in a far wing of the palace. A face the colour of old linen. Sweat, and soiling. The result of a dream from the same old source. He retched without issue into a silver bowl. The physicians dabbed and clucked about him. He pushed their medicines away and wept.

You need to see your daughter. Feed his want.

The king reared in his bed, crying loudly: "Lilene! Where is Lilene?"

The doctors conferred, soothed, nodded. One of them left in haste. The king drowsed.

Now. What is the Crown Prince doing at this moment?

Unpleasantness and waste, decadence and squalor. And above all, purposelessness. Too much wine, and noxious substances. Bad company. How can this be my son? Led by the things of earth. Enial's blood.

Enough of him. A waste of light and sight. Let us feel a moment of real hatred. Seek the mindless one. Honyia.

A lyre, like plucked heartstrings. Honyia, her head on her hand in a little green pocket of the palace gardens. The minstrel sat at her feet. Only the top of his head was visible and his brown fingers attentive to the strings. One of Honyia's tears splashed on his shoulder. He did not look up.

One day you may yet serve us, Thing. But in the lowest capacity.

The picture was visibly darkening. A cloud came over its sky.

We have wasted light. Yet unseen is a matter of paramount importance. Sweep, now. Sweep the plain, quickly, as far as can be done in this fading time. Across our land, to the border and beyond, if necessary. Into cursed Taratamia, our slippery foe.

The light, fitful now, homed in on movement south of the border. The procession, tiny as mice, yet in one sudden burst of clarity, near, as if a telescope had been righted. Horses, banners, weapons, faces. One face in particular.

Oh, Taratamian. You are perfect for our special purpose.

The pearl dwindled, diminished, sank to a little orb. The black mirror lost light. Malkar placed the pearl back in her navel, seating it deep and firm.

She touched her face a little anxiously, and her fingers reassured her. Beauty, palpable, unsurpassed, inviolable.

Special man, you have wakened our appetite. Malkar is hungry.

With the coming of Spring, the Lion lilies had grown tall, their waxen white lips and delicate stamens upheld like chalices in the sun's light. They grew profusely beside a little mere fed from a crystal fall, and their swordshaped leaves were mirrored in the clear water, where swam golden fish. Roses climbed over arbours, sprang wild among the neat hedges. They were red and white and gold, the outer petals serrated, growing like a mane. The Roses of the Lion. Endless green lawns, smooth as skin, were intersected by beds of tulips and yellow daisies. Cypresses, bent from the east wind, framed the garden. A thousand-years-old oak had become a citadel for birds, and the garden was crystalline with their song. And east, beyond a rolling sweep of green banks and little paths, the ocean could be seen; the ink-blue Sea of Infinity, swallowing the horizon.

Beyond the garden, built in an L-shape of amber stone, lay the House of Brides, solid as faith. It was protected on its far side by a row of outbuildings, stables, bakery, infirmary, the main chapel of the Lion of Day. Exhaling fragrance was the herbarium. Small fields, a vineyard, and an olive grove peopled with stone images of the god, stretched beyond the garden to north and west. South and east, the house faced on to the bay.

Ten thousand acres of Taratamian land, that was all. Set on the south-east tip of Karenia, an independent state within a kingdom, ceded to its motherland as part of the Treaty of Braf. That a Taratamian abbess should rule there in perpetuity, and that Taratamian novices—usually those of high blood—should be educated there, were two of the Treaty's clauses.

Karenian girls were admitted in special circumstances. One of these, high-born and special in this and other ways, walked now alone in the garden. She was Lilene, Princess Royal of the House of Karling, daughter of Enial and Malkar. Her beauty, like that of her mother, was extraordinary, but Lilene was an apricot-skinned blonde, a golden blonde, her hair long enough to reach her hips, with a wild ripple in it, like sun on water. Her full mouth was a delicate rose. She was small, with the slenderness that is deceptively strong, and her large eyes were a flawless ocean blue.

Today she was blind to the lush paintbox of the garden. She was worried and apprehensive. She had not dared to keep a copy of her letter; her lips moved silently as she tried to recall its exact content.

Had she said too much? Would the young gardener make the journey safe to Kalvaria? Kalvaria was isolated, north of the capital, but it was not called The Place of Trials for nothing. It was policed; the headquarters of the Draconhood. And they were everywhere, licensed to stop and search as they chose. She sighed. It was done. No sense in worrying.

She would pray to the Moon-Lion, god of the forests and dusk. This matter was not for the light. Oh, how furious those at Karlinkis would be, she thought, if they knew of my conversion to the gods of Taratamia. The Oyster and Pearl are not for me. I only ever wear pearls when commanded. She prayed now: may that boy reach Kalvaria unmolested, and deliver my letter into the hands of Cristarpa . . . seven days since he left with it.

Mayla came running towards her, funny little dark Mayla, with her eyes like black fruit, and her plump childish body. Fourteen, heir to the great silver fortunes of Mayt, with its unworldly philosopher ruler. She trotted up to Lilene, her two serving women panting behind.

"Your Royal Highness," Mayla remembered her manners, even in haste.

"Your Grace," said Lilene. "Are you well today?" She slipped her arm round Mayla's waist and they moved off together on the edge of the mere. Mayla blinked up worshippingly at Lilene.

"What's the excitement, darling May?" asked Lilene.

"The escort is on the road. One of our couriers saw them. Only half a day away. Oh, Lilene! In a few weeks I shall be in Tamia."

"I'll miss you," said Lilene with feeling.

"You must come and stay with us after I'm married. I'll throw parties and revels. You'll be the toast of the Court."

"If you say so," said Lilene with a faint smile. "Would I be welcome in Tamia, d'you think?"

"Of course! You're at peace! And my Duchy has no quarrel with Karenia . . ."

"It's a fragile peace, May," said Lilene softly. Just then a tame robin flew down and landed on Mayla's shoe. Instantly distracted, she bent to it in pleasure. Such a child, thought Lilene. Far more than I was at her age. I grew up too quickly. I hope Prince Rost treats her gently.

"When will you be married?" she asked.

"When my father thinks fit. I wish my mother were still alive." The robin flew away. Mayla leaned her head lovingly against Lilene's shoulder.

"All will be well," said Lilene. "Crown Prince Rost will love you."

"What happens in marriage, Lilene? Will you tell me?"

"No. It's not my place. You must ask the Matrix. Anyway, I should probably tell you wrong."

Oh, what a liar. None could grow up in my mother's court and not know of these matters.

"It will all come right," she said to comfort Mayla, who did not need comforting. They turned and walked back beneath a bow of weeping willows, Mayla still bright with expectation, Lilene again far away, following her secret letter to Kalvaria, the Place of Trials.

The dwarf came for Kipil just as he was closing the shop for his master, who had gone off early to the races north of the river. The shop was a bespoke tailor's, patronised by nobility.

The shop lay in a little court under the palace walls and was shadowed by them. Kipil had seen the dwarf before and recognised his silken breeches, which he had helped to sew. He was worried in case the palace had sent a complaint. But the little man merely smiled, and with a wave of his long arm beckoned Kipil to follow. Kipil, shrugging into his shabby cloak, obeyed.

Although he was only seventeen, Kipil was nearly six feet tall, slender from an inadequate diet, and good to look at, with a light tan skin, a broad untroubled forehead, and curly ash-blond hair. He smiled rather anxiously at the dwarf.

"Where are we going?"

The dwarf beckoned him on. Kipil followed. His dog, which lay all day outside the shop waiting for him to finish, made to come with them. Kipil pointed at it sternly.

"Stay!"

The dog sank its head on its paws and whined in disappointment.

Ungainly, the dwarf led the way. Kipil realised as they passed from one narrow alley to another and through a deserted court, that they were approaching one of the buttressed wings of the palace that lay close to the river. The walls towered, the river smell grew strong. They crossed a short bridge and entered through a low watergate studded with nails. They were in a passage so dark that Kipil was temporarily blinded. The dwarf drew him up a spiral stair, at the height of which torchlight flared.

Kipil said unquietly: "Is something wrong? Was Lord Ing displeased with his new robe?"

The dwarf turned, smiling gently. They had reached a long deepset door.

"Touch his tongue," said the dwarf. "I am too short."

Kipil looked up at the leering stone merman. Obediently he fingered its tongue and the door opened. He half-turned, but the dwarf was vanishing down the little stairs. Kipil entered quietly, and the door closed behind him.

The chamber was filled with a soft whiteness, soothing as moonlight. Pale flames burned in ocean spirals on the walls. The walls were black, but the light painted them silver. There was a tall black mirror. In a bowl carved from a single great emerald, costly lintwood incense plundered from the isle of Despra breathed honey, and wine was set on a low table near a bed covered with rich dark fabric, and on it sat the woman.

He knew her immediately; who did not? And fell to his knees. He could not look at her, any more than a man can stare into the sun.

The one glimpse he had revealed a torrent of black hair streaked with white fire, a radiant flawless face. A body clad in filmy grey as if she had put on sea mist. His heart beat, his throat ached. He was frozen in homage.

Her voice was little, low.

"Look up, my child. You are not here for anything ill. You are here because I wished it so."

He looked up under his brows. She had called him child. She had been on the throne before he was born. Yet she looked scarcely more than childlike herself. The teeming incense crowded his head, and he swayed on his knees.

"Your majesty. There is a mistake." His voice sounded rough and silly, tailing off.

"Yes, I am Malkar. No mistake. You are here, because I dreamed you."

He swallowed, and closed his eyes. She was still there when he looked again, but her beauty seemed impossibly to have grown. He said: "That can't be so, majesty. I am nothing. Forgive me."

"Forgive you for what? Stop being foolish. Get up. Pour us wine. What do they call you?"

He filled two goblets, his hands shaking, slopping the wine. "My name is Kipil, highness."

"Sit by me, Kipil." She drank a little. He sat as if lowering himself on to thorns.

The wine tasted of smoke and roses.

"My name is Malkar," she said. "You must call me by it."

"I can't," he said, biting the edge of the goblet in desperation.

"But yes, you can. Call me."

He took a huge breath. "Malkar," he whispered.

She stretched out and took his hand, his fingers pitted from the tailor's needle. At her touch a charge went up his wrist and arm as if lightning had laid hold on him. Through her fragile gown he felt her warmth against his thigh. She set down her cup and took his burning face in her hand and turned it to look deep into his eyes.

"Tell me of yourself, Kipil. Are you married? Have you a sweetheart?"

"I have a girl," he said shyly. "But we can't marry until I have finished my apprenticeship."

Malkar's face brightened with interest. "And tell me," she said, "Do you make love to her? Oh, you're blushing. Talk to me as if I were your mother."

"My mother is dead," he said, still blushing. "And my father . . ."

"You haven't answered me, my love. Have you enjoyed your sweetheart yet? Was it bliss?"

"No," he whispered. "We are to wait."

"But there have been others, surely."

He shook his head. "No. Never."

The queen laid her hand on his thigh. And at that moment he realised this was a dream. He would wake any minute, and the dog would want to go out. And as this was a dream he could study the queen more boldly.

Through the gown he saw her breasts, the curve of belly and thighs where something gleamed like a star. Kipil had never known lust. Now it rushed in him like a blaze. He heard her say: "I should like to teach you to make love, my Kipil."

He drew back and she pressed on him, whispering: "Come! don't disappoint me. We'll know such joy."

She took his hand and slipped it inside her gown. He shook like a fly in a web. A round young girl's breast was in his hand, the nipple heating and swelling. "Kiss me," she whispered, and he took her honeyed mouth into his shivering mouth and her tongue snaked between his teeth and her fingers busied themselves at his clothing.

"Oh, Malkar," he said, almost crying. And then she was naked and he was in her arms on the smooth couch, blinded and smothered by her kisses.

And still he hung back, the dream becoming too real, and turned his head away.

"Ah, come," she said again, her hands like moths on his loins.

"But you . . . you're the queen!"

"I'm a woman! Love me, Kipil. I dreamed you."

He raised himself. Her eyes were honey and flame. He drew close once more while she kissed his eyes and his hands slid over her silken body.

"Oh, that is good. Kiss me all over." And his face moved on her skin, over her dolphin smoothness down into the sweet salts of her cave.

"My love. Now, my love."

She spread herself and he mounted her. His heart shuddered as he worked on her and she plunged under him, her whispering mingling with the bloodrush in his ears. He pounded her while she cooed and smiled and whispered unbelievable things. She loves me! He thought. Oh, let this be forever.

"Yes, forever!" she said, and he realised he had cried out loud. Then, her breath forced out in gasps from his pumping: "Come now, come! Ride your joy!"

He raised himself on his arms to look into her face. Taken by a mighty spasm, what felt like an ocean jolted into her body. And this pulsing flood was overtaken by a stronger urge, like a fierce suck of tides as she drew him in, spent and lost, taking his essence, his past, his future, his sharp ecstasy now forgotten in sudden panic. For he was falling into her like a bather who drops over a treacherous hidden shelf of ocean. His mouth filled with blood. Something vital burst in him and he cried out in agony.

And he saw her face below him. No longer smiling, nor young, but old, older than prehistoric rocks on a desolate shore. An eyeless face, neither male nor female but having the worst components of both. A face of streaming darkness, fanged, gaping, hollow as bone, entirely inhuman and pitiless. A foul, reeking body.

Kipil fell forward on to the thing that lay beneath him, and it swallowed his soul.

Presently Malkar resumed her known shape. She pushed Kipil's body away—it sprawled, the tongue was bitten through. She stretched her arms above her head as the power she had harvested began to pour through her.

After a little time the dwarf came. The chamber was made pristine once more. Alone, Malkar removed the pearl from her navel. Already it was regaining its intensity. Again, it vouchsafed visions, but it would not last.

Outside the tailor's shop the dog waited. As darkness fell, it began to howl.

They called the abbess Andine the Matrix because she was the fount and source of all goodness nurtured in the House of Brides.

She watched from her apartment as the Captain approached across the cloister garth. He did not know she could see him; she stood a little back from her arched window. Neither did he know that she regarded him with deep affection. She also thought: I wonder if he realises how attractive he is, then: no. He would ridicule the very thought. He has pride, but no conceit.

She saw him mount the steps leading to her tower. Such a straight back—slender—everything about him disciplined. He was tired, she could tell by his face, but he was intent on his mission which was after all of some importance.

And although she had not seen him for years, she knew more about him than he could ever imagine; something not to be told, if ever. Now she rose to greet him as he ascended to her chamber.

The abbess was elderly. She was sister to the late King Valm of Taratamia, and aunt of the present ruler, Valm the Seventh. Her hair was white as frost, braided round her head under a stiff wimple. Her gaze was straight, like that of a clever warrior. Her hands were whiter than her hair but today the palms were marked by a dozen little crescent wounds. Similar old scars lay beneath, and she kept these hidden as she put out her hands to be kissed.

Gracefully he went down on one knee.

"My lady. My deep respects. And I bring most affectionate greeting from King Valm Capashenet and all the royal court. And may the Lion attend you."

Through an open doorway a private chapel was visible, where two gods flanked an altar; the Lion of Day, crowned with a gold sphere and ruler of the mountains, and the Lion of Night, deity of the dark forests, wearing a silver horned moon.

"Welcome, Ricalpa," she said, and as he rose, kissed him on both cheeks.

This, and the use of his first name, was unexpected, but then he felt the radiant peace from her presence and was at ease.

"Now, give me the news from Tam," she said. "Sit with me." She clapped her hands and a young novice, noiseless as a white butterfly, darted in, left a crystal flagon of wine and departed.

"This is the one you like," said Andine. "As I remember."

Tallis poured into ornate tall cups, sunlight through rubies.

"To your health, madam, and all in this House."

"And to yours. And to King Valm and all who serve him."

"To Taratamia and the House of Capashenet. May the gods keep them in their sight."

They drank sombrely, and were both silent for a moment. Then he said: "It *is* good. Like fire wrapped in silk."

"Our vineyards had a splendid year. I could have made a fortune. I've even had slaves from those creatures on Lake Sigillan come begging for a cask or two. I refused, as always. There's nothing in the Treaty that says we have to share our produce with reprobates."

He frowned. "They're still as bad, then?"

"Worse than ever, I hear. I thank the gods my girls are safely cloistered here. Tell me now. How is my royal nephew?"

"The king's in splendid health, my lady."

"That is good." Then, acutely, "There was something you were about to ask me?"

"It was when you mentioned your novices. As we came through I noticed your little guard, working in the garden, warding the gatehouse. Young men . . ."

She smiled. "They are picked for their purity. They would die before they defiled the honour of the house. Also," she leaned forward, saying softly; "they take a certain herbal which annuls . . . the natural urges."

Tallis said thoughtfully, "I know a young lieutenant who might profit from a dose."

She smiled. "Oh. I saw him. So young and comely. But now"—she pointed to the sheaf of documents the Captain had brought: "What have we?"

"These are the papers; this one to release the Duchess Mayla from your care and into mine, and this, for her safe conduct over the border. If you would be pleased to sign them so we can be on our way. And these," presenting further scrolls, "are the lists of tribute to be sent on to King Enial at Karlinkis— a sign of our goodwill." (A costly sop to a prickly neighbour, he thought.)

"It shall be done." The abbess was signing her name, a strong stormy hand. Without looking up, she said abruptly: "Do you know the history of this holy house? It's very old. It was once the province of the old Kings of Kardespra, before Karenia became a state."

"And before Kardespra became a desert." Tallis thought of the trunklike spit of land which hung between the west coast of Taratamia and the Isle of Despra, with Avatal Bay a treacherous oval watched by a Taratamian fort on the coast.

"Sometimes on a clear day you can see Kardespra," he said. "I was stationed at Karetara garrison for a time. I was a cadet . . ."

"That was after you left your monastery," said the abbess. He raised his brows. "The lady abbess honours me," he said a little sharply. "My past would seem an open page."

"When the House of Brides belonged to Kardespra," the abbess continued, "they worshipped the Pearl, if not the Oyster. Young novices were sacrificed in the Gulf of Brides. It's said the bay is lined with their bones. I do not remember the Lion ever wanting sacrifice. He is a god of nature, respecter of all life."

"Yet even after all that, the House is still a holy place."

"Yes. The power has been washed of blood by prayer and grace. Where once there has been a raising of power, it can be shifted and refined into its desired form. Peace. Chastity. Sanctuary."

"You've achieved much, madam." Then he said, because the thought was so keen, "are you ever molested or harassed by Karenia? It's brave, to hold this tenure so deep in their country."

"Oh, the peace holds. I am the king's representative here. The only bond is that Karenian requests regarding their native subjects should be filled without demur. We have the Princess Lilene here."

"I didn't know that. I don't think I ever saw her. My one visit to the court was years ago. I was a young soldier—young and green."

"And did you see the queen?" said Andine softly.

"No, I think not."

"You would have remembered. Let me tell you something, Captain. Beware Malkar. Wrap all your gods close around you, should your way meet that of the queen."

He smiled faintly. "I've heard some tales," he said. "Men take a whisper, like a pat of snow, and roll it round until it grows into a boulder. Legend into truth, and generations believe it."

"She takes away," said Andine softly.

He raised his brows. Andine said, in quite a different tone: "Few know the truth of the queen. They say she was born on the Kardespran coast. That somehow she was taken hostage during the second Despran war. She came to the court at the time of the Treaty of Braf, when my sister Doro was married to King Enial to seal the peace. It was of no moment that the king took Malkar to his bed. The scandal was that he took a serving-woman for his queen. Malkar was present at Queen Doro's lying-in. Doro should not have died."

She lifted her cup and drank, looking steadily at Tallis.

"And so?" he said.

The abbess shrugged.

"Why are we having this conversation, madam?" he said easily. "I'm not a diplomat, or a courtier, or, gods forbid, any class of spy."

"It was my choice to speak so. I still mourn my little sister. Honyia was damaged too, later."

"The queen is a great beauty, they say."

"She is a witch," said Andine.

Tallis finished his wine and sat looking at the abbess under his lids. There was always gossip in a nunnery. For sure, the abbess would regret the brevity of her sister's reign, resent her successor. He smiled a funny little smile, looking down into his empty goblet.

"You are amused."

"I ask your pardon."

"How is my nephew's queen, Sarene?" she asked lightly. "And the sons. Crown Prince Rost, Prince Lepo, Prince Ataret?"

"Prince Rost looks forward to his bride," Tallis said politely. "He takes his duties seriously as heir. Prince Ataret has nearly completed his priestly studies. Prince Lepo . . ."

He stopped. This time Andine was smiling.

"That naughty boy. He'll calm down in time."

"I love Lepo dearly," said Tallis. "I remember the princes being born. I was only little. I lived near the court with my mother." He stopped, as ancient pain nipped him.

"Come," said Andine, noticing his mood. "Aren't our gardens fine this time of year?"

They stood at the arched window. On the lawn the duchess was playing with a kitten, and near her stood a figure, her head and shoulders clothed, it seemed, in sunlight.

"There is Lilene," the abbess said. "She is just nineteen. She's Malkar's daughter, yet in a way, she is also mine. Lately I find her secretive. She sends letters, out of my sight."

One of the coffers of tribute was full of opals from the Taratamian mines. Andine picked up one large stone already set in gold, and turned it, watching the colours merge and fade.

"Guard against Queen Malkar, Ricalpa," she said. "I speak as your friend."

"And I'm grateful." He laughed. "I'll heed you. Though I'm not likely to meet with her that I know."

Andine let a handful of opals slide back into the chest. "Captain. Orders came through today from the Court at Karlinkis. King Enial is sick and wants Lilene with him. As yours is the nearest armed escort, you are commanded, through me, to bring her to the capital."

For a moment he was dumb, then his pale face whitened further and he said: "Madam," (soft with anger) "this I cannot do. I am under orders from my king. I am responsible for the Duchess Mayla's safe passage north. With no diversions. Am I to drag her across the miles west to Karlinkis? It is unthinkable."

The abbess folded her arms in her sleeves and waited for him to calm down. She said: "Captain. I don't like the idea any more than you. But it is part of the Treaty that I obey Karenia in just such a manner as this. King Enial's malady seems grave. There's no time for them to send an escort from Karlinkis, and you are here. You can go north to Treaty Bridge and join the River Braf. Go by barge thereafter. Deliver the princess and continue your journey north. You will be on the western highway to Tam, and save many miles."

"I have sworn," said Tallis deliberately, "not to let the duchess from my sight."

"Nor shall you. You need stay no more than a day at Karlinkis."

He looked hard at her stern face. He knew there would be no merit in argument. He was more than annoyed. He accepted her authority, for he could do nothing else. Suddenly formal, he came to attention before her.

"Madam. May I see the orders delegating me to lead this extra journey?"

"I have them here." He unrolled the parchment, saw his name and that of the Red Royals. He wondered how they knew of his presence, his plans, the movements of the duchess. Lilene writes letters, the abbess had said. Of course: he thought. Through the Princess Royal, Karenia is privy to what is none of their business. Although this betrothal is no secret, this is a strange development, and I don't like it.

"In view of the circumstances," he said stiffly, "we should leave without delay. Tomorrow at the latest. I wouldn't want to harm diplomatic relations in any way." His normal colour had returned, but the scar on his mouth showed very white. He gave the abbess a cold smile.

"Don't be angry," she said. She laid a hand on his scarlet sleeve. She gazed high over the garden to where, in a fallow field near young wheat, the tents of Tallis's company could be seen.

"You need not be anxious," she said. "Your bodyguard are strong and able. Come, Ricalpa. Let me give you my blessing."

He knelt, and she placed her hands on his head.

"The Lion protect you by day. The Lion defend you by night. The Lion be on your right and on your left. Go, in the strength of the Lion."

The blessing entered him like cool water. For the first time he saw the crescent wounds on her palms.

"Stigmata?" he whispered. "The claws of the Lion?"

She clenched her fists quickly, hiding the wounds.

"Nothing so blessed," she said lightly. "I do woodcarving, as a meditation. The knife often slips. I'm clumsy."

She led him down from the tower. "Make your preparations," she said. "Until we meet again, Captain."

She turned abruptly and went back into the tower, a waft of snow-white habit. The three lieutenants met him near the outer gate.

"We're going to Karlinkis," he told them grimly. "With her"—Lilene was entering the courtyard through a postern gate, walking away, too distant to see clearly. Tallis frowned at her back.

"Captain," said Lieutenant Recansky, "We think there may be a problem."

Tallis raised his brows.

"The coffers of tribute for King Enial. We think one may have been tampered with. It's the box of herbs from the High Tiranians. It was heavy when the men loaded it after we left the first inn. Now it's much lighter, and there are holes in the sides."

"Rats," said Lieutenant Narzet helpfully. He was gazing after the retreating figure of Lilene.

"Rats don't eat herbs," said Lieutenant Pinpol. "Some of those medicines are so strong they'd be killed stone dead."

"Where's the inventory? How many sacks were in the coffer?"

"Six hundred. Shall we question the men? It'll take hours . . ."

"Well, go and count the sacks," said Tallis in exasperation. "We're counting now," said Pinpol, and at that moment Sergeant Delvas came running. "The tally is six hundred, Captain." He looked unhappy. "We must have been mistaken."

"I don't accept mistakes," said Tallis frigidly. "Sergeant, make ready to strike camp. The men will march and ride. We shall go by river with the ladies. We'll meet you at Karlinkis."

The sergeant saluted and left at a run.

"Karlinkis," said Lieutenant Narzet, almost in ecstasy. "City of Pearls." Pearls can mean tears, thought Tallis. "And women like pearls," pursued Narzet, overreaching himself. "Oh, I do love women!"

"Lieutenant," said Tallis severely, "There are four things only you must love. Your gods, your country, your sword, and your commanding officer. And love in that case, means obey."

He looked at Narzet, who dropped his eyes. "Yes, Captain. Sir. I will. I do."

Lake Sigillan, blue as pansies and almost always calm, was a vast inland sea. A river ran south from it to the Braf, flowing under the bridge where the Treaty had been signed a quarter of a century ago. On the lakeshore, where ornate barges and boats were anchored, small waves lapped, but the lakebed shelved steeply and a few yards out the water was fathomless. A monster or two was said to dwell there, the most legendary being the grendelfish.

The white villas of the high-born Karenian lords were built close to the shore, encircled by walls and paths of shells and semi-precious stones. The buildings were marble and porphyry, scrolled at windows and doors with malachite and silver. The largest was built around the huge pillared court of cool stone where vines climbed and trailed. Marble couches lined with cushions stood round the walls beneath fans of bright feathers, and further banquettes surrounded a sunken bath where perfumed water rippled over mosaics.

It was early evening during the dregs of the three-day orgy, when the bite of the substances eaten, drunk or smoked had soured, leaving those who had indulged sick, bored and dangerous. Two dishevelled whores lay in a corner, tumbled unconscious across one another. Two young men, glassy-eyed, stood in the bath, apathetically fondling one another's parts.

In a winespotted gold tunic, Prince Vergon, heir to the Karenian throne, sat petulantly on the edge of the bath.

He was muttering to himself: "Welcome, sweet sister, to my domain. This is the House of the Unworld where nothing is real. Where pleasure is stretched like sinews and wine is blood and . . . I am going to puke", he said, and did so copiously into the water of the bath. Mashed shreds of meat and fruit borne on an acid gush of wine polluted the surface. The two lordlings, Fraycon and Bratt, hastily left their dalliance and the bath with noises of disgust.

"Oh, my lord prince, that is revolting!" cried Fraycon. Bratt laughed and made sympathetic retching noises. Fraycon and Bratt were cousins, much alike, with long curling ashblonde hair. They ruled fiefdoms north and south of the River Braf.

The day had been hot, and the bath-house steamed. Fraycon and Bratt came to sit, dripping, at Vergon's feet. Two other lords lounged nearby: Molgon, greying yet handsome, and Wurmol, small, thin, redfaced with an evil temper. Both owned vast tracts of land from the Crown.

Prince Vergon's hair was thin, showing a diseased and pustulent scalp. He looked down with distaste at the others. They were not friends. They were good for an orgy but that was all. It was through his persuasions that King Enial had divided the land tenures among them; they all owed Vergon favours. He scowled at them, tasting bile. Sometimes they even spoke as if they were his equal. Yet they were all he had. He chanted a soft, mad song.

> *"Lilene, Lilene,*
> *Born of our Queen,*
> *Come to my Unworld and be unfurled*
> *Be twirled*
> *At the unending end. Undone . . ."*

Molgon barked a laugh.

"The day your sister sets her luscious toes in our black water I'll go beg my bread."

"Oh, she's pure," said Vergon, brushing his vestige of moustache clean of vomit. "A virgin mare. She doesn't like me," he said plaintively, then suddenly began bawling at a middle-aged slave.

"Fetch me a pipe, you."

A hollow reed came, and fire, and Vergon inhaled. He smoked a mix of herbs, chief being the dangerous aphrodisiac, lankaine, which grew insidiously beside the rhododendrons and roses on the estate.

"Talking of mares," Bratt said easily, "that Tamian beast I bought dropped a good colt. In a couple of years I'll enter him for the Pearl Stakes."

Vergon grunted disagreeably.

"Horses and opals are the only good to come out of Tamia," said Molgon.

"And their black beer," added Fraycon.

"And their herbals. Mother of the Oyster! I tried their blackwort on a slave. It died in seconds, without a sound."

"Yes," Vergon said with a nasty smile. "Tamian roots are useful for disposing of parasites."

Bratt rose instantly and poured wine for the prince. Molgon relit Vergon's reed, which had expired. Wurmol shouted orders and a clean gown for the prince was hastily brought. The atmosphere settled to a dreary calm. Molgon snorted a white powder from his wrist.

"Want some Red Flower, my love?" he asked the prince.

"No. I shall vomit again. Be careful with that, Molgon. You know it makes you ratty."

"Never with you, highness."

"Often with me, you harlot's get."

He could insult them and they were powerless. But Molgon turned crimson, and his hands clenched, and when Wurmol laughed, he turned on him with venom.

"Weary of living, Wurm? Get up, you little prick."

Vergon clapped his hands. "Oh, are you going to fight?" he asked, brightening for the first time. "Kill one another. A fitting way to end our party."

"No," said Molgon, collapsing on to his side. "Red Flower, Red Flower, I love you." They lay propped on elbows round the pool, drinking.

"The whores need paying," remarked Bratt.

"They'll be paid, when they come round. They did well. The fat one especially. Some feat, to take four of us at once."

"I don't remember that," said Fraycon.

"Too much wine and Red Flower."

"Gods, I've never been so bored," Vergon said. "Why is it always like this afterwards? I'll be quite glad to get back to Karlinkis."

"Oh, are we going to Karlinkis?" Two said it at once, loudly. The others sat up straight.

"Who said anything about that? You don't deserve to. I'm going to Karlinkis at the command of my lady mother. The king's sick again."

A chorus of concerned bleats.

"I'll sacrifice my giant eel for his recovery," said Fraycon humbly.

"We'll gladly accompany you, to give comfort," one said.

Vergon jeered. "You only want to see Lilene. My nasty little sister's coming home."

"Oh," said Molgon dreamily, "for one glimpse of that golden slit."

Vergon leaned forward and struck him in the face with his fist. Molgon fell into the pool. He climbed out shortly, abashed.

"Talk like that again, and I'll have your tongue nailed to a tree."

Molgon grovelled. He kissed the prince's foot. All was quiet again.

After a moment came the faintest moan. Bratt raised himself to peer into the darkest corner of the court, where a bound shape was etched against a pillar. Tightly fastened, the girl hung her head. Her face was hidden, and her dress was bloodsplashed and ribboned as if sliced by knives.

"Gods!" said Bratt, amazed. "I'd forgotten all about her. She's been there hours. She's piddled on your marble floor, highness."

To the girl, their voices were vague. Their earlier voices were in her head anyway, their sharp excited cries and oaths. Between her legs there was numbness, as if the parts there had been long since excised. She had even ceased to bleed.

Vergon came from a light trance and craned to look.

"What shall we do with her, highness?"

"The lake, obviously," Wurmol said. "She'll have enough company there."

"Be quiet," Vergon said sharply. "Go and give her a stir."

Wurmol took up a little whip with many leather thongs. He went over to the girl and struck her hard across the thighs. She did not even flinch. She raised her head slowly. All colour had gone from her eyes, as if they had been washed.

"Pretty one," said Wurmol, "don't look at me like that. It's not my fault." She looked over his head as he struck her again, harder. "Father," she said, out of her mind.

"Yes, blame your father," said Wurmol viciously. "Next time he'll pay my lord here his land rent quick sharp on reckoning day. Or it'll be your little sister coming to our next party."

"A very good idea, Wurm," said Fraycon. "Send it home to its dad. I'll wager my bailiff'll be happy for the next ten years."

"Oh, untie her," said Vergon irritably. "Send her home. Can she walk? Give her some wine."

Her bonds loosened, the girl fell on her face. She lay there for some time. Finally she crawled away through pillars and arches, leaving a fresh blood-trail, and was gone from sight.

The silent slaves watched her closely, noting, remembering. They were still as wax. Their minds raged and sang.

"Come," said Vergon, rising with the help of his guests. "I forgive you all. Let's leave this midden. Today I feel benevolent. Gentlemen, you may accompany me to court."

The slaves brought water, perfume and robes and tidied prince and lordlings. The singing in their minds was deafening. Their time was not now, but it was coming.

The Abbey owned a barge with the Sun-crowned Lion of Day at the prow, a snow-white sail, and hired oarsmen to man it. It was kept moored under Treaty Bridge. Now it passed up the River Braf. A strong easterly breeze from the Sea of Infinity, whipping under a Spring storm, danced in the sail.

The Braf was almost half a mile wide, and swelled the tributary from Lake Sigillan. Even with the wind, the westerly current was strong, and the oarsmen had to toil to keep the craft moving steadily on between the distant banks of reeds and meadowland.

The footsoldiers and cavalry had been left on shore to follow the barge to Karlinkis, and with them the pack-mules laden with tribute for King Enial. The horse-drawn litter which had carried the ladies to the river went behind the mules. On the barge's deck the duchess and Princess Lilene sat under a turquoise canopy. Both were veiled; Mayla in a jaunty little flounce of silver brocade, Lilene in a deep purple fall. She had worn the veil from the moment of leaving the House of Brides. None of the men had seen her face, and this particularly frustrated Lieutenant Narzet.

Narzet was extra spruce, his uniform fresh, the stormy sunlight glinting on his silver buttons and windswept bright hair.

He was full of delighted anticipation. By him stood Tallis, his black and scarlet cloak wrapped tightly round him, his mind grim with a dozen doubts.

He could hear the little duchess chattering as she pointed out a flight of heron, a small island of blossom floating by. None would dare harm her at the Karenian court, yet she was his sacred responsibility. He looked for the progress of the escort on land; they had been keeping up fairly well, the footsoldiers moving at the double sometimes. Now they were concealed behind a thick fringe of alders and this illogically enhanced his disquiet. The duchess spoke, and laughed like a bird. He heard Lilene's soft monosyllabic answer, and turned his tight-lipped gaze upon her. She moved her head a fraction, regarding him through her veil.

He frightened her. Not with the same fear engendered by Malkar and Vergon, for that was always supported by her anger. It was his implacability, his severity, the air of cold isolation he carried. And in some mysterious way he was like a ghost, never seen clearly. Why, he is not even of high rank, she told herself, certainly not my equal. His, if anyone's, should be the fear. And yet I do fear him. She lifted her chin a little and stared at him through the veil's purple mist, trying to abash him with her royalty. He stared back, coldly, drawing his cloak about him, as if to distance himself. She looked away.

Tallis looked for the lieutenants Pinpol and Recansky, patrolling the deck forward and aft, scanning the riverbanks for potential enemies. He approved of this. He turned abruptly to Narzet, who wiped a silly grin off his face immediately.

"Go and see if the duchess is comfortable," he said. "Ask if she needs anything." He looked about the deck, which was populated mainly by the serving-women of Mayla and Lilene.

"Where are their pages?" he asked, frowning.

"Ashore, poor little devils," said Narzet with a laugh. "They're not used to marching."

"That was an oversight on someone's part." Tallis glared at him.

"I'm sorry, Captain." Narzet's fair face coloured. Our boss is in a rare mood today, he thought, while Tallis said to himself: dilettante, aristocratic dolt! And instantly regretted it. He's loyal. Nothing else matters.

The oars moved in a stressed barcarolle as the wind dropped. Narzet spoke to one of the serving women, snatched a glance at Lilene's ankles, and returned. "They're happy," he told Tallis. He wandered to look over the side of the barge. A bizarre assortment of debris was floating down; wineskins half-filled with air, a piece of purple underwear, fruit rinds, and a severed human hand.

The barge responsible for all this detritus was a faster craft and the party from the villa was out of sight beyond a river bend. And ahead, nearing with every surge lay Karlinkis, City of Pearls. Its misty outline began to form, straddling the great river in an iridescent arch of towers and bridges and ramparts. Lilene rose and walked slowly to gaze beyond the Lion of Day figurehead. She stood with her breast pressed against its carved hindquarters. She trembled a little, like a bird on a blown branch.

By now the footsoldiers and horsemen and the ladies' pages on the riverbank had fallen far behind. The pace was too much for them. At the very end of the line, one page in particular wearied and stumbled, in tight knee-breeches that were slightly too big in the waist, and a jacket slightly too tight, and a large cap jammed down over a pallid face and a lot of hair.

Barbel had taken a while to recover from her ride in the herb chest. She had emerged in secret, drunk and sick from the powerful odours, for it had taken her some time to bore ventilation in the sides of the coffer. She had hidden among the horses at the Abbey. She had stolen her clothes. She had marched like a soldier, but now she was almost done. Her presence she had cleverly explained: to the pages of the duchess she belonged to Lilene, and to Lilene's servants she belonged to the duchess. She was full of triumph. She was with Tallis. She had joined the army.

The little bride carried a spray of purple valerian and yellow kinewort which matched her dress, for yellow was the wedding colour of the woodland people. They dwelt enclosed by trees, east of Karlinkis, which they seldom visited. They lived off the earth, selling their carvings to neighbouring farms and inns that could afford them. An old tribe, whose elders told fortunes and were wise.

Roze and her groom, Borda, proud as a bantam in his new jerkin of russet hide and with his new wife on his arm, were both fifteen. Betrothed from the cradle, now they had leaped over running water together, had mixed their urine in the sacred copper pot, and had knelt for the blessing of the matriarch, Roze's great-grandmother. Like the rest of the party they were slightly tipsy on grass wine. Their wedding gifts were piled in the centre of the clearing; wooden household implements, a beautifully carved sycamore bed, berry beer in oak casks. As he danced, pulled by the laughing drunken circle of family and friends, Borda cast glances at the bed and at Roze's shapely little figure and flushed face. He had abided faithfully by the ancient honour code not to take her before marriage, and he had never wanted other than her. Now, catching her bright eyes, he knew she was as eager as he was, and his whole body tingled. Round and round went the dance, to the squeal of pipe and fiddle. Borda's father, the wine in his legs, fell and rolled on the grass; the chain of dancers buckled and dropped, panting and fanning themselves.

Borda swung Roze off her feet. "Wife," he said, and Roze looked longingly at the bed.

"I wish they'd all go home."

"Not long now, honey girl." He let her go and hopped about. "I have to piddle, love. That wine fair goes through me."

"Shall I come with you?"

"I'll be but a minute."

She smiled and went to sit at the feet of the great-grandmother, whose shawled head was nodding in the shade of the trees.

Borda walked off into the bushes, through a copse of hawthorn, and made for a willow tree near which a stream was running. He made water, shivering with relief. The revelry came faintly through the screen of bushes. He tidied himself, standing in sunlight that was suddenly chill. He felt an inexplicable urgency to return to the camp, and turned to go.

Something ran through the grass in front of his feet, undulating, swift as a whip, and he let out a muted yell. The grasses parted and he saw the snake, quite small with a round black-and-silver body, down the length of which a white stripe ran. It froze, then raised its head, looking at him obliquely. It jetted out its tongue. Borda hated snakes. He had never seen one like this before, but it looked venomous. He seized a branch, raising it to strike, and the branch was twitched from his hand by something unseen, and flew into the bushes.

"You might have hurt me, my love," said the woman who stood before him.

Without knowing how he had come there, Borda found himself on his knees. One of his hands clasped a small warm white foot. There was a rustle of black and silver as her loosened gown fell from her body over his wrists. She came down naked to meet him in the grass, her red mouth smiling, the fall of her black hair half-blinding him. Her breast touched his. She took his face in her hands and kissed his lips. She was so young, younger than Roze. He felt drunk.

"Who are you?" he whispered. He had never seen a naked girl before. His eyes filled with polished whiteness, white as the froth on new milk. She kissed him again, and his mouth opened at the touch. Tranced and unprotesting, he felt her unfastening his new breeches. She took his hand and laid it between her legs, and his fingers encountered a soft lapping.

Then she lay down on him, covering him with her body and her hair, and in seconds they were joined as if they had never been apart, and Roze was someone long ago, in an unimportant dream . . .

"I am love," she said. "I am lust. I am all men's fantasy. And this is our wedding day."

What felt like a hot fist gripped his untried maleness; he burgeoned with ecstasy. One final atom of thought told him that all this had been destined for some other, and that he should dominate, so he flailed to be free, to master and mount, but the slight, white clinging weight pressed on him like fathomless waters.

Two mouths, above and below, pursed about him. He met her hard, shaking rhythms and danced against them groaning. He was about to beget a child! The tribe would rejoice . . . and so burst and broke endlessly in the depths of her, summoned by her cry of "Come, beloved, come!"

Something neither living nor dead nor even part of nature sucked him through the door of death. The power of all he had been and ever could be was garnered by darkness. By some mercy he never saw the thing that lay over him in the sunlit grove, but small creatures fled and the birds stopped singing.

His friends and father came to look for him after a time, blundering through the trees, laughing, shouting his name. When they found him their silence became absolute. At first they would not let Roze see him but when at last she flung herself in awful grief upon his body, they had closed his eyes so that the void in them should be hidden.

"Poor boy, poor boy," they said. "The wine, the dancing, the excitement. It was too much, his heart gave out. Come away, Roze, poor Roze."

But the old babushka, who had studied the corpse intently from head to foot, signed the air asking protection from the woodland gods, and said:

"A soul thief has been here. Darkness comes among us."

"Doro," whispered King Enial, feeling the cool hand on his forehead. "Sweet Doro. Why have you been away from me for so long?"

At times like this, the wraith of the long-dead queen often surfaced in Enial's mind. As usual, Malkar had brought him to the point of death, husbanding him there like a juggler's plate on a sword, her skill guarding him from the final plummet.

In the beginning, he had been easily revived; these days it was not so easy. The king's brow, which she continued to caress, was ash-white beneath the long iron-grey hair, with the feel of fine white tissue.

The dwarf was hovering near, his ugliness hidden behind a mask, the head of a crow with long beak and gleaming plumage. He leaned his great head lightly against Malkar's thigh, and peeped over the edge of the bed. The king's eyes opened and he looked straight into the black face of the crow. It did not disturb him unduly; the horrors seen over the past days made this vision almost benign.

"Malkar," said the king weakly. "Thank the gods you're here. Where have you been?" He sought her hand. "Oh, I have had such awful dreams . . . I thought my life was done . . ."

"I've been here all the time, my heart. What dreams, my love?"

"Too dreadful to recount!" Malkar helped him to sit up. rang a little bell. Two manservants entered.

"Bring wine. And a little breast of fowl. Tell the physicians the king is with us again. My sweet lord," she said to Enial. "You must get well. I have sent for Lilene."

"Lilene." For a moment he could not remember who she was. He shut his eyes the better to think, and a vestige of the dream returned. He was walking along a desolate seashore, and something was following, slowly then rapidly, with a strange swishing gliding sound that seemed part of the sea. When he turned he saw it—moving unbelievably fast—a giant grey mollusc with a mouth that dripped a viscoid substance and sucked at the air. It pursued him, the distance between them lessening even as he fled. It propelled itself along on a sea-wave, and the taste and smell of the sea was in it, like the drink Malkar had given him before he fell ill. The mouth was following him, wet, hungry, moaning its desire for his life, his manhood, his soul . . .

"Drink, my love." Malkar held wine to his lips. The cure had been roasted in the sun's rays and an amethyst dropped in it. Her heavy-lidded eyes burned him into vigour. Miraculously he felt desire, and strove towards her, clutching at her breast. She lifted her gown and climbed upon him, covering his mouth and nose with the spread flower of her sex.

"Drink."

When she raised herself from him at last, the colour was vivid again in his face. She straightened her gown.

"The physician is coming," she told him. "I will return soon."

"Lilene," he said peevishly.

"She's on her way. We are having a banquet tonight to honour a special guest. You must be well enough to attend, sire."

"I doubt it." He knew he had no choice. A sea-tide now boiled and fermented in him, lending him a febrile energy. He watched the tide of her beauty wash from the room, leaving him beached.

She went through ranks of servitors, to the suite of apartments occupied by Prince Vergon. Even through the thick door Molgon's drawl could be heard and the unpleasant laughter of Bratt. Her entrance silenced them like a slap. She looked on bent heads, silken shoulders. All the lordlings greeted her reverently, and she told them to depart.

Her son was fairly drunk. His face twitched as he embraced her. She disengaged herself sharply and sat, the white eyelids sleepy over bright amber pupils.

"What mischief have you wrought up at the villa?" she greeted him. "You will need to mend some when you are king."

"And when will that be, madam my mother?" he said artlessly. "As for mischief, the villa is as dull as ever. Although we had to chop off a slave's hand, coming upriver. The thing was trying to write! A household list, it said . . ."

"Listen. Be sober. Especially tonight. I have not engineered this visit of the duchess for nothing, so do your part. Stay away from those poisons you love, and keep your friends in line. You do remember my instructions?"

"Ah, the little duchess."

"Yes, the duchess. I have no intention of letting her marry Rost of Taratamia."

"As you say, madam. Leave it to me."

"Make ready then," said Malkar, and left him.

Enial's blood! An empty, valueless vessel. Even were he not male, he could never inherit the darkness.

Karlinkis. A shimmer like a hard cloud. Growing definite, more awe-inspiring the closer it came. Shining with a pearl whiteness which imposed itself on the wide river.

Seven bridges of pearly marble, their parapets carved with sea-creatures and topped at either end by the image of a pearl. A monopoly of pearls, gathered from its southern shore and the uninhabited island of Ruva had made Karlinkis rich.

The oars shipped, the sail furled, the barge drifted under the first bridge. Weed clothed the stone banks and danced under the clear water. White broadwalks lay down on either side. White buildings with damp green feet reared beyond them, government buildings, the mansions of the rich. An armed watch patrolled the bridge as, with the gold Day Lion of Capashenet undulating from the swell, the barge rode
into the heart of the city.

On board the party was silent. No longer could Tallis keep surveillance on the escort. They were still on land outside the walls, seeking entry through the north gate, beyond the chessboard of streets which divided the hierarchy from the mean. Far upriver, beyond the seventh bridge were the slave shacks and warrens of the poor.

The stretch on which they travelled was Royal Braf; further down it became Beggars' Braf. Miles on it changed course and dropped into a valley on its way to the Western Sea, below the southern edge of the principality of Karkis. The river ran clear across Karenia east to west. Its course mirrored the

Takk far north across plains and hills and a great forest. Willow and alder, cypress and olive groves proliferated outwards beside the watercourse. To south and east were the legendary vineyards, a lush green grid marching over hillsides and stretching for miles.

The climate had changed perceptibly since the journey began. Sun leapt and dazzled on the river. Biting insects assaulted Narzet's fair skin. The occupants of smaller craft going downriver gaped at the splendid barge. Women were attending the noble ladies. Tallis, his eyes moving from the duchess, saw Lilene being draped with the device of her House. Pearl necklets, bracelets, anklets, a filet for her head. The veil was lifted for a moment. He saw her small, perfect profile, her skin a paler sun, a reflection of the water but somehow her own, individual light.

With the other officers he had changed into ceremonial dress; snow-white linen with red and gold braid at chest and shoulder. He dabbed sweat from his lip and looking at Lilene thought, rancorously: by now the duchess should be halfway home, madam, but for you.

The biggest bridge was upon them. Oyster Bridge, the great emblem surrounded by stone fish and mer-people. And here was the landing-stage, and marble steps leading to the palace. A line of liveries waited as the anchor fell. The officers came ashore. The duchess safely on land, the Captain held out his hand to assist Lilene. She stepped quickly away from it, up on to the side of the barge. She poised there a moment like a pearl and purple bird, then dropped lightly to shore. She did not look at him, nor he at her.

She had been away for months, and had almost forgotten the dangerous glamours of her mother's bower. She left her women outside the door, straightened the circlet of pearls over her veil, and drew a long breath. The great doors, inlaid with mother-of-pearl, swung open, and Lilene went in.

Malkar sat with her back to the mirror, which stretched from floor to ceiling; her eyes fell fully on Lilene, who peered for the gleam under the heavy lids, blinked at its brightness, and knelt a few feet away. There was good reason for keeping her distance. Malkar's two guardians were with her; two silvery landfish, as big as deerhounds, lizard-like but with barbed tails and fins. They had stunted legs, their foreheads were plated with scales, and their mouths revealed shark teeth covered in salty foam. They wore silver collars and leashes at which, seeing the princess, they began viciously to strain.

"Quiet, my precious ones," said Malkar. "Well, daughter?" And she stared at Lilene, the stare of the implacable ocean that washes sailors away without a thought, finding neither pleasure nor grief in its mindless, elemental swallowing.

"Madam. Mother. I hope you're well."

"I can't kiss you," said Malkar pleasantly, "or these two would tear off your breasts. They're very jealous. How was the Abbey? And that old fool Andine? I trust you were not tainted by their jungle god, that kitty-cat Lion. Remove your veil."

Lilene obeyed. Malkar rose, tugged the slavering landfish after her and tethered them in a corner, where they began savagely to rend one another. She took Lilene's arm.

"Come with me to the mirror."

They stood together. Shimmering black and white, with the lightning-shot hair. Rich rose and apricot, framed by a long cloud of sun on wheat. Malkar laughed.

"You look like my elder sister! Lilene, Lilene. We must find you a man."

Lilene was undeceived. *I see that I am beautiful, although yes, she looks as young as I.*

"I don't trouble about a husband. I was happy at the House of Brides. I enjoyed the books, the knowledge . . ."

"And you have been writing," said Malkar softly. "You learned to write. Letters. To whom, and why?"

Lilene thought: I should have known. She knows everything, down to my least thought. She would even know if I had lain with a man, something that seems to exercise her constantly. It was always so. But this is vital. Let me deceive her. She did not look directly at Malkar; that was a sure admission of lying. She cast a glance at the quarrelling landfish and said casually:

"Yes. I write poetry."

"Poetry?"

"I thought it might be set to music for the Court."

Malkar sat down before her mirror, staring through it at Lilene.

"Very well. Let us hear your offering."

And Lilene, in a voice itself like a song, replied:

> *"Last night I saw a star*
> *Shaped like a rose.*
> *It hung so bright, the child*
> *Of earth or heaven, who knows?*
> *Its face was that of love,*
> *I watched for hours,*
> *Then slept, and when I woke*
> *The sky was full of flowers."*

Malkar was silent.

"I have other songs," said Lilene softly.

"Go now," said Malkar. "Your father has been asking for you. And on your way, attend the Thing. I suppose the creature must be at the banquet. Send in my women. Tonight we shall make an impression on our guest. You're dismissed."

Outside, she dried her forehead on her veil. Her women fell into step behind her. Trailing behind them came a rather grubby little page. No one spoke. Lilene went past tall windows that looked out on to the courtyard. Horses and men were below.

She glanced down and saw the Captain and his lieutenants, elegant in their white dress uniform. She hurried on.

Music was coming from the next apartment, a plangent lyre and a man's sweet tenor voice. A sad song, of death and an uncertain heaven. The Princess Honyia could bear only sad songs.

Lilene entered alone. Honyia sat on a low stool, her dark hair, legacy of her Taratamian mother, tightly bound and shaped like a coffin about her small face. She was engrossed in the music. Honyia had not spoken for five years, when she was sixteen, and was now never likely to.

She acknowledged Lilene with a lift of her dark eyes, neither fearful nor pleased. The minstrel stopped playing and came to kneel before Lilene; a young man with a sharp keen face and a tender mouth. He looked deep into Lilene's eyes with such meaning that her heart began to drum against her ribs. She said brightly, "Good evening, dearest sister. The music is lovely. I'll help you prepare for the banquet."

Honyia looked at her and nodded blankly. Lilene continued in a loud cheerful voice. "Is that a new lyre, little master? May I see? Bring it to the light."

Together they went to a window bay, their heads bent close over the instrument. The musician murmured: "The news is bad. The Draconhood have taken your letter."

Lilene struck the lyre. It dropped one sweet note. Under its resonance she whispered: "The courier?"

"Killed, before they could question him. Shot down with an arrow meant only to wound. But, oh, princess. They have taken Cristarpa!"

He laid his hand over hers as it lay on the lyre. "Your lip's bleeding, princess." (She had bitten it to stop a cry). "We must remain calm. Cristarpa won't talk. You're safe."

"I don't care about that," she said brokenly. "Poor Cristarpa. He was so brave."

"Remember the cause," he muttered fiercely. "Raise up! Or die. The time is coming."

"Thank you, little master," she said, briskly turning. "It's a fine piece. Now, Honyia my love. Let's make you fair for the revel."

Lilene had a silver basin in her hands. Honyia's eyes filled with terror. Lilene put her arms round her. "It's only oil, darling," she whispered. "Perfumed oil to clean your face. No water, I promise. No water."

During her childhood and her growing up, Honyia was put to work in the kitchen by Malkar. She liked this, the cooks were kind and young Household officers sometimes called to collect provisions. Sometimes they did not realise her rank and joked with her, admiring her petite dark looks. That was when she fell in love with Jonakin; he was twenty.

When he was off-duty, he would call a minstrel and a drummer and they would dance together in the little servants' courtyard. One day he kissed her as they danced, declared his love. And in that moment, Malkar, forewarned by one of her minions, appeared and stood in the doorway, watching them.

Any object dropped in the great lake in the palace gardens was lost forever. To this lake Malkar had taken her, dragging her by one arm so that when she fell her body trailed like a sack. Malkar had held her by her legs and neck, submerging her head down in the water. She had held her there for an eternity, while her lungs burst and flamed with approaching death. When she opened her half-drowned eyes, she had seen Lilene watching a little distance away. Lilene had saved her life, but Honyia could never thank her.

Malkar had summoned Jonakin to her private apartments to rebuke him. It was said that he had been sent on dangerous manoeuvres to the western delta of the River Takk. He was never seen again.

And never now would Honyia speak, in case the water should hear her.

"They certainly know how to enjoy themselves," murmured Lieutenant Recansky.

"Even the fish are dancing." Lieutenant Pinpol glanced round the walls.

The Hall of the Sea was shaped like a pearl. The curved walls were faced with mother-of-pearl. They conjoined at the zenith where an enormous silver oyster was fixed. Convex glass punctuated the walls, behind which assorted marine life swam; octopi, swordfish, small sharks, all divided by curtains of silver from swarms of piranhas, dolphins, turtles. And angelfish, and fish so phosphorescent they served as lanterns. All swimming or moving with mirrors behind them, giving the illusion of a limitless marine population. Now and then a small war would break out in the tanks and the water would redden. The Karenian court applauded this, laughing.

"The dinner was very salty," observed Pinpol. "I never want to see another salmon or herring."

"I thought it was marvellous," said Narzet. His blue eyes sparkled.

"It's to make them drink more," said Tallis. He stood never taking his eyes from the dais, where the duchess sat with Prince Vergon and Lilene. He had eaten little, and drunk only water. Even that had tasted slightly salt, like tears. He kept his hand on the pommel of his dress sword. The duchess seemed to be enjoying herself, but he could not relax. He had already organised her night guard, Sergeant Delvas and a dozen of his best men. He had decided to put Narzet in charge of them. Give him some responsibility, he thought.

"Don't drink too much, Narzet."

"No, Captain."

Near the dais but lower, were Vergon's friends. All dressed in silks and sarcenets and velvets, weighed down with jewelled collars and on their best behaviour. Bratt, Lord of the Middle Way, Fraycon, Lord of the Bankside, Molgon, Lord of the Hill Pastures. Wurmol, Lord of the Wells. Tallis watched them too, weighing them up like dangerous dogs, but they remained quiet.

The small dark girl who never uttered he took to be a superior kind of waiting woman. On the dais, Lilene was a distant sliver of cream and gold. Prince Vergon wore a low amethyst crown; he was drinking hard. Performers were employed in the centre; half-watched by courtiers gathered on the perimeter. Jugglers and giants, a ballet of young girls who mimicked the waves of the sea. The musicians played softly, as if saving their best. They were all waiting for the king and queen.

A trumpet blasted the air. The court sank to an obeisance. Tallis had no intention of kneeling to the foreign power. He came to attention, his salute like the silent crack of a whip. The three other officers copied him. King Enial was carried on a silver chair by six men. But Malkar flowed as if borne on a running tide, her feet hidden by the length of her extraordinary gown. It clung and rippled away from the lines of her body. It was both blue and green, with white flecks like wavelets, and translucent so that her nakedness showed; the high white breasts tipped with coral moons, the ebony delta at her groin. Everything visible but then, next instant, suddenly unseen, so that those who blinked at the sight reckoned it an illusion of their own desire.

Her crown was a silver crab under a delicate glass castle in which live fish darted. In her nightblack hair hung line on line of pearls. The long dazzle of white was threaded with Taratamian opals. Her heavy lids were raised, her eyes stars of amber.

Narzet turned pale. He made a little incoherent sound. He even swayed a little where he stood.

"Lieutenant," said Tallis from the side of his mouth. "Attention."

The court had hands in the air, crying praise. "Hail Enial! Hail Malkar! May Karling live forever!"

The two thrones were in the form of open oyster shells, and the great banners behind them showed the personal device of Enial and Malkar, the sea-horse and the crab. The king was gently settled between the lips of the throne. Malkar held out her arms to embrace the Duchess of Mayt, and placed a long pearl necklace round Mayla's neck. Prince Vergon presented her with a jewelled box. He took her hand and led her back to her seat. He gazed at her solicitously.

Malkar made a long speech of welcome to which Tallis hardly listened. He was looking at the King. Enial's very sick, he thought, marking the sunken eyes, the hands spilling wine mopped up by the silent Honyia. He felt an acute unease. Gods grant us soon out of this unhealthy place.

He was uneasier still on hearing his own name.

". . . let us not forget those who brought our daughter safely home and afforded us the pleasure of her grace's company . . . Captain! Will you and your officers present yourselves."

"Quick march," he said through his teeth and the four of them went in pairs up the hall. Close to her, he glanced once into Malkar's eyes. She is a witch.

Andine's words. It could be so. I wager she dabbles in mischievous herbals. Her wine is strong. He looked past her, stony and rigid.

"You may address us, Captain," said Malkar graciously.

"Your majesty is too kind. We merely performed our duty."

"But duty has bestowed a blessing. Now you must enjoy yourselves." She clapped her hands. The musicians became poised. "We will dance. And we are democratic at this Court.

Captain, you may dance with the Princess Royal. I will honour your lieutenant here."

It was happening too quickly. The next moment Narzet, his face crimson, yet courtly, graceful, was leading the queen on to the floor. Pinpol and Recansky had been captured by two Court ladies. Prince Vergon was bowing to the Duchess of Mayt. Then the air was full of bright sounds and forms gliding like ships, bowing like fountains, dizzily plaiting a skein of colour in the round room, meeting and retreating from their partners like the overlapping of waves.

Lilene stood before him, looking at him with her seablue eyes. His hand in its white glove on his heart, he bowed deeply to her.

"I fear I must disappoint your highness. I do not dance. A war-wound."

She was relieved. She was disappointed. Her fear of him drew her; she would like to have tested it out. She looked in his cold, sad grey eyes, at his hard face. She wondered how his mouth had been scarred. He was a liar. He marched too straight not to be a dancer. She turned away, saying, "You are excused, Captain. It is all right. I will dance with my sister."

She had seen Molgon slouching towards her, and seized the reluctant Honyia by the hand, pulling her into the dance. Tallis's eyes sought out the duchess; he kept her in his sight. Once more, he thought, taking his first glass of wine that day, the sooner we are from here the better.

First she led him dancing on to a shore. The beach was white sand strewn with pearls. The sand was pliant and cool, like a woman fresh from a bath. He danced on the sand. And then she led him into the sea, and he was unafraid for he was safe in her clasp, and they circled and bowed and touched lightly among the waves. And then together they began to rise, wrapped in seamist, then higher until the mist was a cloud, shot with the topaz of the sun, and there they danced higher and higher until he touched the stars. Then the stars were below him at the level of his lips, bright coins of amber, and there was a flash of white lightning in the black and stormy sky.

The two dragons gave him pause for a moment, for he thought that dragons no longer existed, but they were leashed, and although they showed him their foamy serrated jaws he did not fear them, because they were hers.

Then there was neither sea nor sand nor cloud but a bed like a cloud that was ripe with the breathtaking pungency of the ocean, and the body twined with his was white as a wave. And he was drawn into the wave and hovered there for long moments of sweetness, and spat the foaming wave out from his loins, and lay spent and jerking in the ebb tide of the pearly sea.

He heard her voice, saying go on! go on! She rubbed the honey of her voice upon his mouth, rubbed his mouth with the raw red slit of her wet womanhood, making all of him her captive, his tongue, his phallus, his heart. She took him deep in her throat and washed him with waves.

"My true love," he said.

"Ah, my beloved," she said, and he looked down to where the splashed foam of his lust clung to her mouth and chin. He looked at her young, young face. They were children together.

At one time, in his toxic heaven, he hallucinated deep gravel voices that seemed to issue from her lower core: "Take, take . . ." then, "No! not this time, it is too useful . . ." fading into his sighs, her sighs, the cries of cataclysm . . .

"My one and only love," he said. She rolled herself over like a delicate porpoise at play in a swell and her gleaming buttocks had the graceful whiteness of washed shells. "Now here," she said. "My love," and raised herself on her knees and her hair washed over the side of the couch like an acre of black weed.

Here, she was hot. He was plunged into a searing oven that narrowed and gripped his parts, grinding him to ash in an insupportable delight. He was in the hot desert now, blown by the white desert wind, choked and blinded and crying in an ecstasy of pain and joy. The world was his, inside Malkar. He moved within the burning core of the world.

"Everything all right, lieutenant?"

There was a man standing before him, a stern man with a pale strained face. Torches flickered on the corridor walls. The man's voice had broken a long silence. He was standing very straight and Narzet quickly copied him. For some reason his body hurt all over, as if he had been in a grave accident.

"Everything is in order, Captain."

"How many guard on the duchess's apartment?"

"Twelve, sir. Sergeant Delvas, as you said."

Narzet was pleased with himself, for the man nodded approvingly.

"Very well. My room is there"—he pointed to where the corridor adjoined an L-shaped wing. "You look weary, Narzet. Get some sleep."

Narzet gave a perfect salute. "At your orders, Captain."

Tallis watched as Narzet turned and walked steadily along the corridor where Sergeant Delvas headed the line of guard. Then he went slowly to his own apartment. He felt drained and not quite himself. He had drunk only half the glass of wine offered to him, but he felt as if he had been on the town all night with Lepo, back in Tam. He wondered how any of the Karenians could stand up straight. But they had all gone in orderly fashion to bed, and at last he could give way to his longing for sleep. He had not liked what he felt. He had watched the duchess continually, had seen her handle the attentions of the Crown Prince modestly and firmly, and had finally seen her to her chamber where two waiting women and a page attended her.

Narzet had reached the stolid figure of Sergeant Delvas. Narzet had the taste and feel of Malkar inside him. He had no memories, only those of her body and her command. Yet as he spoke to the sergeant he was full of calm authority.

Tallis removed his white dress jacket, his belt and sword, and his boots. In shirt and breeches he stretched himself on the bed. It was huge, with quilts of swansdown and pearl moons studding the canopy. He felt for his sword, propped near him at the bed-head. He closed his eyes and prayed briefly.

"Defend us in moonlight and dark. Be at our right hand and our left. Lion of Night, grant us peace and protection. So be it ever."

He thought: will the Karenians be insulted by the presence of such a strong guard around the duchess? Well, let them be. Sleep came down on him like an inky drawbridge, cloistering him in an abhorred dream.

Once more he was a child, still ravaged by the news and manner of his father's death. He craned upwards past the dung-coloured habit of the monk into the fat, wine-ruddled face. He knew in his dream what the year was; Crown Prince Valm was married to Sarene of Karkis, old King Valm the Sixth and his queen, Gilaene, were still alive. There was peace with Karenia at last. "We do not allow weeping, insect," said Brother Sundew.

"But my father was murdered . . ."

"Quiet," said Brother Sundew, and licked his fat red lips, moving closer. The dream ran on faster, there was blood on the stones . . . he was running, running. Then a high voice—one of the other novice monks?—shouting: "Trouble! trouble!" over the pounding of his heart.

"Captain. Trouble!" the page was dancing about in the dimming glow of the night lantern. Tallis leaped from the bed, seizing his sword. The page yelled: "Come on, come on!"

"The duchess."

"Yes. Hurry!"

He shoved the page out of the way and burst from the chamber. He was along the corridor in a dozen strides. The corridor was deserted. From the duchess's chamber came a sound like a small animal being hurt. Tallis threw himself against the door, which opened abruptly.

The two waiting-women were snoring, a wine flagon upturned beside them. On the bed Prince Vergon, naked from the waist down, was straddling the little duchess. Her nightgown was round her neck, her face half-smothered by the pillow. The prince knelt between her legs, which he had forced upwards and apart so that her bent knees touched her shoulders. Her feet waved feebly in the air. At Tallis's thunderous entry Vergon turned his head. Tallis saw everything; the duchess's one desperate eye appearing from beneath the edge of the pillow, the prince's member on the point of penetration.

Tallis's thoughts raced, weighing up the implications in a flash. With a sword-thrust he could have terminated one branch of the Karling dynasty. He was here with one hundred men, within the walls of a foreign power that could muster ten thousand. He acted in the only way possible. He turned his back, rubbing a hand over his eyes as if half-asleep.

"Your pardon, your Grace," he said smoothly. "I heard a noise." Very slowly turning—"It's dark in here. Why, Crown Prince—I see you were anxious for the duchess too. She has nightmares. Perhaps that was what we heard."

And he walked, eyes humbly down, slowly towards the bed. When he looked up, all innocence, Prince Vergon was standing beside it, his dress righted, his expression a mixture of fury and embarrassment.

"Perhaps her grace will be able to sleep now," said Tallis. "May I escort your highness back to your chamber?"

Vergon did not answer. He gave Tallis a look of absolute loathing, and walked unsteadily from the room, kicking the fallen flagon as he passed. It rolled against the door as it closed behind him.

Tallis looked briefly at the snoring women, then went to the duchess. She emerged from beneath the pillow, her eyes enormous, tugging her gown quickly down over her body. Tallis expected tears. None came, and he admired her. He helped her to sit up. She was hot, and short of breath. A quick glance showed him no blood on the sheets or her gown. She was shocked but undamaged.

"Your grace." He found it hard to speak to her. "All's well now. Don't be afraid."

"Thank you, Captain," she said with dignity, and composedly drew a shawl about her. His admiration grew. His rage looked for an outlet. He went to the two women and smacked both their faces, hard blows that woke them with yowls.

"You useless cows," he said. "You moronic bitches. How dare you sleep?"

He beat them a bit more, until they fell to their knees crying. "Attend your mistress," he lashed at them. "Gods help you when this gets back to Mayt." He strode from the chamber and came face to face with a yawning Sergeant Delvas, who thought for an instant his last hour had come.

"I'll have your balls for this, Delvas," said Tallis. "I'll have your head. I'll have you locked up for so long you'll forget you were ever human."

Sergeant Delvas waited. Then he said, very quietly so that Tallis would hear him through his rage: "Lieutenant Narzet dismissed the guard, sir. He said it was on your orders. He told us all to go to bed."

Chaos had brought Malkar from bed; minions had borne the stories of mischance. Now the Crown Prince stood before her in his sweaty bedgown. It was useless to dissemble. For Vergon, there was no place to hide. Her terrible look beat him to his knees. His fearful, resentful hands left damp marks on the floor as he sagged and knelt.

She spoke softly. She uttered things that wounded him in his heart and manhood. She reduced him to tears. This done, she became calmer.

"What possessed you?"

"Molgon put me up to it," he whined.

"I don't care to hear about your excremental friends. My son should have more sense."

"Wurm, Molgon, I . . . we thought, that if she were deflowered, Rost would no longer want her," he sobbed.

"So you came at her in rape. I said nothing about rape. I told you plainly—court, woo, seduce. With kindness, sweet words, adoration. The situation was carefully arranged. She was to have been so charmed she would never wish to leave us. Now we shall see nothing but the dust of her departing."

"Can I make amends?" He was bold enough to rise, awakening one of the guardians, who hissed through its jagged mouth.

"You cannot. I have a mind to lock you up."

A little anger made him say: "You forget, madam, one day I shall be king."

I'd like to kill you, he thought. Steel can bleed you, fire burn you. When I am king. He tried to look her fiercely in the eye, and was confronted by the heavy white lids, through which her spirit manifested itself.

"Yes, you will be king," she said. "You will be king when I choose. You will wear the crown, but I will wield the whip, the sword, the armies. Tonight you've proved yourself a fool. There was more riding on tonight than the puncturing of a child's quim. I planned we should have a foothold in Mayt through marriage. Not only for her silver, but as our stronghold when we make war again on Taratamia."

He gaped at her. She laughed in contempt. "It is all preordained. Bleak Taratamia, with her morals and her justice. Greedy Taratamia, who still demands the sweetgeld from the Tirkar goldmine. That clause in the Treaty should never have been agreed."

"It is only one-eighth of the yield," he ventured.

"One-eighth is too much, imbecile. I grudge the sweetgeld with all that I am. With our armies garrisoned in Mayt, we could have moved on Taratamia with ease. Mayt lies on the coast—our forces could have been augmented from the sea. Would that I had other sons! I see nothing of me in you."

"What shall you do, madam?"

"Do? I had thought in time to wed Lilene to Mayla's old father, though it's not the best of my plans. After your lunacy, we must wait and see if Mayt sends a thunderbolt upon us."

"That little country!"

"Oh, hear the politician," she mocked. "Mayt is a close ally of Taratamia. If war comes prematurely, you will be to blame. Think on that."

"Mayla won't talk," he said suddenly. "She will be too ashamed. As for the captain who foiled me . . ."

"Have I seen him?"

"You spoke with him."

"Not a man to remember."

"Well, I've a score to settle there."

Malkar's eyes flashed wide open. "You'll do nothing. You will leave my court for a moonspan. Go back to your villa and your poisons. Play with your beasts and catamites and whores. I'll hang above you like a sword. Go! take my wound as a reminder."

She jerked the leash of the more evil-tempered of the guardians. It lifted a scaled foreleg and slashed like a cat. Blood and a ribbon of flesh sprang from Vergon's flank. He screamed.

"It will mend," said Malkar. "And you will mend too, or worse will follow. Leave my sight."

The thing that was Malkar entered her sanctum, and slipped into the dark dimension. The human anger faded.

The seas sang of a time when darkness would rule from coast to coast. From the Isle of Ruva in the deep south, to the Towers of Kite. Deadly ambition gathered like a hurricane. And the pearl sang, strong and clear, of the Towers of Kite, the far north gate to the otherworld, and the chamber grew icy with the breath of their snows.

Had it not been for his customary concern for the horses, Tallis would have led his homeward party even faster away from Karlinkis. As it was, they went at the double over most of the terrain, the footsoldiers shedding pounds, the duchess's litter rocking a little more than was comfortable. He took them due north in the hot wind, between the border of the Principality of Karkis and the town of Kalvaria. He was vigilant all day and most of the night. He found he could sleep for minutes astride his mare. His skin prickled with warnings. Danger lay behind; danger lay now to the west, as they forded the Takk, beginning to swell with Spring rains. Not far away was the coast, the Karenian garrison of Fort Nial on the delta, Avatal Bay and the peninsula of Kardespra, whence the Despran raiders sometimes launched their attacks.

Narzet, stripped of his uniform and his sword, marched in chains at the rear of the train. Tallis had not been able to get a word out of him. His face was bland, not unhappy. He fell down once, bloodying his knees, and rose with his face as unchanging as if the hurt had happened to someone else.

Tallis had not decided what to do. He was obsessed with getting the duchess safely over the border. The report of the attempted outrage would have to wait. He put it from him while they crossed the Plain of Tirkar, where for once he forgot to think of his father's death. Only when they began to ascend the Tiranians, heading for Knife Pass, did his tension fractionally ease. The Karenian officer at the frontier glanced at their papers and waved them on, neither friendly nor unfriendly. The Taratamians greeted them with smiles and salutes. Tallis dismounted and went into the post-house.

"Welcome back, Captain. Enjoy yourselves?"

He knew the officer well; at one time they had served together at Karetara garrison.

"It's a cursed country, Jankel."

"We know that, my friend. Cheer up. Spring's coming."

Spring showed itself in hill flowers, tough little anemones, wild daffodils, luminous alpines. On the higher peaks the snows were slow to melt. To the west, Avatal Bay's dark azure was splashed with white.

"No trouble from Despra," said Jankel, following his glance westward. "Spring storms have stopped their gallop. It's quite unlively here, for once."

"Gods be thanked," said Tallis, and went to look at the duchess. She was beginning by now to wish he would leave her alone; he was like a mother hen. Nonetheless she was touched by his solicitousness. Mayla was a resilient girl, and had traded her unpleasant memory for experience.

"What's he done?" Jankel was looking at Narzet, sitting on the ground in his chains.

"Dereliction. Maybe treason. I haven't decided."

Jankel grunted. If Tallis wished, you would get nothing out of him.

They pressed on north-west into Taratamia, to where the two great lakes of Palla and Pen lay in a bower of gently curving hills. The air was cool, graceful stands of larch and sycamore and spruce gave shade to living lakes—wild hyacinths, purple wood-orchids and bluehorn. Here, the Lion lilies were still immature, milky green swords pushing for the light.

There was a marvellous mansion at the lakeside for the last stage of the duchess's comfort before the capital, with room for footsoldiers, horses and riders. Tallis counted everyone in; Sergeant Delvas in charge of the prisoner, the duchess's women, still wary of the fierce captain. The duchess's young pages—six, no seven. Tallis frowned. It had been like this for some time. Now there were seven, then there were six. I must be tired, he thought. The sun was down, the company fed and bedded. All in order. He went to look at his mare, who had carried him so well, to reward her with carrots and soft words.

Barbel's feet were bleeding into her boots. She had been thrown out of the duchess's litter after many miles, as the women complained of her unwashed odour. She was still far from clean, and hated herself. But this was an insignificant price to pay, even the enforced trudge, the dodging for cover whenever Tallis rode down the line. Her great cap stuck to her brow, over the mass of hair she had not been able to bring herself to cut. Now she was among the horses, safely couched, half dreaming.

Tallis had not come back to bed, the night she had given the warning. She had not expected him. She knew he would stand all night outside Mayla's door with drawn sword. So she had got into his bed, still faintly warm from his body, and had slept in total satisfaction. She had served the duchess, the army. She had served *him*.

He came in now, startling her, his lantern swinging in his hand. It was like the old days at the inn, when the fat landlord would come to awaken her at midnight to help clear up the mess after a party. She heard Tallis whispering to the mare, thanking her for her patience, her stamina. In the lanternlight his slender figure was elongated against the white wall. Alone, he was himself, his face defenceless, younger. She came to a decision. No more hiding; over the border, she would give herself up. She rose from the straw. His hand went to his sword, and he swung the light upon her.

"Tallis," she said disrespectfully. "It's me, Tallis."

He came close, lowering his sword. "Well, page . . ." She yanked off her cap. Her hair fell about her, abundant. For a moment he did not speak. Then he said: "You."

"Yes, me, Tallis. Don't shout. Look at me. I joined the army, like I said. Don't send me back. I saved the duchess's bacon."

She spoke so quickly he had hardly time to draw a breath.

"It was you," he said, stunned.

"Yes, and if you send me back I shall be killed. I want to stay here in Tamia with you."

"By all the gods," he said slowly, "Barbel. You were the only one to stay alert. You cunning vixen. I should beat you senseless. Come here."

She went to him obediently and he hugged her, squeezing out her breath. She put her face against his shirt, closing her eyes.

"Tomorrow we shall be in Tam," he said. "What am I going to do with you?"

"Think of it in the morning," she said happily. He had spread blankets on the straw, and his cloak for a pillow. She asked: "Are you going to sleep here tonight?"

"Yes. I've had enough of soft beds. And I want to be with my mare. She's worth more than any human."

She hovered. "Do you know your way to your lodging?" he asked. She did not answer. He gave a light groan.

"I see. You want to sleep with me again. People are going to start talking about us."

Barbel did not laugh. "Please," she said. "Tallis. Please."

He shot her a glance that told her nothing. He took another blanket from a peg and threw it down. "You always get me when I'm weakest," he grumbled. He lay down, pulling the covers over him. "Lie in your place then. Keep still. I don't want to know you're there."

She curled herself snugly against the wall, her head at the level of his knees. After a moment she said "Thank you," with such feeling that he was made uncomfortable.

"Next thing, you'll want to marry me," he said sarcastically. "Well, you can't."

"Are you married, Tallis?"

"Not exactly."

For the first time in weeks he thought of Pancora, waiting for him in his house not far from the Household barracks. Pancora would not be pleased; he had already decided what to do with Barbel.

She stayed wakeful for a time while he slept, remembering how, before, he had held her close in his sleep. No one had ever held her close in her life. He had dreamed unremembered dreams. He had ground his teeth and uttered half-revelations, the source of which she was determined one day to examine. She would find out more about the things that robbed him of peace. She would never, ever leave him.

The thing that is Malkar is hungry again. On the delicate face the skin shivers as if held to the bones by an illusion of magic. The white streak glistens like a chalk road in the night. The body of the Soul Thief is a pulsing chasm, but outwardly there is only sublimity.

Darkness has set its sights on the next Taken. He is new at court, very young, too young to have been corrupted, slightly awed by splendour. His father was a brave Karenian warrior, his mother chaste. His soul has all the potential of power, and will slide down easily.

"Your majesty." He bowed low.

He was slightly embarrassed that the queen should receive him in her bower, but it was a command. His new friends, half-joking, had told him, "Obey the queen's every whim, Freyo. Those who displease her are swiftly banished—never again seen at court."

Any fear he may have had fled once he was in her presence. It would be worth banishment, he thought, for a sight such as this. Perfect, she reclined on a day-bed, clad in emerald silk, her arms and breast gleaming like starshine. The tips of her ebony hair caressed the floor. The landfish couched close to her, their ugliness highlighting her beauty.

"Ah, they trouble you," she laughed. "I will not let them harm you. If you wish, we will move from here." She rose up noiselessly and came towards Freyo, holding out her hands to be kissed. The touch of them sent thrills all over him; he could hardly bear to let them go.

"Are you finding court life pleasant?" she asked, and went on with a sweet, almost ingenuous conversation like that of a diffident young girl rather than a monarch. Had he been to the royal opera, to the races? She had watched him dancing in the Hall of the Sea at last week's revel. He was a fine dancer. Freyo was spellbound. If he had not been in love with her before (and he had never before been in love) now there was no mistake. He felt he could die for her.

She startled him, saying: "Come, talk with me while I bathe. I always take a bath about this time."

She took his hand; the joy of this was almost painful to him. She led him into a large bathing suite where water from hidden springs gushed continually in and out of a golden bath. There was a phosphorescence about the chamber, and green-and-silver plants grew out of the walls.

He said quickly: "Should I not call your majesty's women to attend you?"

And she laughed, and stood on tiptoe to kiss him lightly. "You shall be my abigail, Freyo. Undo my gown."

Her nudity was almost too much to bear. And when she skilfully unclothed him too, he wanted to laugh at the joyous unreality of it all. Impossible it may be, but it seemed he was going to have the queen. It crossed his mind that he might not be the first of her young lovers, but this did not trouble him at all.

"Malkar," he breathed, and she smiled, as they stepped down into the bath together. "Adorable, peerless Malkar."

"Sweet child," she said. "You do well to name me, to have no awe of me. For I am woman, you are man . . ." she caressed him expertly, smoothing the thick crimson stalk of his risen phallus. "Oh, such a fine man. Today you're my subject only in love." She lay down in the bath, and floated, the black hair of her pubes drifting like weed, her limbs outstretched to him. He lowered himself upon her, careful not to submerge or cause her discomfort. But she floated, she carried him on the water as if her body were a boat. It was miraculous. She wrapped him with her legs and leaned back, gasping with pleasure as he drove like a ship into harbour, through water into her hot depths. Her body closed around him, sealing him in. He swam in her, groaning.

He wanted desperately to please her, but there was too much ardour to prolong the encounter, and he lacked experience, and very soon, his lunging brought him to fulfilment. "Yes, come!" she cried knowingly, as his rippling seed discharged itself in her and he felt the gulping of her ghostly womb. He clutched her, crying from the echoes of lust, and she disappeared beneath the water. And rose again, her body still leeching him, milking him with a vice of flesh, while an eyeless face, inhumanly grinning, and dripping with foetid moisture, pressed against his own.

Screaming, he felt his soul go from him, torn out as by an executioner. He tried to claw back from the fatal darkness, and the darkness claimed him.

Malkar swam out from under his body, which sank to the bottom of the bath. With water drying on her, she moved silently to dress. Soon the dwarf would come and drain the bath, and the corpse would be carried through sewers to the sea.

She went to her sanctum, with the glowing pearl in her belly, and set it before the black mirror.

Show me the inheritrix.

She is idle. She is lazy. Her beauty grows. The day will come when she will know the power of her womb. As yet it is untapped. No matter; Malkar is the waiter on change and chance. And there is a time when Malkar, like Lilene, was insensible of her powers.

Show me my chosen servant. Disgraced, he has crossed the border. He is mine. My instrument. We shall watch him work.

The pearl light is strong today. Freyo's soul stiffens it. There are thoughts of war, of conquest, of chaos.

Let us visit Little Taratamia, and strike again at the holy fool.

The abbess Andine was backed up against the wall, fighting for the life of her soul and her House. Behind her the Lions of Day and Night were losing their illumination, as the fierce wind blasted the room from wall to wall. It always started with the wind. Sheaves of papers, heavy bound books dashed about the air like a flock of wild birds. Her lectern was on its side. The chest of opals had been torn apart and the stones scattered. The candles died at the feet of the Lions. The incense flared red in protest then was extinguished. The wind was soundless; that was what made it terrible.

In the House, the novices slept their holy sleep; in the garden, the pure young men dreamed their sacred dreams. Andine was alone with the madness that raged about her. Her wimple was torn from her head, her white hair streaming as in a vortex. Her habit was in shreds, revealing her fragile limbs.

The visitation of this night had been half-expected and she had prepared for it with invocations. The Lions had answered, promising protection. They were stone on their stone and silver plinths, but even they had started to rock a little. If only the wind would cease, then she could call upon the Crystal Lion out of the depths of the ether, and use it as a sword. There was no respite. Battered, indefatigable, Andine of Capashenet fought on, her back to the wall.

There was chaos. She knew it was born out of Malkar's recent anger. Something had been done that should be undone, or the other way about. Malkar was breeding war, and there had been a mental rehearsal of war. Andine's mind grappled for the focus. A child of Malkar's. Could it be Lilene, now in Karlinkis? Lilene with her secret letters and her meek embracing of the Lion-faith? Lilene wore the Lion, hidden next to her heart. Yet again and again, the irrefutable fact: she was Malkar's daughter, bone of her blood. All her life, Andine thought, I have fought Malkar for Lilene, then a blast of air, stinking of a poisoned sea, blew the abbess nearly through the wall.

The spear of chaos had been loosed at Taratamia. Fragments of its impact had found the House of Brides, much as shards from a smashed glass fly everywhere, and Brides was Little Taratamia, a jewel set bravely in the toe of the foreign power.

The low-tide smell worsened. The wind died. A wet rustling was coming from all corners of the room. They came then, the grey things, and she put her hands up, palms outwards, to receive their spite. They were low elementals from a grey dead sea, but they could spring.

Their mouths bit at her gown, leaped at her face. She held her hands before her face, crying from the pain, retching at the stench. One attached itself to her foot and worried there like a wet grey dog. Andine began to pray.

She sent her torn spirit out beyond the gross torment. Into the soul-forest where the Moon-Lion stood with the crescent on its skull. She cried out with all her silence, while the grey mouths lapped blood from her wounded palms. And the Moon-Lion turned its noble head and heard her.

From the Moon-Lion a strange ethereal shimmer detached itself. Flame sprang suddenly on the altars. The incense poured out smoke, forming a shape. Crystalline smoke, like glass blown from a furnace. It grew, filling the chamber. Transparent, almost invisible, stronger than diamonds. Majesty. The Crystal Lion, rampant. Andine closed her eyes.

The chamber vibrated under the shimmer. The grey elementals sprang and scattered and were seared by the curved shimmer of the Crystal Lion. The mist of its body leaped like a vicious cat, destroying the grey ones until all that remained was a small black ash which vanished before it settled.

When Andine looked again the room was still. The holy flames burned steadily. With her bloody hands upraised, she praised the Lion. Then, drained almost to extinction, she sank to the floor. The chamber filled with the scent of roses. The battle was over, until next time.

Kalvaria, the Place of Trials, was more fortress than city. It was also the seat of justice and the habitation of the Most Holy Order of the Draconhood, whose summary powers had nothing to do with justice.

Around Kalvaria was a thick stone wall. The legend ran that there were more deaths than births in Kalvaria. Men and women lived and worked therein, but the main industry was death. Its gate would open for field workers, traders, and the riders of the Draconhood and their prisoners, under their standard, a green shell on a white ground. Visitors were reluctantly admitted and glad to leave.

The city had its mansions, and its hovels. Every facade was vulcanised from the smoke of years, as in a mining town. Nearly every day black smoke suffocated the city from the great central plaza, the Square of Burning. Adjacent to this, the main execution ground, a steep flight of stairs led to the Drowning Place. The city stood over a fathomless spring, and a vast square well provided a less agonising death. It was rarely used. The Draconhood was omnipotent, implacable and savage, familiars of a high court who could by tradition override the decision of any civil judge.

The House of Questions looked unremarkable, set in a narrow street. But once through the iron-studded door the way led down, until the chill of the hidden spring was palpable. Flights of steps ended in a long subterranean corridor lined with cells. At the far end was the surgery of pain.

Weeks earlier, when he was first brought in, Cristarpa had been a young man. Now his face had shrunk almost to the bone, as if he had been long dead, with death's pure pallor. The eye they had not removed stared out, not yet beyond pain, but beyond fear. White and naked, he hung on a large wooden diagonal, his hands nailed high, gloved in blood.

Six of the Draconhood sat under torchlight at a long table. They were dignified in their green robes, and very quiet. In the corner on a low stool the Truth Doctor waited with his bloody instruments for orders.

Lilene's letter was creased and slightly freckled with blood. Colonel Zairopo sat in his Grand Master's high-backed chair, a jar of wine to hand. He had been silent for so long that one of the Draconhood had fallen into a meditation, and came quickly alert to respond to Zairopo's loud voice.

"Could it not be the hand of a woman?"

"Colonel, with respect. We have been over this twenty times. The pressure is too strong. This was written by a man, a young man."

"May the gods blast whoever shot that courier," said one.

Zairopo said suddenly to the Truth Doctor, "Put out the other eye," and the Truth Doctor picked out a crusted gouge from his array of instruments. At its approach Cristarpa turned his face away.

"Wait," said Zairopo. He got up and held the letter in front of Cristarpa. "My poor friend," he said. "One name. One name, and you shall be nursed, healed, given a pension. I'll read the letter to you again, in case you have forgotten. It says: 'Five hundred karins in the old place. One thousand karins and fifty pearls in the new place'. This is to buy arms, is it not? 'Raise up! or die.' and more. Where are these places? Who are your leaders? Save yourself, you have my word . . ."

Cristarpa let his hoarded spittle fly. It trickled down Zairopo's neck.

"Talk to me," said Zairopo, no longer wheedling. Cristarpa shook his head.

"Geld him," said Zairopo savagely. He turned back to his chair as the Truth Doctor went to work. The Draconhood became suddenly talkative.

"He doesn't break easily."

"Tough bastard."

"Has he no family we could pull in?"

"No one. He worked alone."

The sounds from Cristarpa found a resonance in the Draconhood's own private parts. They talked more loudly.

"That slave of Prince Vergon. He could write."

"He died. But all those at the villa are too quiet of late. A little surliness is the sign of true servitude, oddly enough."

Cristarpa was no longer screaming. Something was happening to his consciousness; the agony was losing its edge, becoming almost a balm. He closed his one sighted eye and saw a rose, frilled at the edges with gold. He was adrift on the sun-gold rose. The voices of the Draconhood receded.

"Then tell me, is docility a sign of unrest?"

"It's a consideration. At the Tirkar mine, those stopped work who had toiled long in silence. They attacked the overseer."

"This has happened before. A few hangings brought them into line."

"There's been a bit of trouble, north of Sigillan."

"And in Karlinkis, down on Sluts' Wharf. The rebel preacher..."

"Who vanished before we got to him."

Zairopo scored the tabletop with his nails. He smoothed out the letter. "If only you could speak," he whispered. "Truth Doctor. Ask him once more. Tell him it's the fire next time."

"I think he's going to talk," said the Truth Doctor. He shouted, "Who?" brandishing the letter, and Cristarpa raised his head.

Oh, but it was a near thing. He almost said her name; not in betrayal, never that, but in greeting. Because at last she stood with him in his mind, smiling, with her rose-mouth and sunshine hair. Without a sound he spoke to her. I kept the faith. And the bewitching smile spread throughout his torn body, and he was suddenly sailing on the crescent moon of her smile, into a sweet freedom of nothing . . .

"Colonel," said the Truth Doctor, embarrassed. Zairopo rose and peered. Blood gushed from the artery in Cristarpa's groin. A red lake widened on the floor where the dropped letter, indecipherable now, floated like a raft.

"I cut too wide," said the Truth Doctor. "He's gone. My apologies."

Zairopo did not waste his anger. There would be others. There would be answers. But the waiting was deadly. He tipped back the last of his wine.

"Sometimes," he said reflectively, "I could almost wish myself back in the army, carving up the Tamians on Tirkar Plain. Those days were lively. There's no more to be done here, Brothers. I'm for getting drunk."

He limped from the place of death, a big man with reddish blond hair and six fingers on one hand.

PART TWO

Secrets

"The general will receive you now, sir."

General Camlot's orderly, a little man invalided out of the army with a hip wound, went with his peculiar twisting gait up the marble stairs to the general's quarters. The house stood a little back from the barracks square, where cadets were drilling. There were paintings on the walls, large battle scenes and trophies—wolves' heads, bears' heads. The drill sergeant's bawling grew faint as they progressed upward. Tallis straightened his tunic and brightened his sword-hilt with his sleeve. Far below, through a turret window he caught a glimpse of Barbel, sitting meekly on the crupper of his mare, where he had left her with strict instructions to behave. A couple of off-duty cadets gave her the eye; she ignored them. Barbel looked almost like a lady, until you saw her tough childish face. Tallis had given her a thorough bath at the last stopping-place, scrubbing her almost raw, and had appropriated a gown from one of the duchess's women. Her hair, in two long clean plaits, shone in the morning light.

The orderly showed Tallis into the room. Its austere familiarity lifted his spirits. There were more trophies hanging beside countless weapons, swords, cutlasses, and various antique braincrushers, dangling on rusty chains. There were paintings of severe old military men. There was a small painting of Tallis's father. He knew it was there without looking. Eyes straight ahead, he whipped out a salute.

"Captain. Welcome back."

The scarlet-clad general, a little portly, chest aflame with decorations, skirted his enormous table and came to shake Tallis by the hand.

"Are you well, Tallis?"

"The general honours me. Very well, sir."

"I've read your report. The commission appears to have been executed almost without incident. Very successful, by all accounts. At ease, Captain. Take a chair. I was surprised by the speed of your return. You must have set a record. Relax, man. We're off duty."

They sat facing one another. General Camlot, thought Tallis, had hardly changed in twenty-five years. His face had always matched his scarlet uniform, his black villain's moustache was as lustrous as in youth. He had lost some hair. His eyes were long-soldiers' eyes, wealthy with old wars. It was twenty-five years since Tallis had seen the tears in them.

The orderly shambled in with tankards on a silver tray. "Nothing to beat our black beer," said the general, smacking his lips. "Though I suppose you've been spoilt by the Karenian grape."

"On the contrary, sir. There's mindrot in that stuff. To your prosperity, general."

"Thanks. I'm to retire next year," said the general, without enthusiasm. "Younger blood, you know. Uppers and comers. Now then, Tallis. What's all this about Lieutenant Narzet?"

Tallis put down his beer. He said: "Narzet, sir, has lost his wits. He showed gross dereliction of duty. Fortunately no harm came of it."

He closed his lips up tight. So far the duchess had said nothing. He was more or less certain that she would continue in silence. There had been a little vague gossip in the Household barracks, but Sergeant Delvas had soon put a stop to that. Gods grant, he thought, that the whole affair blows over.

"What should be done about him, d'you think?" said the general thoughtfully.

"I was his commanding officer, sir. I'm equally responsible for his conduct. He should be court-martialled, I suppose. But on the other hand, the man is sick. He sits in his cell, all smiles. He'll eat nothing but fish, and puts salt in his drinking water."

"Gods," said General Camlot in wonder.

"What should be done, general?"

"Have you seen him lately?"

"Not since our return. The surgeons have. He's fit and healthy, but his mind . . . I don't know, sir."

General Camlot frowned. "You know who his father is, of course?"

Tallis took a drink of beer.

"Sometimes," said the general heavily, "the Red Royals must bend beneath the crown they serve. Narzet senior has always held a high post at Court. Since you've been gone, he's been promoted. Under-Secretary of the Wardrobe. Politics, Tallis. Shall the lad be invalided out?"

"If you think it, sir. It's a pity. I thought I was bringing him on. I was wrong, naturally."

"A heavy reprimand," said the general suddenly. "Then let him slog it with the footsoldiers, if he's able. If he improves, make him up to corporal. It's in your hands, and that contents me well enough. By the by, I believe you're due for the Little Opal. Only a minor medal, but deserved, I'm sure."

"Thank you, general." Barbel should have the medal, he thought uncomfortably.

"Of course, we could always send him for a term to Fort Opal. With the Desprans just down coast, that's enough to shock anyone into sanity."

"I hear they've been peaceful of late."

"Only because of the weather. Sooner or later, we shall have the knives out. You served at Fort Opal, didn't you, Tallis, when you were a sprig?"

"Not until later, sir." Almost unconsciously, his forefinger stroked the diagonal scar across his lips. The general observed the gesture.

"Old wounds," he said quietly. "They often ache with the heart's weather."

He looked straight at Tallis over the rim of his tankard, and they both fell silent.

Tallis thought of the least of his three wounds; this one he could remember almost with ease and humour. Ten years old, one of the very junior cadets at Karetara garrison. And Karetara, with all its harshness, was a haven compared to that which he had just left. Almost too small to perform the duties of baggage-boy, he was even so subject to the disciplines and traditions. The cadets' initiation ceremony fell into three parts. The first two were unpleasant—retrieving a helmet from the spire of a highish tower; walking a narrow beam over water (if you fell in you were committed to eating a small piece of horsedung); the third was undeniably dangerous. You were suspended upside-down on a quintain, while the cadets took turns to rush at you, slashing with the flat of their daggers. The daggers were sheathed, even so, if you failed to turn your head away in time, your face was badly bruised. Major Vica's son—already conscious of privilege and superiority, was a big boy, a bully. He had it in for Tallis, calling him The Monk, an allusion to Tallis's sojourn in the Bay of Moons monastery. Tallis ignored him.

He scaled the tower without hurt. He fell in the water and consumed the dung, which tasted of bitter straw. They hung him by his heels from the quintain, and charged him with their padded weapons. Major Vica's son swore that his knife had accidentally slipped from its sheath at the last moment. He was lightly scolded; none of his superiors heard his later boasting of how he had marked the Monk.

Tallis had not sought vengeance; so low was he in spirit at this time that he fancied the scarring no more than his deserts. It was not until years later, when General Camlot found it timely to show his favour, remarking: "It will make you more desirable to the ladies," that he had thought more about it. For a long time, while he kept close within himself, he thought nothing about ladies either.

He realised General Camlot was addressing him now, saying something about the Desprans.

"Yes, yes. Quiet, until next time."

"Captain," said the general impatiently, "I was telling you. They have a new weapon. We're calling it a quebus. A stray raider came ashore and we took him. Observe."

From beneath his great table he produced a long firing-piece shaped rather like a bugle, with a wick and powder, which the general now prepared to ignite. He then raised it to shoulder height, and Tallis, observing its aim, hurriedly rose and flung open the window. The general advanced, holding the weapon steady.

"See that pigeon?" He indicated an innocent-looking bird taking the sunshine on a roof. "Now."

Fire streamed up the wick; the powder burned, and with a loud bang, an iron ball was discharged. Below, the cadets' drill fragmented, Barbel's mount reared, nearly unseating her, and the ball sped high across the square, amputating the left ear of a gargoyle. The pigeon flew away.

"Damn," said the general cheerfully.

"It takes practice, I imagine," said Tallis diplomatically.

"Even so, it's a damn sight more lethal than ballistas," said the general grimly. "Our armourers are working on one now." Then he said suddenly, "what's the temperature down in Karenia?"

"Warm. Someone spat on our colours at an inn. I brought him to his knees."

"The colours!" said the general, as if to himself. "I remember, Tallis, how you brought the colours home when your general had fallen. With a hundred Despran prisoners too. That's when I knew you would make captain. A Red Royals Captain, nothing less."

"I'll always be grateful. But I know this—I'd rather fight the Desprans—than Karenia."

And his eyes moved automatically to the portrait of his father in uniform, smiling sternly.

"It's history, my boy," said General Camlot.

"Never to me, sir. It's like yesterday."

"You're still seeking that assassin?"

"In a way, I was glad to go into Karenia. I'll never rest from it. Every step of the way, I looked for him. It will happen one day. I feel it."

"If we only had a name to work with." The general drank, snorting foam from his moustache. "The hostage we saved never learned it, and he's dead anyway. Put it from you, Tallis. Be glad you knew your father. Never forget I loved him too. A great man. Now then. How's your lady?"

"I haven't been home yet."

"Well, you must." The general walked to the window, below which the amazed drill sergeant was examining the fallen quebus ball. "Who's the wench waiting for you? Bit young for a camp-follower, what? None of my business. Come and see me again. We shall have the betrothal affair soon. No sleep, too much eating and drinking. I can't wait. You're dismissed, Captain. My regards to your woman."

Palbo came to meet him. Almost blind with age, his legs clumsily arthritic, he weaved purposefully across the small court in front of the house, down the path to the gate guarded by small stone lions, and shoved his long nose into Tallis's palm. His hairless bow of a tail swung majestically from side to side.

He gave a tremendous sigh of joy, and overcome by emotion, sagged to the ground.

"You old fool," said Tallis. "Are you glad to see me?"

I knew you'd come, said the sweep of the tail on the path. I nearly died without you. But I knew. The day, the hour.

"Cold nose," said Tallis, pulling it in rough love. "Come on. My boy. Foolish old boy. Good dog."

"He's enormous." Barbel walked a pace behind them. She sounded, and was, nervous.

"You should have seen him once. I got him from out of the river, trying to swim with a rock round his neck. Six weeks old. Rat-size. Still a rat, aren't you, my lad?" He ran his hand over the dog's narrow skull, and Palbo sighed again in ecstasy.

The house had been his father's private dwelling. Colonel Tallis had left it to his only heir; when Tallis had been appointed to the Household Red Royals, he had been able to claim it as his quarters. It stood in a quiet courtyard. More stone lions climbed the portico, the windows were of shining mullion glass. There was a small orchard at the rear, stables, a rose arbour, fishponds and Pancora's knot garden. The door knocker was a gilt lion. He thought: never have I been so glad to be home, and I don't know why.

Servants greeted him, keen to take his baggage. A groom ran from behind the house to see to the mare. All faces were familiar, welcome sights, yet somehow strangely, subtly altered.

He had hoped that Pancora would be waiting to welcome him, like Palbo. He went upstairs to her solar, where the Spring sun blazed in. He could smell her perfume, musk and Lion-lilies. She was playing her little harp. He had bought her that harp on her last birthday; she was adept, almost professional. Her dark husky voice wafted down the stairs as he climbed, with Barbel trailing uncertainly behind. Pancora sang: —

> *"Three loves have I; one dark as night,*
> *One like the sky, a shining light.*

And one like rain, a man of mist,
And none of these has ever kissed
My hand, or won me for a bride.
I can't decide.
The night for love, the sky for prayer,
But in the mist, what passes there?"

He wondered if she had been unfaithful. He had his suspicions. He was often long away. He knew that during the last Despran campaign she had been beset by admirers; young officers serenaded her nightlong, sent her poems and sweeteners. Tallis would probably never know the truth, and to question her would demean them both.

Pancora was the young widow of a brother officer. She was so good-looking that Tallis had been genuinely amazed when she had attached herself to him, with great determination to set up house with him. They had spoken of marriage once only, and that some time ago. He halted at the solar door. She had her head bent close to the harp. He turned to Barbel, who was tripping over her gown. "You've got the package?" To Palbo, crawling painfully upstairs after him: "Lie there. Stay." He took the package from Barbel. "Wait," he told her, and stepped into the solar. Palbo sneaked in after him.

Pancora was wearing a long yellow gown with a split skirt that showed her leg. Her crow-black hair was cut as short as a young boy's, an outrageous style copied nonetheless by the Court ladies. It was sleek hair, with curving tendrils on her cheeks and brow. Her eyes tilted up at the corners. The eyes moved from the harp to Tallis. He went swiftly towards her. She rose, and he took her hands and kissed them. He could not tell whether she was pleased to see him or not, so he kissed her to find out. She had a full voluptuous body which he gathered close in his arms.

She locked her arms round his neck. "So you're back. Uncorrupted, I hope, from the wicked South."

"I'm incorruptible," he said, in the same joking tone. "How are you, Pan?"

"The same, Ricalpa." Her eyes fell on the package he had laid down while he kissed her. "You've brought me a present."

"Don't I always?" She was tearing off the wrappings. "Silk," she said.

"Yes, Karenian silk, from Karenian worms, fed on Karenian berries. The abbess sent it, and it's a miracle I remembered, what with everything."

"You had trouble?"

"Nothing that couldn't be handled."

"I hear Lieutenant Narzet has gone off his head." Tallis raised his brows. "I heard it—from a friend."

"An admirer. Gods, this place is still like a hive. You can't fart without everyone knowing before you do."

"Poor Narzet," she crooned. "Such a lovely young man."

"Yes, and nearer your age," said Tallis. The more she provoked him the more he wanted to take her to bed. He kissed her again with more intent, running his hands down over the curve of her bottom. Then she opened her eyes and saw, over his shoulder, Barbel lurking behind the door-jamb. She dropped her arms from around his neck. "Who's this?" she asked, her voice rising a few semitones.

"Come in, Barbel," said Tallis. "I want you to meet your new mistress. (My old mistress)", he added, trying to lighten things and succeeding in the exact opposite.

Barbel entered with her usual gracelessness and stood before Pancora as if on a slave block. Pancora had cherry-coloured eyes, a rich blackish-red, riper now with temper.

"What in the world can you mean?" The two females looked at one another. There was hatred at first sight.

"I've brought Barbel to help you in the house," said Tallis. "She is good at most things. I'm sure you'll find her useful. She could help you with your clothes, your hair," he said hopefully. Pancora burst out laughing, a cold laugh. Even Barbel smiled a little, looking down at her feet.

"I think not," said Pancora, queenly. "I already have a trained maid. I do not think we are reduced this far, Ricalpa."

Tallis began to seethe inside. He waited. Pancora said: "Where did you find it, for the gods' love? It's . . ."

"This is Barbel," said Tallis quietly. "She is a girl. A free girl. Only in Karenia do they have slaves whom they refer to as 'it.' Barbel has no family. She has come to us for protection."

"I'll not have it," said Pancora in a great temper. "You bring this brat here and expect me to cherish it. Really."

Tallis said gently, "Leave us, Barbel. Go down to the kitchen. Eat something. Tell them I sent you."

Barbel went quietly away, with a last keen look at Pancora. At the door she said, almost whispering: "It's good to meet you, my lady. Tallis has been very kind to me. He let me sleep in his bed." And left, having fired the fuse.

Pancora stood as if turned to salt. For quite some time she was beyond speech, which gave Tallis the chance to say: "It isn't what you think, Pan."

Pancora let out one shriek of rage, as if she had been stung. Then she said, "I am amazed at you. I really am. You're almost old enough to be her grandsire. And she calls you Tallis. And to bring her here—to me. I'm lost for words. That wretch, that waif, that unformed camp-harlot . . ."

"Be quiet, Pancora," said Tallis, in a voice that made the old dog lower his head to the floor, whining. Pancora was quiet. She did not often hear that voice, nor did she like it.

"Barbel," said Tallis, "is one of the bravest girls I have ever met. We all owe her a great deal. It is nothing I intend to talk about. You will have to take my word. She is a child. I do not seduce children. You will be kind to her, Pancora. Do you understand?"

"I understand," said Pancora. She did not look at him. She picked up the silk and smoothed its rich folds. "I'll do as you say. You know best."

"That's better." He felt suddenly tired beyond words. He put his arms round Pancora.

"How about welcoming me home?" He made to kiss her again. She turned her cheek to him.

"I see," he said. "Is there anyone in your bed at this moment?"

"Of course not!" She sounded outraged.

"Then we'll go there." He took the silk from her and threw it across the room. He picked her up, all her solid flowing curves, without much effort, bore her through an archway and tossed her on the bed.

"You devil," she said, and fought him, just enough to excite him to a pitch. He did not trouble to undress either of them more than was necessary.

He lay hard upon her, and drew her supple legs around his waist. Peace, he thought. The first warning frisson of the approaching tide began in his loins and the base of his spine. Warmth. Home. At the last moment he opened his eyes to see the look of the animal, the red-brown eyes, the short black hair tousled where his hand gripped it. And, for an instant that nearly stopped his heart, drove back his flooding seed, he saw, close beneath his own, another face. A mouth like a blown rose, the full lower lip in a half-smile. Great sea-blue eyes. Hair of clear sunlight. He cried out in passion, in terror.

Pancora lay beside him, a cat after the cream. He lay rigid, thoughts pounding like his heart. *Malkar's daughter has bewitched me. Lilene has bewitched me. Thank the gods I got home safe. I feel still that I've brought a little of Karenia, dangerous, devilish Karenia, away with me, inside me.* He pulled Pancora closer, breathing in her perfume as if it were incense. *Gods protect me.*

"She's in love with you, you know," said Pancora in her muted, after-love voice.

"What?" He could hardly answer.

"The child. Barbel. Yes, Ricalpa. I will be nice to her."

He doubted very much whether anyone was in love with him. Pancora certainly wasn't. They fitted together like well worn shoes. Fondness, that lukewarm word, was appropriate. And it looked to be continuous and indefinite, if war or disease didn't carry him off. Even horses could be hazardous, and this thought took him naturally to the day when he, quite abruptly, first crossed paths with Prince Leporet, youngest son of the House of Capashenet.

A day of storm. Clouds racing, black streaks across the uplands and river, darkening the temple roofs. Autumn had advanced. Brown and amber leaves scuttled around the red rooftops, swirling in mad pirouettes in and out of the marble columns either side of the main thoroughfare.

He was walking back to barracks. His mare was slightly lame and having attention at the horse healers. He was seldom on foot, but cared nothing for it, being cheerfully warmed by his new promotion to captain.

Mad as a trapped wasp, but glorious to behold: here came Prince Lepo, storming down mid-road on a foaming, frothing bay horse, its eyes swivelling white, while its rider clung on in an unregal manner. Handsome, fair-haired Prince Leporet, out of control, sawing on the reins, red with embarrassment, fright, or both. Unthinkingly, Tallis stepped into the road. He blocked the gallop with outstretched arms and his body. He stared into one of the wet, rolling eyes. Fire flashed as hooves skidded on cobbles. Everything quietened suddenly, as if the world had held its breath. Prince Lepo swayed in the saddle, then managed a dismount which, though undignified, was competent enough for a face-saver.

Tallis held the bridle. The wet bit slipped in his fingers. Foam splattered the new uniform. He spoke to the horse, the same calming tongue that bound his own golden mare in obedience and trust. The beast snorted and dipped its head against his chest. Its hide was inky with sweat.

"This is a new mount" said the prince. "Should I send him back, I wonder?" He looked at Tallis as if for some reason he was the arbiter.

"Highness," said Tallis. "The horse is beautiful." He rubbed its velvet nose vigorously.

"Then, why the devil did he run away with me?"

"The leaves spooked him, your highness. It's rough out, today. This is a rich blooded animal. Sensitive."

"Ah," said the prince. "Yes. You may be right. You *are* right."

Tallis handed back the reins.

"May I help your highness to remount?"

He looked straight at Lepo and quite suddenly wanted to burst into mad, reasonless laughter. Behind the fair, comely countenance, there was a joke waiting to be told. The man carried joy within him.

"Have we met, Captain?" Lepo's bright merry eyes had marked the insignia on Tallis's sleeve. "You saved my skin, whoever. I shall reward you, copiously."

"Tallis, Ricalpa, sir. Red Royals Horse. I have seen you before, sir, on duty." He saluted. "No need for a reward, I assure you." He resumed stroking the horse, gentling its fine brow, drawing its ears through the palms of his hands. They liked that.

"Indeed there is, Captain Tallis. I could have come a cropper. That makes us friends. I like new friends. I need 'em. You must come to my party. Do you enjoy a party, Tallis? I'm throwing one tomorrow night at a little house of mine. It may degenerate into a riot, if you don't mind."

"I go to very few, Highness. Regimental dinners aren't usually too riotous."

"Right!" cried the prince. He grabbed his saddle-horn and, hopping on one leg, remounted the calmed horse. "I shall send a man to show you the way. You will enjoy yourself, I command it. We'll have a time." He turned his mount, heading back the way he had come. He bawled over his shoulder: "And call me Lepo, dammit! Everyone does."

He remembered that party, the first of many.

He remembered the woman he had met there.

The prince was waiting for him at the top of a flight of narrow stone steps, chiding him for being late: "We've been partying for hours!" waving a welcome, tankard in hand. Lepo was dressed in yellow velvet, and for some reason known only to himself, was wearing a half-mask in the shape of a small blue dragon.

Seductive music, from harp and viol and tabor was issuing from behind a stout little door. The house was decked throughout like an exotic garden. The long room tapered off at the end into a further flight of stairs. The trellised walls and ceiling supported a profusion of vines heavy with full fleshed purple grapes. Blushing overlarge peaches and apricots hung down begging to be picked and eaten.

The little orchestra played sweetly near a fountain from which splashed a constant stream of rose-red wine. Tables were laden with choice food and the nation's favourite, Tamian black beer. Everywhere were flowers. A pyramid of Lion-lilies whose scent sang through the room. Purple roses. Striped green orchids, translucent and delicate.

The air was potent enough to stun. A hundred coloured lanterns blazed.

There was no overcrowding. The guests were obviously Lepo's favourites, picked for their capacity for revelry. A stiltwalking jester stumped among the company, rapping out a succession of rude jokes and mockery, cleverly dodging swipes from those he insulted. There were officers in uniform and out of it, and a few royal cousins. There were a lot of unbuttoned jackets. All round the walls were gold velvet banquettes upon which reclined gorgeously dressed women, to whom various guests were paying ardent court. The party was, as Lepo had said, at its height.

"Pancora would like this."

He spoke absolutely without thinking. Prince Lepo roared with laughter, pushing his dragon-mask up to the top of his fair head, where it looked about to take flight.

"Tallis, Ricalpa, my good new friend. You don't bring your own bottle to a winery. Just look around you."

They were all young, slender as eels or flowingly voluptuous. There were some who were boyish, with mock-innocent or knowing eyes. They twined in and out of the men, pouring strong liquors, offering dainty viands.

Two girls, both red-headed, one a copper beech colour, the other a flaming rose sunset, came to the Prince with goblets and radiant smiles and sweet light kisses, cheek by cheek, and clinging arms and prospecting eyes.

The copper-hair stroked Tallis's back, a feather touch up and down. It was strangely unerotic. Next moment the sunset-hair began stroking his shoulder and arm from the other side.

I am being groomed like a horse, he thought, and smiled, not to hurt their feelings by laughing as he wanted to.

"They're sisters," said Lepo helpfully. Behind Tallis's back one gave the other a nasty pinch. Combat was in the air, and he was in its zone. The Prince leaned closer, bending from his height until his dragon-mask grazed Tallis's ear.

"They're real beauties. They're miraculous together. And they've taken a fancy to you. I can vouch for them, I swear."

Tallis politely moved from the little stroking hands. He suggested copper-hair should bring him a fresh drink. Instantly both were off, shoving each other on a race to the wine-fountain. Lepo looked after them, thoughtfully.

"Perhaps that wasn't such a good idea," he said.

Tallis said: "Lepo, it's an honour to be in your house. I need nothing more."

"Is the wine to your liking?" Lepo asked hopefully.

"Excellent, your highness. This is a great party."

Lepo so anxious to please. It came to him suddenly that Lepo's princeliness would have gladly been exchanged for Tallis's soldier's freedom. He felt the germ of a lifelong affection begin in his heart. He raised his goblet and drank to Lepo, who had brought forward a stately blonde girl in a large green wig.

Tallis felt strangely detached, seeing the kisses and caresses being exchanged the length of the room, along the gold banquettes, and noticed couples quietly leaving, entwined, to climb the flower-draped stairs and disappear into privacy.

Lepo came to sit by him on one of the banquettes. He was not drunk, but in the musing, mad-philosophical state that precedes drunkenness. A small pretty dark skinned girl came to sit on his knee.

"D'you know, Tallis," he said. "I still remember my first woman. She was my nursemaid, so sweet and kind. She made up for my awful mother. I love my family, but, d'you know . . ." he leaned forward, the blue dragon slid down over his brow and rested on his throat. Its spiny back pressed on his gullet, choking him. "D'you know . . ." and he ripped the dragon off and threw it across the room, where the jester, still doggedly playing pranks on his diminishing audience, caught it deftly.

". . . I've always wished for a brother."

"Your highness has two brothers." Tallis murmured. The stately blonde, starved of attention, got up and began to dance on her own.

"One's the royal heir, the other's a priest. Now, you could be my brother. Brother Tallis, how d'you like that. Weren't you nearly a monk?"

"I do remember my first woman," said Tallis softly. "I never talk about her. She died."

In his last year at cadet school. The widowed mother of a fellow student. It was a precious memory, not to be spoken of. The other cadets knew nothing of what had passed; they were too busy, what with learning to fight, drinking and roistering, while he was still "the Monk." Quietly practising with arms and horses, saying little, never rising to their half-serious, half-malicious banter . . . He never talked of her, any more than he spoke of Brother Sundew at the monastery on the island, and what Brother Sundew had attempted to do before Tallis ended him . . .

He looked up and away before Lepo could question him further and went off on the excuse of taking their goblets to be refilled and came face to face with a woman who looked into his eyes as he stood at the wine-fountain, and her gaze swallowed him, and the empty cups he carried clashed together as if held in the hands of a very old man.

Because this was the face. The very face he had refused to speak of. Now before him as if conjured, or like a talisman hidden somewhere in the recesses of his soul and revealing itself this moment, as if summoned from out of time. Impossible that it could be her; the years would have taken their dues, especially the final one because Katela was dead. And yet the resemblance was so extraordinary that he spoke her name. He said it so softly it became almost swallowed by the revelry coming up from below, but she heard it, and her little frown showed non-recognition.

"Katela."

Then she smiled at him and he filled his eyes with her: the dove-white skin of the small pointed face, throat and breast, the ash blonde hair like silk, the straight nose with delicately carved nostrils perfect as those of a classic mask, the full mouth with well defined lips as rich as summer fruit.

The immense eyes, lucent topaz like the eyes of the Lion. The full breasts, the tiny waist.

For an instant he felt his heart move, and when she took the goblets from him and clasped his hand in hers, he obeyed as if under orders.

He cast one look back to where Lepo was feeding grapes to the dark skinned girl; he went with his first-love lookalike where she wished to have him. Up the slow, sweet scented flower decked staircase, and into a quiet candlelit chamber where there was a large couch trimmed with golden feathers and not much else in the way of furnishings, other than a brood of ivory Lion-lilies luminescent in a tall green vase.

What she did then was almost a replication of that which had happened to his sixteen year old self, and what he did was also a reprise: he cupped her right breast in its glorious fullness and slid his hand into her gown to caress with great tenderness the hot white flesh, while all the time she held his eyes in her topaz gaze and deftly, expertly, began to unfasten the laces of his clothing.

No words were spoken. Her clothes were jettisoned in seconds.

Later, he recalled their coupling as a dream, in which she opened like a flower into which he drove deeply. It was a quiet, seamless rapture as natural as the mating of birds, and yet it made him think of death.

He lay with his lips against the pure white throat. Her hand covered his heart until its racing slowed, and then he heard her say: "Take care, my dear."

He roused to look at her, the one who was Katela and who was not, concerned and wondering, for he had *not* been careful in the business of impregnating her, the deed was done. But she only smiled. Eyes the colour of a honey-bee now, smiling.

"Too late," he whispered.

"No, I mean, always be careful. Take care for *she* will come for you."

Then before he could find out the meaning of this, she was up and enrobed as swiftly as she had shed her gown, seeming to become a flickering of shadow and lilies and candleshine, still smiling her lion-amber smile, and then—gone. Leaving him embalmed in a memory that was sad, happy and uncomprehending, with only the Lion-lilies to watch over him.

And Lepo, when asked later, had not known her name.

Those eyes—cat eyes, awesome, but not terrifying! Not like that recent blue shock!

For now, awakening from the long memory to Lepo in a tavern telling one of his jokes . . .

"And the colonel said to the major: 'Major, I warned you to keep your mare well ahead of him. He always stands up for the Tamian national anthem.'"

Prince Lepo was on form. It was his joke, but he roared louder than any of the others, thumping the man next to him on the shoulder so hard that beer flew everywhere.

"You've spilt your drink, Carne," he cried. Then, accusingly: "Tallis isn't laughing. Laugh, damn you. I command your mirth."

"It's a good story," said Tallis, slowly mopping the table. "I've always liked it."

Prince Lepo howled in rage. "Now you've spoilt it. Throw him out, lads."

Nobody moved. "Tell us another," someone said. Lepo swung round in his seat, almost falling out of it. "Where's the girl? More beer, sweetheart." A fat woman came, grinning, with jugs, and Lepo pulled her on to his lap.

"Do you know who I am, my darling?" he demanded. "Your beautiful bottom is in close touch with a royal root."

"There, there, highness," she said soothingly. She whispered something in his ear, pressing her plump cheek to his. Lepo roared even louder.

"You mustn't call me that," he said severely, "I'm a poor merchant. From a far-off country. Leon the Long. Long legs, you see. And long . . ." he muttered in her ear, sneezing as her frizz of hair went up his nose.

"It's as well that I know you," she said, getting off his lap. "Happy drinking, gentlemen." She left them, smiling, shaking her head.

There were six of them, three lords, the prince, another army captain, and Tallis. They were in the private upper chamber of the Crescent Moon, near the east gate of Tam, where a window looked out on dark water, for like Karlinkis, Tam stood over a wide river. It was getting late, the beer strong, the jokes weaker, but Tallis could have stayed there all night. Lepo had greeted his return with delight, anxious only to take him where pleasure was, incurious about his southern expedition, too full of life's joy to feel any nuance of Tallis's disquiet. This night was what he needed. And yet, it seemed he was taking more than he put in, absorbing the camaraderie, the basic decency of the company. It assuaged the last tremors of unease; only by remaining quiet could he feel the benefit. This did not suit Prince Lepo.

"Hey!" he shouted, banging Tallis on the back. "What ails you, in the Lion's name? You've scarcely smiled, your stories stink. Gentlemen! what say we toss him out of the club?"

"Give him one more chance," suggested Lord Carne.

"He at least pays his way," said another pointedly.

"And I don't?" The prince was indignant. He rummaged in his robe, and hurled a small fortune in Tamian karins on to the table. They bore the heads of King Valm and Queen Sarene on the reverse, and the Lion of Day on the obverse.

"That ought to square it."

"It was my round anyway," said Tallis. He went in his pocket. Among the coin were a few Karenian karins unchanged at the customs post; he had been in too great a hurry to get home for that. He stared at the Oyster, turned it over. The profiles of

Enial, wild hair and fragile bones, and the mystical loveliness of Malkar leaped to his eye. He leaned back in his seat, and tossed the coins through the open window into the river.

"Throwing his money about as usual," said Lord Carne.

"Madman," said Lepo, as to a kindred spirit.

"I hear Narzet has boiled his brains," said one of the lords.

"Has he?" said Lepo with interest. "That's the wine. Gentlemen. I suggest we take a vow of total abstinence."

"I'll do it," said the army captain. "The day I turn into a woman."

"Oh, gods!" cried Lepo in rapture. "That reminds me. We must do it again one day soon."

They had dressed Lepo as a tall girl one night, complete with cosmetics, hairpieces, breasts and jewellery, and taken him round the taverns.

"I nearly lost my honour," said Lepo.

"The look on that fellow's face! When he caught you in the alley."

"He had a knife on him too. You nearly lost more than your honour."

"What's these?" he said. "By the Lion's tail, he was angry."

"He was like a boar in rut. He thought he was right for the night."

"But you rescued me. Dear friends," said Lepo, all maudlin. "My dear, dear friends."

"We'll always rescue you," said Lord Carne gloomily. "It seems to be our mission in life. Open the window more, Tallis. I'm bursting."

"Give the fishes a drink."

Four of them stood at the window, relieving themselves over the sill. Prince Lepo looked sharply at Tallis, turning a coin over and over.

"What's the matter? You're two flagons behind already."

"I thought you were drunk."

"I am drunk, thank the gods. But you're not, and it worries me. You're acting all monkish. It must be your upbringing."

"Don't bring up my upbringing," said Tallis, and Lepo roared again. "I like it. That's good. Oh, you're not a bad fellow."

"You're all right too, highness."

"Talking of the priesthood," said Lepo, taking a copious swig, "my brother Ataret is going to officiate at the troth ceremony. I'm to hold the rings for Rost. I expect I shall lose them. You'll be honour guard, of course. What do you think of my little sister-in-law?"

"Her grace? Very gracious. Surprisingly mature. I wish her every joy, and the Crown Prince too, of course."

"She'll be all right with Rost," Lepo said. "They liked one another from the start. He's very honourable, our future king. He won't touch her until she's ready, and I have a feeling that won't be too long. Anyway, the ceremony's not for a moonspan. Listen. This should cheer you up, you dreary dog. I'm giving a party in a week or so. Rost's last chance to let down his hair. On the Royal Barge—she's anchored in the Bay of Moons. We'll have a splendid time. I want you there. And Pancora."

"I'm honoured. Mind you don't get too drunk and fall overboard."

"Don't be insulting. Anyway, the holy men on the island will watch over me."

"That place," said Tallis slowly, "that place has changed since my day."

"Beyond words. There are good priests and monks there now, not like the rough old beasts of yore. Since they've had my brother Ataret there, their sanctity fairly glistens. Even the fish in the bay sing psalms."

"The sea is dangerous," said Tallis thoughtfully. "Beautiful, and dangerous."

(He had run into the sea, away from the island where the great white cloister reared like a cliff. He had tried to swim the bay, to reach the mainland, find his mother again. The salt had seared his wounds. He had swum as if through blue fire, the disinterested, death-dealing ocean. The brothers had taken a boat and brought him back before he drowned. He had waited long and in vain for retribution to fall. Sometimes he felt he was still waiting).

"But you will come, won't you?" Lepo was saying. "I want you there. If you don't mind me dancing with Pancora."

"As long as I can have her back at bedtime."

"Done, then. Shall we move on from here? The river air's chilly. Let's go to the Tears of the Moon. They've a new singer-jester there. If he's gone to bed we'll get him up, make it worth his while. Come on!" he yelled suddenly, making the company leap. "Let's live. Then you can all carry me home."

The little shoemaker had never been so honoured in his life. He was short and thin, with most beautiful blue eyes, clear as glass and devoid of all but tranquillity and compassion. The eyes were slightly strained today, for he had worked in bad light all night to finish the work commissioned by the queen. He was a perfectionist, and the slippers were perfect. Made of the skin of a young hind, the right foot had an M sewn in pearls and diamonds, the left a K for Karling. The little heels were glazed with the wings of thirty blue butterflies varnished over. Four different colours of coral ran round the uppers. The buckles were crabs of amethyst. No stitching or glue could be seen, and each slipper weighed less than an apple.

He knelt at the feet of the thing known as Malkar. A proffered slipper lay on each palm. He lifted his bowed head and looked anxiously up with his great eyes.

"Do they please your majesty?"

He could hardly believe that the queen was here in his lodging. He had tried hurriedly to tidy things, pushing his workbench into a corner, throwing a rug over his narrow bed. When he had heard she was coming he had bought the best refreshment he could afford, but she had already declined it. She was alone; her guard were somewhere outside with her litter. She sat before him in his best chair, smiling. The smile, her perfume, her presence, all were overwhelming, but he was a craftsman first, and kept to the matter in hand.

"They are quite wonderful, Master Cedril. You are a genius. And now you have my royal favour."

Cedril, pink with pleasure, said humbly: "Will your Majesty fit them on?"

She lifted her gown above the ankle and extended a foot. For a moment he was afraid he had fashioned the slippers too large. Never had he seen such a tiny, beautifully shaped foot. He took it gently in his fingers, and eased foot into slipper. All was well.

"Ah," he breathed. "And now the other one."

"You are a master indeed. I am well pleased."

She smiled at him, so young, so lovely, lovelier even than those he had lost. On his knees, he worshipped her.

"They are not good enough," he muttered.

"Nonsense, Master Cedril," said the soft voice. She looked curiously about the little chamber.

"Do you live here alone?"

"Quite alone, madam. My wife and daughter died two years ago. A summer fever."

"I am so sorry." She placed her hand on his head. The touch made him shiver. It was strange, like the blessing of a priest and a lover's caress in one. He found himself rubbing his head against her palm as if he were a cat. All his dead male desires awakened with frightening suddenness. His hand was on her ankle.

"How soft your hands are, and how gentle. My feet are tired, and my legs. Too much dancing, I expect. Will you rub them for me?"

She raised her skirt higher. He did as she asked, and more. He found his hands climbing smooth forbidden slopes, while his brain chattered, no, you must not, this is the queen, what are you doing, for the gods' love! but he was powerless against the ascent of his fingers, and when he heard her sigh in rapture, his loins ruled, and Malkar came down softly into his arms. His head went beneath her gown and he caressed her with his mouth.

"Love me," she whispered.

They were soon together, the sordid little bed creaked alarmingly and the rug was rough to their skin, but she did not seem to mind. She clung to him, her arms like lianas, her vulva a gentle grasping sea-anemone. Something touched his heart and spirit and he wept while he sank kisses into her small smooth body and felt a poignancy of joy as pure as he was.

"Come, my love, come, Cedril!" he heard her cry, gasping, and he arched over her and spent luxuriantly in her and she was his dead wife and all that was dear, and she was death.

The paroxysm that shook him cancelled out all pleasure. He was gripped in an inhuman clamp, he was drowning, he was burning. He fought desperately to the end, his blue eyes bloodied and bulging with the struggle. The darkness was leisurely, almost thoughtful, as it devoured his soul like a rich morsel. The darkness purred and gloated as it ate him up, and before it tossed him away like the core of a fruit, he saw its terrible face. The darkness had taken its due, the deeps received him.

She took the pearl from her navel. The purity of the Taken was so powerful that she needed no mirror to have the sight. She whispered: Show me Taratamia. What passes?

So. Princes are revelling, complacent and carefree. How little they know.

There shall be tears for wine, and lamentation for music.

The soul-glutted pearl vibrates, clear as a moon.

The tiny feet don the new slippers. Their maker lies still, his face written with agony.

Darkness rises in beauty, to walk the world like a pestilence.

"I concede," said Lord Carne. He wiped the sweat from his forehead and threw the towel to one of the pages who stood in admiring rows round the walls. Like Tallis, he was dressed in white open-throated shirt and breeches, with soft shoes on his feet. "You're my master with sabres today. Can I persuade you to a sword-bout? Say, two out of three?"

"My pleasure." Tallis took his sword from a page. It was his special weapon, the pommel the slim gilt body of a lion, supple and twisted, leaping-cat-fashion, and it fit snugly over the knuckles of his sword-hand. They were in the Sun-gallery, the walls covered with armorial bearings, weapons and shields. The colours of long-dead lords hung in bright rows overhead. The floor was a long mosaic of suns and lions.

They saluted each other with raised blades. Sunlight streaming through oriel windows ran like wildfire on the dancing steel. The blades hissed upon each other like snakes, kissed and locked and parted, came together with knotted hilts, parted. Tallis's point pirouetted and lunged, made harsh music on his opponent's blade, knocking it askew. A tiny piece of fabric floated from Carne's sleeve. The pages applauded softly and their master glared at them.

These unguarded games were so dangerous that only the crack swordsmen were allowed to adventure them.

"You're tiring, Tallis," said Lord Carne, catching his breath, and Tallis laughed. "Am I?"- with a thrust so quick that even the sunlight missed it. "Keep your guard up, my lord. I feel like picking apples today."

"Just because" panted Carne, "you're going to the palace. You're getting above yourself. Ach!" as a riposte sent his sword gliding away to the end of the hall. "I'd hate to meet you in earnest, Captain."

"That's not likely." Tallis presented the retrieved weapon to Carne. "On guard."

The second and third bouts ended in much the same fashion. As ever, Tallis felt the sword as an ally, an extra limb. The supple Lion leaped on his hand, warm as if imbued with his blood; at the height of conquest he seemed to feel blood actually beating in the body of the Lion. The Lion had its own brain, controlling disaster; he knew no harm could come to his friendly opponent. He gave himself to the Lion; guardian of all things, arbiter of safety. He thanked it as the armourer took it away for cleaning. Some warriors called their favourite weapon by a female name. This sword was neither male nor female; it was too pure for gender.

"One day I'll avenge myself." Carne had thrown off his soaked shirt and was towelling himself. "Look at you. You don't even sweat."

"I have to change for the ceremony." Tallis had not removed his shirt. He sat, relaxed, hands on knees. "Thank you for the exercise. I feel good."

"And I feel out of condition. You can buy me a drink tonight. What time are they giving you the Little Opal?"

"Towards sundown. The gods know why they're honouring me. I only brought the lady home."

Tallis got up rather suddenly. "You'll excuse me. Before I go home, I have to go to the prison."

"To see Narzet?"

"Yes, but that's not my prime reason. I've been asked to see the Despran—the one who brought us the magic weapon. Apparently it's because I speak a bit of the language. I ought to. I've tangled with those bastards often enough. As for Narzet, I want to see just how mad he is."

"I'll see you at the palace. Lepo has promised me a medal too."

"You? For what?"

"For outdrinking him last week."

Tallis laughed, and left him, putting on his jacket, fastening the tight collar at his throat. As he passed the armourer returned his shining sword to him.

The prison was within walking distance. It was a military prison, and a holding place for suspected traitors to the Crown. Even so, it had windows high up which let in the sun and there was even a little garden, tended by cadets on punishment duty. He was admitted through three sets of stout doors. As the guard conducted him to the Despran's cell, a girl was let out, awry and giggling.

"Home comforts?" remarked Tallis.

"The governor said it was all right, Captain. He is a very well behaved captive, after all."

Tallis went in and the door was locked behind him. The Despran was lying on his pallet, much at ease, with a tankard of black beer. He was huge, with small mad black eyes, and a black moustache so profuse that its thick fall touched his collarbones. At the Captain's entrance he came in leisurely fashion to his feet.

"I should have known it was you, Mervhu," said Tallis.

"Tallis-Cap!" The great Despran came forward as if to embrace Tallis, changed his mind and wrung him painfully by the elbow instead.

"Tallis-Cap, I often think of you," said Mervhu. "That last scrap. How I admire your fighting."

"That scrap, as you call it," said Tallis grimly, "cost us both a few thousand men. Your High King signed the peace, if you recall. That didn't last long."

"Pouf! Who wants peace? It makes young men old. Ah," he said rapturously. "You and I, hand to hand. Have you still the Lionsword? You let me live. Such honour."

"I should have stuck you through, you." He was going to say "you bastard" then remembered this was no insult to a Despran. He sat down on Mervhu's pallet and helped himself to beer. The Despran lowered his great weight beside him, and smiled ingenuously.

"Tell me, Mervhu," said Tallis. "What in the name of all true gods, yours and mine, were you doing ashore in Taratamia? Was it a one-man invasion?"

"Oh," said Mervhu, suddenly switching to bad Taratamian. "Invasion good. We invade you again soon, carry off all your opals and nice women and steal your gold. One day soon. Not for a little while though. Then you and me, we have good scrap again, and I kill you."

"I can't wait, tortoise," said Tallis, having found the best Despran insult at last. "But never mind that. Why were you here with your quebus?"

"What quebus, what he?"

Tallis aimed his arm and mimed the firing of a weapon. Mervhu gave a bellow of comprehension.

"Ah, see, so! Turineko. Our spitter. Named for our god -" he rolled his eyes upwards—"great Turinek. Thunder man in sky."

"So why?" pursued Tallis. "Was the que- was the turineko a gift for us? to show you're sorry for all your past evil?"

"Despran never sorry. Turineko—he not for you. Great wind she blow me nearly on to Bitches' reefs. I sail into Avatal Bay without the meaning."

"What is meaning?" said Tallis, feeling his brain addled from the dialogue. "Is meaning you were sailing south?"

"I say no more," said the Despran, and grinned at Tallis with all his sooty moustache.

"Yes, you do say. To Karenia? You were sailing to Karenia?"

"Karenia bad land," said Mervhu, pulling the ends of his moustache as if at the reins of a horse. "Tamia bad. Karenia badder."

"Who was the turineko meant for? King Enial? Or Queen Malkar?"

The Despran's expression changed. His fingers extended themselves in the Sign of Horns for protection. He was silent.

"Then who? And why only one? Was it"—he said suddenly, "a sample of your armoury?"

"For you," said the Despran with a winning smile, completely changing his tune. "For brave Tallis-Cap. Shoot ducks. Shoot rivals. Blow off head. Blow off ballocks. Good fun."

Tallis waited. Then he said: "Mervhu. I can probably get you out of here. Just tell me what it's all about."

Mervhu shrugged his giant shoulders. "No tell. Turineko no use to you anyway. Need rocks."

"It fires rocks? Like a ballista?"

Mervhu narrowed his eyes cunningly. "Not fire. Rocks. What is in rocks. No tell. One day you find out, then we have good scrap and I kill you again."

"Wouldn't you like to go home?"

Mervhu shrugged again. "No care. Nice here. Play dice. Have young fat woman. Plenty beer. I stay. Until end of world come."

"Is it coming?"

"Oh yes. Plenty blood. You watch. We all fight then, and Despra High King lord over all."

Tallis, defeated, got up. "I'll see you again, Mervhu. Perhaps you'll tell me next time."

"You torture?" asked Mervhu brightly.

"No. We leave all that to Karenia."

"Gods-bye, Tallis-Cap," said Mervhu. "Send me young fat woman."

Tallis went out, shaking his head. "Nothing," he told the guard. "Ask his lady friend if she can get some pillow-talk."

He went to another wing of the prison where Narzet was being held. Narzet, he saw, had comforts too; books, dice, even a vase of flowers. But no women, and no drink. He was sitting crosslegged on the floor. Tallis thought how well he looked; high-coloured, bright-eyed, his hair like mint coin. He got quickly to his feet, tried and failed to salute, and his eyes brimmed with quick tears.

"Private Narzet," said Tallis unforgivingly.

The guard, who had lingered, said: "He won't speak to you, Captain. He'll speak to no one."

"He'll speak to me," said Tallis. The door clanged shut.

"Captain," said Narzet. His voice sounded sore. "My Captain. Pardon me, forgive me. Forgive me. Send for the hangman, but first, forgive me." And he sank to the floor, crying, his face against Tallis's boot, his hands round Tallis's ankle. Tallis had a strong inclination to kick Narzet in the head, but suppressed it.

"Get up. You were a soldier once."

Narzet struggled upright. His bright bright eyes seared into those of Tallis, who thought: this man isn't mad. Something, but it's not madness.

Narzet stood more or less at attention while Tallis dressed him down. He lashed him with words, exorcising all his past anger and unrest. He surprised himself with his vituperation. He continued for a very long time. Narzet cried silently. His tears flowed and flowed, wetting his chin and chest. Narzet dipped a finger in his own tears and licked it; a momentary look of bliss flitted across his face. It brought Tallis to sudden silence. He had finished anyway, and for a second he revised his opinion. Perhaps Narzet's wits were indeed lost. He said fiercely: "Your explanation now, Narzet. It is your last chance, and my last time of asking."

"It was the wine," said Narzet simply, looking at Tallis with his big blue eyes. (Oh, the sea-eyes of Lilene . . .) The little frisson of fear straightened Tallis's spine. He looked with something like loathing at Narzet.

"Take me back, Captain," said Narzet. "I'll serve you, so faithfully."

"You sound like a woman," said Tallis in disgust. "Take me back. I'll take you nowhere. If you're lucky, you'll be sent to Fort Opal. The north wind should clean you out there."

"Thank you, sir," said Narzet, and bowed his head.

"As the lowest ranker."

"It's more than I deserve."

"You're correct. I suggested a court-martial . . ."

They were interrupted by the door opening. The jail sergeant ushered in a tall, corpulent figure. The Under Secretary of the Wardrobe, Narzet Senior.

"I have come to see my son," he said. "I heard his voice. Has he recovered, Captain?"

The only son, thought Tallis. The father's pride. My reprimand might as well have been kept under my tongue.

"Shall I leave you, my lord?"

"Yes, leave us, Captain. I see my son has been weeping. He is contrite. Contrition means a healthy soul. Now my son has recovered he can tell me all and I will see if he merits absolution."

He talks like a priest. Tallis, fuming, saluted and went quickly out into the passage. Instantaneously, painfully, he thought of his own father. Had I broken faith with my colours, as Narzet did, he could not have excused me. He might have understood, but duty bound him first and last and he expected it of others . . .

Narzet Senior did not keep him waiting long. He had made up his mind, and had the power to be adamant.

"Captain Tallis." He arranged the stiff lace at his wrists. "I believe this was a temporary lapse on my son's part. He is young. I know the king would not wish him to be punished quite as severely as General Camlot has intimated. I agree with the loss of rank—for he can always work towards his restoration. But Fort Opal—no, Captain. It is suggested he remain with the Household Guard in a menial capacity until he has learned his lesson. He can be useful; he is cognizant of the niceties of royal apparel; there are vacancies in the Guard of the Wardrobe. Yes. I myself shall see General Camlot and see that this arrangement is satisfactory. It pleases me well enough. Good day to you, Captain."

And good day to you, you dandified, upper-crust idiot, thought Tallis, saluting. He was no longer angry; it was pointless. He was not even surprised. He went smartly from the prison, home to change his clothes before going to the palace to collect the Little Opal.

Tam was older than Karlinkis. By accident or design, it stood on a nearly exact alignment with the Karenian capital, miles over the border in the deep South. Tam had been built by the Old Kings of Tamia when they founded the Opal Kingdom. The River Milesa flowed beneath it; like Karlinkis, the city bore seven bridges. Taratamia had existed before Karenia had been founded by the Old Kings of Kardespra, the peninsula west of Avatal Bay. They had migrated there from some unknown source in the Western Sea, south, to the hot fertile lands and there, like their pearls and silkworms and cattle and oils, they prospered. Since the Treaty of Braf, trade between the two countries had been quietly flourishing. Taratamia exported silver, exotic herbs, wheat, opals, beer and fine horses bred at the feet of the insurmountable Towers of Kite, the barrier to the Far Lands.

No one knew the Far Lands. It was the abode of dead souls deserving of bliss.

The River Milesa flowed sweetly west where it forked into the delta and ran into Avatal Bay. Eastwards it ran sluggishly into the arms of Besla, capital of the Duchy of Mayt, where it became the River Soge. The Palace at Tam was set back from the river. You entered by a sloping marble path, many yards wide, a gentle incline up which horses and vehicles could be taken. The palace was built on a high point of the city, below the principal temple. On an even higher eminence, a massive stone representation of the Lion couchant overlooked the city's destiny. There was a legend that one day the Lion of Stone had risen and strolled through the city to drink from the river, returning to its station for an unknown further season, during which the wars began.

On this day in late Spring Taratamia was in full flower. The Lion-lilies were out, spiked trumpets upheld by the thrust of silver-green leaves. They lined the marble slope like a guard of honour, punctuated by rosettes of purple buglehorn, red spellwort, blue gentians. Tallis rode towards the rear of the procession going up to be honoured, lords and Crown servants and militia, including General Camlot, who was to receive a long-service medal.

Tallis felt ridiculous in his ceremonial helmet. It was thin gold but still too heavy to be worn for long. It came down low on the nape of the neck and was surmounted by the Lion of Chivalry rampant, one paw raised, soaring high above the wearer's skull. As he dismounted and entered the first of the great rooms he found himself walking almost on his heels in an effort to bear his headpiece erect. I am not a Court animal, he thought. This is all a farce. Riches flowed past him as the procession went reverently towards the Opal Throne. Tapestries coruscated with the national gemstone, great vases of gold and silver. Trumpeters cracked the eardrums with their announcements. The party approached the thrones. King Valm and Queen Sarene occupied the highest tier; a little below them sat Prince Lepo and Crown Prince Rost, close beside whom was seated Mayla, Duchess of Mayt. Musicians burst suddenly into the national anthem.

*"Let tides run high, let arrows fly
And highest mountains fall,
Courageous Taratamia
Shall triumph over all.
So friend and foe her power may know
And honour every scion
Of peerless Taratamia
The Opal and the Lion.*

*All hail to Taratamia
Capashenet her son,
Glorious in their majesty,
Now and forever one."*

    Tallis forgot his discomfort. The singing swelled and floated to the gem-starred roof. The occasion ceased to be a farce. Taratamia. It was all contained there, in the verse, in the music that made him shiver: her glory, her honour, her steadfastness. He saw the crowned, stiffly garbed rulers in their gold and silver and opals. King Valm looked well, younger than his fifty-five years, with a very little of Lepo's sweet insouciance in his eyes. Lepo of course, although draped in royal honours and tidier than usual in white silk, looked about to burst out in fits of laughter. Crown Prince Rost, the tallest, the heir, stood to award the major honours. He looked, thought Tallis, as if he had a spear up his spine. His face was as serious as that of a high judge.
    Tallis hardly recognised the Duchess of Mayt. In a few weeks during which Rost had lavished her with devoted respect, she had become almost womanly. Her little rosy face had filled out. She wore a fortune in Mayt silver. The man in front of Tallis knelt to receive a medal from Prince Rost. Mayla smiled like a sunbeam. Tallis glanced past her, his eye caught by the Queen, Sarene.

Sarene of Karkis, the rich principality in the south-west, which had always kept itself independent of strife between north and south, had not even been a pretty girl. Now, at fifty-four, her long face and wide nostrils gave her a distressingly equine look. Her eyes were small, and her hair, scraped back under wimple and crown showed too much of her lumpy white brow. She looked back briefly at Tallis, with peculiar hostility. He had never spoken to her; to King Valm once, after the Despran campaign when he had been taken into the Household Red Royals. He removed his vast helmet, taking it under his arm, where the Lion's paw jabbed into his axilla. He knelt. The Duchess of Mayt rose and came down one step to him. Very deftly, she pinned the Little Opal on the breast of his uniform.

"Captain, I asked to present this honour to you in person." Even her voice had changed; it was richer, assured. "I am grateful to you, Captain, for bringing me safely to my destination."

"I thank your Grace. The honour was mine. Your servant, always."

Their eyes met. I know what you saw, hers said. And he silently replied: Yes, and it is locked away.

And then the ceremony was over, the musicians began to play Court music. Flagons were circulating in the hall. Tallis laid his helmet on a chair with relief. The royal party made their exit, except for Prince Rost, who began a conversation with the Chamberlain, and Lepo, who came dancing down from the dais to wring Tallis's hand.

"Congratulations," he said, screwing up his eyes in mirth. "Gods! I thought I should die. If you'd tipped your head forward you'd have speared my mother through the foot."

"Whoever designed this headgear should be shot with arrows," Tallis said.

"Hush," said Lepo, shaking with laughter. "Your future king thought them up. My esteemed brother."

"He should try wearing one." Tallis looked down at his medal. It had the Lion of Chivalry etched within a circle of opals.

"You're right there. Good day, general."

"Good day, your highness." General Camlot came respectfully to attention. "I'd like a word with the Captain."

"Oh, military stuff," said Lepo gaily, "One moonspan in the army was enough for me. I prefer the artistic side of life. I'll leave you splendid fellows to your war-talk." He drifted off in the wake of one of the duchess's pretty waiting-women.

"Tallis," said the general. "Did you hear the latest about Narzet?"

"Only that his father has had his punishment reduced, sir."

"More than that. His father has somehow managed to have him attached to Prince Lepo's baggage team. Guarding his highness's best boots and the like. This sort of thing would never have happened in the old days. Dereliction of duty meant a flogging job then."

"Times are changing, general sir," said Tallis inanely.

"Too damn right. And not for the better. Congratulations, Captain. Her grace did the honours very prettily, I thought."

"Indeed she did. I think you're wanted higher up, general." The Chamberlain was beckoning; the general swallowed his drink and went smartly towards the dais, his spurs scraping the mosaic floor.

Lepo caught up with Tallis as he was leaving. "Don't forget my party," he said. "Have you told Pancora?"

"Oh yes. They've been sewing a new rig-out for days."

He swung down the slope on his mare, the dreadful helmet lodged on his saddle-bow, glad in a way to be from the palace. He thought of Lepo's party with mild anticipation. It was to be held at the next full moon. He rode across the principal bridge, past the Crescent tavern and came on to the main thoroughfare, lined with stout willows. He heard the hoofbeats behind him and turned, drawing on the mare's reins. It was one of the palace servants, flushed from a swift ride.

"They want you back, Captain."

Even before he turned his mount and started to follow, Tallis knew it was bad news.

The first thing he saw on arriving home was Palbo. The great dog was lying on his side on the path. Barbel was sitting beside him, cradling his head.

"Tallis. I don't think he's very well. I've tried to give him a drink, but he won't take it. Look, Palbo, here's your master."

Tallis knelt in the path. Palbo raised his head; the big bald tail stirred a little.

"Don't cry, Barbel. He's had these turns before. Has he been eating anything?"

"I cooked him a rabbit." She wiped her nose on her sleeve.

"That's probably it, then. The rabbits eat the sulphur grass near the mountains. Starve him for a day. Then try ringwort, only a little. That usually does it. Look, he's on his feet."

"It's because you've come." Palbo and I are one, she thought. Before you, I was flat on the earth, never to rise.

Palbo stood, legs splayed, and shook himself. The tail waved more strongly.

"There. You damned old fraud. Cheer up, Barbel." He gave her shoulder a squeeze. From the window, Pancora watched, silk in hand, her mouth full of pins, frowning slightly. Tallis looked up and saw her. He groaned inwardly. Better break the news fast, get it over with.

He went upstairs and told her. She sat down hard, her black-cherry eyes already dangerously alight.

"You mean you won't be going to Lepo's party?"

"We shall neither of us be going. I shall be, may the gods help me, in Karenia."

In a very quiet voice, Pancora said: "Tell me again. I can't take this in."

He sat down. He said, carefully and patiently, "I seem to have carried out my duties too well. The duchess has expressed a desire to have her Karenian best friend at her troth ceremony. The Karenian best friend, who also seems over-impressed by my efficiency, has further requested that one Captain Ricalpa Tallis should go down to Karlinkis and fetch her. With a cavalry escort, and a pretty carriage, and suitable pomp and care. And said Captain is to leave within the week."

"And," said Pancora in a voice of snow, "who is this friend, without whom the ceremony would apparently be joyless?"

"The Princess Royal," said Tallis in a flat voice. "She's sent a letter by swift courier. Lilene apparently does a lot of letter-writing."

There, he thought. I said her name, and my wits are still in my head.

"I don't mind her coming to the ceremony," said Pancora. She sounded as if she were choking. "But why, in the name of all the holy Lions, can't she bring her own escort?"

"I've told you. She was pleased with the way we carried her. King Valm is pleased too. It reflects well on Tamia. It will be another little dab of mortar in the bridge of our relations."

Pancora was holding a needle. She thrust it suddenly into her own hand, the Mount of Venus below the thumb. Tallis watched the blood come up and trickle down her hand.

"Don't do that, Pan," he said.

"You want to go," she said angrily, sucking at her blood. "You want another chance to look for your man."

"I do not want to go," he answered. "I shall always be looking for him until the day I die. But I don't want to go. Believe me, Pancora, I am sorry we shall miss the party."

There had been a short scene with Lepo, beside himself with disappointed rage. It's ridiculous, Tallis. They won't listen to me. Damn that spoilt duchess, and damn Lilene too. I wanted you at my party. It won't be the same without you. (Nearly crying with frustration). You're like a brother to me, damn your eyes. Better than a brother. Curse them all.

Now Pancora said, without looking at him:

"You may be in Karenia. But I don't intend to miss the party. I shall find someone to escort me. I have always wanted to go on the Royal Barge. My dress is nearly finished. I'm going."

"I forbid you," he said. "Absolutely."

Pancora gave a short nasty laugh. She gathered up her sewing and went like a strong gale from the room.

He could not forbid her. She would do as she liked. He went slowly downstairs, outside, to the undemanding presence of Palbo and Barbel, with a weight on his mind heavier than the great golden helmet.

The Karenian beekeeper wept as he went among the hives. He had told his bees why he cried, otherwise his grief and shame were private. He missed the boy, Hajil. He knew it to be his own fault. Passion had driven him away.

This was a palace apiary; the honey jars bore the mark of royal appointment, a crested Oyster. Standing in line was a score of hives. Generations of bees had bred in them, in the suntrap of orchard fringed by noble elms.

Hajil had been rather like a young bee himself, with his brown body and big shining eyes. He had been good with the bees. He had hardly ever been stung. Yet Hajil had been frightened by the beekeeper, who one day had moved to embrace him too quickly, unable to control his longing. Hajil had been gone seven days, and the beekeeper was worried. The Draconhood swooped where they would, always vigilant for moral malefactors. People were disappearing frequently these days. Yet Hajil was pure, as he himself was pure; there was nothing in his heart but love.

The bees were noisy today, and he suspected a revolution in the northern hive. They had all been happily drunk, but now they sounded intense, like a man with a hangover.

"Quiet, my pretties. Nothing's afoot. No deaths or births or marriages, you'd be the first to know. Oh, I would never have hurt him. Stop your rebellion, little ones. Acceptance is the only way."

A half dozen scouts flew out of the hive and arrowed away towards a stand of oaks. He knew now what was wrong. The hive had become overcrowded. In secret, a rival queen had been hatched and a new colony was about to come forth. The drones would have mated with the queen and died from it, the sterile workers would have nurtured the pupae, and now the process was about to start afresh.

The swarm began to emerge, darkening the immediate sky. The cloud lifted and moved, a suntouched mass coloured honey and dark treacle, and thickened, nucleating around the queen. A few outfliers whirled round the beekeeper's head; he was stung twice. Then the swarm followed the returned scouts. At a distance, he went after them.

They came to rest on the lowest branch of an oak. A crawling almost heartshaped mass, they clung, drowsy and gorged with sugar, stray outfliers circling the perimeter. I mustn't lose them, he thought. He was turning to fetch smoke to make them biddable, when something extraordinary happened.

The swarm lifted away, leaving the queen, and dispersed fast, lost in the air, mere specks going over the tips of the trees. The queen was alone on the branch; enormous, pampered, regal, her translucent wings quivering gently.

The beekeeper closed his eyes in disbelief for a second. When he opened them, Hajil was sitting on the branch, his bare tanned legs swinging, and smiling. His eyes glowed amber. On the crown of his head was a comical white patch where some bird had made him a target.

"Hajil," whispered the keeper, and held out his arms. Hajil sprang down on bare feet and came to lay his head on the keeper's breast.

"Forgive me, my friend," he whispered. "I've had time to think. I was wrong."

"The bees have missed you," said the keeper through tears.

"I was foolish to run. Life without you is unbearable." He wound his tanned arms round the keeper's neck.

"Never would I cause you pain."

"I know, I know. I want us to be lovers. Do you still love me?"

"I'll love you lifelong," said the keeper, weeping.

Hajil drew him down on the soft ground. The swarm had disappeared. Even the hives were muted. "Then love me" said Hajil, and bared himself.

Gently he laid the boy face down while his tears fell on Hajil's neck. He slid a hand under his haunches and caressed him. Close to the earth, Hajil vibrated stiffly in his hand. The keeper penetrated him slowly, the warmth of the tunnel glib as with honey. "Did that hurt?" he whispered.

Hajil laughed softly against the earth. He jutted his buttocks voluptuously, engulfing the keeper's tumult. As the keeper, crying in rapture, prepared to launch his orgasm into the body of the boy, he felt Hajil turn impossibly beneath him so that they came face to face. And there were breasts beneath him and a woman's face, and he cried out again in revulsion. And the lovely face laughed as Hajil had laughed, and dissolved, into something of infinite darkness. A long fanged skull, blind pits of eyes, a vicious clenching at his groin. A liquid, low-tide stench like the corpses of the long-drowned. And the reeking thing spoke, a deep, gravelly gobble: "Babby, babble, bubbie, come to me, my darling!" against his dying mouth.

The seed was drawn out of him like a tide at the moon's pull, and his immortality went with it. The hives broke into sudden life, like the roaring of the sea.

The swarm returned when he was at last alone, and covered his body with a sorrowful pall of black and gold. Buzz! they will blame us! he was stung once too often. Buzz! Shapechanger! Let us fly, let us spread the word. But who will listen?

The picture was as precise as a diamond, doubled in the black mirror. She sat there, doubly beautiful, white and white-gowned, urgently following all that she was shown.

The light is bright on the Bay of Moons. Capashenet is in festive vein. Minstrels, baggage, food, all going aboard. There are casks of drink, and pretty women. And my sworn man, his arms filled with bunting to dress the ship.

Malkar closed her eyes, preparing to deliver from the gorged vein of power.

She had dreamed of him every night for weeks, and now he was here. The dreams were more like visions. She had floated along with him in different situations. She had ridden with him, she had been with him in an inn where, troubled and pensive, he was trying in vain to get drunk. And once she had even witnessed his lovemaking. She had watched him embrace the pretty dark woman, mastering her with grace and power. She had seen his supple movements, heard him cry out. It had made her weep. She had never made love herself, though she knew what went on in her brother's villa and between the lords and courtesans. She knew too that all that had nothing to do with love.

"I do not dance, highness." So he had rejected her, sounding final. And she wanted him, wanted him more than she had ever wanted anything or anyone in all of her nineteen years of life.

That was one of the main reasons she had asked for him as her escort. Not the only reason; a Taratamian guard would be easier to manipulate.

Malkar was oddly detached concerning the expedition, and had not troubled to greet the foreign escort. To Lilene she merely said: "Woo the duke, Mayla's father. He is half-crazed with philosophy, almost a recluse. But hear me," she looked acutely at Lilene, "if you should succeed with him, on no account let the duke bed you. That must come only when the alliance with Mayt is signed and sealed."

Lilene said nothing. Malkar thought: as yet she is still unaware. As I was until the first time, when I knew that Malkar's powers were limitless, infinite. The duke is old; it will be a good test. The inheritrix has my beauty, my blood.

Lilene said: "When I return, may I be permitted to return to the House of Brides?"

"If you don't manage to snare the duke," said Malkar, "you may go where you please. Yes, go back to that wretched Lion-house, and take the Thing with you."

Lilene was secretly pleased. Honyia's minstrel could accompany them, and at the Abbey there would be freedom to work. Not that the palace was as yet impossible. Gardeners came and went, field workers brought produce, itinerant entertainers were admitted. And Lilene knew them all, and they, her.

She had decided on no more letters. It was too dangerous. It would have to be word of mouth from now on.

Beneath her gown Lilene was wearing the tiny gold Lion of Power; around her throat and head the Karling pearls. Her women, chosen specially for the journey, were devoted to her, and one was slightly deaf. Perfect. The day was hot; Lilene wore russet and yellow silk under a white sharkskin habit, white silk stockings and slippers of pearl. She had three chests of baggage.

And he was here. He had not slept within the palace, not he nor his smart cavalry troop. They had this time set up bivouacs in the orchard. But she had seen him from her window, quite close. She had heard his voice. He had been addressing his junior officers, very serious young men, all taller than he, yet subjugated by his presence. His voice had been very quiet, but so forceful and precise that it carried to the rear of the ranks. And cold, like the grey glitter of his eyes. He stood so straight, so pale, with the white scar on his mouth that she had kissed, with trembling dread, in her dreams.

Her women were closing her baggage. She turned to her window. And he was there, one hand on his sword-hilt, the other straightening the nose-band of his mare's bridle. He did not look up. She judged his height—a few inches taller than herself. So if they were to lie down together, they could kiss with ease . . . in pain, she clutched her own breast, her legs shaking as if she had been running. "Wait for me," she told the women. "I must say farewell to my father."

As soon as she entered, she knew that the king was ill again. Not sick unto death exactly, but in his own horrible world. He had been so handsome, she thought sadly; now he was cadaverous.

"Doro," he said to her. "Doro, why have you bleached your lovely dark hair?"

"Enial," she said, "Doro needs more money to take home to Taratamia."

His thin hand came from beneath the covers and waved feebly at a chest.

"Take all you want, sweet Doro. Only come back to me soon."

She went quickly to the coffer, knelt, and loaded herself with loot. She weighed down the big pockets in the lining of her habit; bags of gold and silver pieces, even some sea emeralds, the rare coast jewel which grew in the rocks. They'll like those, she thought. With those they can trade anywhere, everywhere.

"Doro is so grateful," she said. She bent to kiss his lips. His breath was rotten with a smell of fouled estuaries. He had been left quite alone. "Goodbye," she whispered. "The Lion protect you." A little of her pity faded. How could you have been so blind all this time? Why was it left to me? You were the king. Karenia is your shame.

She went next to bid Honyia farewell. The minstrel was with her and she pressed a few karins into his hand.

"For any of our needs."

"Gods go with you, princess. Take every care. The Draconhood are abroad." Lilene nodded. She looked at Honyia. "Do you think she understands?"

"Oh yes." The minstrel went to kneel by Honyia. He took her small limp hand and kissed it lovingly. "She speaks with her eyes," he said softly.

"Make her happy." Lilene kissed Honyia's sweet dumb mouth. There was no response, but Honyia's eyes filled with tears.

"I'm coming back," said Lilene. "And then we'll go to Brides together."

"Watch for a man called Alpac," said the minstrel. "He's Cristarpa's younger brother. They never knew he had a brother. Alpac has taken on the mantle. He's a fisherman."

"That's good to know. I must go now. Captain Tallis is waiting."

"How pretty you are when you blush, princess," said the minstrel lightly.

"I want your solemn oath," said Tallis in a voice like a knife in the ribs, "that none of you have disobeyed orders during your stay here."

There was a communal muttering. "We swear, Captain. No wine. We've drunk no wine."

"Then let's go," said Tallis. "Here comes our noble charge. Gods help us."

The litter, tasselled with gold and harnessed to four white horses, was drawn up at the gate. Tallis turned to Lieutenant Pinpol. "Assist her Royal Highness, lieutenant."

He did not look at her, as she stepped high and delicately into the litter. She slid one sidelong glance at him as he stood to attention beside his mount, his lips set tight, his profile remote as a falcon's. When will he ever look at me? she thought despairingly. She sat down in the cushioned litter, carefully quietening the treasure in her clothing.

"Mount up." She peeped through the curtains. She saw the tender way he handled his mare, the tight muscles in his thighs as they gripped the saddle, his careless yet absolute control as the mare pranced forward. She leaned back, her eyes stinging. They set off at a tremendous pace, almost a gallop, the three officers at the head together with the standard-bearer.

"Look at that bloody Oyster," Tallis muttered. They were flying the Karenian standard quartered with the Crab of Malkar in the colours of a diplomatic mission.

"We're going to shake up the lady at this rate," remarked Lieutenant Pinpol.

"Where's the first stop?" asked Lieutenant Recansky.

"Near the borders of Karkis. I want to avoid Kalvaria if possible. That place gives me a damned bad feeling."

Tallis was wearing his military medals on the breast of his uniform. He looked down idly at the Little Opal. Up until now he had not had a chance to study it. Now he was touched to see that the palace had had it engraved on the reverse with his personal motto.

CEDA PEFUR GEVAC. I face what most I fear.

They went north like an intermittent thunder, veering west. The sun was fitful, the day cooling with the faintest sea-breeze. There were vine-covered slopes, small hills, over which the good roads ran. Troops had marched this way countless times during the Tirkar Plain war. It was travelled now mainly by farm workers, itinerant artisans, beggars. Sad people: the unfed belly of Karenia.

Lilene was disturbed. The way was not as she had anticipated; they were too far west. Sergeant Delvas rode close to her litter. She parted the curtains and was about to call to him, when hooves, drumming faster than the procession which had slowed to a jog, sounded on the road. Twelve riders, their faces half-hidden by the cowls of their green mantles, and mounted on tall black horses. The Draconhood, flying their green-and-white standard, out on the evening hunt.

Colonel Zairopo rode in the middle of the pack. His face and head were sheathed in green. He was full of wine and ill-humour. For days he had been trying for an interview with Malkar, who, closeted away, was not receiving petitioners. Between him and Malkar was a mutual dislike. He had wanted to discuss the sporadic risings of the commoners, abortive though these were. He had been told she had bigger fish to fry, that she understood the Draconhood had powers, and why were they not being used?

"Here's a pack of grasshoppers," said Tallis irreverently. He held up a hand to halt the column. "I suppose we should see what they want."

He knew perfectly well who they were. He would not dignify them by naming them; they were beneath his contempt. In her litter, Lilene had seen them. Her heart rose to her throat. She slipped out of the treasure-heavy habit and stuffed it beneath the cushions. She adjusted her pearl diadem and sat straight. And waited, listening.

The lead horseman rode up to Tallis. The others circled their mounts, blocking the column's passage.

"Greetings, Captain. Have you come from Karlinkis?"

Tallis saluted, staring straight ahead. His foot nudged the stirrup of Lieutenant Pinpol, who duly answered.

"We have come from the palace, sir. You will observe our standard."

"But you are not Karenian," said the Dracon affably enough.

Tallis could foresee a long and infuriating dialogue. He turned suddenly in his saddle and yelled: "Your Royal Highness!

Here are your fellow countrymen, anxious to greet you in homage. I pray you, reveal your noble presence." (And let's get on, for the gods' love.)

Lilene, her mouth like dust, her hands running with sweat, drew back her curtain. Colonel Zairopo rode from the middle of the bunch and halted before her. She saw his sun-red forehead, then the green-clad crown of his head, deeply inclined in an obeisance. She knew and hated him; she had seen him limping about Karlinkis on occasion.

"I beg your highness's pardon for impeding your journey," he said softly. "We are merely performing our holy duty. We are patrolling for criminals—traitors to your highness's royal House." His hood slid back a fraction, revealing his hair. He adjusted it quickly, anxious for his dignity. He was wearing green gauntlets. She answered him, amazed to hear herself sounding calm, and a little vexed.

"I commend your duty, colonel. Traitors must be hounded at all costs. I am sure, however, you would not wish your duty to cost us a night in the open. We are seeking lodging before nightfall."

"Again, your pardon, highness. Why," he said, looking at her more closely, "your highness is trembling. I trust our interruption has not alarmed you."

"Colonel," said Lilene in an even calmer voice. "I am trembling because I am cold. The night is coming. I am hungry. Now, we will pass on. May your search be fruitful."

Alert, Tallis heard all this. She sounds very regal, he thought grudgingly; then Zairopo, with another low obeisance, left the side of the litter and spurred his mount to join the others. He passed close to Tallis, whose mare, usually insensible to all but her rider's will, flinched and reared a few inches above the ground. And a chill ran through Tallis, an unearthly thrill almost of excitement, anger, gone in a flash, to be replaced by the feeling of a heavy stone in his chest. Now what's to do? he thought, unnerved. He turned to see Lilene still leaning from the litter. She was smiling, her lips drawn back hard over her white teeth.

It's her, he thought. Again. Stay from me, witch. He turned roughly in the saddle to watch the green ranks of the Draconhood riding fast away into the evening, going north-east to fresh hunting-grounds beyond Kalvaria. His hand crept beneath his scarlet tunic to where, against his heart, he wore the little gold Lion of Power. Protect me. His hand went next to the Opal medal. Ceda pefur gevac.

He turned and rode back to Lilene as the cavalcade moved on again. He rode beside her. He looked into her blue eyes.

"Are you comfortable, your Royal Highness?"

He had no idea of the expression in his eyes. He was only relieved that she shrank away as he spoke to her. He kept his wits. He felt the Lion beating against his heart.

The little country temple stood on a hill overlooking Karlinkis. The priest had finished his evening office. He placed a black cloth over the great Pearl on the altar, and bowed reverently before it. The stained glass window behind bore a great representation of the Oyster, immaculate Mother, who had conceived without congress. The priest was young, and very devout. Although he disliked some of the things that were done in the name of the Pearl, he observed his duties in blind faith. This was his first living; he kept the temple spotless and pretty; mother-of-pearl faced the walls, aromatics burned in the censers, and there were many candles, which he now prepared to extinguish before leaving.

He thought himself alone except for the confetti of black bats that swooped in and out of the doorway, until he saw the cloaked figure kneeling in shadow towards the rear of the aisle. She—for he saw it was a woman, had come in as noiselessly as the bats. Her head was bent in penitence and sorrow. He left the last candle burning through the dusk and approached her. Her back was stooped as with age.

"Well, Mother," he said softly, "you are too late for evening prayer. How can I help you?"

"I wish to confess," said the voice from beneath the cloak's cowl.

"Then come to the altar." He turned and strode back to where the shrouded Pearl nestled. The woman followed, her feet soundless on the tiles.

"What is your sin?" They faced one another, and she threw back her hood. She was young.

Her beauty lit the temple and stunned the priest. He swallowed hard, and said the first thing that came into his head.

"Is it a sin of the flesh, my daughter? If so, you are not alone . . ."

The woman laughed. "Oh, priest," she said. "You speak the truth." And with a lissom bend of her shoulders she discarded her cloak. She stood stark naked before him and the altar. Everything around her was illuminated by her whiteness, her blackness.

The priest, his mouth falling agape, stepped back. He leaned against the altar to steady himself. He was speechless. One thought raged in him: this is a demon come to tempt me. A demon, that knows all my shameful secrets. I always imagined demons to be ugly creatures. My soul is pure, pure, he told himself frantically. But now my body betrays me.

She moved forward so that their bodies touched. The priest was transfixed against the altar.

"I think it is you who should confess to me, sir priest," she said very softly, and laughed.

The light touch of her changed the priest, and he saw an angel now; more, an angel who could see into him, and not to his comfort.

"You have dreams," said this angel tenderly. "Pearls issue from you as a result of these dreams. Pearls are holy. I would like to have your holy pearls within my body."

She reached out and took his hands. He became riveted to her. It was a visitation of the highest order.

"Lift yourself up," she said, and seemed to levitate up on to the altar, laying herself down in the shadow of the shrouded Pearl. Effortlessly she drew him up with her; he felt he had wings. He lay with her and she pressed him close, and he did that which he had never done, the mere thought of which had brought a shower of lashes from his own hand. So doing, he found himself within a miracle. He saw sights and colours undreamed of; he heard celestial choirs. He wrought upon her furiously, and within minutes felt the dreaming ghost of himself pour out in a flood. A grating voice issued from the lovely mouth near to his. "Sacred seed!" it chuckled, and he knew himself lost forever, no hope of earth or heaven, a nothingness here and hereafter. The soul mourned desolately, calling on its gods, as it slid into the infinity of the black deeps.

The thing that sucked out his essence rolled the Taken off the altar. Malkar drew the cloth from the Pearl. The token in her belly a minute facsimile, she used the altar's image as an eye.

Show me my servant now. Ah, there he is. Soon, soon. The unsullied power of the priest is enough to transport the vision.

Glorious Taratamia! Here is a strike to bring you low.

A cloud of black bats left the temple precinct, fragmenting into the night sky. One bore a snow-white streak between its ears.

Narzet, in the drab grey uniform of a common private, worked in silence, industrious and efficient. He had been fearlessly up the rigging like a tall grey ape, leaving the vessel festooned with decorations as if ten thousand butterflies had settled on her. It was by no means dark yet, but the full moon had appeared, a silver sphere in a cloudless sky.

The Royal Barge was more of a schooner although she had galleys. She had three tall masts and her figurehead was the Lion of Grace, the deity invoked during holidays, flowers in its mane. Hundreds of lanterns swung from rigging and gunwales. Green, yellow and blue lights, their colours obtained by the burning of different aromatics.

The vessel lay a mile offshore in the Bay of Moons. The main deck had been holystoned fit for royalty to dance on. Various large animals and birds were being spit-roasted aft. The drink had already come on board; casks of Karenian wine, black beer, flagons containing a mixture of long-fermented grapes and barley known as Poleaxe, Prince Lepo's favourite beverage, and even some wrapped, hilarity-inducing substances for chewing and smoking.

The surface of the bay was as smooth as the cheek of a baby. The guests were already arriving, and a long line of boats brought them in dozens. Narzet was not allowed to assist as the royal party and favourites boarded the vessel. Officers of unimpeachable character did that, glittering in stiff festive uniforms. Narzet did not care. Wet overshoes were thrown his way and he stowed them. But most of the time he remained crouching behind a stanchion, gazing over the gunwale at the sea, as the ocean turned from turquoise to indigo and the risen moon opened a silver road across it. Narzet fixed his gaze on the sea as if at prayer, unwinkingly looking south.

It was a bachelor party, but unsurprisingly Lepo had invited a whole flower garden of chosen women, some whose reputation was slightly tarnished, all witty, stunningly dressed, beautiful. Lepo, already merry, staggered up the ladder with a beauty thrown over his shoulder shrieking while he laughed uproariously. Prince Rost came aboard in more dignified fashion, but even he had within a few minutes a lady on either arm, and smiled, then laughed, and began to forget his sombre destiny.

Bright music commenced to float across the bay. The still water carried it to the ears of the monks on the island, where the priest-prince Ataret meditated for the future happiness of the Crown Prince his brother. And miles away to the west, the Duchess of Mayt sat in state with the king and queen, wistful like all brides-to-be excluded from such an occasion, and comforting herself with the thought: Lilene will soon be here.

The fiddlers and drummers and pipers and harpists played fanfares of court music, then mountain gigues, meadow capers, circle dances, and when the last guest, Lord Carne, came aboard, he found the revelry well advanced. Lepo was drunk, and as always even more amiable in that state, roaring at Carne for his lateness, kissing him on both cheeks, shoving a drink into his hand and a slim girl in a great purple wig into his arm, and howling at the boatman unshipping his oars below: "No more boarders! You can come back for us in a week!"

Prince Rost sat in the place of honour, his collar undone, one of Lepo's prized mistresses feeding him with grapes and quail and glasses of Poleaxe, and suddenly the musicians ceased all but for one harpist, who began to sing—an ocean ballad, opening a window of peace in the wild night, so that the guests swayed and sat, drinking, happy, their arms round one another.

And Rost turned to his brother, for once condoning his wildness and said, "This is a wonderful evening, Lepo. I shall remember it for the rest of my life."

Even under the dancing, the sea was so calm that the vessel scarcely vibrated, merely breathed its faint creaks as an accompaniment. The moon was so bright that the lanterns lost their colour. All the sky was silver, superimposed on palest blue, the ghost of the day.

Narzet lifted his eyes from the ocean and looked up into the face of the moon. There was one cloud. It slid tranquilly, secretively across the moon's face. A very small cloud, shaped like a crab. Narzet drew a shuddering breath. He crept, unseen, on hands and knees beneath the gunwale to an uninhabited section of deck and stood up, facing south. He whispered: my true love. I am here.

The cloud dissolved. Narzet looked down, deep into the dark water where it caressed the keel. There was a crab-cloud again, just below the surface, and Narzet whispered incoherently in fear and longing. And she was there in her loveliness, her hooded eyes beckoning, just below the water's skin, her long black hair with its white streak a gleaming island about her, her peerless white body revealed to him once more. Narzet moaned softly. My love, my true love. I thought you had left me. And heard her watery whisper: "I will never leave you, little one. I have come to join the party."

He leaned dangerously far over the high gunwale and stretched out his hands to her, and she began to rise, naked, flawless, smiling, from the shadowed ocean. She whispered urgently: "Call me. Call me to you, or I cannot come."

He cried at the top of his voice: "Malkar, come! Come, come, Malkar! My love, my dream, come now!"

Their fingers brushed, hers like the touch of water, impalpable, fleeting, and he called again: "Come! My Malkar! Come!"

She rose and caught him in arms of water, salt, burning, as if the sea were fire. He sank crying his delight into her depths, his whole body attenuated in the succulence of hers, in the long-remembered agony of pleasure. She rose, and with her came a wave, from an ocean bed so deep it could have been the grave of the universe; a wave that reared to never-ending heights, rising up and up, tipped with a head of foam like a monstrous white flower. A wave so high that it was seen by the monks on the island several miles away. And the wave was Malkar and Narzet was in her, dying in delight, drinking her and being drunk by her, while sudden lightning whitened the sky, the boat, whitened the upturned fearful faces on deck, being followed by a roar of thunder like a thousand drums all struck at once. And the wave covered the Royal Barge, swallowed it as a whale swallows a minnow, and the Bay of Moons began to boil.

"She is adamant, Captain." Sergeant Delvas, dismounted, stood by the head of Tallis's mare. "I respectfully suggested you wouldn't like it. She wants her own way. Ask the lieutenant here."

"It's right, Captain," said Pinpol. "Perhaps you could speak to her." He saw Tallis's grim face and looked down at his own dusty boots. Tallis said, in the quiet hard voice that always made the troop uneasy: "Does she give a reason? Where exactly is this place she must visit at all costs?"

"No reason, Captain, except that she has business there. And it's a village called Rulen, north of Kalvaria. Only a hamlet; I've been there. A poor little place. I doubt they've an inn grand enough for her."

"I'll be damned," said Tallis. "It'll put hours on our journey."

He was furious, his nerves on a knife-edge. He was longing to get home. Today he had been thinking much about Pancora, strange, for she was not often in his thoughts while he was away. He wondered whether she had behaved herself at the party. More than likely she had been seduced by one of Lepo's more raffish friends; someone not in the tavern club, for none of those would dream of such a thing. Pancora couldn't handle her drink too well. He feared the worst. And now this: Lilene's doing again. No. He would not speak to her. Just do as she requested and bite on his anger.

He gathered up the reins. "Tell the others," he said to Pinpol. "We ride north-east towards Kalvaria. I hope her highness knows the road."

"I do," said Pinpol. "We have to go through the forest."

"Lead on, then," Tallis said shortly to the standardbearer. "And when we get there I must rest my mare." He glanced back to make sure the fresh horses trotted behind; glanced past Lilene's carriage. The curtains were tightly drawn.

It was around mid-day, with a little thunder about. The small procession left the vineyards and crossed a plain yellow with rapeseed along a less trodden path where sycamores grew in an avenue. Once the mare stumbled and Tallis cursed while he gentled her. The four white horses pulled Lilene's litter easily along; they seemed to tire less than the others. More of her sorcery. Tallis thought: I must put this from me. She's just an ordinary wilful woman, a thorn in my side.

"Here's the forest" said Pinpol. "We're on the right track."

It was an oak forest, where villagers drove their pigs for the mast. Great trees darkened the sky; squirrels played in them. There was a choir of birdsong, otherwise it was very quiet. Paths, some of them overgrown, traversed the main way. They came to a clearing. Someone had been here recently, the remnants of a wood fire still smoked. All around was a faint rustling.

They were deep in the womb of the forest, hemmed in by paths and trees. Tallis felt the arrows of warning prickle up his spine. He turned to the lieutenants, about to speak, when the way before them was suddenly filled by a mob. A very determined, menacing mob; at least two hundred of them. Tallis's first thought was: Desprans. It's not too far from the west coast for them to be raiding inland. His next, on scanning the faces and clothes was, no. Not Desprans, but out to make trouble nonetheless. And, in sudden fury: she engineered this, that we should be led into an ambush. In the name of the gods, why?

He said quietly to the lieutenants: "Tell them to form ranks," saw that this had already been done, and that Pinpol, Recansky and Sergeant Delvas had drawn up their mounts alongside his. Tallis unsheathed his sword. His mind drew itself together in a concentration like the steel blade. He looked at the weapons carried by the crowd. There were a couple of swords, but in the main they were nasty-looking farm implements: sickles, pitchforks, choppers. He recognised now that these were Karenian peasants. Thin, wild faces. Grubby smocks and breeches. Desperate eyes.

"Speak to them," he said softly. Lieutenant Pinpol stood in his stirrups and called: "In the king's name, let us pass."

His Taratamian accent seemed to puzzle the leader, who frowned, hefting a rusty broadsword to shoulder height. He was a big man, wearing the leather apron of a smith, bearded, gaunt, hollow-eyed.

"Get out of our way," said the lieutenant, more commandingly. The big smith came forward. Pinpol's horse threw up its head nervously.

The man said, in a guttural dialect: "Not until we have what we want," and Tallis got down from his horse. He walked slowly towards the smith, sword in hand. The smith towered above him.

"What do you want?" Carefully, so the man should understand, "what you may get is some steel under your jerkin."

The man's eyes blazed with determination.

"We want your swords. Your daggers. Some horses. We'll leave you enough to get away with."

The crowd behind him heard this. There was a growl of dissent. "Kill them all," someone said. "They're palace guard. Send them to hell."

Behind him Tallis heard the metallic slither as his troop unsheathed their weapons. He stood there, calmly eyeing the smith, waiting for him to lose his nerve. He prepared to strike the rusty sword out of his fist. He felt their weight of numbers pressing him. What a way to end. Chopped down by Karenian farmers. The crowd began to move forward, with little growls like muted war cries.

"We are Taratamian," he said, playing for time.

"Liar," said the smith. "You fly the cursed Oyster. Who's in the carriage? Eh?"

And someone in the rear of the peasants called out: "It's Vergon. Cursed Vergon. Let's get the swine."

"If we die for it!" The shout went up and, strangely, faded on the last word, into absolute silence. The smith fell on his knees before Tallis. Amazed, he saw the crowd following suit, laying down their weapons. And a murmur began, and swelled, and Tallis followed their eyes to where Lilene stood, balancing unsafely on the high step of her litter.

"It's her," the smith said, tears running down his face. "Beloved one. Lilene."

It was a praise-song, a love song. The trees took it up as a wind arose, and the name washed through the clearing, liquid with homage. Tallis looked at the princess. She was trying to come from the litter. He heard her call him.

"Captain. I wish to speak with my friends. Will you please assist me down?"

He hesitated for only a moment. Then he went to her, stood below her, seeing her in her entirety for the first time, from her pearl slippers to the sublime shape of her slender body. Like a goddess in miniature she stood swaying on the step, her face with its lovely apricot bloom quite calm, her full mouth a blown rose, her eyes a tranquil sea, and her hair a streaming cloud of gold like the sun coming through the window of a temple at high noon.

She held out her hands, palm down, and he took them in his. A mutual spark of fear flashed between his hands and hers, gone the next second. It left in him a feeling never before experienced, or anything like it. Her hands, warm, slightly damp with nerves and the day, became part of his hands. An overwhelming tide burst over him, transfixed him, filled him from edge to edge. It was more than lust, although lust was certainly a part of it. It was desire, more than he had ever felt. Far more than with Pancora in their first days together, more than with any of the fair women passed around by Lepo on occasion. More even than that felt with Katela, the sweet older woman who had painlessly relieved him of his virginity. Desire it was, and more. It was like a death.

Now she stood with him on the ground, still holding his hands. He could look down into her eyes. She was so close that her breasts almost grazed the front of his tunic. Trembling, he held on to her hands, as if to release them would be to die. He forgot the gathered soldiers, the silent peasants. He knew nothing but the desperate urgency of longing: to be in her arms, and to have her in his.

He saw her lips move; her voice broke through a second later, almost drowned by his own racing heartbeat.

"Captain, would you please hand me down my habit?"

He looked down dazedly at their joined hands. She wore a large pearl ring, and her finger was oozing blood from where he had crushed it. She did not seem to notice. He let her go. The spell broke, leaving him light-headed and bereft. One of her waiting-women was handing the bundled habit down, and he gave it to Lilene in silence.

She walked steadily to the kneeling peasants. Some were weeping, most were smiling; they gathered about her like a crowd of dirty children, kissing her slippers, the hem of her gown. She disappeared into their midst. Her voice could be heard, calm, faint, only a word here and there. Pinpol and Recansky looked at Tallis with raised brows. He stared straight ahead, saying nothing.

After a few moments Lilene turned and came from the throng. The peasants rose slowly to their feet, watching her go, their thin faces alight. The big smith was holding the bundle she had given them. Lilene walked past Tallis to her litter, and Lieutenant Pinpol assisted her in. On the step she paused and turned and looked once more at the crowd she had left, her head high, smiling, and a cheer went up that sent the birds flurrying out of the trees.

"Well, gods help us," said Sergeant Delvas, watching the mob disperse and disappear like giant mice down various of the forest exits.

"Captain." Her voice again. He walked to the litter. She leaned out, looking directly at him.

"Your highness."

"Captain, I must ask you. In fact, I must entreat you. Say nothing of what you saw today."

"There is no need for entreaty, princess. Do you still wish to go to Rulen?"

"Yes. It is necessary."

He nodded. I saw nothing today, if you say so. So the peasants love you. So be it. It is nothing to do with me or my company. But I saw you, for the first time. He looked again, covertly, as if it were forbidden now, at her face, her throat, her breasts. Her collar was undone against the day's heat, open quite low, so he could see the gold image on the chain she wore. Only for an eyeblink, for she moved and the silk hid the Lion. Was it the Lion? He thought, and, sickly: am I still bewitched?

He rode up to the head of the line. "Ride on, to Rulen," and the cavalcade moved on through the forest of anarchy and sudden love.

There was an inn. It was called the Lobster. It was a poor place, standing athwart the rough track and surrounded by ill-nourished fields and orchards. The landlord suffered shock when the party descended upon him. He hastily cleared rooms for the princess and her women, mercilessly evicting the present occupants. There was dust and flies, but the big taproom had a cool stone floor and there was shade. The landlord got out his expensive hoarded candles and made the place bright, for night was coming. The moon was just past the full.

The landlord was relieved when the escort raised tents in the field and broke out their own rations. Now he could feed the princess plainly but adequately. His awe bemused him; when the quiet man arrived in moonlight asking for the royal guest, he showed him to her room unquestioningly. The landlord knew a little of what was happening in the remote rural areas and it terrified him, for he was not a brave man.

Lilene spoke quietly to the man in moonlight, dousing the candles in her room so she should not see his face. It was better that way. He was not Alpac, but his cousin.

"Alpac is on the west coast with his boats," he murmured. "He waits. The Despran emissary never came. He's in a Tamian prison. So we're no further on."

"You must not move without the weapons."

"We know that, princess. Weapons we'll have in plenty, especially after your gift today. That's already on the road west. We've horses, not many, but enough. And we can travel through Karkis, even at night. Of course, the Karkian frontier guard needs a sweetener. It's worth it, to miss Fort Nial and Karlinkis both. Then Alpac can put to sea and wait for more Desprans to contact him. The hiding places are still secure. Number one"— and he laughed, "is an oyster bed."

Lilene laughed with him. It was an effort. The moonlight came through the window and seemed to creep coldly beneath her skin.

"I don't know your name," she said. "I don't want to. But I tell you, be careful. Say to the leaders: there must be no uprising until all is ready. Gods!" she shivered. "We are so near Kalvaria."

"It is useful," he said calmly, "to work near Kalvaria, inside the city sometimes. We can watch the Draconhood, see who goes in and out. They are fairly predictable. Tonight they have hunted and are back in their lodge."

"Go," she said. "Back to your home while there is safety. And remember: nothing, no one is to move until victory is assured. There will not be another chance."

"I hear you, highness. We'll do as you say. Everyone is alerted week by week. From the slaves at the villas to the goldworkers in the north. We've a good courier system going now..."

"Go," she said again. "The gods protect you and yours. We work for the day to come. Raise up! or die."

"Princess." He kissed both her hands. "I'll go out through the window." Smiling, "anyone who sees will think you have a lover. Forgive my impertinence, highness."

"There's nothing to forgive. Keep to the trees."

He hesitated, one leg over the sill. "Your Tamian escort," he said. "How much do they know? If they thought we traded with Despra..."

"Nothing will come of it," said Lilene. "I have the word of their Captain."

He went out, only the faint rustle of the apple tree down which he climbed the measure of his going. Lilene's women came from next door to prepare her for bed.

"Leave me," she said. She was shivering, so they wrapped her in a white fur. She sat by the window, under the streaming whiteness of the moon. And there she gave herself up, finally, to the agony of her wanting.

She could see his tent, pitched quite near to the inn. He had a lantern burning and she saw him moving silhouetted against the tent wall; then his shadow disappeared and she knew he lay down to sleep, although the light remained undipped. She pulled the pearl ring from her finger with difficulty, for it had stuck to her flesh from the wound his grip had made. He has drawn my blood. Would that he could make me bleed in another place. His beautiful hands. Slender, strong, long-fingered. The hands of a nobleman, no, the hands noblemen should have and seldom do. She unfastened her bedgown, baring her breasts. She caressed her breasts, watching her hands, his hands. Her hands slid lower. She tipped back her head. The moonlight shone silver on her tears. She cried out softly, just as the light in his tent went out.

I could go to him. I should be seen, and my honour smirched, but does it matter? The Tamians think little of our morals anyway; all Karenians are thought to be whores or rogues. I could go to his tent before he sleeps; the moon would show me to him, naked, willing. I fear nothing now but his honour. If he turned me away, that would kill me. That cold honour of his. An upright soldier and a gentleman. But oh! Love me, Ricalpa—for that is your name, isn't it?—give me your love, your arms, your body. And a clear image of his stern eyes arose, to shame her thoughts into silence.

Tallis was lying on his pallet, completely rigid, as if encased in full armour from head to foot. His mind climbed the apple tree. He was in her room; she was in his arms. Already he had made love to her several times with the almost total participation of his flesh. Now he lay naked on her body, but not at peace. And how easy it would be to go to her! Awakened, she would not scream, she was not the sort. She was so near . . . Desperate, he tried to deflate the madness. Just a woman. A pretty . . . no, an exquisite woman. The love of my life. And he sat up violently at this last imprudence and swore aloud. He found some cold water and poured it over his head.

Pancora, I forgive you, he thought. Whatever you are doing under this festive moon, you're not to blame. I shall not say a word. I have done foolish things myself in drink, and Lepo's parties addle the most virtuous minds. We are good together, despite your tempers. He came to a decision. When I get home, I shall ask Pancora to marry me.

The Opal Throne was draped in black. The tapestries had been taken from the walls, the opals extinguished like a thousand little eyes going out. The walls were hung with black. Black was everyone's garment, from the Chamberlain to the Court fools. No footsteps were audible; everyone went barefoot. From the temples all over the city came a constant requiem. The palace was quiet, its population thinned. There was an ambience of the end of the world, which in a way, it was.

Prince Ataret, only recently crowned High Priest of the Lion, stood before the throne where King Valm sat, his face in his hands. With Ataret were two other priests from the island, the Chamberlain, Narzet Senior, and a couple of the Household Guard in mourning uniforms. Queen Sarene was in her chamber, attended by six Court physicians. The inconsolable Duchess of Mayt had hidden herself away.

Kneeling before the throne was the fisherman who had witnessed the cataclysm. The Chamberlain continued to press for details, as if their repetition could in some way turn back the clock.

"I was just about to cast off. I was going to set my traps by moonlight. Then I saw it. At first I thought some sea-monster was awakening—the grendelfish again after a thousand years. It was a wall of water, a cliff of water." He shook his head. "I thank the gods I had not entered the bay. The wash from the wave carried my boat up the shore for half a mile like a cork. When I came to myself, the Royal Barge was gone. Not a splinter of her left behind. I've fished that bay for thirty years. Never have I seen the like."

He muttered and shook his head. Then Lord Narzet broke down in tears.

"Oh gods! my poor boy. I should have let him be sent to Fort Opal."

"There are so many to mourn," said the Chamberlain softly.

"All the young, high-born men. The young women too. The flowers of tomorrow gone."

The king made an inarticulate sound. He pressed his hands so hard against his eyelids that a reddish-blackness swamped him. In it were the faces of the dead. How could they be dead when they came so clear? Rost, tall, elegant, born old before his time, his kind mouth looking as if it would like to laugh were it not for protocol; his slow voice weighing every pronouncement so it should be fitting. Oh, and Lepo! the dearest, the secret favourite, naughty Lepo, with his father's eyes and quirky lips and handsomeness, and his jokes and joy in life. Lepo gone. It was impossible. It was one of Lepo's bad jokes. Any moment he'd walk through the door, shouting: "Fooled you!" and dripping from the sea . . .

The king bared his face. All the vessels in his eyes were broken from crying.

"Dead," he said. "My beloved sons. Dead, as I am dead. What sin did I commit? Tell me, Prince Ataret. A curse has fallen on Capashenet. Why?"

Ataret took his hand. "Father. Majesty. No sin. No crime. Yes, I am learned in the mysteries. But this defeats me. I can tell you nothing. I can only mourn."

Ataret had the Capashenet strong attractiveness, but his head was shaven for his calling and indelibly tattooed with the Lion. He had had a dream. It came before the moon was full. He had been undergoing a vigil and in a lapse of fatigue, had dreamed, short and disturbing. The Abbess Andine was standing before him. She had raised hands dripping with blood and cried: "Chaos! chaos is coming!" He had jerked awake and, negligently he thought now, paid little heed to it. He felt ashamed.

"Father," he said, thinking he should speak of it now, but the king forestalled him.

"The kingdom is without an heir," he said, for the twentieth time. "The House of Capashenet will die. Ataret, you are the sole heir."

And for the twentieth time Ataret replied patiently, "Majesty. I am a High Priest of the Lion. I am chaste. I can never marry. I could never rule."

The king began to shake convulsively. Foam appeared on his mouth. The Chamberlain beckoned to a physician. "I fear for him," he said softly. "What have you?" and the man produced two vials. "Soulbane, and heartroot."

"Then give it to him," said the Chamberlain. "And some for all of us. Though these are hurts well past healing."

Ataret slipped away to pray in the temple. Wandering the corridor came the Duchess of Mayt. She tried to put herself in his arms. He shook his head, evading her gently, for he must never touch a woman. She was crying bitterly, repeating: "Lilene! I want Lilene!"

They were on the last leg of their journey, with Tirkar Plain behind them and Knife Pass straight ahead, cutting through the majesty of the Tiranians. Lilene was no longer in her litter.

She had been too restless for its confined space. She was riding one of Tallis's best horses. She wore loose silken breeches and rode astride like a man.

She tried to ride as close to him as possible, not easy, because the lieutenants were mounted on either side of her for her protection. But now and again he looked back to see how she did, and she could watch his straight back and the sleek black fall of his hair, and once she got too close so that his mare grumbled and swished her tail in the face of Lilene's mount. So then he beckoned her to come beside him, and although he seldom spoke, she could see his remote profile from the tail of her eye and his wonderful hands like feathers on the reins. And once he complimented her on her horsemanship. It was a fine morning, with the sun making rainbows on the last snow-caps of the mountains, and where the lion-coloured plain gave way to lush meadow, larks shot up like sparks, singing.

And his whole body ached from the rack of her nearness, and his mind cursed and desired her alternately, and so he kept much within himself, though the rest of the company were talkative, glad to come home. The first hint of tragedy came at the Karenian customs post. The officer there, a dour taciturn man, said, as he perused their papers and made a deep obeisance to Lilene: "My condolences, Captain," and disappeared into his lodging before he could be questioned. They saw the knot of black at the other end of Knife Pass. The officers were waiting for them. Tallis rode forward, his first thought: Sarene must be dead. The queen was not well at the best of times.

"What's the news, Jankel?"

And Jankel told him, holding Tallis's bridle as if for support, one fresh tear rolling from each eye.

Tallis dismounted, clumsily for him, and Jankel steadied him as he stumbled.

"Let me come inside." They stood together in the gloom of the posthouse.

"All of them," said Jankel, weeping openly. "Not a soul left. The boat crushed small as plankton. I still can't take it in. Nobody can."

"Lepo," said Tallis. "Lepo."

"Yes, Lepo, and the Crown Prince, and all their friends. Everyone." And Jankel let out a stream of multi-coloured curses, and cried.

Tallis could not curse or cry, not yet. He heard Lepo's voice, very plain. "You're more than a brother to me, damn your eyes." Lepo, gone.

"It's wrecked the dynasty. Capashenet is done for. This is the worst day of our lives. The—the remains are being washed ashore. Some on the island, some on the mainland. It's terrible. Prince Rost—it looked as if a big fish had mauled him. Lepo"—he gulped back tears, "Lepo just looked as if he'd been for a swim."

Tallis did not speak. He sat down very slowly.

"Speak to me, Tallis," pleaded Jankel. "Another thing—people have been having dreams. My wife had a nightmare—something about the Karenian Queen. I told her it was nonsense, but there was water in it. I see you've the princess with you. So don't mention this last bit."

"She was coming to the wedding," said Tallis in a very faint voice. Then he looked up at Jankel, his face so deathly that Jankel hastily poured wine, which Tallis gently pushed away.

"Pancora," said Tallis. "Tell me they didn't all drown, Jankel."

"Oh, gods," said Jankel.

"She could swim," said Tallis, his face lime-white. "We went to Lake Pen together once, and she swam."

"They all drowned, Ricalpa," said Jankel quite gently.

Tallis jumped up, upsetting his bench and the wine. He rushed from the posthouse and leaped on to his mare. The next moment the company saw him whipping the mare up the pass and out of sight.

The news had already passed down the line of horsemen. There were exclamations, oaths and tears, but mostly a stunned silence. Lieutenant Pinpol came to Jankel, on foot, leading Lilene's horse.

"Your highness," said Jankel.

"Where's he gone?" Pinpol asked.

"It's his woman," said Jankel. "His wife-woman. Pancora."

Jankel looked at the princess. Tears were pouring down her face. Lieutenant Pinpol gently touched her arm.

"Your highness. Shall we continue on to Tam?"

Lilene dismounted. She shrugged off his assisting arm. She walked to her litter, climbed up into it slowly and with difficulty, and closed the curtains tight.

He did not go home. The truth was, he did not know where he was going. Vaguely he realised he was in breach of his duty; he had abandoned the princess on the road, and there were still bandits in the mountains. He did not see any, however, as he rode the mare uncharacteristically hard to the gates of Tam. The city was a sea of black. Tallis's scarlet uniform stood out like a blot of blood. He dismounted. In his saddle-bag he had a black blanket, and this he wound round himself, slinging it across his shoulder and through his belt, where it reached the top of his boots. On the road to the palace he was caught up in a weeping throng; black-clad families bringing more bodies home. Black horses pulled the biers through the city. The biers were covered with flowers thrown haphazardly on to the covered bodies. The occasional foot stuck out, or the wet fold of a dress. At a distance he saw General Camlot, his face creased in grief for a lost son; then the cortege moved on.

Still he could not weep. Very clearly, from out of the ether, he heard Lepo's raucous laugh that never had malice in it. He remembered Pancora swimming like a seal in Lake Pen. She had come out naked and cold and he had dried her and warmed her, had brought her to boiling point there in the secluded meadow. It had been one of their happiest days. He had never even said goodbye to her properly, he thought with sorrow. He had chided her over the party and she had flounced off without giving him her usual blessing. Still he could not weep.

He had to make his journey report to the Household, but no one wanted to hear it. So he went to the palace, walked unhorsed up the marble slope now covered in all its great length by a black pall. He spoke to sentries and guards and officials, some crying openly, others numb and blank-faced with shock. Everything seemed like a tired old dream, with the fatigue of an illness. In the hall of reception he came upon the High Priest, Ataret.

He did not know Ataret well, but had met him in the company of Lepo sometimes. Now he went to him, quite desperate, as if the Lion could give him the answers he wanted.

"Your Holiness."

"Captain," Ataret's dark eyes searched and saw. "There were no survivors, Captain. Everyone in this city has lost someone."

Tallis, like so many others, asked "Why?"

Ataret shook his head sadly. "I cannot tell you why. I had a dream . . ." Now it came out. "A dream of chaos. From afar. If a leaf stirs at one end of the world, a landslide can follow at the other. The further away, the more momentum it gains. And if there should be a focus near to the doomed end, it finds there the force on which to feed."

"A woman had a dream also," said Tallis. "Of water, and Malkar."

"Ah," said Ataret, and frowned.

Andine warned me, thought Tallis. And here was I, lusting after the witch's daughter, with poor Pancora drowning, dead. A small commotion at the great door made him look round. Lilene was entering with her servants and the escort. She was wearing black. She had her mourning clothes ready in her baggage, he thought savagely, forgetting that these were customarily carried by all royal travellers. Was she the focus of disaster of which Ataret spoke? My lust had forgotten she was Malkar's daughter.

He saw her moving through the hall on her way to comfort the Duchess of Mayt. He was careful not to meet her eyes, nor did she look at him. Next, he came on General Camlot, looking as if he had aged ten years. Tallis said, his voice shaking:

"General. May I put in a request here and now? As there will be no wedding, I assume the Princess Royal will be returning to her homeland. May I be excused the duty of escorting her this time?"

General Camlot looked at him tiredly.

"Request granted, Captain," he said, as if the matter were entirely trivial. "You should stay here anyway. A number of the senior Household Guard perished on the boat. Your services will be needed." He sighed deeply. "I have sent for troops from Fort Opal. They will need to be schooled in protocol—you can train them." He came suddenly to attention. "Her majesty comes. Gods grant she is somewhat recovered."

Queen Sarene, supported by attendants, passed through the hall. Her long face was yellow; she came slowly, making for the outer door, hung with black flags. They were bringing the bodies of Prince Rost and Prince Lepo home. They had lain in state for the past few days beneath the Lion of Stone in the temple on the hill. The queen moved slowly past. As she came level with Tallis she gave him a sidelong look of venom, as if the tragedy were somehow his fault. He felt it like an undeserved blow.

As he left the palace, wandering, as most were wandering, a Major of the Household caught up with him.

"Captain. Go to the prison. There is an amnesty in view of what has happened, to placate the gods. General pardons. The Despran is to be released."

He went to Mervhu's cell. He found the Despran slightly subdued, not triumphant as might have been expected.

"Big bad water spell," he observed. "Came down river. Came west, swelled Avatal Bay."

"Yes." Tallis had noticed how in the heart of Tam, the River Milesa had burst its banks.

"Capashenet all finish now," said Mervhu. "No more princes. King die soon. Queen die too. Then High King of Despra sit on Tamian throne."

"Dreams, Mervhu," said Tallis wearily.

"All very sad," said Mervhu unexpectedly. "Poor young men. Go Far Lands. Be born again. Thousand years, maybe less. Tamians bad, but more good than Karenia."

"Yes," said Tallis angrily. "Why don't you go down and wipe out Karenia? You haven't tried that for a long time."

"Oh, we go," said Mervhu cheerfully. "You watch. Blow Karlinkis into sky. Then we sit High King on Karenian throne as well."

"You'll have blown up the throne. He'll have nowhere to sit. You'll have blown it up, I suppose, with your famous Turinko."

"Tur-in-ek-o," said Mervhu. "You no fire it any more. No more powder. No good without powder. You know where powder come from, Tallis-Cap?"

"Tell me," said Tallis, and Mervhu laughed. He tapped his nose, and pulled at his ebony moustaches.

"Well," said Tallis, knocking at the cell door for the jailor. "You're free to go, Mervhu."

Mervhu got up. "I say prayer for souls of princes," he said. "Wish them well in Far Lands. Then I come back with army. Where my young fat woman? I take her home with me now."

"She's a Tamian citizen, you can't." Tallis could see the girl, bundle packed, leering at Mervhu in the passage.

"She want to come. Nice girl. You got girl?"

"No," said Tallis; he felt like choking. "Not any more. Take the slut, then. Get out of Tamia while you've the chance."

Mervhu embraced Tallis. "Stop that," Tallis said, angry.

"Gods-bye, Tallis-Cap. We still friends. When end of world come, I spare. You keep ballocks. March with new army."

He and the girl went off at a lumbering dance into freedom. It was time for Tallis to go home. On the bridge he turned and looked up at the Lion of Stone, watching over the city. He blinked. The Lion had moved. Only a fraction, but one paw now splayed outwards and the massive head was raised a little and slightly turned to the south. The Stone Lion will move in time of danger. Tallis walked slowly on through the city and came to the gate of his house. Barbel and Palbo were waiting for him on the path. Barbel ran to him, Palbo came more slowly. He went down on his knee and clutched Barbel in his arms. "It's all so mortal sad," she wept.

There was a sound near the house. He looked up over Barbel's head. Pancora's ghost stood there. He felt his heart stop. It seemed forever before it resumed its beat. She was wearing black; she was very pale. Then she smiled a ghostly smile. And spoke.

"Ricalpa," she said, trying not to laugh. "Why are you wearing a horse-blanket?"

They met, running, on the path. She nearly fell from the force of his embrace. He felt her warmth, her plump luxurious curves, and wept at last, sobbing into her soft neck.

"You'll be the death of me," he said, wiping his eyes with a bit of Pancora's wide collar. "I thought you were at the bottom of the bay. Oh, Pan."

"I didn't go to the party," she said. "At the last minute, I changed my mind. It wouldn't have been the same without you. I was sorry. Thank the gods you had to go away."

It was not until much later, after they had eaten, and talked, and remembered Lepo with love and sadness, that the realisation came home to Tallis. It was like a sharp stab over his heart. *Lilene has saved my life. And to what end?*

"Have a little rest," said Pancora comfortingly. "Sleep for a few minutes. Then we'll try again."

A blackbird sang in the garden outside the window. Sun was gilding the horizon. Vibrant light washed over Pancora's body as she lay exposed, her legs apart, her arms thrown up above her head.

Tallis lay still, staring up at two flies circling near the ceiling.

"It used to happen to my husband at times," said Pancora. "Don't worry about it."

"It's never happened to me," he said through his teeth. "Never. Least of all in the morning."

Pancora crossed her legs, brought down her arms. "It must be me," she said. "You're tired of me, I expect."

"It's not you. It's that bloody witch."

"What witch? Have you been near a witch? You didn't tell me. And how . . ."

"This is a witch's favourite trick. They take away manhood. Suck it out. Then use the power to their own ends."

"Let me help." She wriggled down the bed, and began to caress. After a moment she sighed and raised herself again.

"You're tired," she said. "And still sad. Mourning for Lepo."

"Lepo's been dead for a moonspan. I've shed all my tears. They won't bring him back. All the funerals are over.

Even the duchess has gone back to Mayt. All that has nothing to do with it."

"I didn't know the duchess had left. Poor child. What about Lilene? Has she gone with her?"

"Lilene leaves this morning for Karenia. Wretch. Witch."

Pancora sat up, amazed. "She's no witch, Ricalpa. She's a beauty. And doubtless she knows it."

"I detest her," he said, his eyes closed. "She's a witch and the daughter of a witch." He rolled over suddenly, violently, on to Pancora. "Fight me. Bite me. Pretend I'm a Despran pillager."

She obligingly smote him about the face, writhed under him, sank her teeth into his shoulder. He lay still, cursing. Then he left her, and flung on his clothes.

At the door he looked back. She was frowning slightly. "It's not your fault, my love," he said. "I'm off. I have to try to make gentlemen of those clods from Fort Opal. Today they'll wish they'd never left it."

It was early. Few were about. I'll get those bastards jumping, he thought savagely. Teach them not to wet their breeches every time a royal asks for a hand up. Put some steel in their arses, straighten them out. He yelled at his groom to throw him the mare's bridle. She was out to summer grass this week, sleek and fat. He came round the corner of the house, still in shirt and breeches, and saw Lilene.

She was alone, standing by the stone wall that ran by the path to the gate. She was still in mourning, but her hair was down, thieving gold from the rising sun. He dropped the bridle on the path and went slowly towards her. Ceda pefur gevac. He looked without fear into her eyes.

"Your Royal Highness. Why this honour? I am alarmed to see you unescorted."

Her soft soft voice, her Karenian voice.

"My escort is waiting for me outside, Captain. I came to thank you for your kindness to me."

He bowed low. "It was my pleasant duty, highness. I trust your return home will be uneventful."

"And," she said even more softly, "I came to say goodbye."

He bowed again. She had moved a little closer. Chills began to attack his spine. She was standing in the shadow of the wall, but her hair still shone as if the sun were trapped within it.

"Goodbye, your Royal Highness. May your gods go with you."

"I should like," and she swallowed a gasp, "I should like it very much if you would kiss me goodbye."

Speechless, he watched as she slowly held out her hands to him. He took two or three involuntary steps and found himself standing close. Close to her and full of sudden fury. You ask this of me, you, who have unmanned me. And then he suddenly found that he was far from unmanned, was in fact more man than he had ever been, and driven by madness.

And his madness said to her, very low:

"I could do more than that to you, highness. I could take you where you stand."

That could earn me a hemp necklace, he thought, in a kind of dream. And in the dream he heard her say: "Yes. Yes, Ricalpa. Do it."

And she put her arms about him and covered the scar on his mouth with her open rose-lips. And madness engulfed him like a hot red cloak.

He seized her by her hair and pushed her against the wall, slamming his body against hers as if to drive her through the stonework. She had her arms tight around his neck while he kissed her, kissed her as if to suck out her life. She was very slender and he held her without mercy, brimming and bursting with a terrible desire, as he wrenched up her skirt and kicked her feet apart. She raised herself on her toes so that he could come into her the easier, clutching him, kissing him endlessly . . . and the hot madness of the embrace was shattered by the voice of Barbel, calling his name from very near.

The bond broke, with her still unbroken. His seed leapt from him and flowed down her thigh. They let out a simultaneous soft cry, in a kind of anguish. She let her skirt fall quickly and he put himself to rights just as Barbel came running round the corner. Barbel stopped in her tracks.

"Oh. Your Royal Highness, excuse me." Barbel essayed a curtsy so inexpert she nearly fell backwards.

"This is Barbel," said Tallis in a choking voice. He was shaking so much he could hardly stand. The princess was trembling too, but more quickly composed.

"Good morning, Barbel," said Lilene.

"It's a lovely day," said Barbel in daft fashion. She peeped acutely at both their faces, caught the tension, tried to guess, dismissed the guess, to be pondered at a later date. She was standing in the same shaft of sunlight as Lilene. Good food and comfort had filled out Barbel and she had grown taller over the months. Even in his delirium Tallis noticed that their hair was almost the same gold and the same length. There the resemblance ended.

Lilene said softly: "My escort awaits me. Good day to you, Captain. Barbel."

She turned and they watched her walk down the path. "Oh," breathed Barbel. "She is so beautiful. Somehow she's not like a Karenian."

"She's Malkar's daughter," he said. He watched her go. She turned at the gate and looked at him, a long intense look of such sadness it was like a last farewell.

Malkar did not often interview her generals. They were old men. This day, however, she was excited by chaos. It whirled about her. The old generals caught something of it, and fidgeted as they stood before her in the Hall of the Sea. The queen sat very erect in one of the shell-thrones. Beside her sagged King Enial. A little drool ran from his lips, which Lilene regularly wiped away.

Vergon, morose at being commanded from his villa, was also present. Malkar was speaking war to the generals, and Vergon hoped he would not be expected to lead an army.

She leaned forward, flashing her eyes at the old men.

"Well? General Dabinol, what have you to say?"

General Dabinol, resting on his sword's ornamental hilt, wished he could be seated.

"Most high," he said, "and revered majesty." He shot a glance at King Enial's lolling form. "Since we last had the honour of an audience, my brother officers and I have conferred. We are agreed that this is not at all an auspicious juncture for a declaration of war on Taratamia. It would seem . . ."

She would not let him finish. "General. Taratamia is demoralised. A nation on its knees is easy to floor. Strike now, and see Karenia rule over all the territories from Ruva to the Towers of Kite."

The military men glanced at one another. The general said stubbornly: "Greatness. It may well be as you say. The loss of his heirs was a mortal blow to King Valm. But I would humbly ask: how many fighting men went down with the Royal Barge? I believe a few dozen officers at most. What happened has not lessened Taratamia's force, which is more than ever one to be respected. And again: grief can breed anger. They might well welcome any aggression as a chance to exorcise some of theirs. Again, we do not think the time is right. Your majesty?" and squinted, hopefully, at the king.

Enial responded with surprising coherence.

"The Treaty was sealed with my marriage to Doro," he said. "The Treaty cannot be broken. We are sworn allies." He closed his eyes.

"Indeed, majesty," said one of the other generals. "And we need their alliance against Despra."

Malkar sat even more upright. "Despra! I am surfeited with threats of Despra! They are barbarians—primitives with no real idea of tactics. They can be swatted like flies any day. We need no Taratamia to nursemaid us."

The generals were quiet. Her rashness disturbed them.

"Your Majesties" said General Dabinol. "According to the reports of our agents, the Taratamian army has, since the Treaty, become much stronger. It is certain that in number their troops exceed ours . . ."

"Then recruit!" cried Malkar. "Train up the common people. Take them from the fields, the farms."

"This could be done, greatness, up to so far. But workers are essential to tend the Crown estates and those of other lords . . ."

"That's your affair to resolve," said Malkar briskly. "The country teems with labour. Exploit it."

Poor oafs, to be swiftly speared on Tamian blades, thought the general dispiritedly. One of his colleagues, whose temper had risen during the interview, said: "May I speak, greatness? Now we are on the subject of peasant forces, can you not speak with the officers of the Holy Draconhood? They interfere with the efficiency of our armies. Last week near

Kalvaria our military exercises were interrupted when the Draconhood chased a number of suspected heretics through our lines. They lost them, incidentally, and we lost our competence. The entire manoeuvre was ruined."

"The Draconhood's methods do not concern us," Malkar answered. "They are capable of working independently of the Throne of Pearls. We are interested only in the outcome, not the method."

The general bowed. Malkar was silent for a long time, her eyes distant. "Taratamia has been weakened," she said softly. "Her back is broken. I intend to lean on her. I shall see that a proclamation is made by our parliament. No more sweetgeld is to be paid to Taratamia."

King Enial stirred faintly, but said nothing. Vergon stared at the queen. Lilene remained apart, pale and golden and far off. The generals exchanged glances, mentally counting their troops, their faces long. There seemed nothing more to say, and quite soon Malkar dismissed them.

Lilene had gone half-heartedly to tend her father. He had not missed his treasure and relief made her kinder to him. He clung to her, calling her Doro, and she petted him abstractedly for half an hour, until Malkar sent for her.

The bower's walls mirrored the finned fanged guardians precariously on leash, and the great round pearl of a bed. Little snow-white hands summoned Lilene near.

"There is a change in you," said Malkar intently. "The way you move your body. Your eyes. You have lost your virginity, I think. Is the Duke of Mayt well?"

"I am still a virgin," said Lilene. "I never met the duke."

"Never lie to me. There was someone. Who had you?"

"No one," said Lilene, in grief and rage. "I wish by all the gods they had."

"I shall watch you," said Malkar silkily. "Even when you are in the House of Brides. I am all-knowing. Never forget it."

As Lilene passed, one of the guardians reared from Malkar's restraint and slashed at the princess's arm. She went weeping from the room.

"The scratches will heal," said the Abbess Andine. "I give my word. This is a rare herb. It is called hatebalm. It grows at the feet of the Towers of Kite. It's said the seeds are blown on the wind from the Far Lands."

"I wish I were in the Far Lands," said Lilene. "Dead."

"There is no need for that." The abbess lidded the little pot. "These will heal without trace."

"I want to be scarred," said Lilene. "Scarred, as he is."

Andine walked to her tower window and looked out. The novices were seated in their sacred formation, the oldest forming the head of the Lion, the little ones the tail, in the middle of the green lawn. The youths, and young manservants, were busy tending the herbaceous borders, cleaning the ponds. For all the notice they took of them, the girls might not have been there. All was in order.

Her gaze moved from the Brides of the Lion, went inward. For a moment she was back in Malkar's birth-bower. The beautiful little demon emerging from Malkar, formed from her blood and brain and Enial's seed. The knowledgeable eyes, primed for the stamp of sorcery. The ocean of chaos ready to claim its own. A new witch had been born. The battle for Lilene had been terrible. But had it truly been won?

Lilene was crying quietly.

"So you are in love," said Andine. "A state not guaranteed to bring felicity." She held out her arms. "And I think I know who it is."

"Talk to me about him."

"What would you know? I've known him since he was born. He lives much within himself. Evil things happened to him when he was a child. The monastery was a bad place in those days. Perhaps he has forgotten, who knows? The worst wound was the death of his father."

"Why was he sent to the monastery?"

"Queen Sarene ordained it. He was orphaned. Before you were born, the great plague occurred. Some say it was sent from the south. Karenia escaped it. It took its toll in Tamia. It was one of the turning points in the war. His mother died of it, a month after his father was murdered. The monastery was thought to be the best place for him."

"Tell me about his father."

"His father was one of King Valm's most beloved officers. He fought most gallantly in the war. He was captured by the Karenians and imprisoned near Fort Nial, and held there with others as a hostage. A large ransom was negotiated. But the night before the hostages were due for release, a drunken party of soldiers went into the prison and killed the colonel. They had sport with him. They brought that brave soldier down as far as a man can go before they let him die. One of the hostages who got home safely reported this. He said that what was done sickened the most brutal. But one stayed behind and tortured the colonel to death. No one ever knew his name. We only had a description."

"Let me know it."

"There's nothing you can do, princess. It's in the past, and there it must stay."

"Tell me what the man looks like."

Andine told her.

"I know him," said Lilene. "I could write."

"What for?"

"Because he would want to avenge his father. That is how well I know him."

"You're right, of course. But if you do this, you may send him to his death. Think long."

"I shall write," said Lilene.

"As you think best, princess. But is it that you wish to lure him back to Karenia?"

The abbess went again to the window. The novices had finished their meditation, rising from the grass. The young men bowed low as they passed with averted eyes, and walked away in the opposite direction. The sun turned to the amber of sunset and then to a lowering purple.

Last night the creatures had assaulted Andine again, and there had been another, more terrifying manifestation. A moving pearl had appeared on her chamber wall, darting like wildfire. And a voice, low, menacing, with a chuckle in it. "Wait for the trick!" it had gabbled. "A little joke, Andine, very soon!" Only the Crystal Lion had warded off the assault. And it had taken longer than usual.

She turned to Lilene. "Princess. Hear me. Take Honyia to your room tonight. Lock and bolt the door. Hold a small office to the Lion of Night. Don't stir till morning."

The minstrel had brought Honyia flowers. She held a blue delphinium in her fingers. With each phrase played by the minstrel she tore off a petal. When the song ended Lilene called the minstrel over to the far side of the chamber.

"Have you the latest news?"

"The Desprans met Alpac out to sea, north of Fort Nial. They were very pleased with the bargain. Alpac has some weapons hidden away. They are getting the powder. Your holding instructions are clear."

"Would they join forces with us?"

"It's difficult. Never forget, princess, a Despran puts his own interests first. They would be uncomfortable allies. Any triumph of ours they might use to their own ends. At the moment they seem content to watch and wait. I say, let it be. Have faith."

She nodded, her mind moving on. "Has our courier left for Tamia?"

The Abbey's courier system had been brought to a peak of efficiency. Relays of swift-horsemen made the journey north.

Letters could reach Tam in days, sometimes hours, according to the weather. Lilene took up an inkhorn, quill and parchment. "We'll walk in the garden."

Lilene and Honyia went down the stone spiral and out into the garden. A thrush sang vespers. There was the scent of stocks and lavender, and to the west the sky had a bloody glamour. Honyia took Lilene's sleeve and urged her away from the lily pond.

They sat down together on a stone bench where red and white roses grew in trails. The thrush came down and heaved a worm out of the earth. Lilene dipped her quill and wrote:

The name of your enemy is known to me. And, in her heavy bold hand signed it: Lilene of Karling.

She sat regarding what she had done for a long time. Then she rolled the letter and addressed it ready for her seal. And sat again, reading the name thereon, over and over. And tore it up, and scattered the tiny pieces on the grass, where a little breeze, suddenly arising, blew them seawards. She took up the quill again and applied it afresh.

Not until Honyia was asleep in Lilene's bed did she read over what she had written.

"Today I heard the song
Of your old sorrows,
And all your yesterdays
Are my tomorrows.

The road is long between
Your rage, my bliss,
Until we reach its end
Your soul my dwelling is."

King Enial was gravely ill. All the royal physicians, not to mention healers and charlatans from Karlinkis and its environs, had been summoned. The psychic poisons inflicted on him by the pearl, the infestation of his dreams, had overtaken him. Now and again he rallied, lapsing at similar intervals into short agonies. He wanted the dark; the heavy drapes were drawn in his great ancestral bedchamber. He called continually for the queen. She sat beside his head, very still, her face and hands and the white streak in her hair luminous in the gloom. She watched dispassionately; his demise was part of the preordained pattern, a linkage of the circle of chaos which now ramped from coast to coast since the crippling of the Capashenet dynasty.

The king opened his eyes, and turned his head to look at her. She was wearing a dress the colour of weeds at the bottom of a clear pond. He called for light to see her better.

"He is fading", said a physician hearing the weak, cracked voice.

Round her neck Malkar was wearing a glass bauble containing a small live crab. Enial felt its claws in his heart.

"How long?" asked Malkar softly.

"His majesty is sixty-five years old. A good age. He could live a day, a week. No one can tell."

Malkar's High Steward murmured: "Should not the Crown Prince be sent for? and the daughters of the king?"

"Not yet." She knew how impatient Vergon was. She had already made up her mind. There would be a full year of mourning before his coronation. A year during which she, as regent, would bring him down until he had irrevocably lost his way. There was no necessity for Lilene to be involved. Honyia was not worth a thought.

The king lay staring at the ornate ceiling rippled by shadows far above. Darkness lay all about him; the only light seemed to emanate from the hand clasped on his. He held on it, and the vibrations of her thought came down into his fragile flesh.

The thing that was Malkar, invisible, encapsulated by her flawlessness, was dwelling on war. *As yet, these foolish old men will not jump to our tune. Wait, until Taratamia is provoked. We shall make King Vergon's first decree the mustering of an army. Then eventually, for the first time in memory, north and south will be under Karenia, and what is left of the Taratamian royal family paraded in chains . . .*

"Stay by me, Malkar," said the king in a whisper.

"I am here. Forever here." To the physicians she said quietly: "You can do no more. Leave his majesty alone with me."

The room was very still when they had gone. The shadows waited. She bent close to his head, smoothing his forehead.

"Do you remember the old days, my lord? When you and I first lay in love?"

He tried to smile. "I remember," he murmured. "You came to me, soft as a cat. A little black kitten, creeping to my couch for warmth. I was fit to love you, then. I was comely . . ."

"Yes. Your hair was like a silver field of wheat, more gold than silver. Your eyes were like discs cut from a summer sky. How long, my lord, since we lay together?"

"So very long," he whispered. "I can scarcely remember the joy."

"We could know that joy again."

He laughed, a horrible, phlegm-choked sound. "I am dying," he said.

"You need not die in agony and grief. I can give you the sweetest end."

He did not answer. With great care she turned back the coverlet, raising his gown to his waist. The withered legs and the crumpled grey scrotum were revealed, and the shrunken flaccid penis. Malkar drew whiteness from her gown, eased sinuous whiteness across him. She pressed her lips to his, shaped her body upon him, imbuing him with the restless energy of the sea. He groaned. Beneath her silken groin came a flicker of response, a miraculous testament of arousal. The king stood stiff and strong between her thighs in a terrible renewal. She raised his gown higher, to the level of his throat, kissing the grey sinews there, and with the pressure of her breasts coaxed thunder from his heart. He glided into her body, impaling her on a febrile spear of lust. She twined her legs round his and, with the strength of high-running tides, rode him through the gate.

The soul was strong. It was ancient and royal. It had its own puissance and fought the darkness that lay sucking and strangling over and around it. Silver threads of the soul sought wildly to escape bondage; the darkness, venting its anger in a wordless black yammering, spread its net wider to trap them. Darkness ate up every atom of the king's final flood. Darkness conceived once more, and Malkar rose from the corpse like a fountain.

She drew the covers over Enial and sat quietly for a time.

The Taken did not have to be virgin, but it was far better if they were. The decadent and corrupt all lent power of a sort but it was weak and short-lived. The pure had more to offer; the gift of flight, of shapechange, of seeing far and true.

Enial had been celibate almost since the birth of the Princess Lilene, and his heart was very pure. There was more than enough here for the next blow to be released on Taratamia;

a strike to be witnessed with satisfaction through the mirror of the pearl.

The eldest of the boys awoke first. He was employed as a general factotum, and one of his duties was to make and repair the shoes of all in the House of Brides. This day had been busy and he had fallen asleep as soon as his back touched the rough pallet he shared with one of the gardeners. For some minutes he lay, watching the moving light on the ceiling. The dormitory, which lay to the east of the little olive grove and faced on to the bay, was arched and pillared with stone, with broad windows through which came the sight and sound of the Sea of Infinity. The round white light, like a mobile moon, had come from beyond the window. Now it chased shadows up and down the pillars and cornices as if at play.

The boy's name was Charlo. He was virgin, like all the rest. He knew nothing of the flesh, its images and urges. He knew nothing of the dominions of lust. The white light hovered. He thought it beautiful and stretched out his arms to it. It bounced gently on the air, like a hawk on a thermal. Then it glided gracefully down, and settled on Charlo's groin, which became instantly, grossly, tumescent.

"Oh Lion!" he whispered. "What is happening?"

The pearl left him and moved to the parts of his neighbour, who awoke instantly. And on and on, touching the bodies of all the young men who lay sleeping in gentle rows like flowers. Soon all were sitting up, murmuring softly. Murmuring into themselves, to the beast that had awakened at their core; greeting it, half in fear, half with a terrible excitement.

The pearl lifted from the last of the youths and, a soundless luminous bubble, bounced and floated back whence it had come, through the window, into the night sky where planets hung like dew, and the moon hid behind the hand of a cloud.

The boys, the young men, stirred from their beds. Their murmuring, at first like the buzzing of a hive, grew deeper, more intense, a growl of purpose. Charlo turned to look at his neighbour, who was staring down at his own engorged phallus. "I am man," he said.

"And I," came the twentyfold echo.

They came and stood together, slowly divesting themselves of their modest nightwear. Naked and rapt they stood, entranced by virility, and, as one, moved out into the garden towards the east wing of the House of Brides. Charlo led them. Their bare feet printed dark ovals in the dew of the grass. Unerringly they went to the door behind which the novices and their little handmaidens lay asleep. They did not speak. They raised their heads and snuffed the air like stallions. At last, chaos laid one word upon their tongues, to be breathed at first, then growled into the night. *Maelikali. Maelikali.*

They had all eaten of the herb that negates desire, but against chaos it was powerless. The door had been bolted and barred this night, but lust was iron, and iron was the tool they found to force their way. They needed light to savour their work, and Charlo found a lantern just inside the door. The maidens were awake, alarmed by the noisy breaking-in. A score of frightened faces grew up like blossoms in the gloom.

The first girl spoke, quite softly, uncomprehending. Her eyes grew big and dark at sight of the army of pale rampant bodies.

"Charlo? What is wrong?"

He did not answer. He knelt across her. He ripped her gown from neck to hem and grasped her breasts. Her screams, the first of many, thrilled around the chamber like a peal of agonised bells. He caught her ankles and split her legs wide and, unerringly, plunged his new manhood deep into her virgin place. About her neck she wore the Lion of Night, and this he seized and broke and threw away. She cried in pain and terror as he ravished her. And even while he drove into her and pumped her full of his burning seed, he too felt pain, as if his phallus were bursting, and the spurt of blood which issued as, panting, he withdrew, was not from her alone.

The other white shapes padded swiftly past and fell on the occupants of the beds. Some of the girls were clinging together, shrieking and crying for the Matrix. But Andine could not help them; she was besieged, embattled against the whirl of chaos, the darting white light, the grey mouths; protecting her face with her bleeding hands, Andine vainly sought the Crystal Lion.

The youngest novice was eight, and she was not spared. Her tiny maidenhead was brutally torn by one of the gardeners, who then thrust his member in her mouth and stifled her with an ocean of lust. The eldest girl was twenty; one of the grooms raped her twice without pause, penetrating in turn both orifices between her legs. One of the novices was exceptionally pretty. Three went for her: one lay on his back and pulled her on top of him. He ravished her while another mounted her buttocks, forcing himself into her anus. The third stood at her head, ejaculating over her hair and brow. When they rolled her away on to the floor, she was insensible.

As the orgy progressed, the young men were no longer silent. They laughed. They emitted animal sounds as they reached a succession of unending climaxes. They shouted to one another like a triumphant army, they bellowed like stags in rut. The girls had no voices left with which to scream. And many fell silent through unconsciousness as the rapes continued throughout the night.

There was the briefest of pauses, during which the young men became aware of pain in their parts and realised that they too were bleeding, that the semen issuing from them was mixed with blood. Even so, the terrible urges returned, unappeased, and all of them fell once more upon the novices in a relentless attack, though by now, as they thrust and drove and spat their venom into the bodies of their prey, they too cried out in agony. And after a very long while even chaos tired of the game; besides, the dawn was breaking, revealing a battleground where those who once were virgin lay as the dead in rumpled sheets soaked with semen and urine and blood, and the others who once were virgin began to creep away, doubled up, holding groins that burned and bled.

So dawn came, and with it the most terrible awakening, as the trance of lust left the young men like driftwood on an insane shore. The sun was lining the horizon. The gardeners, the grooms, the servants looked slowly at one another almost without recognition. Naked, themselves violated by chaos, they drew together and began to weep. And as with their seed, disgorged countless times, there was no end to their tears. Their grief was limitless, they cried like babies, they shook like trees under storm.

And finally, weeping, Charlo looked towards the bay, gleaming in dawnlight beyond the slope of the green lawn, and his feet began to run towards it, faster and faster, and the others followed him like lemmings. And the young men, who had been so pure, cast themselves and their unbearable pain into the Sea of Infinity, and the waters closed over them.

The Treaty House, on the bridge over the Braf, had not been used for nearly a quarter of a century. There were cobwebs in the cornices, and a musty river-smell. The great chamber was crammed with diplomats of both countries, the ambience anything but cordial.

King Valm's representative, a tall thin man named Plumel, sat at one end of the long table, opposite Malkar's envoy, a squat fair man named Ing, and stifled a belch.

"My belly is in revolt," he whispered to his Taratamian neighbour.

"Mine too. It was the funeral feast. I think my liver will never be the same."

They had come straight from Karlinkis where they had represented King Valm at Enial's lavish funeral, which had been followed by three days of eating and drinking. Everyone was in dark blue, the mourning colour of Karenia. Malkar had shed two crystal tears, which had been ostentatiously collected in a silver flask. Vergon had sobbed loudly. Lilene and Honyia had both been heavily veiled. Now there were more vital matters to hand. The talks had been called as an emergency. Twenty-four representatives of either country sat opposite one another, more stood round the walls, and the rest of the space was filled by slaves and servants. The miasma from the river oozed through the window.

Plumel had the distinct feeling that the disagreeable outcome of the talks was already decided. Lord Ing of the Pearl had been speaking for half an hour, not saying very much. The whole occasion was provocative. They all knew it.

"Lord Plumel, will you reply?" said the Speaker. Plumel got to his feet.

"My lords. It is my unpleasant duty to remind you that Karenia is already in breach of the Treaty of Braf. The sweetgeld revenues, being one-eighth of the yield from the Tirkar mine, have not been forthcoming for two moonspans. Of this we should welcome an explanation."

He sat down. Ing of the Pearl rose lazily.

"My lord. Our countries have both undergone a sudden change in circumstances. We have already expressed our grief at the loss of his Majesty King Valm's heirs. You have mourned with us over the death of our beloved sovereign King Enial. A new day is dawning, however, with regenerative changes. Our new monarch, whom the gods preserve for many years, has decreed that the terms of the Treaty be revised. Taratamia has gold in her mines near Kite garrison. The Tirkar mine is our only source of gold. King Vergon has decided that the terms of the Treaty have, in today's climate, become inequitable."

"They can't do that," whispered Plumel's neighbour. "The Treaty is inviolable."

"I know," breathed Plumel testily and got to his feet again.

"My lord, what is suggested is illegal. The Treaty has already been read over to remind us that its terms were sealed by the marriage of the late Queen Doro with the late King Enial of blessed . . ."

"Just so," said Ing triumphantly. "The Treaty has undergone a deterioration in validity. We have a new king, who has empowered his sacred mother, Malkar the Wise, to act as regent. Both these noble beings are in accord that the Treaty shall be re-written."

"Over my dead body," said Plumel rather too loud. Ing smiled.

"There are other clauses which are to be revised at the suggestion of our new ruler. The House of Brides, for example . . ."

"What about it?" Plumel interrupted, undiplomatically.

"This as you know, is Taratamian land, enclosed within our realm and subject to the privileges of its homeland. We hear all is not well within the House of Brides."

"I know nothing about that," said Plumel truthfully.

"The Princess Royal and her sister have already been removed. Enquiries will have to be made as to whether this is still a fit place for young women to be raised. It may be that the land should revert to Karenia and the Abbey closed."

Plumel's offended liver gave a stab. His neighbour whispered: "They're trying it on."

Quite coolly he said, "Naturally the Princess Royal and her sister are no longer in the Abbey, being required to attend their father's funeral. Of the rest, I know nothing."

"You will, my lord, very soon."

A violent roll of thunder rattled the window. The chamber grew icy. Sweat broke out on Plumel's brow nonetheless. For a few moments he lost concentration. When he regained it, one of the other diplomats was speaking. What was being said he had no idea, but as another crash of thunder sounded, Ing's voice rose in reply.

"Let us not mince words, gentlemen. Taratamia has no male heirs to inherit the throne. In time, your great northern country will be without rule. Your king and queen are no longer young. Queen Malkar the Wise is of Kardespra, which lies within the sea-boundary of Taratamia. It is the natural law that in due course, her son will advance a claim upon it."

Plumel became speechless. His neighbour, seizing the chance, spoke out firmly and deliberately. "My lords. Your country has no claims, never had claims, and never will have claims on Taratamia, which is the hereditary realm of Capashenet through the Old Kings of Tamia." He drew a deep breath and said: "Taratamia can only be gained by right of conquest."

Outside the chamber it began fiercely to rain, as if someone had upended a bath. The window shook with thunder.

"I hear you, my lord," said Ing, smiling. "But I have conveyed the message of our sovereign, for you to take back to King Valm."

Pouring with sweat, Plumel braced himself.

"My lord," he said, and in that moment ceased to be a diplomat: "We believe that these are not King Vergon's dispositions at all, but those of his mother, Queen Malkar, who, men say nowadays, does not fight by natural methods, but by spells and charms . . ." His pale northern face went crimson. He bit his tongue, too late. He heard Ing saying, "Be grateful, my lord, that you are not a subject of our realm. Otherwise you would be handed over to the Holy Draconhood for heresy and treason."

"Yes," said Plumel angrily. "I thank my gods I am not a Karenian subject."

"I think," said Ing of the Pearl, "these discussions serve no purpose. You have heard our terms. The payment of sweetgeld is to be terminated."

"And the House of Brides territory?"

Ing shrugged. "To remain, if wished, until such time as our ultimate aim is fulfilled, a neutral enclave, ruled by a Taratamian Abbess."

The thunder crackled again. Plumel said: "Lord Ing, may we then hear your ultimate aim?"

"Gladly, my lord. Our ultimate aim is to join the territories north and south of the Tiranians as one, with King Vergon head of the joint state and all persons living in the demesne subject to his rule."

Plumel came slowly to his feet. "My lord, this sounds remarkably like an invitation to join not territories but hostilities."

"You can so interpret it, my lord."

The diplomats around Plumel stood up. More than a score of pale, blackhaired men regarded their blond opposite numbers. Plumel said:

"Hear me now, in the name of King Valm the Seventh. We do not accept your terms or even contemplate your ultimate aim. The sweetgeld shall be paid to us with two moonspans' interest. If a letter of acquiescence restoring the payments is not received within one moonspan . . ." he drew a breath, "then we shall assume that war between Taratamia and Karenia is again declared. I trust I am understood."

Lord Ing and his companions rose. "You are fully understood, my lord. We shall deliver this message at once to the palace. I wish you all a safe journey back to your homeland."

He bowed low. The whole chamber bowed. The slaves and servants remained motionless, digesting what they had heard. The sun burst through as the storm rumbled away east. In a few minutes the chamber was empty.

Riding fast towards Karlinkis, Ing of the Pearl said ruefully to his nearest companion: "Well. We've done it. She has her war. I only hope we can afford it."

"Scum of the earth," said Tallis. He walked slowly up and down the line, gazing in turn into the face of each sparklingly turned-out recruit to the Household Guard. The eyes stared straight ahead. At the end of the line he came upon a man whose eyes were slightly crossed, who was doing his best to look straight. Tallis stared at him, fascinated. "Scum," he repeated. "You were scum when you came here. Now you are polished scum. You!" he said, in the quiet voice that was worse than any sergeant's bellow: "Why are you slouching? Is your back broken, or what?" The man, who was standing as erect as if impaled, whispered: "No, Captain sir."

Tallis walked back down the line, slapping his boot with his stick, and turned to Sergeant Delvas. "Dismiss them," he said, and Delvas roared the order. The men, shining like washed jewels, turned as one, and marched from the square.

"Congratulations, sergeant," said Tallis with a grin. "They're a credit to you."

"Thank you, Captain. I'm afraid there are a few curses laid on your head."

"Well. A soldier's curse is worth a civilian's blessing. They'll have a soft life. No doubt they hope I'll be killed within the first week."

"You and me both, sir. I must say it'll be good to see some action." He gave a little cough. "I rather thought, sir," he said, "that you would have been retained on the palace staff. Let the others do the fighting."

"So did everyone," said Tallis. "I had to do some persuading. General Camlot put in a word. He knows how I feel."

"I hear the general's coming too."

"Yes. He fancied one last scrap before he hangs up his helmet. He's looking forward to it."

"So am I, Captain."

"And I. Back into Karenia."

He left Delvas with another word of praise and made for home. *Never did I think half my days would be spent back and forth to Karenia. I shall be fighting where my father fought.* He bit his lips to stop thinking aloud. *This time I'll find him. How old will he be now? Not young, certainly, for he was old in wickedness all those years ago. We may even meet in the field. I should like that. Yes. I'll find him.* He kept to these thoughts as he might hold the reins of his mare, directing them undeviatingly forward. Avoiding the thickets of even more obsessive thoughts. But as ever, he found himself ensnared.

She was raped. They raped her, spoiled her. Didn't they? She could never have escaped the sexual carnage of that night. They tore her lovely body. She will never be the same. They raped her, and she is mine.

Just how insane am I? he thought dispassionately. *She is mine. It comes to me again and again. And it's not knowing the truth of that night that keeps my mind in turmoil. How can I say she is mine? Another moment and she would have been mine, irrevocably mine, had Barbel not . . .*

Off-duty, he reached the gate of his lodging. *I could ask Prince Ataret. He has not yet returned to the island. The abbess would have written to him for guidance. No one will ever know what brought that night about, but all suspect. The rapes were somehow Malkar's doing.*

He greeted Palbo, taking the sun. There was already a tinge of autumn in the air. The Lion-lilies were beginning to hang their heads. He thought: *we must get afield before the winter.* He went up to the solar. Pancora and Barbel were sitting together, very companionable. Pancora was utterly unpredictable. She had taught Barbel to cook, to sew, and how to look after herself. She had confessed that she was very fond of Barbel. Barbel herself remained inscrutable.

There was a bloom on Pancora. He noticed it as he undressed her and laid her back on her bed. Her short black hair had an almost silvery sheen, her limbs were like glazed ivory.

It was because he now made love to her regularly and frequently. And she no longer indulged in tantrums. She behaved almost dutifully. He reminded himself now, as he lay down over her and took her in his arms, that he could have lost her. He reminded himself what a prize she was, how every man in the Household envied him. And, as ever, part of him remained aloof now. Part of him was in Karlinkis, or wherever Lilene was. And even in those hot final moments, the spirit of Lilene grasped him, heart and vitals, tossed him into a vortex of longing, where nothing could ever be the same.

He lay with his arm flung over his eyes, and heard Pancora say: "We haven't talked about it for a long time, Ricalpa."

"Marriage, you mean."

"Yes. I am getting old, Ricalpa. I am nearly twenty-five. Being with Barbel makes me realise I should like a child."

"Stop taking your herbals, then."

"No. I want to be married first. I know there's no shame in bastardy these days, but even so."

He raised himself and looked at her. "We'll get married," he said. "When I return from the war."

"You may be killed."

"No chance. I've always been lucky. I'll come back, then we'll have a big wedding. You'd like that. An arch of swords. Me in my dress uniform, and that awful helmet."

She was still laughing when he rose and dressed. She looked happier.

"I want to try to see Prince Ataret," he said.

"You're surely not thinking of asking him to officiate at the ceremony."

"Scarcely. Since when have you and I been of the blood royal."

He left the house, going through the kitchen, where Barbel shoved a hot spoon towards his lips.

"Taste that," she commanded.

"It's wonderful," he said, with a burned tongue.

"My own recipe. I can make enough to feed a hundred." He frowned deeply at her, guessing what came next. She put the spoon down and faced him, her hands on her hips. She looked like a dangerous young boy, with very long hair.

"I'm coming with you, Tallis," she said.

"That you are not."

"I am coming with you. I've decided, and there's nothing in the world you can do about it. I can come as the page, or even as a camp-follower, though I'll kill any man who tries it on with me. Or I can come as a cook. An army has to eat."

"Go away," he said. "Go upstairs. Help my lady."

"I'm coming with you, Tallis. I shall be with you when you reach the front. I'll hide away, like before. Or you can let me come visible. But I've sworn an oath to myself, you see." She set her lips very tight; suddenly she looked years older, and grave. "I shall never leave you, when you go into danger."

"Oh gods," he said, and she smiled a little, knowing she had him.

"I shall have to look after you. You will be a liability. I can't guard your virtue among a lot of soldiers."

"I can look after myself very well," she said. "It's you who need looking after."

"You may well be right," he said, and went to the palace.

He was lucky. Ataret was there, hearing confessions and accepting tributes from members of the Household. Little stone Lions, gold Lions, Lions made of topaz and onyx lay before the private shrine where small fires spun webs of light from the jewelled altar. Tallis had a large sea-emerald which he carried about as a kind of talisman, and this he gave to Ataret, kneeling.

"This is my prayer-price for the souls of Lepo and Rost."

Ataret bowed. He looked sombrely at Tallis.

"You came to ask me something, Captain."

"Yes. The lady abbess, Andine. How is she?"

"She is almost confounded. We do not discuss the details. They are too heinous."

Tallis waited, then he said very carefully: "I appreciate that, your Holiness. But there is something of great concern to me."

"Captain. You may ask, and if I am able, I will answer."

"During this year, I have been responsible for the safe escort of the Princess Royal of Karenia. I still feel some residual obligation—why, I am not certain, but . . ."

"You need not fear for her," said Ataret. "Apparently neither she nor the Princess Honyia were subjected to any violation. Does that satisfy your sense of obligation, Captain?"

And he looked very hard at Tallis, almost as if he knew. Tallis said carefully, "I am grateful to your Holiness. And relieved. Please give me your blessing."

He went from the palace in even worse turmoil. No, my Lilene. You were not born and bred to be a victim. And the fear returned to him, the fear and the anger. Yes, of course. Malkar would protect her own.

PART THREE

Enchantments

Alpac had beached his coracle in the rocky cove, beneath the high cliffs which ran along the whole of the west coast, sparsely punctuated by small inlets and coast paths leading to deserted meadows. This particular cove lay near the northern frontier of the Principality of Karkis. Not too far to the north was the Takk delta, in whose arms lay the Karenian Fort Nial, overlooking the ocean. Alpac's landing was well out of sight.

He stood with Solon the big smith on the shining sand, their feet kissed by the small waves. The coracle was lined with the day's catch of mackerel and dabs. Alpac was ostensibly at his trade; Solon had travelled cross-country from the Forest of Rulen with mule-cart laden with the tools of his; mending farm implements, shoeing horses wherever there was a forge and anvil. He covered miles this way, ploddingly, like the pace of the planned revolution. Alpac's growing impatience was shared throughout the land.

Often he thought of Cristarpa, whose battered remains had been hung on display in Kalvaria. Raise up! or die. Lilene had invented the war-cry. So, some died bravely that others should be raised. Yet every day of inaction brought more tales of abused miners, tortured servants, slaves used to test venoms, and punishment of families unable to pay the impossible taxes levied by the Crown. There was work in the land, on the farms, but the tenants still lived on the narrow edge. The merchants, the rogues and tricksters, the minor government officials, they did well enough. Those beneath them seldom knew a grey day without hunger.

"Here they come," said Solon. The galley, which had high curved gunwales and a figurehead of Erun, the Despran Stag god, danced in from the south, her shimmering yellow sails coming down like furled sunlight, her oarsmen skilfully prising a way between the low sharp reefs guarding the shore. Mervhu stood on deck, arms raised, laughing with great white teeth under the flowing black wealth of moustache.

"He always seems happy," said Alpac wonderingly.

"They're like that. And they breed like rats. It's part of their religion."

"Who's that with him?"

"Gwch. The chieftain from Ogor in the north. He's an alchemist."

The galley dropped anchor. Several Desprans boarded small boats. Mervhu was the first ashore, wading thigh-deep through the shallows. In one hand he carried a long sack. Over his shoulder, herself like a sack, was a plump plain girl.

"My woman," explained Mervhu. He spoke ungrammatically in the Karenian coastal dialect. He set the girl down on the sand. "Tamian. Nice girl. Pregnant now. I bring her for trip. Revolution go all right?"

"Revolution not begun," said Alpac grimly.

"Oh so. You still wait. This Gwch. Clever fellow. Invent turineko." Here he patted the sack he carried. "More turineko for revolution. Blow ballocks off new king."

"Gwch, Mervhu," said Alpac patiently. "We are very grateful. I'm glad you were pleased with -"

"Green stones very nice," said Gwch sonorously. "High King put round throne, drape antlers of Erun in temple. Want more."

"Lord Gwch," said Alpac with respect. "You shall have more. But it's difficult now. Our movements are somewhat restricted." The Desprans frowned, trying to follow Alpac's swift dialect. "It isn't so easy to talk now with the Princess Lilene . . ."

Mervhu interrupted with a shout. "Ah! The Lilene! Our High King want her for fifth wife. You tell her."

"You see," said Alpac patiently, while Solon scuffed the sand with his boot in frustration, "we are about to go to war with Tamia. We have to be careful, or we shall be conscripted. People hide away. They are called traitors if they do not come out to fight for Karenia."

"Turineko very good for war," said Gwch.

"Mervhu," said Alpac. "I am trying to tell you. The turineko are wonderful. Lord Gwch is a genius. But they don't work without . . ."

"The gwgli," said Gwch. "Gwgli needed for big blow-up. No can do yet."

"Why not?" said Solon impatiently. Alpac nudged him and frowned.

"Gwgli put in pan and set fire for bang," said Gwch. "Gwgli come from rocks. Only Despran know where. Towers of Kite, western side, hidden. Only one secret place where gwgli grow. Now war begin, ships sail down coast, from Fort Opal round past El of Kardespra, near our coast. Too much seagoing. Despran gwgli miners no go while ship lanes full. Might be caught. Same way, Desprans let shipping past their coast. Want to watch and wait for war. Till then, gwgli not possible."

"We must have it," said Alpac. "It's our only chance of victory."

He felt his stomach sinking. He stared at Mervhu, who was caressing his Taratamian bride fondly. "Mervhu," said Alpac. "You'll have more payment. We do not break our word. Only get us the powder."

"Despran word good too," said Gwch proudly. "We swear by great Erun. We help you. But now we wait to see who win war."

Solon spoke, gruff with anxiety. "Who do you want to win?"

Gwch shrugged his shoulders. "Does not matter. Tamia perhaps. We see."

"You revolution boys," said Mervhu suddenly, "you no fight for homeland. You help Tamia? Yes?"

"It's a thought," said Solon.

"You join up with Tallis-Cap. Whatever," said Mervhu, playfully belting his woman's backside so that she fell over on the sand, "you no harm Tallis-Cap. Good fighter. He give me woman. He let me out of jail. We promise to kill each other one day. You meet Tallis-Cap in war, you spare."

"I hear you," said Alpac. He picked up the sack of weapons. "I'll keep these safe until we have the gwgli. If you only knew," he said sadly, "how much we depended on it."

"Swords any good?" suggested Mervhu brightly. "I bring you swords next time. You got swords?"

"Only a very few," said Alpac. "Swords would be most welcome."

"There we are then," said Mervhu happily. "We go now, tide on way. Tell The Lilene. When High King sit on throne, she sit at his side."

Alpac and Solon watched as they boarded the boats and rowed out to the waiting galley. The head of Erun clove through the air as the vessel skirted rocks and reefs. Mervhu's woman waved gaily as the ship rode the waves and vanished in a drizzle of spray.

There was just a little sharp wind, puffing the occasional snowy cloud sideways. It was a perfect day on which to go to war. The sun blazed as the company began its vigilant file over Knife Pass between the high cliffs that formed a vantage point for snipers with bows and ballistas.

This was the advance party, with large reinforcements lying not far behind the Taratamian frontier. After a week of being cloistered in Karetara garrison where the strategy council had been held, the men were glad to be on the move. In the north, more armies were preparing to stream down from Fort Opal. The force from Kite garrison in the far north under the unscaleable Towers had marched down two weeks earlier and, under the command of General Camlot, were preparing to advance over Singstar Pass in the east. Lines of communication borne by swift-horsemen had been set up between east and west along the frontier under cover of darkness. These missions were dangerous, for there were Karenian guards on the gold mines.

General Lindo, the commander from Karetara, was in charge of the force in which Tallis rode, and, under the General, Colonel Pog, a rather foppish favourite of King Valm. Directly responsible for the captains and their troops was Major Sirban, under whom Tallis had fought in the Despran campaigns. Tallis was none too pleased: he suspected the major of incipient idiocy.

Two thousand advanced down the pass, footsoldiers in the van, cavalry behind them, and more footsoldiers and camp servants in the rear. Among these were surgeons, stretcher-bearers, armourers, blacksmiths and cooks. Barbel was somewhere in the throng. Tallis had caught one glimpse of her before the advance commenced. She was dressed boy-fashion, with her hair concealed under the slouch cap, with huge boots in which she strode out purposefully, and over her shoulder, baggage which weighed her down; mess cutlery, butcher's knives (she had learned how to skin and joint a beast for cooking), and even her own small tent. Tallis knew the cook-sergeant had accepted her presence. The sergeant was a huge man with fists, and daughters of his own. It had to be enough. She would be protected, if not by the sergeant, then by the gods.

Kestrels, buzzards and red kites sailed overhead, their eyes diminishing the long steady file as it moved beyond the frontier into the no-mans-land of the pass. Deeper into the defile, the column divided into two, so that each marched or rode as close as possible beneath the overhang, out of range of missiles from above. Men raised in the mountains had been sent aloft, scaling the cliff on either side. They were armed with long knives, short bows and catapults. Their adversary was the force of ballista handlers and snipers upon the cliff.

The army was very quiet. Only the chink of bridles and weapons and the thud and crunch of hooves was audible. The wind, rising from the north, funnelled down the defile behind them. The cavalry officers wore scarlet under breastplates and greaves of branzel, a stout alloy formed from metals from the mines of Kite. They wore plumed helmets blazoned with the Lion of War, rampant with raised tail, like the device on the great banners. Above all flew the Opal of Capashenet, worked in iridescent threads, next to the Red Royals' own colours.

Tallis was riding a war-stallion, seventeen hands high. It rolled beneath him like a great warm ship. Sergeant Delvas, also mounted, rode close behind him. All the horses were armoured at breast and face. These were the tall steeds of the north, bred, according to legend, in the Far Lands, the first two foals being blown by a gale over the Towers, millennia ago, on to the plains of Kite. The horse-archers rode stout little hill ponies, fast on the turn and swerve. Bows and quiverfuls of arrows were carried on the riders' backs, and chests full of arrows followed on mules. The footsoldiers, their armour similar to the officers' but with a bascinet on the head, carried broadswords, axes and knives. The officers were armed with sabre, dagger, sword and axe. Tallis had his Lion sword. Under his hand the gold curve of its hilt felt alive.

The drummers and trumpeters were quiet. The enemy above knew of the army's presence, but it was not about to be advertised. Ballistas, great thonged catapults, trundled along on carts. And there were a few big royal dogs in the company.

King Valm had spared no expense in equipping the army. As Malkar's generals had suggested, he had welcomed the chance to subsume his dreadful grief in war.

The High Priest, Ataret, had held a witchbanishing service of protection for those men who marched this day.

"All in order, lieutenant?"

Lieutenant Pinpol spurred his horse to ride by Tallis. The pass had widened slightly and they could come side by side under the overhang of the cliff.

"All in order, Captain. Just waiting for the rocks to start falling."

"I doubt there'll be much before the frontier." Tallis ducked in time to avoid being brained by a stone outcrop. For an instant he saw a face in it.

"The coastal scouts are back," said Pinpol. "Our supply ship is moving down Avatal Bay. Not a sign of Despra."

"Nor will there be," said Tallis. "They're going to sit back and enjoy the show."

"Captain," said Pinpol. "We're out to capture Fort Nial, right?"

"Right. And if there's too much to handle our reinforcements will come in from north and east."

"I was wondering. Suppose we were ordered to march on Karlinkis. What then?"

"That we'll learn from orders. Right now, I can't answer you. I only know part of our orders is to remember we're Tamian. We don't rape or pillage."

A quivering flame rose in the base of his spine.

There she is. With me again. The prospect of conflict hardened his sensibilities. I could have raped her, loved her so hard and so long that she finally melted away, never more a danger to me . . .

Angry, he crushed down these thoughts, and said abruptly: "Lieutenant. Tell Sergeant Delvas to make sure the men empty their bowels and bladders before we attack the Fort. They won't get another chance."

A small avalanche began to rain down on the path ahead. The horses threw up their heads. The fall suddenly stopped.

Then a body plummeted down, followed swiftly by a snaking rope, down which one of the Taratamian mountain men came like a monkey. A Karenian sniper lay dead in the path, face down, a knife in his back.

"Good work," someone said, and the mountain man shook his head.

"Not me. Him." And he pointed upward where, just visible on the heights, a large hairy shape was striking another Karenian sniper over the head with a club. "Bandit", panted the mountain man, coiling his rope round his waist. "Thought he was a wolf or a bear at first. Thought he was Despran. Then he yelled something in a Karenian accent."

Major Sirban came riding up, jostling his mount through the ranks.

"What's going on, Captain?" The mountain man repeated his last speech for the major's benefit.

"Bandits, eh. Want flushing out, what."

Tallis, remembering something, said: "With respect, major. There was a saying that the Tiranian bandits were the lost generations."

"Lost generations of whom, Captain?" said the major sceptically.

"Escaped slaves," said Tallis. "Come up from Karenia."

"He was Karenian," said the mountain man, taking a swig of water from his flask. "He was blond. I was just about to kill this man -" he poked the dead sniper with a foot, "he muscled in. He wore a lot of furs. Thought he was a bear."

"Well," said Tallis. "Useful bear."

"Carry on," said Major Sirban disdainfully, and rode back up the line.

The company moved on towards the frontier fort; already fierce fighting was taking place overhead. The mysterious allies were embattled hand to hand with the Karenian slingmen and ballista wielders. Bodies hurtled down into the pass, and boulders. There was some arrow-fire. A few Taratamian soldiers fell, but it was soon over, and the company, in their long file, came out the other side at a gallop.

Oh, Tirkar Plain. Once more, over there, where the Lion gave way to the Oyster, where the lion-colours are suddenly tinged with grey. There was the crumbling pile of stones where murder had been done. And he recalled how he had been asked, so many times: did you really know your father? Tell me, Tallis, my dear friend (that was Lepo, who had known his secrets): you were only a little boy.

I remember everything about him. His strong honest eyes (not grey like mine, but black), his smile. The things he told me almost before I could speak. Of honour, and love of my country, and respect—never to be used as a shield for fear, but to be surrendered when the person concerned proved unworthy of it. And love of horses and how to treat them so they gave of their best. Of self-preservation tempered always by courage. Of clear thought and knowledge of the will of the gods. He was not away very long before he met his death. And by all the gods, would that he had died fighting with honour. By all the gods, I will never rest until I find you, red-blond, limping six-fingered drunkard with your love of pain, where your victim is helpless . . .

King Valm loved him. It was said he shed tears. General Camlot, even now coming down over the peaks, he loved him too. And my mother—well, they said the plague killed her. My beautiful mother, Carilene. You couldn't wait to join him and leave me alone . . .

"Captain."

He found his eyes and brain unfocussed. This was no way to be at the start of a campaign. Uncharacteristic, and unprofessional. He straightened on his tall horse, flashed a look round to see all was in order with his company, and answered his lieutenant.

"Shall we send out scouts to sweep the terrain? The major says to look for an eminence to set up camp."

The major needs his brains exhuming, thought Tallis.

"Ride back. Suggest with respect to the major that we make camp in the lee of the mountains where there is shelter."

There was a pause in which the major found the suggestion acceptable.

"We shall attack by night, Captain."

You learn fast, major. Now, Lilene. I am about to slay a few of your countrymen. How will you like that? And then he put such thoughts away, becoming all soldier, heart and blood and brain.

"Let tides run high, let arrows fly . . ."

The song was in his blood like an infection. It went with the noise, the tension, the turmoil.

"Courageous Taratamia, shall flourish over all . . ."

They had come south-west by night, moving fast with caution, with Avatal Bay on their right and the upper arm of the Takk delta swiftly crossed with pontoons. The fort, massive and amorphous in the small hours, rose on the lip of the bay. The sea sang on the reefs far below.

Two thousand men surrounded the fort. They had broken down the inner and outer rings of the palisade and laid bridges across the moat, making good headway until the alarm was raised. Now a constant exchange of missiles was airborne, making parabolas of light from the fire-arrows and ballistas as they arched across the gap. Far out to sea, the Desprans stood on their rolling decks and counted every spear of light.

General Camlot and General Lindo had joined forces to the east and were holding their reinforcements ready. Barbel, the baggage-boys and the civilians were tucked into a cave at the edge of the mountains with a view of the combat. The Karenians defended their fort energetically. Blazing arrows and stones hurtled down. A Taratamian force was using rams to batter the great iron-studded door, working in a lurid glare; part of the burning palisade lit up the night, making it easier for both sides to find their target.

The major was issuing fairly sensible orders. A party of men was sent up with scaling ladders, hooks and ropes. Tallis's horse suddenly curvetted under him in terror and rage; it smelled the devil's-kitchen stench of burning oil, which descended in an amber sheet, wounding with splashes, stripping flesh. The ground smoked. Men shrieked and swore. The colonel and the major, beyond the blazing palisade, were shouting orders in quick succession. Tallis wheeled his horse in among the men working the battering-rams. The horse struck out with an iron-shod hoof as if to help. Damn, this is a good horse, he thought, and in that instant, the door crashed apart and Tallis, the other captains and cavalrymen charged through into the stone hall of the fortress, followed by an army of singed, howling footsoldiers.

Sabre in hand, he felt the familiar rush, the glory that had something hateful about it, until, confronted by the swinging steel of a big Karenian sergeant it became no more than a dirty necessity to be washed clean by blood. Tallis leaned clear of his saddle and took off the Karenian's head with one sweep. The head rolled open-mouthed into the wide fireplace, where evening embers still smoked.

"Courageous Taratamia, shall flourish . . ." He could not resist a lightning glance at the dead head. Too young. Not him. Then the hall was black with fighting men, the horses skidding on the stone flags, sparks flying from the anvil of their hooves, the footsoldiers embattled, using clubs and maces and knives, pressing forward, fighting on the tables, fighting up the spiral stair, moving the battle higher and higher with Taratamia gaining ground, as the bodies of dead and wounded Karenians came slithering over the inner ramparts or down the stairs.

Tallis and the others left their mounts and pursued the fight upwards, clashing with assailants on the curves of the spiral, wounding and maiming. There was a door on the left where a round room faced on to the bay, and the soldiers broke it down. A score of women and many children were revealed. A half dozen Taratamians stormed at them. Tallis roared an order and they stopped mid-run.

"Close up this door!" The soldiers retreated, leaving the occupants of the room motionless, except for a boy of about seven. He left the side of a woman and rushed forward. He kicked the leg of one of the sergeants, then leaped high and bit Tallis in the hand.

"By the holy Lion, I'm wounded," said Tallis. He laughed and swung the boy off his feet. The boy glared at him; although Tallis was an awful sight, with blood-splashes on his grinning teeth, the glare was fearless.

"You'll make a warrior." He tossed the boy back into the arms of the women. "Put a guard on them." The door was slammed shut. The tail-end of the battle was still going on above their heads, but the oil vats were empty and the ballistas exhausted. Only a few archers continued to loose their arrows over the parapet.

They found the commander of the fort barricaded in an upper chamber. A small slim Karenian, he came proffering his sword across both arms. Tallis and the others stood and waited until Colonel Pog and Major Sirban came up the stairs.

"Lieutenant-Colonel Volt, at your service, gentlemen," said the Karenian mournfully. "We concede defeat of Fort Nial. Our wives and children are below. I would deem it courteous if they are unmolested."

"Your son is very brave, colonel," said Tallis, guessing accurately, and the Karenian gave a pallid smile, as Tallis wrapped a rag round his bleeding hand. The party descended to ground level. Bodies and blood lay all around. There were several Taratamian casualties, some of them mortal. Surgeons crossed the burnt palisade to attend to the wounded. Dawn was breaking, creeping along the mountains in a pale gleam and finding a response in the waters of the bay.

"Captain," said Colonel Pog, "Have our colours run up."

"And make provision for our prisoners to be held secure." This from Major Sirban, who added: "This was very good work, you men." Tallis saluted and went to his horse. He let it outside the gate so it should be calmed, and, looking up saw, rising, the Opal and the Lion of War. A nimble boy was climbing a high tower with them over his shoulder. On the morning breeze the Lion's body was filling with gold light. A cheer arose from the army. The boy came down again, no rope attached, only hands and bare feet to grip protruding stones. As the feet landed on the ground with a slap, the boy's cap fell off. Tallis went forward in three strides. He caught Barbel by the shoulders and slapped her face.

"What in the name of the gods -" and a lot more oaths as well -"do you think you're doing, you wretch?"

She grinned at him. He had not hit her very hard.

"Raising our colours, Tallis. Didn't I do it well? They tried to stop me, but I was too quick."

"You unnatural creature," he said. "You might have been killed."

"Oh no, Captain," she said with respect. "My father was a mountain man, remember? Look at us flying there, Tallis! Just look!"

He looked. The anthem sang in his brain. He felt the lithe, blood-warm Lion on the pommel of his sword.

"Yes, Barbel," he said, suddenly weak and tingling all over. "Courageous Taratamia."

"Tourageous Caratamia," said Barbel, and yawned as if she would never stop.

Darkness was flying. A black sea-bird, not a chough nor a hooded crow nor a raven, but smaller, like a cloud-shadow, almost amorphous, with a brilliant white stripe bisecting its poll.

West of the Palace of Karlinkis, downriver to Beggars' Braf, where the hovels stood, the chill wind, skipping with malice down the little alleys, found hunger and weakness for playthings, and scratched at the lungs of the poor.

Radek sat by his mother's grave in the paupers' cemetery. The wind blew through his rags. A week ago that same wind had drawn the last red cough from his mother's lips, and since then he had come daily to the rough hummock of earth, dully amazed that there were more tears for him to shed. Radek was alone now, his father long-gone, and some time ago the recruiting officers had come and taken away his three brothers to fight in the war against Taratamia. Him they had discarded as unfit for service, leaving him alone with his leg, withered from birth, and his mother, now beneath the ground.

He had been left to look after her, he, her precious one, and he had failed. He rested his head on his knees and wept more, under the grey sky. On the grave lay a broken brown lily. He whispered against his rags: "Come back to me," and the wind mocked him and blew a light debris against his head. He put up his hand to brush it away, and encountered sleek feathers, black wings that lightly touched his eyes in passing.

The bird settled on the grave. It looked at him, perfectly calm and tame, with a piercing intelligence. Its amber eyes were unblinking. It seemed to understand his sorrow, and foolishly, he spoke to it.

"I miss her so much," he said. "My little mother."

The bird was suddenly galvanised. With both feet it began to scratch frantically at the mound. Clods of dirt flew. The earth caved in, and the bird vanished downwards into the hole it had made, swift as a rabbit into a burrow.

The shock dried Radek's tears. He stared at the spot where the bird had disappeared and thought: sorrow has driven me mad. And then the earth began to move, spraying outwards, the mound rose and divided, leaving a bare chasm as neatly squared as when it had been dug.

Radek's mother rose smiling from the grave.

Not a mark on her, her shroud unsullied, her face blooming with health. Not skeletal as he had seen her last, but full and rosy, with her blonde hair which, when he was little, he loved to play with and plait, glossy on her shoulders. And the beloved voice, which he had thought never to hear again, spoke to him, and she held out her arms.

"Don't cry any more, Raddie."

He was not in the least afraid. Grateful joy flung him into her arms. She held him fast, and she was warm. "Mother," he said. "Oh, Mother."

She kissed his brow, she rolled him in her arms, lying with him on the turned earth of the grave. She held him close.

"Come home, Mother," he sighed into her neck, crying a little again with joy.

"Yes, in a little while," she murmured. "Let me rest for a moment. I am very tired. I slept too long down there. Kiss me, my Raddie, my boy, my babe."

He flung his arms round her neck and kissed her rapturously on the cheek, and she turned her lips to his. She had never kissed him so before, but he found it lovely, this strong kiss, and thought: dying has made her strong. He lay lax in her arms, as she began tenderly to undress him, just as when he was a little child.

He allowed it. Nothing else mattered; she had come back. Even when she lifted her shroud to her waist and, turning him on his side, slipped her legs round his, he did not deter her, only whispered: "Oh, Mother! My sweet little mother!" closing his eyes to savour her embrace. He had an erection but ignored it, for nothing mattered—she was wonderfully, miraculously alive. Only when, next instant, he found himself inside his mother, feeling her warmth and wetness, did his eyes fly open in shock.

The blonde hair was gone. There was whiteness and blackness and a hungry red mouth. And the strength of the world's oceans, drawing in instants from his frail little body his ultimate essence, the part of him that was everlasting.

When it was over, the darkness let Radek's body fall into the grave to lie with the redolent remains there. Grief killed him, said those who came later. One less beggar in the city.

Malkar sat before her mirror, hardly daring to look. All was well; the tiny line between her brows had been ironed away.

Beauty was power; power was seeing. They fed one another, and Malkar must feed well and often, or be discarded.

The pearl illuminated the chamber, showing Taratamia armed, afield, and in council in their war pavilion. The light wavered and diffused; the Lion of Taratamia was blazoned on banners and tabards, setting up protective vibrations which marred her seeing.

There were several generals; she chose one. It would not be easy.

He came with his maimed ungainly walk up the middle of the Hall of the Sea, purposefully heading for the twin Oyster thrones where king and regent waited to give him audience.

Zairopo hardly troubled to look at Vergon, who was finding kingship frustrating. He could order punishments, but that was nothing new. He could sign documents, but their content was always arbitrated by Malkar. The war was his mother's tool.

Courtiers flanked the thrones, but Malkar could have occupied the chamber sole. Her glitter was challenged only by the angel-fish, the tiger sharks, the rays and electric eels captive in the glass walls. Her glass crown housed a small live squid, dancing above her midnight hair.

Colonel Zairopo bent his wounded knee in secret pain. There was the smell of bonfires about him.

"Colonel. Welcome to our court," Vergon said hastily, knowing it was possibly his only chance to speak.

"I am grateful to your majesties."

"Please be brief," said Malkar. She looked at him under her white lids. He thought: they call her the most beautiful woman living. To me, she is like an avalanche of freezing night.

"Gracious King," he began, and Vergon brightened attentively.

"You may speak," said Malkar.

"Greatnesses, I am troubled. I am greatly exercised by the situation in the dioceses of the Most Holy Draconhood. I understand your majesties have seen fit to arm the peasants, the common artisans and people."

"What of it, colonel?" answered Malkar.

"Why, madam. We of the Draconhood are responsible for the loyalty of these people. Lately we have met with much resistance. If these people are given weapons, our task will be greatly hindered."

Malkar laughed. The fish vibrated behind the glass.

"We are at war, colonel," she said. "The enemy has already been victorious in a meagre way. This will not last, when they meet our armies to the south of Fort Nial. They have their quota of battle-fodder and so have we. Karenia has men who will fight for her if commanded. That is, colonel," she said, "if there are enough remaining who have not been roasted alive in your holy city of Kalvaria."

Zairopo concealed his anger. "Madam. You surely do not condemn the work of the Draconhood? In each barrel of apples we find dozens that are rotten. For the physical and spiritual health of the realm it is our time-honoured vocation to root these out. The Draconhood has worked loyally for countless years. This is no time to rob us of our power!"

"You speak to us of power? We are omnipotent!" The white lids revealed the burning beautiful amber beneath.

"Majestic one," said Zairopo, furious and servile. "Of course."

"The peasants shall be armed and commanded into battle for Karenia. Remember, colonel, when we are victorious from the far south to the utmost north, places in my favour will be carefully chosen. Think on this, but do not think of interfering with my army."

Zairopo, his leg paining, inclined his head. Woman, keep apart from me, he thought angrily. Talk power, but Zairopo goes his own way. The gods of death looked on me in my cradle. One day, great madam, you may have need of the arm of the

Draconhood. He looked up at her quite gently, feigning acquiescence.

"Majesties. I appreciate your wise concerns. We must work together for the good of Karenia. May the sun never set on her."

"Thank you, Colonel Zairopo," said Vergon pompously, and Malkar slid her unrelenting eyes towards him, then back to where Zairopo knelt.

"You may stand before us, colonel." Zairopo tried to rise, finally lurching upright when softly, from a round door in the chamber's highest curve, Lilene entered.

She had held back as long as possible. But she wanted desperately to confirm what was vital, and this meant speech with the monster. He looked at her as she entered and she at him. Reddish-fair hair, crippled leg. Deformed hand.

"Your Royal Highness."

Lilene inclined her head. "Colonel Zairopo, I trust you are well."

"My health has improved. I thank the Princess Royal."

I didn't know the creature was sick, thought Lilene. She said: "Is it your leg that troubles you, colonel? Was it a wound taken, valiantly no doubt, in battle?"

Zairopo was pleased at first, then suspicious. He answered nonchalantly. "Yes, madam. Shortly before the end of the First Tirkar Plain War." With a polite smile towards Malkar, "We have to think of it as the first, now we are fully embroiled in the second?"

It's him, thought Lilene. A little well of triumph bubbled within her. Zairopo's next words gave her an unpleasant jolt.

"I recall," he said, smiling, "the last time I had the pleasure of meeting your highness. It was in the Forest of Rulen. I was alarmed for your highness; there were renegades in the vicinity. I trust no harm befell you."

Lilene's hands became icy. She felt herself grow pale. Zairopo's smiling eyes held hers; she bowed her head as if in politeness, to avoid them. She felt on the point of collapse.

"No harm at all," she heard herself say. "My trip north was quite uneventful."

"I'm glad to hear it," he said. "I almost decided to send a few of the Draconhood after you as escort wherever you wished to go. But that was obviously unnecessary."

"I had an escort," said Lilene. "They were most efficient."

"I would not recommend Taratamians as your escort these days," said Zairopo, laughing. "They would be more likely to cut your highness's throat. Or hold you to ransom."

"Yes," said Lilene, and before she could stop herself, "and ransom does not always pay. Sometimes throats are cut prematurely, am I right, colonel?"

She saw his puzzlement, realised with relief that her reckless jibe had not registered. In no way could he connect her with anything in his past. But Malkar was looking at her curiously. Without taking her eyes from Lilene she said: "Colonel, we thank you for attending us today. There should be no discrepancy in our future aims: the supremacy of Karenia throughout all lands."

"So be it, madam," said Zairopo as humbly as he was able. He bowed, knowing himself dismissed, and went from the Hall.

"Madam," said Vergon edgily, "I think the colonel has a point. The peasants will be running amok, with weapons to hand. We shall none of us be safe in our beds."

Malkar stood up, like a rising wave. "Get from this throne room, sir. You try my patience. Remember who rules here. Go back to your villa. I have seen enough of you to surfeit me."

He opened his mouth to protest, then went rapidly from the Hall, a few minor cronies trailing after him.

"Now, Lilene," said Malkar.

Oh, she knows everything, thought Lilene. No, not everything. Surely not.

"What were you doing in the Forest of Rulen?"

There are things that are dear to me. There are also things on which hang ten thousand lives. Now I choose. She hung her head as if embarrassed. Malkar gestured to the courtiers, who hurriedly departed. She and Lilene were left alone.

"Well, daughter? Come, divert me. What a little secret thing you are. You intrigue me. What, who, and why?"

"I went to the Forest," whispered Lilene. "It was a ruse. I fell in love. I wanted a secluded inn where I—I could seduce someone."

"So," said Malkar softly. "So."

"Yes."

"Tell me all about it," Malkar said even more softly. "Was it pleasant for you? And was it pleasant for him?"

Lilene stared at her. She said simply: "I failed."

For the briefest instant, the queen's image seemed to waver and shift. Something that was not quite Malkar gave a little jeering laugh. And the fish in the tanks went crazy, attacking one another. The water ran red and clouded. Fragments of small fish rose, the jaws of big fish overspilled with fragments of flesh. Then the tanks grew quiet again.

Malkar said casually: "And who was he, that escaped your embraces?"

"Taratamian. One of the escort guard."

"A commoner? His name?"

"I never knew it," said Lilene. Malkar sat back in the shell of the oyster. "I am weary," she said. "Go away, princess."

"Where shall I go?"

"Go back to the House of Brides. It is still a neutral territory until we win the war. Go and see what chaos lust has wrought. It should be an education for you. And take the Thing."

"Yes, I'll take Honyia. I'll stay until you call for me again. And if I am taken hostage by the Taratamian army," (oh, blessed thought!) "it will be on your head, Mother."

Lilene turned and went from the Hall. The piranhas in the tanks darted, following her progress round the walls of glass.

The pearl was white and vital in the dark mirror. It pulsed gently, like a heart.

Oh, it is cold down here in the deeps, in the dark of fallen days, where mortal man has never lived. The damned drift about crying their emptiness into the black pillow of the waves. The damned have a slight phosphorence; they feed the pearl. The pearl feeds Malkar. Now Malkar would like to see what happened in the Forest of Rulen The inheritrix failed, but why? Shine, pearl, give forth the retrospective. Show me Lilene, and the man.

Time has laid a veil; but here he is, and she. Oh, there is certainly lust. But something else? What was it?

With her there is love, and what is love? and fear. She should not know fear, not Malkar's daughter.

Oh, and now I know him. We met once, briefly. This is a soldier, and no innocent. But there is honour. The soul has great purity. I would take him myself, but she has chosen him.

In the fullness of time she will have him. Her beauty like that of Malkar is an irresistible force. Captain Tallis, you shall be her first Taken.

"For the gods' love, Solon, don't sing," said Alpac. "The likes of us don't sing."

"It was hearing about Fort Nial," said Solon, whacking the white-hot horseshoe on the anvil. "Gods bless the mountain men. Gods bless Tamia."

"Steady," said Alpac. "Better the devil you know."

"I know no devil like a Karenian lordlet," said Solon. "Let me have a little sing. I only got the news this dawn. By the gods, our communications system is working well. Now wait for the lads from Tirkar Mine to move. Not only the lads. The women too, and the poor little brats."

"It makes me shiver," said Alpac. He hoisted his fish-basket on to his shoulder. They stood together in Solon's smithy on the outskirts of a village between Rulen and Kalvaria. To the west, where lay Karkis, the morning was sunny and clear, but south there was a drifting pall and a scent more acrid than the singed hoof that Solon was shoeing. A couple of villagers strolled by, one of them with a child, who pulled back to watch Solon at work. Alpac and Solon became quiet. Then Solon said: "It's all right. I know him."

Alpac put a finger to his lips and turned his back to the open doorway. "Every child has a father," he said softly. "The Draconhood has been known to pay informers."

Solon worked his bellows viciously and the fire blazed. "Tell me,"—for the people had passed by, "did you see Mervhu?"

"I did. And I got the swords. He met me further north this time. The swords went up to Tirkar, safe and sweet."

"That madman, Mervhu. Where's the gwgli, I ask?"

"I like Mervhu. No gwgli yet."

"They're biding their time. Playing games."

"The swords are damned good. I just hope they know how best to swing them."

"Where are they hidden?"

"In a mountain cave. There are guards on the mine but they've found a way through. Mountain men again. Told them about the caverns and tunnels. And they've got wind of the Tamian army's next movements. They're moving south-east, towards Incana-on-the-Takk. A good place for battle."

Solon trimmed the horny hoof and blew smoke away to see that the horseshoe fitted. "What do you know about battle?" He let the hoof fall and straightened up.

"I know about battles," said Alpac. "Battles for the right. Raise up! or die!"

"Gods bless her, the darling," said Solon. "And gods bless your good brother and his close mouth. May he have joy in the Far Lands."

"I doubt I could be as brave," said Alpac.

"I could," boasted Solon. "I would never betray the princess. They could cut out my liver and burn it."

"Oh, they would," said Alpac. "And I say again: remember what she said. No action here until the time is right. There are some hotheads in our movement, especially down south."

"There's a lot of grief down south," said Solon, and spat into his forge.

"Should you do that?" asked Alpac. "I always heard it was bad luck."

The first thing Lilene saw was the birds. Little puffs of feathers, they lay on the lawn in the unmistakable state of non-being that is death. She could see no marks on them, not on the robin who had sung so blithely, nor the goldfinches, nor the tiny wren. Some lay in the grass, which was now long enough to cover them almost completely; some had fallen into the rosebushes where suckers proliferated, dead-heads hung withered and brown, and buds grew abortively misshapen.

She had come by river from Karlinkis, accompanied by a few servants, whom she had sent back to the city. She was alone now in the garden. Honyia had flatly refused to come with her. Honyia could write, not as fast or as well as Lilene, but enough to communicate her dread. In a scrawl she had put: "No, no. Don't make me. I am afraid of Mother's rough boys." And

Honyia, who had heard the screams on the night of chaos, trembled almost as much as at the sight of water.

Lilene could not be cruel to her, but she was deeply troubled. The minstrel, who would have been her sole agent regarding the rebellion, was also staying behind.

"Goodbye, my sister. The Lion protect you by day and night" (uttered softly). "One day I'll take you away, to a place of safety."

These were empty words. There was no "one day." The future was intolerable, precarious. At the House of Brides, the grapes were withered on the vine. In the ponds fish floated belly-up or were being systematically devoured by one enormous carp, which Lilene did not remember having seen before. On the grassy slope leading to the bay a straight swathe was scored as if it had been burned, and along it no vegetation grew, not even a plantain. The door of the novices' lodging lay amid rubble. Rats ran over the couches and nested in the pillows. One scurried behind the little altar where the Lion of Night lay on its side. Lilene went in sadly, without fear. She tenderly righted the figure of the god and left, her feet leaving marks in the dust.

Her steps barely echoed on the spiral as she ascended the abbess's tower. The door was open and she could see Andine, lying on her bed.

"Enter, princess." Andine's voice was strong, and Lilene was almost heartened, until she saw the abbess's face turned slowly towards her.

"Matrix," said Lilene. "Mother."

"I prayed you would come. I needed to see you before I went to the Far Lands. There is something I must know, for my peace."

Lilene knelt by the couch.

"My work is ended here, not by my choice. Lilene, tell me. Can you remember, far far back, when you came from the womb of your mother the witch? Can you remember your birth? Can you remember me?"

Lilene shook her bent head. Her tears fell on the skeletal hands with their crescent wounds.

"Do you remember the mist?" said Andine urgently. 'Try, try hard. You call me Mother, often. But do you truly belong to me?"

Lilene looked up, her eyes full of fresh tears.

"The Crystal mist," said Andine in anguish. "The weapon and shield of purity." She began to cough uncontrollably. Lilene got up hurriedly and fetched water from a ewer on a chest. A letter with the signet of Capashenet lay rolled beside it. She supported Andine so that she could drink; the abbess felt almost weightless.

"My thanks, child." She followed Lilene's eyes, her own half-closed from the effort of beating back death. "A letter there from Prince Ataret. So far their army is triumphant. You should be pleased."

"I wish I knew, Mother," said Lilene. "I wish I knew how and where he is. I wonder sometimes if he has been killed in the fighting. Sometimes I think he would be more mine, if he were dead."

Andine frowned worriedly. "That is a strange thing to say," she whispered.

"I dreamed of him, with his woman. He was making his will. His possessions are hers, as he is hers. I feel as if a snake were coiled in my heart."

Andine succumbed to another spasm of coughing. Blood streamed from her lips, tainting the water she drank.

"Is there no doctor?" asked Lilene in a panic.

"No doctor, nor do I wish for one. No one is here. Only you and I."

Lilene sat holding the abbess in her arms. "You cannot stay here alone," said Andine.

"I never fear to be alone. Here is where I want to be. When the war is over, I could restore the House in your memory."

In a weaker voice, the abbess said: "There is not much time left for what I have to tell you."

"Is it about him?" Lilene whispered. The abbess was silent, thinking: the letter from Ataret should have been burned. Yet, if commanded, Lilene will not read it.

"No," she said. "It is this. Help me up. This is vital, for it is the greatest of all the mysteries. I shall try to teach you how to summon the Crystal Lion."

Much later, when dusk hung purple over the wild garden and the incense still streamed and curled, the abbess said in the faintest whisper: "Have I failed?" and while Lilene hushed her trying to breathe comfort—"Oh, my dear child. I beg you, spare Ricalpa. He is such a good man."

And then, quite suddenly, she closed her eyes and died.

Lilene washed her and dressed her in the gold robes of a high Priestess of the Lion. She carried the leaf-frail woman down to the rose garden and cleared the grasses from a patch where the morning sun would strike and the sea-winds blow. It took her well into the night to dig the grave. She placed the small gold Lions of Day and Night on Andine's breast as she lay with her face free of the pain Malkar had laid on it. And because Andine had loved the little birds, Lilene gathered the bodies of the finch, the robin and the wren, and covered them and the abbess with earth, so that Andine should have sweet music in the Far Lands.

With first light she went back into the tower, and saw again the letter from Prince Ataret. As the command not to read it had been overlooked, she did so, and what she read made her exclaim out loud. She let the scroll fall, and became very still, for a long time.

"It looks a damn fine place to me." General Camlot stroked his moustache with a hand which to his chagrin was not as steady as once it was. His face was the scarlet of his uniform and a pulse throbbed hard under the tight gold trim of his collar.

"Isn't the hill a bit too high?" said General Lindo. He said it in a lackadaisical fashion, much as he might have said to his tailor: "Aren't the sleeves a little too long?"

General Camlot called for a jar of wine. Tallis, who had been called into the pavilion with other officers, brought it to him.

"General Lindo," Camlot said quite patiently, "from this eminence we shall have a clear view of the enemy advance from the south. I am posting an additional force on the north of the river, ready to entrap any who come through our lines. Hence the hill."

"There's the town of Incana," said General Lindo, helping himself to Camlot's wine. "And the bit of forest. They'll block off our view of you even so."

"I understood you to say you thought the hill too high." How in the Lion's mouth, did this man ever get where he is? Another of King Valm's privileged. Younger than me, too.

"Our scouts will be in constant communication," he said. "What have you done to your hand, Captain?"

Tallis looked down to where the fleshy part of his thumb was red and swelling. It came up a little more every day, and hurt.

"A Karenian dog, general sir," he said, and grinned. "A very small dog, with two legs."

"Have the surgeon look at it," said Camlot testily. He turned again to Lindo.

"Perhaps we should run through the battle plan once more. My company will line up south and north of the Takk. General Dalit" (he turned towards a lugubrious, stooping man festooned with decorations), "will command the left wing to perform a pincer movement cutting off the enemy from the rear. General Lindo with troops under Colonel Pog will occupy our right wing position and complete the pincer. The ground here is lower; there's not much to the west except plain and eventually sea. Those enemy troops not crushed by our two arms will be lured into the River Takk by our force on the north bank and finished off there." He sat down, feeling dizzy.

"Splendid," said General Lindo and Colonel Pog.

"What's their number to date, general?" asked Major Sirban.

"The last scout party reported somewhere in the region of eight thousand regular troops. Plus about four thousand conscripts. Poorly trained, badly fed, their heart's not in it. I'd say we had ten thousand to deal with in truth."

"But two thousand more than us overall," said Major Sirban.

"Don't forget most of ours are crack troops," said Camlot. It was very hot in the pavilion, and he called for water.

The camp sprawled, line on line of tents. Not far to the north the wide river ran between banks of green rushes where waders fed and herons stood like sentries; to the west a thin line of sea was visible. Beyond the river troops were readying themselves. Scouts on fast horses came and went across Tirkar Plain. At the little town of Incana there were no chimney smokes. Even the scrawny cows and other beasts seemed to have been deported for a season. A couple of miles south, hidden by distance and oakwood, lay the enemy.

On his way to the surgeon's tent, Tallis saw Barbel. She was stirring a giant pot of stew over a smoky fire. She was not wearing her cap, and actually wore a dress, her hair in long braids. As Tallis watched, a young private passing by spoke amiably to her and gave her waist a squeeze. Barbel yanked the vast ladle out of the pot and whacked the soldier with it so forcibly that he fell down. He picked himself up and went off ruefully. Barbel resumed stirring the stew.

"I pity your husband, when you get one," Tallis said, coming up behind her. She said something rude under her breath, then:

"How's your hand?"

"Worse."

"Get it seen to, Tallis. You don't want to miss the scrap."

"As I said," he mocked. "A nagging wife is an ugly thing."

She laughed. She watched his departing back. Her laughter died. She watched him into the surgeon's tent.

Daybreak came, sunny, with a little fast-dispersing mist, and with it the first movements. The scouts came back in ones and twos, reporting to the generals, who had moved their pavilions over the pontoon across the river. The Karenians appeared to be an orderly force, the conscripts being spread among the ranks of the regular soldiers, the main army stretching across the plain in two tight formations.

Priests of the Lion moved early among the men of the Taratamian army, hearing confessions and giving absolution, as well as a tincture of the holy lionweed to place under the tongue. Morale was good; only a few, mostly familiars of the Royal Household, thought briefly of Malkar's unnatural powers.

"Have no fear, my son," said one of the priests. "She works only in the nasty darkness. She cannot sway armies."

"It's said she can control the sea," said one who had helped pull the princes from the Bay of Moons. The priest blessed him and told him not to worry.

"General Dabinol has the cavalry on the wings, the horse-archers in the van, and ranks of swordsmen in the centre," a scout reported. General Camlot scratched his head. His face was redder than ever in the rising sun.

"That's a departure for Dabinol. I know the old devil's tactics. He usually brings in the cavalry last. We shall see."

"And the dismounted archers spread out very wide, from east to west," said Tallis.

"After our flanks, yes. That makes sense." He peered from his pavilion to where General Lindo was leaning against a tent-prop in animated conversation with Colonel Pog. "My compliments to the general. Suggest battle order. Same to General Dalit. I think they want to get this over as quickly as we do."

Spaced out, a line of trumpeters stood ready, to be echoed across the river where the main force was flanked on the hillside by the two battalions. The Lion of War and the Opal of Capashenet flamed on the great standards. A very faint glitter from afar signalled the Karling Oyster and smaller banners belonging to her crack troops flew the Crab of Malkar. King Vergon's Seahorse flew half-hidden in the enemy ranks. The Karenian uniform was the pale purple of a stormy sea.

General Dalit and Major Sirban waited, alert, on the left wing with the horse-archers and cavalry. The main body was composed of footsoldiers, sword-and-sabre men, men armed with clubs, spears and battle-axes. General Lindo on the right wing had cavalrymen under him, and the longbowmen were deployed evenly in each battalion. Tallis, the throbbing in his bandaged left hand forgotten, sat on his warhorse, which was barbed and visored with branzel. His weapons, sabre, axe and mace, were attached to his saddle. The Lion sword lay under his fingers. He felt it glow in the sun. Lieutenant Pinpol and Lieutenant Recansky were with him, also Sergeant Delvas; he was warmed by their company.

General Lindo sat outside his pavilion, holding his detachment in readiness. A map of the area was spread out before him. Forest, hill, river, troops. There seemed to be movement around the edge of the map.

Something swift pulsed beneath the map across his knees and jumped down on to his boot. He saw it was a fish, with legs, all black and silver with a thin white stripe. It looked up at him and uttered a word, in no language known to man, then whipped away. He looked at the map again; it had changed. The hill was a rising wave, the forest waving seaweed. He began to chuckle . . .

The Karenian army was a blur like a lavender hedge. Their trumpets sounded like a distant gnat's whine. The hedge became a wood, the ground began to vibrate. "They're coming!" yelled a very young scout, his voice breaking. The civilians raced across the pontoon for cover. Barbel was among the last to go, turning, jumping in the air for a sight of Tallis, losing him in the press of movement amid the horses' haunches already glassy with sweat, and the silvery forest of spears slicing the air. There was a crashing staccato of drums. The Taratamian trumpets ripped the air apart, from the trumpeters of General Camlot; Advance, advance, and then the old cry, heard on this plain a quarter of a century ago: "Capashenet! Tamia! For the Lion!"

The drums beat louder and faster. The trumpets screamed. There was a thrumming heartbeat of hooves as the main bodies advanced on one another across the plain, the Taratamians gaining impetus from their surge down the hill, the horse-archers with their bows notched, riding without reins, tough little men strung out between the mailed cavalry on their great destriers. The two armies came on one another in minutes. They piled into each other, in the wake of hundreds of arrows that blackened the air. The crash of the impact was so tremendous that immediately afterwards it seemed that a second of silence fell. Then the screams and groans of wounded men and horses began to rise; severed limbs and pieces of shattered armour lay on the ground, and the noise rose again like a storm renewed. Those unhorsed were fighting hand to hand with swords and sabres and axes, the Lion held high by the standard-bearers on their whirling mounts, somewhere in the rear the Pearl banner dipping and shining like a moon unsure whether to rise or set.

General Camlot had crossed the river and stood on the top of the hill with his keen-sighted scouts. They had a birdseye view of the melèe, the scarlet of Taratamia glimpsed in flashes beneath the branzel armour, the sea-purple of the Karenians running like a wave-pattern through the field, the yellow-green of the plain already darkly puddled with blood. The general turned to his couriers.

"Tell them it's time." They sprang to horse and rushed east and west to where Lindo and Dalit waited.

Below in the centre the fighting was fierce. Many of the Karenian conscripts were hacking unskilfully at their opponents, their terror often lending luck to their blows. Two of the captains went down, one dead, the other wounded. The two armies fell back from one another; trumpets shrilled and they charged and clashed again, and again a rush of arrows preceded them. The Karenian horse-archers were nimble and experienced; damage was being done to the cavalry, when General Dalit's pincer movement began. A healthy force of fresh men and horses came galloping down from the east; they smashed into the Karenian right flank, rode straight over the phalanxes of archers, almost before they could draw a bow. General Camlot, riding downhill for a closer look, muttered approvingly.

The main Karenian force began to fall back a trifle, and the Lion troops pressed them. Most were unhorsed and the carnage spread through the ranks. Gouged entrails made a slimy carpet for the hand-to-hand combat. The Karenians rallied and pressed forward; the Lion standard wavered as its army gave ground. A severed head bounced against the legs of the standard-bearer's horse, which reared and fell backwards into the bloody mire. Someone seized the standard and hefted it high again, but there was a growl of rage from the Taratamians. They set to with inspired vigour, swinging sabres, chopping with swords and axes, lunging with spears, being chopped and slashed and gouged in turn by the Karenian warriors and their desperate recruits. The pincer movement coming from the rear wavered a little but held firm, but to the west there was nothing, and a massed stream of Karenian cavalry and armed warriors began to encroach on General Lindo's territory.

Camlot began to shout at his couriers and aides. "By the Lion's holy balls! where in the name of the gods is Lindo's lot?" He gave a quick order to a courier. "Send troops from north of the river. Now!"

General Lindo was sitting admiring the map. One of the mermaids had come off the paper and was insinuating her naked body into the pocket of his uniform. He felt sick, and his bowels had moved so that his uniform stank. There was someone shaking him by the shoulder and he looked up with a vacant smile.

"General! On guard!"

He was a soldier, and old disciplines cast out the incantation whispering in his ear, removed the sea-fog from map and brain, and brought him into a terrible reality. He tried to stand. He whispered, "Send down the troops" to whoever was shouting at him, and began to shiver as if plunged into icy water.

Colonel Pog had been doing the shouting. He was appalled, watching as his force sat on their unstable mounts and looked at him with their desperate eyes. The longbowmen were nearly out of their minds, hanging on the loose of their bows, cursing. All the company was cursing. Tallis was cursing more colourfully than most, some oaths invented within the last few minutes. The lieutenants let him do the cursing; Sergeant Delvas added a few of his own.

"Move down!" cried Colonel Pog, in what was almost a shriek. "Go, go!" The trumpets brayed. Tallis launched his mount forward, followed by his men. They crashed down a little slope and met the enemy head-on, men who should have been cut off minutes ago in the rear of the main body, coming now in a pincer movement of their own. Tallis's horse was killed under him instantly. He felt it sag to its knees as an arrow caught it in the neck-artery, deep, so that only the fletch protruded. Tallis continued to swear, a monotonous song of curses, lifting himself quickly from the horse's body and encountering the blade of a Karenian footsoldier who was attempting to sever his head. He sidestepped, off balance, which saved him, and felt the Lion jump in his hand as he spitted the Karenian through the bowels.

Now he was fighting for his life, sword in one hand, dagger in the other, his axe and sabre buried somewhere in the debris of dead men and horses. Lieutenant Pinpol, still on horse, caught the rein of a loose horse and held it for Tallis to mount. Tallis flung a glance behind; half his force was embattled with the Karenians who had come up from the south-east, and who were gaining on them. He turned back on his rearing horse in time to face a yelling Karenian cavalry officer who sideswiped him with a sabre, loosening the pauldron joint at his shoulder so that it hung loose, leaving his left arm defenceless. And behind the Karenian he saw, as he struck at the blond face and cut a swathe through it, the standard of Malkar, the spidery Crab, bristling with spells.

Still they came, in a rush, steel and yells and trampling hooves and a goosewing hail of arrows. Men were falling all about him. He saw Lieutenant Pinpol take a sword through the neck, between cuirass and gorget, and knew he was dead. And Tallis thought: I'm going to die, despite all my boasts. And he found himself praying: Lilene. Save me!

Farewell, Lilene, witch, love of my life. All right to say it, as now I shall never say it.

The Karenians were pressing them, coming on with yells of triumph and encouragement to one another. Tallis fought, his horse wounded and staggering, he fought mechanically, a slice there, a chop here, fountains of blood in the air, on his battered armour, in his eyes as a mace-blow struck his helmet away, leaving his head ringing and vulnerable—thinking, now I shall die. Am I dead now? dead, and still fighting? but the noise of the battle, the hot stench of blood and ordure and frenzy was still too real.

Then suddenly there was a change in the note of battle. A louder cry, bereft of triumph—a rising sound of surprise, confusion, overlaid by a roar—a new strange roar, a young roar, a fresh balance in the carnage all around, as the rebels of Karenia came into the fight.

They came from the caverns of the gold mines, and from the forests. They came from the sea where Alpac and others had beached their boats. They came from the rocks on the coast and the underground tunnels beneath the mountains. They came from the town of Incana where they had hidden long in cellars and dens while the battle-preparations went ahead. They came from the Tiranians, men like bears, the relics of old slavery. They came in thousands.

They came armed with swords, maces, axes, pikes, bows, cudgels, weapons from Despra, weapons forged in secret, weapons stolen at an earlier date from the unwary conscripts. They took the Karenian army by complete surprise. They smashed into their own countrymen, desperate people willing to die, with no thought of tomorrow. They killed and maimed like seasoned warriors, young men and old, women dressed as men, and even children, who, having suffered in the mines, were hard enough to fight for freedom. And even some of the conscripts turned and joined them.

They came between the two armies like a wave of fury. The Karenians, completely off guard, reacted too slowly. The Taratamian army, although equally amazed, rallied. Tallis gathered up the remnants of his troops and they charged across the lines to the east where a large party of Karenians, having seen enough of the terrible auxiliaries, had decided to retreat. The pincer movement joined at last, and the Karenians were trapped. The Lion, lifted high, ramped and snarled on its opaline ground as more and more of the enemy troops fell back across the plain, were pursued by all three of the Taratamian battalions and cut to pieces. And very gradually, as the stragglers were chased and caught, as prisoners surrendered, the little cheer of victory arose, as the shameful battle bled to its close.

It was not until many hours later that the confrontation with General Lindo occurred. Two factors lightened the occasion; first, that the Taratamian casualties were less than had been feared, and second, that General Camlot was feeling far from himself.

"It was a close call," said the general. He sat in his pavilion, sweating profusely, and the sight of Lindo, drinking wine as if nothing untoward had happened, made him hotter. "Your troops were somewhat late in coming, general, to say the least."

General Lindo smiled. His orderly had taken his soiled uniform away and he was pristine and smart again. The whole incident was blurred. Something I ate gave me a transient fever, he thought. All is well now, anyway. The sight of the flag of truce proffered by the Karenian generals had revived him.

"They're off to lick their wounds," he observed blithely.

Major Sirban entered, looking exhausted. He held out a parchment. "This is the preliminary count, sir. The Karenians lost upwards of four thousand. Our lot amount to no more than seven hundred. Not all our wounds are mortal. It was a good day, sir. My felicitations." He bowed towards all three, General Dalit acknowledging him with a nod, Lindo still smiling, General Camlot looking grim.

"You think so, major. In some ways I call it a disgraceful day. That Taratamian troops should have to be rescued by . . ."

"Yes," interrupted General Lindo. "By rabble, general. Traitors to their own country. Peasant pigs working off a grudge. Appalling."

"I wouldn't go so far as to say that," said Colonel Pog, coming through the flap of the pavilion. "Without their intervention at that precise moment, there'd be a lot less of us to tell the tale."

"I have to agree," said General Camlot with a hard look at Lindo. "I was ashamed only by the failure of our tactics. Whatever their motives, we owe these people a great deal."

"I need to ask you, general," said Colonel Pog, "what are we to do with them?"

"Where are they now?"

"I've had them put in a compound across the river," said General Lindo proudly, "I have disarmed them, although some have fled. I have questioned their leaders, without success."

"Have you indeed," said Camlot. "I think that fencing them in is a strange way to show our gratitude."

"They're Karenian, general," said Lindo brightly. "Our enemy."

Camlot, his vision strangely blurred and red, gazed at Lindo. "Then I wish all our enemies were as helpful," he said. "All the same, I'd like to know what's behind it. Send for Tallis," he said to an orderly, "He's been travelling the country around Karlinkis recently."

"He's having his wounds dressed, general," said Major Sirban.

Tallis was not with the surgeon, who was too busy to deal with his minor injuries. He had an enormous bruise on his shoulder and a headache, but the hand where the child at the fort had bitten him was now black and swollen to three times its normal size, the skin pulled tight and festering. He was across the river, talking to the rebels, who stood or sat silently behind the palisade. They were tending their wounded. A dead child was laid out on the grass with flowers at its head and feet. Some of the fierce blonde women who had fought were bloodstained too. There was an air of ill-contained jubilation. Solon stood at the fence, towering over Tallis as they spoke together.

"I remember you," Tallis said. "You confronted me in the Forest of Rulen."

"What are you going to do with us, Captain?" He glanced over his shoulder where Alpac stood looking in the direction of the sea where his boats were anchored. Tallis shrugged.

"We came to fight for you. We expected—not gratitude, but acknowledgement. But it doesn't matter. We have shown our strength. Our time is coming."

"Who supplies you?" asked Tallis.

"I'm not saying. Only this. We've suffered enough. We don't want to rule, only to live without fear. Have you seen the children in Tirkar Mine?"

"Yes, I've seen them." He glanced at Alpac. "Is he your leader? Who's behind all this?"

"I don't know who our leader is. And if I did, fire nor water nor steel wouldn't bring it from my mouth."

Tallis was silent. Then he said: "I'll ask you no more. I'll speak to the general on your behalf."

"Thank you, Captain."

Tallis said: "Never did I think to admire traitors. But I admire you. Look after your women and children." He winced at the pain in his left hand. "By the gods! Karenian children have teeth." Fever was rising in him, awful chills. His head spun for a moment.

When he entered where the general was, Camlot's face was the colour of ripe strawberries. Lindo was lounging, laughing. Tallis was reminded of Narzet at his most witless.

"Well, Captain? what do you know of our auxiliaries, who came so timely?"

"Hang them all," said Lindo, and laughed hysterically. Tallis looked only at General Camlot.

"They appear to be the abused masses, general. The big man is a blacksmith. Apart from that . . ."

"They should be hanged today," said Lindo, a fever-like sheen on his eyes. "Traitors."

"But our saviours, general," said Camlot. "I would not think of executing them. Captain?"

"I've really nothing to add, sir. Except that perhaps, with respect, they could be given . . ."

General Lindo started to make strange noises. Foam appeared on his lips, and he rushed from the pavilion.

"By the Lion," said General Camlot. "I believe Lindo is about to have a stroke."

"I was going to say, general," Tallis began, then stopped. General Camlot was changing colour, from ripe red to a dewy parchment. "They could at least be given their liberty," he finished quietly.

"Absolutely, my boy," said the general. His eyes were closed. "Give the order. Remove the palisade. Brave people . . ."

He stood up, teetered a moment, then crashed face downwards on the grassy floor of the pavilion. Tallis, Colonel, Pog, Major Sirban and the orderlies rushed to lift him to a sitting position. His mouth drew upwards in a rictus. He was silent.

Tallis ran dizzily through the lines of tents. He had the surgeon on his way to the general in minutes. The pavilion flaps closed. Tallis stayed outside, shivering uncontrollably. Barbel found him there. She touched his wounded hand, and he started with pain.

"Come," she said.

"I have to stay by the general."

"Do you want to lose that hand?" she said sternly.

"The surgeons are busy."

"Damn the surgeons," she said fiercely. "Come with me."

She was frightened. However, once she had Tallis in his tent, stretched out in surrender to the fever, she calmly went to work. She left him only for a short while. The cook-sergeant had killed a suckling-pig for the generals' mess. The pig was small and pure, and Barbel took its entrails away. Hot and glutinous, they were wrapped round Tallis's hand and bandaged tightly there. He was icy, pale. He cursed her for bringing such a filthy cure into his tent and, as night fell, he became delirious.

"It works, Tallis," she said, biting her lips. "My grandmother used it. The evil spirits think they've found fresh flesh and go to it, greedy things. Rest." He couldn't hear her. He was burning up. She mopped his brow. During the night General Camlot's orderly poked his head round the tentflap. "He's asking for him. He's very ill." He frowned at the sight of Tallis. "I'll tell him he can't come."

The night was long for Barbel. She took his right hand and laid it on the golden Lion on the pommel of his sword, so he could gain strength from it. Once, when he was deep in his fever sleep, she kissed his forehead. Her head ached, and she unbraided her hair so that it hung loose, damp with her efforts, and in the small hours he opened his eyes, and took a strand of it in his fingers.

"Gold," he said. "My darling."

Then he slept again, cooler, and Barbel cried a little, silently, knowing that what she had guessed at that day in his garden was true, and powerful and dangerous for him.

The general had regained his speech, but it was obvious he was finished. It had been advised that he be not moved, so while the camp was putting itself in order, he remained in his pavilion. He lay on the giant soldier's bed which had travelled with him over the years, under the bright hangings of the Opal and the Lion. The weather was humid and the pavilion clammy with the breath of all those who thronged in and out, disturbing the general's rest. Lindo had been back, saying wildly and inappropriately, "Put those people in chains." General Camlot had tried to say: "Take them over our border. Give them sanctuary," but his words became garbled again, and it was left to the rebels to decide their own immediate fate, which presently they did.

When Lindo left the pavilion, Tallis was admitted. His hand had gone down to its normal size, and he felt cleansed. A heavy sadness possessed him as he looked at the general. Camlot was a last fragile thread spun from the old days.

"You should have promotion," were the general's first feeble words. "You fought bravely, Tallis."

"No, general. I did nothing but save my skin. It was a shambles."

"Have you found your man?" It was a hoarse whisper.

"He could be among the dead, but I think not, somehow That devil must still be living."

"Bones, long ago. As I shall be, soon."

"No, general. You're a giant."

Camlot beckoned him nearer. "Did you know they've signed an armistice?"

"I did, general. They got their feet burned, as they say in Despra."

"They'll be off to report to the moron and the witch. We don't need any more scraps like this one, Tallis. I only wish I were going out on a better tide."

Tallis looked down at his feet, his eyes blurred. He and the general were alone save for the surgeon-general and an orderly. It was very quiet.

"I hear my son calling me," said the general. "From the depths of the sea."

The surgeon approached with lancet and bowl. "I must bleed you again, general."

The blood was sluggish, almost black. The general watched it fill the bowl as if it were someone else's.

"My son," he said again. He looked into Tallis's eyes. "There will be orders for you," he said faintly, "General Dalit and I have conferred. You are to go south again. Find out what goes on in Karenia. And see that all is well in the House of

Brides. There's a safe-conduct for our men while the truce holds . . ." he closed his eyes. Tallis thought he was dead. Then he drew a stertorous breath.

"I hear the orders, general." Tallis thought: back down into Karenia. My fate is there. That's a certainty. He heard himself saying: "I was going home to be married."

The general smiled, without opening his eyes. Almost inaudibly he said: "Tallis. While you are there, talk to the Abbess Andine. She has something for you."

"Why, the lady's dead, sir."

"Talk to her. Never forget that the House of Brides belongs to Taratamia. Glorious Taratamia."

"Has he seen the Lion priest?" Tallis whispered to the orderly, standing hopelessly by.

"An hour ago, Captain."

"He's gone," said the surgeon suddenly. He looked into the blood-bowl. "The spirit flies."

Tallis went sadly from the pavilion, thinking: farewell, old friend. Gods speed you to the Far Lands, the high lands, where the silver eagle flies and there is no night.

Malkar is hungry. Commanded by the deeps, her hunger whets itself on satiety. The longer the intervals without, the more the pearl aches in her belly. The beauty trembles, always on the brink of dissolution. Its very fragility makes it a thing of wonder and dreams.

The Taken come from the lonely farms, the peasant shacks, the periphery of the Court. Sometimes but not always the dwarf brings them. The chaste, the virile, the solitary. Already they are becoming more rare, the young flowers of men.

What went amiss with the battle? Is something moving against us? What, and who?

She leaned close to the mirror. The pearl was small and mournful. The brighter jewel, the small oval of her face, seemed pristine as ever, until she turned to study it obliquely. A mark between eyebrow and temple. The ghost of a chloasma, the deeper pigmentation that comes with age . . .

The blind seller of lottery tickets was going home to his lodging on Sluts' Wharf. He had sold little that day; the streets of Karlinkis were barren of folk. He tap-tapped his way through the granite streets between the tall walls, and stopped to rest in one of the deep alcoves where the whores took their customers. It smelled in here of gutter sex, of past passion and greed. Nevertheless he wanted it, that bad, cheap glamour, had always wanted it, but who would trouble with a blind man, even if he were young?

He set his tray of tickets down and leaned against the wall. He felt a sudden warmth, as if he stood against a fire. A body pressed on his, and he nearly fainted with fright. It felt like the body of a richly furred beast, standing upright. Paws with claws locked at the back of his neck. The hot furred thing pressed him back into the wall.

"Poor sweetheart," said a voice like a violin. "Would you like to see me?"

The young man, paralysed with terror, let out a faint whine. He put out his hands in an attempt to push back the hot weight, and the fur began to peel away under his fingers. There was skin smooth as blossom, two yielding goblets of firm flesh, a ripple of ribs, a curve of belly warm at the centre. And below, a residue of fur, cleft like a plum. His terror turned to lasciviousness.

"Look!" said the voice, and for the first and last time in his life, he could see.

It did not last. The darkness was urgent. This time it was a rape. He glimpsed the sublime and the monstrous almost simultaneously with his climax. Lost and damned, the Taken lay among a scatter of tickets and small coin, while the white-maned darkness panthered away, shadow of shadows, through the deserted streets.

"**B**ring it over here," said Molgon.

The young girl's two brothers hesitated only for a moment but it was enough. Molgon uncurled a lash and sent a long black arc round the little group. It caught all three of them across the loins.

"Yes, jump," he said.

Wurmol lounged beside him at the poolside, where mosaic reflected ripples on floor and pillared walls.

"They don't jump very high," he observed.

"They will."

"I doubt this is going to be very exciting."

"Vergon employs professionals, you know."

"We don't have his money, the bastard."

Smiling, Molgon flicked the whip again. The trio shuddered. A little blood flowed from the leg of one of the boys. They were no more than fourteen, the girl even younger.

"Get on, pigs," Molgon said. "Take its clothes off."

"I thought their father was going to watch," said Wurmol.

"He's fetching the instrument."

Saturnine Molgon, his sallow face reflecting thunderclouds that gathered overhead, unfastened his pearl-crusted robe. Reflectively, he began to stroke his own parts.

"Gods. It's warm today."

"Storm coming," said Wurm, also half naked, his feet on an onyx footstool shaped like an oyster. The humidity was such that dew had collected on the friezed portico and trickled slowly down the pillars. Lake Sigillan, its pansy-blue a little dark, was as still as a corpse.

"Where is he?" said Molgon.

The slaves' father was on his way, bearing a flagon of wine and several gold cups. The cups were arranged in a precise pattern on the salver. Another slave walked behind. The two faces were impassive. They came on to the patio by the pool, the one slave holding the instrument referred to: an immense dildo grown in the sea, looking somewhat like a fibrous corncob, with a belt and straps attached.

"About time, swine," said Molgon. He waved his jewel-heavy hand at the group of three.

"Strip her, I said. Strap it on."

The girl was crying very softly. The elder of the two boys bent close and whispered: "I won't look at you, Sagina, I promise." The other breathed in her ear, "Be brave. I love you, my sister."

A gentle growl of thunder, like a dreaming dog, rolled round the villa. "Stop whispering," said Molgon sharply, "or I'll put you in the piranha pool." The girl's body was revealed. Undernourished, breastless, she cried and trembled. The lords watched hungrily as one of the boys fitted the false phallus about his brother's loins.

"Wine, my lords?" murmured the girl's father. He set the salver on the table at Molgon's elbow. With a steady hand he poured from the flagon into the goblets.

"Get down," said Molgon to the girl and her brothers. "Not like that, fools. Like dogs, to begin."

The girl sagged forward on all fours. Molgon picked up his goblet. He gave a bark of laughter and squinted at the slave who had served him.

"No, not this time or any time, you thing. You'll taste it first—as usual. Your whelps can watch you die."

"It's pure, my lord," said the slave mildly. He lifted the cup and drank, smacking his lips. Wurmol and Molgon observed him keenly. The tableau by the pool crouched, immobile, obscenely posed. Minutes passed; the slave remained upright.

"Very well. Serve us, then. And I don't want to drink after your filthy lips."

The two slaves filled the goblets on the north and south sides of the salver. They filled them to the brim.

"Here's to us, and to sin," said Molgon. He leaned and touched his cup lightly to that of Wurmol. They drank. The slaves stepped back a pace.

"Start the fucking," said Molgon.

The boy wearing the dildo pressed its point into the cleft of his sister's slender rump. Wurmol laughed. Something happened to the laugh; it turned to a strangle. His cheeks acquired an interesting purple. Sharply Molgon looked towards him. His head remained turned, in a rigour. The goblet slid from his hand. Both lords were suddenly stone.

"Well, my dears," said the slave to his masters.

"Well?"

And he walked over and slapped his lord hard across the face. Molgon's eyes rolled and remained fixed, staring to the left. Wurmol gave a gasp, his mouth stayed open upon it. The slave drew a knife from his loincloth.

"Gods bless Taratamian herbals. All the way from the feet of Kite."

"What's it called?" asked the other man.

The first slave strolled near to Wurmol. He smiled terribly into both the stricken faces, a smile containing decades of pain.

"Its name is paralyn. Just a trace rubbed inside the cups before pouring. The Tamians use it for restraining dangerous madmen. It lasts about an hour."

"But they will be able to feel pain?" said the other anxiously.

"Oh yes. Have no fear of that. Children. Get dressed. Go quickly to the Forest of Rulen. Take the horses. Solon will be waiting for you. Ride due west. We'll follow." He smiled. "Victory's ours in the north. Now watch the south follow. Raise up! or die!"

He bent and sharpened his knife on the patio stones, and, leisurely, approached Molgon, from whose throat came the faintest gobble of terror.

He had forgotten everything in this moment of glory. Forgotten the everlasting counsel of Lilene, not to move until the word was given. All he knew of were the victorious miners, slaves and bandits on Tirkar Plain. And this, this moment of requital. He parted Molgon's robe gently, and as the thunder growled nearer and the heavy rain began, laid the razor knife against his master's thigh.

She kneels before the mirror and the pearl. Not in worship, for the pearl is not a godhead, merely the symbol of sight; but because her need is more urgent these days.

The landfish are hungry too; they lie in their kennel, the fur and bones of some kittens scattered around them, but neglected; they have not been fed for days.

The damned swim feebly in the blackness of the deep, crying, and some have lamented their loss, their state of non-being, for a thousand years. The pearl womb of time yearns for more.

Show me my son. Enial's human son.

He weeps. He has been frightened.

He rides merrily into the garden of Fraycon's house, where Bratt is staying. A week's revel had been planned, with girls, boys, animals, food, drink and drugs. The first things noticed are the absolute silence and the smell of burning.

The grass on the large lawn is patched and stippled with red. The garden is a slaughterhouse. The faces of Fraycon and Bratt have been savagely mutilated. They have been disembowelled. The other lordlings, who had come from their upcountry houses on the banks of the River Kes, are similarly used. Their hands and feet are severed. The bodies are black with drinking flies. The slaves have fired a wing of the villa, it burns still. Before fleeing, they have stripped the house of treasure. Someone has drawn, in Fraycon's blood, the rebel sign on the wall; a soaring arrow crossed by another plunging to earth. Vergon vomits into Fraycon's pool, where float the corpses of noble catamites.

The pearl relays all this to darkness, with the dispassion of demonkind.

Vergon stood shaking before the throne.

"They could have killed me too, madam. I am King Vergon the First of Karling. And I hear that the Tirkar mine overseers and guards were butchered where they stood. I warned you, madam. The peasants should never have been armed."

"These were slaves. The betrayal in battle was something else, my lord."

"But there is a link! What shall you do about it?" He was almost hysterical.

Malkar looked at him with her heavy lids.

"I? Why, you are the king, my lord. So you constantly remind us."

Oh, I wish I could kill her, thought Vergon. Would that I had her power. That power defeats me. He paced the floor before the throne. His own slaves had also disappeared from his villa, taking horses and silverware after killing their superiors.

"Do something, madam!"

"Curb your tongue," said Malkar softly.

Vergon became bolder. "I shall act, then," he said roughly. "I am the king. I shall send for Colonel Zairopo."

Malkar showed emotion at last. Her face darkened.

"You do not have my leave."

"I do not need it. Let the Draconhood use their arm. These are atrocious outrages."

Malkar came slowly to her feet. "I will hear no more. The Draconhood can hound their heretics. These are royal slaves, to be punished by the Crown. Some are very young men. I'll not have Zairopo meddling."

Consult the darkness, the black depths. Darkness rises in the fount of power, shivering, pulsing between Malkar's lovely human thighs. But the pearl burns low. And Malkar is hungry, hungry as the darkness.

Show me the remnants of the battle. Show me the lie of the land. Malkar, there is chaos, and it is not of your making.

There are young men. There is just light enough to see them, men on the run. Boys. There are slaves, horsed, and running. They go in packs, or in a diffused mass like a kicked antheap. There are conscripts, deserters. There are young men in their thousands. There is soul-food on the run. Power in flight. And there is chaos in the land.

Again, why was the outcome of Tirkar Plain not foreseen, when we stand on the lip of a thousand years of conquest?

All is not well. The pearl is dull.

What is power, without control?

Seek then, the instrument of control.

Colonel Zairopo. That son of mine, who is no son of mine, spoke wisdom for once. The Draconhood are needed.

But no. They are too fierce, indiscriminating. But only they can round up the rebels and fugitives, the chaos-makers who hinder the dark design. But at my command, they must spare the innocent, the chaste, the chosen ones. Those who shall be Taken.

And spare the male children that they may flourish and be Taken. The inheritrix shall have them. She who comes after Malkar. She who even now lives and breathes and prays for the holy old fool, unaware of what lies within her, or the teeth in her womb.

Oh, Malkar, Soul Thief, Shapechanger, Swallower, she is hungry. She cannot wait. The pearl burns low, and there is a tiny freckle of ageing on Malkar's left hand.

Dusk began to creep into the palace. The minstrel's throat was dry. He had played for Honyia most of the afternoon. At the end of each song she had looked at him with the large dark eyes of dead Doro, tranced and spellbound. His hopes that she would ever speak were fading. Only when a waiting woman of the queen came to him with a summons did Honyia show emotion, rising to write NO! in a jagged hasty hand.

He kissed the hand that held the pen. "Until tomorrow, princess."

Many passages and stairs brought him to the queen's apartments. Still holding his lyre, he knocked. Perhaps the queen wanted him to play for her. He felt resentment; she was unkind to Honyia.

He heard Malkar's faint voice like the clear note of some bird, bidding him enter. He saw the mirrors, repeating the room into infinity, the great round jewel of a bed. There was no one in the room and he turned, disobedient, to go, but the lyre struck the jamb of the door, betraying him with its little sweetness.

The queen was sitting in the centre of the bed, dressed in frills of white and blue. A moment ago the bed had been unoccupied. The minstrel blinked, and knelt, then looked up, uncertain of his own eyes. The queen looked very small; she sat hugging her knees, her black hair a glossy curtain about her.

"I sent for you. You are becoming too familiar with the Princess Honyia. What passes between you?"

He drew in his breath. "Nothing, your majesty. I swear there is nothing improper. Never."

"I do not know your name."

"I am Chauntir, majesty. After my profession and that of my father."

"Are you a good boy, Chauntir? I believe you are. Come, sit with me. I shall not rebuke you." She patted the bed.

He rose, and stood firmly on the spot, deeply suspicious. There was a glow about her, emanating from her skin and eyes. It seemed to him unearthly. He thought of Honyia.

"Will you not come to me?" she said in a little voice. "I have never heard you play. The princess is more fortunate. I know how fond . . ."

Her voice tailed off. Chauntir stood like stone, looking over the queen's head at some tapestries. Then he heard her say very softly, "It is always the same. No one will approach me unless I command it."

"Madam," he said diffidently, "What would you like me to play? An aubade, or one of the Salt dances? I can even play a little martial song, if your majesty pleases."

And she said: "No battle airs, I beg you. I fight my own battles, deep inside. No one knows my sadness, my loneliness."

Now he looked at her sharply, for she was weeping. She seemed to be growing smaller, shrinking into herself, a woeful little creature lost within the frills and folds of her gown. She said, swallowing a sob: "You see this big bed, Chauntir? Night after night, my bedmate is loneliness. And my throne is lonelier still. This is the way of sovereignty."

She hid her face in her hands. A great well of pity opened inside the minstrel. He put his lyre gently on the floor and went to sit on the edge of the bed.

"Madam," he said gently. Why, he thought in amazement, she is like a little girl. And there is something in what she says, to be apart from the world cannot be easy. Tentatively he laid his hand on the hem of her gown. "Shall I sing an evening song? Something to soothe . . ."

She uncovered her face. Her eyes were a lost child's, her red mouth was pale and trembled. She was so small; he could lift her with one hand.

"Only stay with me a little, Chauntir," she whispered. "Stay because you want to, not because you are afraid to leave. Hold my hand. I have not held a hand for so long."

He obeyed. Her fingers curled into his palm like a baby's. She stopped crying, and smiled at him tremulously.

"How brown your skin is against mine, Chauntir," she murmured. "Have you mixed blood?"

"They say my ancestors came from the Isle of Ruva, yes."

"You are beautiful," she said, and he blushed. "Are you the same colour all over? Let me look at you . . ." and she crept near him on the bed, and unfastened his shirt and held his eyes with hers, which the tears had washed to a sparkle.

Dusk fell like a blow.

The black deeps were irked and rapacious, angry at the unfamiliar reluctance to surrender. They were vengeful. The deeps heard the music in him and snatched at it, tearing and torturing it into waves of discord in the ears of the everlasting damned. The thing that was Malkar did not dismiss its beauty; the demoness held its form all night long. And all night long she used the minstrel, his nakedness writhing in sweat, his flesh eroded by her spells and pressures and torments. She played with him as she had played with and husbanded Narzet, but cruelly, a hundred and one times bringing the minstrel to the brink of death, showing him the abyss of ecstasy then withdrawing it, so that his desperate hunger was unappeased and he cried for release like a wounded animal. Time after time she plunged upon him, savouring him with her maw, coaxing his orgasm then slamming shut the gate upon it, so that he howled and clawed at her and at himself, his eyeballs filled with blood and his loins swelling with agonies. Time after time she urged him on and flung him back. She wrought upon him the most subtle tortures. There seemed to be a hundred Malkars, mouths, hands, orifices, all strong as dragons and burning like fire.

She unpicked him nerve by nerve. He became insane, and at dawn, the black cat, darkness, tired of its mouse.

When finally she drained him, the soul wailed piteously, and darkness swallowed up its last scream. There was much power to feed on; the minstrel had been in love.

With the soul's capture the body became a husk. And the dwarf bore it easily away. The skin would go to join those covering the couch in the dark sanctum.

In her chamber, Honyia sat alone, unmoving. Then she took up a lute left behind by Chauntir, and began to strum, a tuneless eternal monotony, her fingers knitting up the chords and discords like spiders.

"Hé mandw, hé mandw,
Scwlch ma hé,
Oh hé na o hé u,
Cateclch mw,
Mwch a gu,
O hé an a hé u."

The singer was Maeh, third Queen of Brwcwch, High King of Despra. She sat on green rushes in the packed meadhall in the northern capital of Ogor, accompanying herself on her little harp. The harp was gold, studded with some of the sea emeralds stolen by Lilene from her father.

The high voice, which had blown like a breeze sharp as a cold knife, came to a dying fall and ceased. The lords stamped their tankards on the long boards and gruffed their appreciation. The three other queens crowded round Maeh, stroking her with kisses and compliments.

The throne of King Brwcwch was fashioned entirely of stags' antlers polished until they gleamed like topaz. The back of the throne was a lattice of similar antlers towering almost to the rafters. The king was young and strong and slender with a bright face and ink-black hair dressed in twenty braids reaching to his knees. He wore a yellow kilt and thongs about his legs. He raised his horn cup and saluted his wives.

"Your music is mighty, Maeh," he said. "Play again. Crwdwn, Ankrwr, Pelch, show us your steps."

The four queens arranged themselves, Maeh taking her harp to a low stool, the others joining hands in a circle. The long black hair of the queens was curled tight as chain-mail. Shan, the king's eldest son, came to sit by the throne with a little drum made from the skin of a man slain long ago in battle.

Maeh struck a chord; the queens began to step round high and gracefully. The drum began slowly then with an urgent rattle and fret, the soft dance moved into a springing slipstep. The queens' rush-green kilts whirled, their rings of hair flew in tight black clouds. Their slim thighs flashed like the diving of dolphins. Their seven children, three of them babies, watched and yawned.

The music was in a minor key, slightly threatening, beautiful. A fiddler joined in, then a man with a mouth whistle, and more skin drums, rattling and booming, and the queens danced into a wild frenzy, feet, hands, hair brushing the rushes as they dipped and weaved. The lords began to shout. Mervhu, richly dressed in chieftain garb, beat on the table with a great gem-starred knife.

"Ay-yee-hah!" he yelled, and the ear of Alpac, sitting meekly beside him, crackled with pain.

The queens fell exhausted to the floor. Cheering beat at the rafters. Alpac gazed at the women in admiration and fear. He had been frightened from the moment Mervhu had persuaded him aboard the ship. He did not know any living being who had been to Despra. He had imagined the court to be a place of squalor and bogs, and had been unprepared for this magnificence. At any event, the unknown hazards of Despra were more palatable at the moment than Karenia, which was anything but a place of safety.

Mervhu turned to him with shining eyes. His moustaches were plaited now as part of his revel gear. Round his head he wore the band of his clan, stamped with the agate image of a wolf.

"How you like our kingdom, little fisherboy?"

"It's a great honour to be here," muttered Alpac, trying out his Despran.

"Oh, it is, it is," said Mervhu. "Soon the High King will question you. Ah, there is my woman. Tamian woman. Not pretty like our women, but very strong. I am a big man. She is to bear my twins."

Brwcwch had taken two of the queens on to his lap; they were small women who could perch on either knee. Maeh had her arms round the other queen, Pelch, and was kissing her on her dance-hot cheeks.

"You all seem very happy," Alpac said.

"We Desprans worship great Erun, Lord of Joy and War. Look, the king is donning the crown. He is ready to speak with you now."

Brwcwch was putting on the head of a stag over his long plaits. Alpac's legs brought him unsteadily from behind the table. He passed the insolent gaze of the twelve-year-old Shan, skirted some chiefs who sat round the throne, and knelt before it. The High King was older than he had first thought, and his nut-brown eyes were very old indeed, and like the eyes of an animal. The stag must also have been aged when it died. White showed on its muzzle, which was lodged just over the king's brow, so that the face of Brwcwch was revealed.

"Yes," said the king softly. "We never slay our god. This stag was one who had shed many antlers. The leader of his tribe."

He could read Alpac's mind.

"Yes," said Brwcwch. "You are afraid, little Karenian. Have no fear. You are under the guest-law. But you do well to fear Despra. All this year, the warriors of Despra rest. They grow impatient. But we are content to wait. For everything there is a season. Change comes, second by second." He drew his dagger, and Alpac quailed. The king pointed to the design on its haft, which showed a myriad coilings and broken webs, broken yet entwined, coiling eternally back and forth upon one another. "No beginnings, no endings," said the High King. "We live, we change, we die, we live again. You are not the same as the man who approached my throne a few moments ago. There is no time, yet time has changed you. Everything comes to change. So we wait, we dance and feast, while your country founders in a web of its own making; while Tamia shudders at the prospect of the death of its dynasty. We have brought you here for us to learn more. Be at peace." He put the dagger away.

The boy Shan, the king's heir, was listening. He was looking at Alpac's clothes, saltstained and the worse for wear.

"The stranger has been weeping," he said, with a nasty laugh. Then he said something else, a Despran insult which Alpac did not catch. The High King had set down his wives from his knee. Now he leaned and fetched Shan such a blow across the face that the boy fell backwards into the rushes.

"Tell me the latest news of your country," said Brwcwch, calmly settling back on the throne.

Alpac found himself weeping indeed. He could not stop, or speak. He wondered if he would be thought discourteous. But Brwcwch merely sat serenely, while Alpac sobbed. Finally the king made a quick movement with his hand, and Alpac found someone standing slightly behind him, close. A woman. He looked at her, and her appearance was such that he could not believe what he saw.

"This is Gwldas," said the king. "She is unique, as you can see. A healer. Comfort him this night, woman."

Gwldas bowed her head. She put her arm lightly about Alpac, and suddenly he was able to speak.

"Lord King. Karenia swims in an ocean of blood. Karenia burns in fire, day and night. The people should have learned from you, learned to wait until the season showed itself. Now they pay the price. The Draconhood have combed the mines, the villages, the forests. They are cruel beyond belief. And they . . ." he choked on the words, "they have taken Solon!"

Mervhu, listening, spoke now in his fractured Karenian for Alpac's benefit.

"Draconhood bloody bad. Not warriors. Cowards."

The High King raised a jewelled hand, and Mervhu said no more.

"He is right," said Brwcwch. "The Draconhood are puny little souls, grown great from the essence of their terror-god. Not like Malkar. She is ancient as the rocks, and far more dangerous. She has unleashed the power of Woman in its darkest form. She is water, beached. She came from the sea, and there she will return. She was found, new-born, in a cave on the Kardespran coast, near great El, across the water from here. She is not of the earth. Her real name is Maelikali, the Voracious One."

For a moment he was silent, thoughtful. Then said: "But we speak of the Draconhood. I am sorry for you, Karenian. When the time is full, we shall rule Karenia. Taratamia too, maybe. We will remember you, and spare you if you bow to us."

"I bow to you now," said Alpac, and did so. "High King, we are desperate for your aid. When may we have the gwgli? Not all of us have been captured, though many are suffering now. If only we had your gwgli, we could re-arm." And he said: "You could sail up the coast to mine for it, while the truce holds."

The High King smiled. "When the time is full. When the change speaks. Go now. Go with Gwldas."

Alpac, despondent, knelt and kissed the hand of the High King. He went to the rear of the meadhall, followed closely by the woman Gwldas, and took a seat next to Mervhu, relaxing with his pregnant wife. She is really ugly for a Tamian, Alpac thought. Why did he take her? And unerringly Mervhu read his thoughts.

"New blood", he grinned over his plaited moustaches. "My clan getting flabby." And he pinched her so that she squeaked and simpered.

Alpac and the unbelievable Gwldas left the meadhall. She led him to her dwelling, which was built of cane wattle and was warm as love. There she held him in her arms. She lay with him and he took the essence of change from beneath her tongue and from the font of her womb, and before the dawn, both of them wished fervently that Alpac had been born in Despra.

Sometimes he dreamed he was at the forge, and that he had fallen into his own furnace. He struggled weakly against the white heat until it blackened and grew cold, and there was nothing. But this was always during the times when his nerves refused to acknowledge any more torment. Also he dreamed he travelled far, under hot sun, over the Taratamian border to the cool of the mountains and the ice of the Towers of Kite, shivering under their everlasting snows. Then as ever came the return to the stone table beneath his naked back, the eyes, the implements, the fires.

The Truth Doctor was a new man, the first having fallen from favour for bungling the confession of Cristarpa. This one was far more skilled.

"Awake now," he said to Zairopo, sitting with his wine in his high-backed chair.

Solon groaned constantly. It kept his tongue occupied, as a mantra aids meditation. In the top of his brain was his own voice, saying: my body, my blood, my heart. Tear them apart. Forget what they want most. Pretend they are only asking me the time of day, which I do not know.

And there was the knowledge that not one, man, woman or child, had said a word. As the weeks had progressed they had been put to the question, and died, silent. All they had said (and some truly believed it) was: "Solon the smith is our leader."

They had broken his heart.

In the beginning he had been profoundly grateful that Alpac had got clean away, and that before escaping he had hidden Solon's wife and child in a place of safety. Now very little mattered, except his constant prayer for death.

Zairopo rose stiffly from his chair. He was frowning. This big, strong man. The strong ones usually broke the fastest. Not this one, however.

"Who is your leader?" he asked. The thousandth time of asking, and the inflection, like the drip of water, had never changed. He stepped around the blood from Solon's severed fingers. The Truth Doctor had cauterized the wounds so that Solon should not bleed to death.

"I am the leader," said Solon for the thousandth time, and moaned. He had no feet; they had been very slowly burned away.

"But there was a letter, and you cannot write," said Zairopo for the hundredth time.

"I am the leader." (My body, my blood, my heart).

"Tough man, oh, tough man," sighed Zairopo. He walked back to his chair, and flicked a finger at the Truth Doctor.

"Eyes."

"I am going to blind you." The Truth Doctor took a white iron from the fire.

"Tell us the name of your leader," said Zairopo almost sadly.

"Solon the smith."

The Truth Doctor raised the iron, so whitely burning it hurt everyone's gaze. He waited for Zairopo's nod. The door opened and one of the younger Dracon came in, slightly breathless. He whispered to Zairopo, who sat up straight and smiled for the first time in hours. He made a quick signal to the Truth Doctor, who put the iron back in the fire.

"That was well done," Zairopo said to the Dracon. And, to the Truth Doctor: "Revive him. Let him sit. Solon, we have a surprise for you."

The door was pushed open a little more and a nine-year-old boy entered. He saw Solon. Burned, bleeding, swaying upright. He ran towards him, saw what had been done to him, and stopped. From the ravaged depths of Solon came a cry, louder and more anguished than any elicited by the torture.

"You have a fine son, Solon" said Zairopo. "Hiding away like a badger with his mother. She unfortunately is dead. But this mite—" he ruffled the child's golden head, "you must be very proud. Let us see, Truth Doctor, how he looks without his eyes."

"Our leader is the Princess Royal, Lilene of Karling," said Solon, collapsed, and died.

Zairopo walked very slowly back to his seat. The Dracon who had brought the child came to him. He waited a long time for Zairopo to speak. Then Zairopo began to chuckle, as if he had seen the point of a joke told minutes ago.

"You laugh. You aren't surprised?"

Zairopo shook his head from side to side, still chuckling. Then he frowned. "When will I learn to trust my intuition? I suspected her in the forest. I suspected her at the court. Well, well. My lady. I must say your followers were true to you."

"You'll tell Malkar?" asked the Dracon. Zairopo frowned again.

"Not yet. That witch and I do not walk on the same ground. I must wait now, see which way the cat jumps. I can wait until the time comes when I can use Lilene as a pawn, to find out Malkar's weaknesses. I know where the princess is. She is on Taratamian territory, but completely unprotected, and could be mine in a few hours if I so choose. I have my answer. Meanwhile, say nothing of this, any of you. Lilene!" He laughed, heartily, in the face of the shivering child. Suddenly the boy rushed at him, shrieking, beating Zairopo's chest with his fists. Zairopo held him off with one hand, still chuckling with pleasure.

"What is your name, little one?"

"My name's Timbel. You killed my father! I'm going to kill you . . ."

The Truth Doctor made a throat-cutting gesture and raised his brows at the colonel, who shook his head.

"I am too pleased not to be merciful. Take the brat into the forest. Leave him for the wolves. Our real work is just beginning."

Sergeant Delvas had been badly wounded in the Tirkar Plain battle and could not be with the company going down once more into Karenia, but Lieutenant Recansky was, and Tallis was glad of his and the other few familiar faces. It was only a small party, not counting the grooms and orderlies and of course, Barbel. They came down the swifter way, past Incana-on-the-Takk, now putting itself in order after the scrimmage at its gates.

Barbel was dressed in her page's gear, her hair concealed beneath the large dirty cap. This time Tallis had not even tried to dissuade her. She had come out the other end of a battle unscathed, and he had come to regard her as a kind of grubby talisman. She rode at the end of the line, in a quiet ecstasy, for Tallis had loaned her a mount from his own stable.

There had been autumn in the air over the Tiranians and during the river crossing, but into Karenia there was a tinge of the southern breeze. They had ridden due south to begin with, avoiding the disputed mine, and there was no way of telling whether it was being worked during the time of truce.

Lieutenant Recansky had the safe-conduct in his saddlebag, and the standard-bearer flew the diplomatic Lion of Chivalry. They were a long way from Incana, and the lieutenant asked: "Shouldn't we be heading east now, Captain? I thought we'd go along the rivercourse and straight down past Lake Sigillan and over Treaty Bridge."

Tallis shook his head. The lieutenant thought he had aged somewhat in the past strenuous months. His face was thinner, more lined, and his eyes were tired.

"Up and down this bloody road, eh, Captain?" said Recansky cheerfully.

"We'll not go east, not yet," Tallis said, disregarding the remark. "I want to go down south and cut across to the Braf. Avoiding Karlinkis, of course."

"Through the Forest of Rulen? That's a bit near Kalvaria, isn't it? That place gives me the heaves."

"You'll follow orders, lieutenant."

He wanted to see the Forest of Rulen again. He thought: I've a strange feeling I will find him there. I don't know why. The Forest draws me to my longed-for vengeance. And it's the Forest, where our hands met; the inn, where she lay, with me outside, crazed with longing for her. Their last meeting came back to him vividly—her mouth, the feel of her silken secret body—so that he drew a deep breath and pulled involuntarily on the reins of the mare, making her toss her head. Lilene would be in Karlinkis now, with her witch-mother.

It was a wonderful morning. They passed through stands of birch and ash and oak, with the faint amber of autumn on the edges of their leaves, and little streams, sunbright and laced with graceful ophelia weed. The party was lightly yet efficiently armed, and a little song of steel mingled with the music of the horsemens' spurs.

"It was strange, wasn't it, Captain?"

"What was?"

"The way they just folded up after the battle, offering a truce. I really thought we'd be embroiled again in short order."

"The generals didn't want a battle," said Tallis curtly. "They were following Malkar's whim. Let's not dwell on it. Our first job is to get down to Brides and see if it still stands. If they touch that land the truce is void."

"Oh great and merciful gods," said Recansky, staring ahead.

The company all saw it at the same moment. They were just about to enter an avenue of sycamores, with wide sweeping branches. From every branch there hung the body of a naked man, woman, or child, some of them no more than six years old. Strange white fruit, they bore wounds at which the carrion birds dashed, fighting among themselves. Some of the people had been crucified, and those whose extremities had been destroyed by fire were impaled with a spike through the middle. The trees themselves bore a dreadful air of sadness, as if mourning their part in the atrocity, and the silence was broken by the tumultuous buzzing of feeding flies.

The party came to a halt. From the rear one little shriek from Barbel arose, then quiet. Someone leaned from his horse and vomited into the grass. Recansky, staring up at the body of a young boy, began silently to weep.

Tallis found the hilt of the Lion sword under his hand. The metal was hot; the Lion seemed momentarily to leap, reflecting the anger that began to surge and boil in him. He looked at the torn and tortured corpses. So was my father used.

"This," said Tallis softly, "is the work of the Draconhood." He rode slowly under the trees, looking up carefully at what was left of one face. "I recognise this one, I think, he helped us in the battle. That one, I think, challenged us in this forest. This is the blood-price." He exhaled long and deeply, turned to the company. "Ride on. We can do nothing here. Be vigilant," he told them. "It makes me wonder just how safe our safe-conduct is."

Eventually they came, silent, from the avenue of the dead. The forest grew thicker, with small hillocks and banks warrened with caves. There were clumps of thick brushwood, trailing wild roses and blackthorn. From one of these densities Tallis heard the faintest rustle, too loud for wolf or fox. He held up his hand for a halt, watching the place. There was a flash of white. He dismounted quietly, drew his sword and parted the undergrowth. The frightened face of a boy looked out at him, and a man's voice spoke.

"Touch him and I'll kill you with my bare hands."

"Come out. We're friends. Tamian. No one will harm you."

Timbel crawled out, followed by Alpac, whom Tallis recognised from the compound after the battle. Both man and child were filthy, scratched, and shaking with fear. Tallis waited for them to calm down. Then he asked Alpac: "How did you escape? Is this your boy?"

"I fled west, to where my boats are. But I had to come back, to see . . ." he choked, glancing behind towards the trees of death. "They killed Solon. This is his son."

Timbel suddenly let out a loud shriek, startling Recansky's mount into a rear. He began to rush round in a small circle. "He killed my father!" he yelled, over and over again.

"Colonel Zairopo," said Alpac. "Grand Master of the Draconhood."

Tallis found Barbel and beckoned her to the front of the line. "Take the child," he said. "Look after him." To Alpac: "There's spare horses. You'd better come with us, to the inn. From now on, you're Tamian."

Barbel took Timbel up on her saddle-bow. Alpac mounted, and the party moved on through the forest. The child's words resonated in Tallis. *He killed my father.* Child, you have a name, a face as target for your vengeance. Would to all the gods I had.

The lobster was empty, the landlord pleased to have the trade. There was enough space to accommodate all, some doubling up. The innkeeper made no mention of the local atrocities, as if to speak of them might bring down a similar fate. Tallis put sentries all round the inn, taking no chances. Now he sat on the bed in the chamber *she* had occupied, looking through the open window past the apple tree towards the meadow where his tent had been pitched. Barbel, who with the boy had been given the room next door, came creeping, late, to scratch on his door.

"You should be asleep," he said crossly, "We've a long ride tomorrow."

"How's your hand, Tallis?"

"Better. Thanks to you."

"I heard you just now, talking to yourself. I thought you were feverish again. Damn me if you didn't say some stuff that night when you were ill."

"What did I say?"—sharply.

"You said: 'A seven-year-old can kill. It's a judgement.'"

"I said that? I was thinking of the child who bit me."

Barbel sat cross-legged on the floor. "Who's Brother Sundew? Did he put those scars on your back?" She stared him out.

"I never knew you'd seen those."

"You forget. The first time we met. You had nothing on."

"Barbel," he said, and sighed deeply. "No one knows about this, and the gods know why I'm telling you."

"You have my word, before you begin. As an honorary soldier. Wild boars won't drag it out of me."

"Well, it's a long time ago," he said. "After my father was murdered and my mother died. I was supposed to go to Tam, to the court, to be trained as a page. All that seemed to change. I was sent to be trained as a priest in the Bay of Moons monastery by command of Queen Sarene. I would have made a damned bad priest. But they were nearly all bad on the island. Especially Sundew, that whore's son."

"He beat you."

"He lashed the life out of me from the first. I was new, and afraid, and very little. There are some evil things men do, especially men who are supposed to be holy. It's as if evil is attracted to a holy place. It was when I wouldn't . . . well, never mind that. I pushed him down a flight of cellar steps. I killed him. No one ever thought other than that he was drunk, and had fallen."

"Good," said Barbel. "Well done, Tallis."

"I tried to swim home. It was a long time before I could trust anyone again." He became silent.

"Thank you for telling me," said Barbel humbly. "Wild boars, remember."

"Go to bed," said Tallis heaving off his boots. He blew out his lantern and lay on the bed fully dressed. The moon was declining slowly from the zenith. He felt a strange release, as if poison had been drained away. He remembered how thankful he had been when the monastery's ill-repute had reached the mainland. General Camlot had brought him out, sent him to cadet school . . . he closed his eyes. He tried to think of Pancora, sewing her wedding gown. Sleep folded over his mind. No bad dreams tonight.

He woke as a dog wakes, sentient of the slightest vibration. Someone was half in at his window, one leg on the branch of the apple tree. The moon flashed on steel. A long knife, carried in the left hand. His first thought was rage at the sentries who must have dozed on this side of the house. His second was gratitude that the man was left-handed. The Lion sword was propped on the right of his bed, away from the sight of the assassin. He closed his hand gently round its hilt, and lay breathing as in sleep.

The man was not clumsy, he was as light as a cat. Tallis's brain flashed coldly over the possible origins of this visitation. Malkar? No, I am nothing to her. The Draconhood? No, I am not a Karenian subject. Finally: a Karenian soldier unhappy with the truce and come to wipe out the enemy single-handed. He decided on the last, just as the black shadow sprang, the moon's play sparkling on his blade. In that instant Tallis rolled across the bed, almost to the floor, and came up with a jump, his feet on the pillows, the Lion sword lively in his grasp.

The assassin had stabbed the pillow so deep that it caught him off balance and he fell forward, straight on to the point of Tallis's sword. He gave one screech and collapsed, impaling himself through the heart. For a moment he writhed on the point, then with a gusty sigh, expired.

"Damn!" cried Tallis, almost as loudly as the man's dying cry. All along the passage doors opened. Recansky and the others came running with lanterns. Tallis withdrew the sword, and the bed swiftly became bloody.

"Who is he?" asked Recansky. "Are you all right, Captain?"

"Just annoyed that I killed him. Turn him over."

The man was small, rather yellow-skinned, with a tattoo of a crow in flight in the centre of his forehead.

"Well, I'm damned," said Recansky. "A Karkian, of all things."

"I thought he might be a Despran." Barbel peered curiously at the corpse.

"Not only a Karkian, but a Koonilite," said Tallis. "They're mercenaries, professional killers. Not thought too respectable in the principality of Karkis. I'd love to know who sent him. Too late now." He tenderly wiped blood from the Lion sword.

"What now?" asked Recansky. "Does Tamia declare war on Karkis?" He gave a shaky laugh. He was slightly rattled; he had wanted Tallis's bedroom, which was the best in the house.

"Karkis is neutral," said Tallis.

"It's beyond me," said Recansky.

"They used to say," Tallis said, "that the Forest of Rulen was enchanted. This is a forest of blood. Let's get rid of this. Is he carrying anything to show who he is?"

"Nothing."

"Very well. Try not to disturb our host until morning. Close that window, sergeant. I must get some sleep. Barbel, I'll have to move in with you." And in an undertone to Recansky, "don't smirk like that, lieutenant. I think of this creature as my son."

She was trying to raise the Crystal Lion. There were horsemen approaching the House of Brides, nowhere near yet, but certainly on the road, and she needed protection. There was so much chaos abounding in the countryside from Lake Sigillan, round the perimeter of which slaves had been crucified, from Kalvaria and from the Forest, that it was impossible for her to ascertain whence the party came, or its intent. Lilene had two perfect opals in her right hand which she rolled constantly round and round. They were not essential for the raising of the Lion, but they calmed her. Her meditation was patchy.

If I am to restore the House of Brides one day, my thoughts will need to be disciplined. I shall dress in coif and wimple, not like this. She smoothed the thin rose-coloured silk of her gown, over the breast of which hung the gold Lion, shook out her long full sleeves as she rolled the opals round and round. Her feet were bare. She was not cold, but some of her thoughts made her shiver. Her room was high in the tower, overlooking the garden with the distant sea a smudge of blue.

The clean room was bare save for the big bed, a Lion icon and a few functional pieces of furniture. She had brought the last of the Lion-lilies in; they stood in a crystal vase. They did not cheer her spirits. There had been no word from Honyia's minstrel, and her every instinct told her that things had gone badly awry.

She did not mind being alone, she was never lonely. She thought much about Honyia however, wishing she were here under the protection of the House.

She resumed her meditation. The Crystal Lion was somewhere on the edge of the ether. One did not summon it unless there were danger; if there were no danger it would not come. The atmosphere in the room remained still. There was no charge of power. She placed the opals away, wrapped her arms about herself and bowed her head.

One more dream-vision of him had come to her within the last week. He had been with the strange boy-girl. He had been giving that one a knife. She had even heard, very faintly, his longed-for voice. "You should be armed, Barbel. I have often thought so. This knife has a little Lion-power..." Then the vision had faded, like a dream at dawn.

She sat on, fragile, beautiful and sad, while the evening came down very slowly, and she lit a lamp and set it in the window. She took another lantern and set it burning on the spiral stair outside her door. She did this every night to ward off anything that might like the dark.

A small black owl, with a white tuft on its head, came to perch outside her window. Motionless, intent, it watched her through the glass.

The little boy, Timbel, and Alpac the fisherman followed in Tallis's company without uttering a word. Alpac knew they were travelling further and further east away from his home on the coast, his escape route by sea, and more significantly from Despra, where Gwldas was. He was further distressed when they crossed Treaty Bridge, on which the severed heads of young rebels had been spiked. As they approached the little enclave that belonged to Taratamia, the awful sights diminished and were no more.

It was a long road, this last leg of the journey, down a track seldom travelled these days, and thorny in places, but the birds sang of twilight and in the west was a sunset of such glory that it seemed an augury of eventual hope out of misery.

They were all weary. The streams and lakes of the House of Brides beckoned the horses and they blew into the air and pricked forward eagerly. There in its L-shape of amber stone at the very end of the road lay the Abbey. The cypresses still stood, bowed by the sea-wind, and the giant oak housed small birds, who had returned at last to their ruined home. But the garden, and the Abbey, were sealed off by an almost impenetrable barrier of cruel blackthorn, man-high weeds, teasels and thistles, and beds of nettles carpeted the tangled gap which was once the gate. Sunset glowed on the weeds, the thorns, the Abbey, lighting the panes of glass on the western side like fire. The rest of the building had a secret darkness about it, a melancholy.

"We've arrived," muttered Tallis. "Hail, Taratamia." He was distressed, remembering the glories of Brides, once so pristine and kempt. He surveyed the garden, standing in his stirrups to see over the climbing obstacles. The roses, gone wild and rotten, the neat flowerbeds a maelstrom of goosegrass and dandelions, with valerian spreading a purple veil overall. The lawns were waist-high grass, coarse as in a field. The ponds were scummed with algae. Some of the outbuildings were crumbling where stones had been dislodged. There was the atmosphere of a recent spiritual earthquake.

"Well," said Recansky, "It's deserted, that's for sure." He jumped down from his horse. "I'm going to blunt my sword on this lot." He began methodically slashing away at the weeds and thorns; the rest of the party followed suit, clearing an entrance into the grounds. Tallis was watching the windows, where the flaming sunset lit them. The glow in the sky was so bright and all-encompassing it seemed that even the side of the building facing the sea shared the gleam. For a moment he saw a rose-coloured cloud reflected before vanishing into the dusk.

"Yes," he said. "Everyone's gone. We have to put this place to rights. And I want a guard on the outer wall. This is still Tamia."

"Where do you want us billeted, Captain?" One of the sergeants, dripping blood from blackthorn, came up to Tallis.

"Better stay below. There are plenty of billets in the outbuildings. Change the guard every four hours. I'm not expecting trouble, but you never know."

They entered the garden at last, the horses making for the stream. Tallis dismounted and walked to where one of the lawns seemed less unkempt, and stopped. There an oblong of earth was planted with sweet herbs, rimmed with round stones, with a wooden marker at its head. A lion was carved thereon, and the legend: Andine of Capashenet. Matrix Bonimac. Source of goodness. He went down on one knee and bowed his head. Pray for us, Andine. I remember your kiss of peace. Your place is near the stars. Lion Woman, I salute you.

They came at dusk, the gaudy ones, coloured like peacocks, with great eyes in their wings. Or the modest brown ones, as fair in their way, their wings silk-fringed. They flew in from the hot coast and the forests, attracted by the light placed in Fastet's window.

He was always careful they should not burn themselves, and caught them gently in a fine net. Never would he harm them. He placed them in a jar with a tiny drop of paralyn to stun them while he made his drawings, then he let them go.

Other creatures came out of the night; poison-green beetles with heads like hawks, earwigs, mosquitoes. They were Fastet's life. He was a recluse, and content.

He had just released a sapphire-blue moth when a small shadow came swinging down on a hair-fine thread from the top of the casement. It settled on the sill. Arachnida ruvaensis, Fastet said aloud. Very rare. Strange, to see one so far inland. He sat very still. The spider approached, feeling about with its delicate black legs covered with silky fur. The two long front legs probed the air. Suddenly it took a run forward on to his hand, where it sat serenely. It was black, wasp-waisted, with eyes like polished obsidian, which gazed at him intently. No, he said. You're not what I thought. There was a brilliant white star on its head. Fastet reached quietly for his drawing block with his free hand.

He felt a drop of moisture on his fingers. It issued from between the spider's back legs; he felt a very slight burning. He watched while the moisture was followed by a sticky white thread. The thread was paid out at astonishing speed. He watched fascinated while his fingers, then his whole hand, were wrapped round and round. The creature scurried in a kind of desperation. I'm not a fly, he said to it, and laughed softly, so as not to frighten it away.

And then the spider laughed too, a tiny silvery laugh.

Fastet nearly leaped from his chair. And found himself bound, arms, chest, thighs, by gossamer as strong as sinews, and the black spider, its eyes now large and jewelled as lamps, scampered up and lay upon his breast.

The weight grew heavier than the world. Arms were round him, and legs, and darkness laughed sweetly in his face. Her loins mischievously continued to emit the glutinous white thread. It burned; he saw his garments shrivel from his body. As she lay over him he was incapable of speech or even thought. He had kept apart from womankind but now he was more than ready to possess one; as she took him he was swept by a shivering fire of pleasure and moaned into her kissing mouth.

The soul was buried deep, niched in a lifetime's tranquillity, and the darkness reamed it out with some effort. She rode him, pushing at him until the chair and its bound victim fell backwards and he lay half stunned beneath her thrusting. In its impatience the darkness issued venom and he screamed as agony surged up through the pleasure and his genitals burned.

Now there was anger in the darkness and she let him see the truth; the mouth that crawled over his face was black and beaked with little dripping fangs. The eyes were holes in the long bone skull, the hair rank weed in which moved a jellied life. The two long front feelers crept and probed inside his ears and eyes. Even while he moaned in insane terror, what she did to him was irresistible; her loins leeched him with a tidal force and his seed-borne soul gushed forth.

The darkness unwrapped him, and needled a bite into his throat. Fastet played too long with insects, they would say who found his body.

The pearl is like a moon at the full. The face and body are without flaw. Power speaks with its sonorous note; of the deeps and their fallen days, of the black days to come.

The thing that was Malkar regarded itself. The pearl shone through the mirror. It opened its round eye generously, swelled with the souls from Maelikali's belly.

Show me Little Taratamia.

Ah, there she is. She is lovely, there is no question. I have high hopes of her. Female, blood of the darkness. Heiress to the deathmating.

Her time draws near. And when her power is proved, we shall swallow souls like sweetmeats, and together rule the kingdoms of the damned.

Fly again, darkness, and bear witness.

The men, after thoroughly searching the grounds and chapels on the lower floor, came back to Tallis.

"Nothing there, Captain." The sergeant was eating a few blackberries plucked from the overwhelming briars. Tallis frowned at him.

He was possessed by a feeling of uneasiness which grew as the sunset crept lower, an intense crimson and gold that faded at its height. The smudge of ocean showed violet, captive of the coming night. Only a faint glow remained on the mellow walls of the building; the windows had lost their gleam.

"Shall we search aloft now, Captain?" asked Recansky.

Tallis cast a further look up at the walls. At one broken window swifts were flying in and out. Apart from this, the stillness was absolute.

"There's no one here," he said. "You can always tell." Even as he spoke he knew he was lying. The knowledge was part of his unease. Something was making him tremble deep within.

"You can set up the watch and bed down," he told them.

"Shall I sleep with the horses?" Barbel gave Tallis a look. No, Barbel, he thought. Guard only the horses tonight.

Thus he dismissed them and watched them go yawning to their rest or their posts. When they had dispersed he began to walk very slowly round the building, past the fading overgrowth of buglewort and bluehorn, the rampant valerian and the sad old roses. He stopped near Andine's grave and looked directly up at the tower. And saw a very faint yellow glow, like the ghost of the sunset.

He turned and went decisively to the great door, its hinges rusty, its Lionhead knocker forbidding and yet serene. He leaned on the latch; the door swung open revealing darkness on the spiral stair. And he was suddenly terribly afraid, and murmured "Ceda pefur gevac" to remind him of his integrity.

He began to ascend. It was as if he had never climbed these stairs before, with Andine waiting to receive him. For the stairs had become, by some tricky mischief of the night, endless. He went up and up in total darkness, his hand always on the serpentine curve of the wall, the dizzying undulation of the spiral. There was no end to the climb, to the dark, and he swayed a little and felt his strength begin to fail, as if the stones' curve was leeching it as food for its darkness. And as he struggled round steps which had become a way for giants, so tall and steep were they, he saw the lantern placed upon the stair.

He halted for a moment. The lantern gleamed up at him,: beckoning. He took it in his hand.

The light led him upwards a little way, to her door.

He knocked on the door briskly, a martial rat-a-tat. After a moment, while the lantern lit the shadows, he knocked again, and, in the continuing silence, entered. He came in slowly, and the last low rays of the sun and the lanternlight illuminated them both.

He was very pale, against the dark scarlet flame of his uniform. Every detail of him rushed upon her; his hair had grown longer, he wore it tied in the nape of his neck. The Lion sword emitted one spark as he moved forward. His severe eyes, the shape of his mouth and his hands were as remembered, more poignant now after all the longing that had been like a bereavement. And the reality of the moment struck her like a blow. There was a carved pillar behind her, and she took a step backwards, to feel its hard comfort under her palms.

And she was all rose and gold as he looked at her; her cloud of hair a spun aureole, her full mouth and sea-blue eyes a remembered shock of beauty, her perfect body tense as she stood against the pillar. She seemed part of a dream from long ago, perhaps in another lifetime.

"Your Royal Highness." His voice, though he spoke softly, seemed to wrench the chamber out of a kind of trance. "You're here, all alone? Are you safe? Have you been harmed at all?"

"Captain," she said. "Yes." Then: "How are you, Captain?" He found he had moved several steps towards her. She had drawn him there. Out of respect he unbuckled his sword and leaned it against the wall.

"I am so very glad to see you," she said. He saw two tears roll from her eyes. She smiled a little.

"What are you doing here, all alone?"

"I live here," she said, still smiling, a tense, unhappy smile. "I am quite safe, Captain Tallis. I saw you ride in. I am so glad you came."

Something rose in his chest; he felt his heart was about to burst. He could almost hear it in the stillness. "Are you comfortable here, princess?" he said. His voice sounded odd, his words foolish. She stood, her hands against the pillar, her body unrelaxed, leaning slightly towards him.

Then she said suddenly, in quite a loud, desperate voice: "Welcome, Ricalpa." And, "I want you to kiss me. Again, I want you to kiss me. Ricalpa, I love you so much."

One moment they stood apart, the next they were close. She stood with her mouth lifted to his, her eyes half-closed, and unhesitatingly, yet without haste, he kissed her. He put his hand gently behind her head and his arm round her supple waist, and she leaned into him like a wand. He could feel every nuance of her body, it curved fluently into his, and suddenly it was as if he possessed her already, her thighs parting, her breast and belly and legs pressed against his. His heart was racing like hers, as he tasted and explored her beautiful mouth as if it were a ripe fruit. He stroked her breasts and her back and caught her to him round her loins so she should know the desire she had created. And kissed and held her for long moments, while she moulded herself to him, uttering low soft cries as if wounded, and they both began to shake from head to foot.

It was as if a mighty wind blew them together, as if they hid within each other from a storm, time hanging on the moment; mouth to mouth, body to trembling body, lost for speech even when slowly they drew apart.

Even then, he began to kiss her neck, the goldflushed skin where the soft fine coils of golden hair clung, and moved his lips over her throat, holding her tightly, and turning her so that he stood with his back against the pillar and she lay against him, supported only by the closeness of his embrace. Her eyes were closed. She held him, her hands on the back of his neck under his hair, gentle and lax, like the hands of someone asleep. My love, my witch, my own, he thought. Whoever and whatever you are, you are my whole and sole desire, now and for all time. And she said again, her voice full of tears, "I love you, Ricalpa. I love you forever."

There were words inside him. They had been striving and pleading for release for months, and they came from him now, gladly like a freed bird, painfully like the searching of a wound.

"Oh, my own Lilene. My beloved. Love of my life," at which she began to weep.

"Ah, don't cry, my love, my little dove," he said, almost laughing with joy and relief. "Don't weep, my sweet, all's well. I love you. I love you. Oh, kiss me again. Give me your lovely mouth. My darling."

She flung her arms round him, kissing him with such passion that he became almost unbearably aroused. He held her so tightly she could hardly say: "I belong to you. I've always belonged to you. You never knew."

"I knew," he whispered. "Always. You were mine from the beginning. Lilene . . ." Trembling, dangerously sick with desire, his hands on her body, in her hair, his lips on her tear-wet face:

"Lilene. I must have you. If I don't have you now, I think I shall fall down dead."

"Oh, yes!" she cried. "Yes, Ricalpa, yes! I've waited so long. Come now, to my bed."

The small black owl which had crouched outside the window throughout, sidled along the sill. It raised its white crest and waited, unseen and shadowy.

He was not cruel; yet finally he possessed her fully, her shriek at his thrust coming into his brain as if from a long marble corridor miles and years away. He drew her on to his body like a hot velvet glove, silencing her, drowning her mouth while she tangled and gripped him with her limbs and her core, fused and melted to him like a candle in flame. And he was suddenly at the beginning of his life and the world's life from its birth gathering momentum in a rush towards infinity, hot with love, seethed and baptised with love, all things coming together in one tremendous consummation of flesh, soul, blood and spirit, suspended together on the high curved wave of the most wondrous of oceans, and all mysteries revealed as to a priest . . .

Outside the window the thing that was Malkar watched eagerly to see the Captain die.

"I'm so sorry I hurt you, my darling."

Oh. *His* voice, broken now, not terse and unsparing as when he addressed his company. He belonged to her; that voice with the shaking exhaustion in it, was token of his life poured into her wounded body. The gate through which he had pushed himself to become hers. And so quick!

"I'm so sorry."

Hers.

"I love you," she said.

Like him, she was naked, among her long gold hair. A slick of red coursed down her inner thigh. Her sex was pulsing, it beat out her conquest. For although he lay on her spent and trembling, she was triumphant beneath him.

"Mine." Her whisper, but he caught it, and moved his mouth in an echo against her neck at the place where a moment ago he had cried out in a deathlike ecstasy.

"My love," he said. "My life's love."

He raised himself and leaned above her so he could fill his eyes with her, lifted a shaking hand to touch her body. The long fine hand, the palm calloused from weaponry and leather, began its slow exploration of petal flesh.

His eyes were downcast, as he caressed her belly as if to sooth it. His face was so rapt it had taken on a kind of youthfulness, the furrows in the lean cheeks softened, the hard mouth given over to tenderness. She realised that it was a beautiful face, uncorrupted and noble, and his body was everything that had occupied her most hot and chambered thoughts. So she began to touch him boldly—the slight, strong torso, the muscular belly and narrow waist, and remembering how she had yearned for him as he carried himself so erectly (unaware of her eyes) she reached to stroke his straight back and found the dozen stripes from an ancient beating, like corrugations on a parchment.

"What's this?" she said, more sharply than intended. And he chuckled, his hand moving to mould the shape of her hip and thigh and waist, up and down.

"Who did this to you?" Tears blurred her sight, for his distant pain and also from jealousy for the long ago, where she had not been.

"Oh, my beautiful girl. Why are you crying? It's over, only a few people know of it." His hand moved lower, brushing damp silky hair between her legs, and against her thigh she felt his arousal. She had never before seen a man's cock (averting her eyes every time the vile Vergon chased her with his weapon out). Now she looked down amorously, watching as it stirred and grew in its soft black nest.

She fingered the old scars on his back.

"Only a few people?"

"Yes," he said patiently.

"Your brother officers, and servants?"

"Naturally."

"And . . . your woman."

It had to be said. She gazed at the ceiling, while he gently caressed her breast.

After a moment he said, "Yes. Pancora. We have lived together for five years. I was thinking of marrying her. Until you came into my heart and possessed me for ever."

She lay still, then, very carefully: "Did you love her, Ricalpa?"

His hand moved lower, and she felt a gush of moisture leaving her body.

"I never knew what love was. She was always there, a habit. She cared little for me, and I was not troubled. I treated her fairly and with honour. It all seems far away. Even the time when I thought she had drowned. I was grieved over that, she didn't deserve such ill fortune. But now . . ."

A deep look into her eyes.

"I know what love is now. It is the most terrible thing. My love for you has burned inside me for months like a torment. Even in battle, I felt you beside me. I was nearly killed, and in that moment I thought of you. You will never be free of me, Lilene, just as I was never free of you. I'm yours, as long as my life lasts."

She said softly: "Oh, I have longed for you. I was so sad when you wouldn't dance with me."

"Oh, I'll dance with you, my lady."

She was like a child, he thought tenderly. He said:

"I had to be on guard. I wasn't easy in that company. The Queen . . ."

She shuddered slightly. "My mother."

"Yes. But I will dance with you, I swear. For ever, I am your sole courtier."

"Oh, that night in the forest, in the inn . . ."

He blew a long breath. He twined his arm round her waist, pulling her closer. His heart seemed to beat within her, becoming part of her bones.

"That was the worst night of my life."

"I nearly came to your tent. I caressed myself . . ."

"So did I, I'm afraid."

He laughed out loud, hugging her tightly in a joyful release. She said:

"I've never seen you laugh before, or be merry. You were so stern always, so serious. I was afraid of you."

He said quietly, "As I was of you."

"But why . . . ?"

"I was sure you had ensorcelled me. I could think of nothing but you."

"It was only my love you felt." Then: "I beg you. Never leave me."

"You smell of lilies. I have told you, we are bound, you and I. To death, and beyond. My life is worthless without you."

The room had darkened, a strangely accelerated dusk now the radiant sunset had gone.

"I'll make a light."

He left her arms. A stand of white candles. A jewelled lamp. He set flame to them all. The bed bloomed, shimmered and revealed its secrets, the stains of consummation.

Passing the window the tail of his eye caught the faintest movement, small and dark on the sill outside, vanishing to nothing.

"I can see you now, my darling," he said.

He laid his body down over her naked body, set his mouth upon the eager rose-lips, while she raised and opened to receive him, held his head, his shoulders, pressed up hard for the hot slide of penetration that seemed to touch the tip of her womb. She wanted his hand on her breast, imperiously seized it, wrapped him round with her slippery sex and her hot thighs, sobbing in passion over the thudding of their hearts.

Her cries shivered the candle-flames. He lay on her breast as if struck by storm.

After long moments, he said shakily:

"Sweet gods! we've wasted so long! We could have had all this—this joy—it's like being in the Far Lands, it must be how it is after a good life . . ."

"It *is* the Far Lands," she whispered. She looked and saw the strain on his face. She said: "Oh, are you tired, my Ricalpa? . . ." and he laughed, saying: "it takes more than loving you to make me tired. Give me time and I'll show you how tired I am."

He pushed the covers away, exposing her. The candlelight played on her honey flesh, the shadows dappled her amber and rose, limned the gloss of moisture in the dip of her belly and the gilded nether mouth.

He leaned and began to kiss her throat, slow kisses over breasts and belly and mount, parting the soft pink and gold juicy with the distillation of love, for his tongue to lap and soothe. When she drew up her knees he pushed them down.

"Don't keep me from what is mine," and went on and on, his tongue like a cat's, while she rolled her head back and laughed and sweetly moaned with pleasure.

Eyes closed, he lay with his cheek against her thigh.

"I'm thirsty." Her mouth was like sand, her skin parched from sweat. "There's wine. On the stone slab."

He rose, went to an alcove. A silver flagon and two goblets—a miracle of convenience. Love-sorcery.

"This is Brides' wine," he said, without turning round. "Never in my life did I dream I would drink it with you. The gods are good to me."

She was watching him, her eyes full of the flat muscled back and the tight buttocks, the long cavalryman's legs, the waist as slender as a girl's but strong as oak. Candlelight on man-flesh as beautiful as her own, even the whip scars marks of pride. She slid out of bed and caught up with him before he could pour the wine, standing behind him, rubbing her sex into the cleft of his buttocks, mad for him again after all the heat and the coming, hands moving round between his thighs to cup the firm sac and the rod of her pleasure which moved and reared obediently into her hand.

"You're making me spill the wine," he said, choking on laughter.

He turned and drew her body against, kissing her mouth, full again of lust and love.

"What a beautiful arse you have, princess. I can fit my thumbs into the dimples . . ."

A joining, instantly, flesh moulding together as if crafted, she was off her feet, his hands clamped round her buttocks, her legs gripping his thighs, and an explosion inside her, hot! crying Oh, sweet gods, sweet Lion . . .

"Yes." (gasping). "Bless the Lion . . ."

"For this."

"For you . . ."

"And against a wall . . . do you remember? when I came to your house?"

"How could I forget?"

"Your little maid caught us. I was so upset."

"I nearly had a seizure."

"You were almost in."

"But not enough, unfortunately."

"Oh, Ricalpa . . . all the way home, I kept the wet patch against my leg. Your seed dried on my dress. It was all I had of you. I cried, all the way home to Karenia."

He moved a little away, and looked intensely at her. "You loved me that much?"

"Oh. You never knew."

He said shakily: "I thought we were going to have a drink." He was more moved than ever in his life. He poured the wine.

"One cup. We are one."

They drank. To the Abbess, blessed Andine, he thought. It is as if she had made this possible. They drank, and poured, and drank more, standing naked at the wall.

"Your health, my darling."

"You're weeping!" she said softly.

"So are you, beautiful girl."

"Too much wine."

"Too much loving."

"Too much joy."

"Hold me close. Hold me."

Wine and goblet in hand, they stumbled back to the bed. They slept. Tranquilly, the candles burned down.

He sighed deeply.

"Is all well with you, Ricalpa?"—little anxious voice.

He opened his eyes. He pulled her roughly to him in a rapturous embrace.

"Well? Never, never better."

He turned on his back and drew her over him. "Cover me," he said. "Take me. My life, my soul. Take all."

He entered her easily and they both cried out from the piercing pleasure suddenly renewed. He clasped her and surged in her while she moved on him, her head thrown back, her hair a rain of gold over his thighs, her eyes closed, her face enchanted. They spasmed and shivered together like a field under tempest, and then he turned her and mounted her, striking deep into her womb, his seed springing with a violence that made him groan, while she cried her pleasure, like the blissful cries of some exotic bird. And he thought: this is the best moment of my life. Better than triumph, or peace, or prayer, or laughter, or food or drink. Better even, than bringing home the colours. That old loneliness gone at last. Here in my arms, is the other half of my soul. I am complete.

There's my scarlet uniform, thrown down, stripped in my haste to take my beloved. Scarlet red, so the blood won't show when one is wounded or dead.

"But I am alive!" he said out loud. "I have never felt more alive in my life."

The small black owl crouching on the sill outside spread its wings and flew away, dark as cinders against the risen moon.

PART FOUR

Lateglow

"Colonel Zairopo awaits audience, greatness," said the High Steward.

Malkar was like an unmoving storm cloud in oyster silk coruscated with tiny mirrors. A ruby like a gout of blood depended from the centre of her crown, fashioned of branched sea-coral.

Vergon was present, in a pretence of authority, and Lord Ing of the Pearl stood uneasily behind the throne, ready to act as Malkar's mouthpiece should she deign not to address Zairopo. The colonel entered with two younger members of the Draconhood. They doffed their green hoods and knelt.

"Welcome to our Court, Brothers Dracon," said Vergon.

"We thank your majesty."

"You are not all that welcome, colonel," said Malkar. "For one thing, you took long in answering our summons."

"Omnipotent ones" said Zairopo with a little smile. "We have been much exercised in putting down the rebellion. Surely you will appreciate that zeal here was paramount, more even than the honour of being in your presence."

Boiling within him was the shock he had in store for Malkar. He had not decided when to launch it at her.

"It is this we wish to address to you," Malkar said. "We applaud your zeal. But we feel, colonel, that this time you may have overstepped yourself. Never have I seen so many corpses in our realm, outside of the fiercest battles against Despra or Taratamia. At this rate there will be no future generations for the

House of Karling to rule over. Neither will there be armies. For I note that many of those you are executing are strong young men. Why do you smile, colonel?"

"Only, great madam, because it is these very strong young men who are prime movers in the rebellion. These are the common people who have been so sadly misled by their leader. These are the strong young men who deserted their commanders to fight for our grand enemy. We do not execute grandfathers. Unless they too are privy to this wave of treason."

Vergon suddenly burst into speech from the recess of the Oyster throne.

"This is what I said!" he cried. "They should never have been armed! It all stemmed from that! It sparked the murder of my friends. I myself escaped by a hair. You did well, colonel, to discipline them."

Malkar shot lidded venom at him. "Yes, colonel. You served us well in putting down the rebellion. It has been a bitter lesson for the traitors. But I feel enough is enough. I command that these people be released and returned to their homes with a warning."

Vergon broke in again. "You cannot command him, madam. I say, continue the executions. Burn, hang, until all these assassins are wiped out."

"His majesty speaks in haste," said Malkar. "He is still sickened by the fate of the lords."

"Well, Madam Queen-Regent," said Zairopo, "we appear at an impasse."

"Not at all," said Malkar quietly. She looked hard at Zairopo. "I know that in his heart the king wishes to stay the executions. Otherwise, our Parliament might find it expedient to temper some of the Draconhood's powers."

"That would be difficult, madam. The Holy Draconhood has many arms, to which your ministers are affiliated. Some of your priests of the Pearl work closely with the Draconhood. It would undermine tradition if its powers were in any way curtailed."

He watched her hands. They swam together, like little white fish.

"Of course, madam," he said softly, "Matters would be very different if the instigator of this rebellion could be put down. Peasants are much like sheep."

Malkar said to Lord Ing: "Inform the colonel I am displeased that he still intends to butcher these sheep of mine."

"Lord Ing," said Zairopo, even more softly, "Would you inform the Queen-Regent that not all the rebels have been apprehended. That their leader is of more importance than any realise. And that I would recommend the information I have be imparted to her in total secrecy."

Malkar's eyes opened wide. "And why, colonel, should I give you secret audience?"

"Because, madam," he said, bowing, "it is of the utmost moment, particularly to you." Something in his tone made Malkar say: "I will receive the colonel in private."

She rose and went through to an antechamber. The fish in the tanks darted fiercely as she passed. A sea-spider pounced and swallowed a tiny squid.

Alone with him, she seated herself. He seemed at ease as he limped to stand before her.

"Well, madam," he said without waiting for her to speak first, "I am aware of your deep desires. Spare the young men, awaiting torture and execution. I have many such, strong, pretty boys . . ."

And he looked into the heavy eyes, guessing at truth, and far from it.

"I can release them to you," he said quietly, "but there is a price."

"You dare bargain with me?"

"A contract then, madam, between us. All I require is this chief culprit, this one adored and followed to the death, who has financed, guided and advised for months. The leader."

"And why," she said, "do you ask me? The capture of the leader is your affair. By now you should have tracked him down."

"Not him, madam," he said gently. And very daring, approached, and bending his big gaunt form, whispered in her ear.

"I do not believe you," she said after a moment.

"It is the truth. Have you not missed the best part of King Enial's treasure?" And listened again to her silence.

"It all went to buy arms, we think," he said. "I ask you now to hand the princess over to the Draconhood."

"She is the Princess Royal of Karling, and above the law. One day I hope to see her married to Karenia's advantage."

"Then, madam," he said, "I suggest you consider whether one life, however noble, is worth saving, if the cost is a realm peopled by impotent old men." And he looked again into her eyes.

"I will not play games, madam," he said. "Her fate would not be pleasant. She would be put to the question. The penalty for treason is burning or drowning. Since this latest outbreak they are all burned. It is more salutary." He took a step backwards. "I beg leave to depart now, greatness. I will leave the matter to your wisdom. And I will offer special prayers that you may be guided to the right."

The pearl turned in the hollow of her belly like a fretful sleeper. She removed it and placed it within the aegis of darkness. The mirror showed its pallor, and her own. A tiny swelling, like an oedema, showed beneath her left eye, as if the muscles there were feeling their age.

Days and days, since Malkar has taken. How long, until the damage can be repaired? The Taken do not succumb to ugliness. How long, before the damage becomes irreparable? And how long until there are no souls left to take?

She slipped into the vortex of darkness and became one with it. The mirror reflected a being the sight of which would have killed any who witnessed it. The dark chamber quaked and boiled with anger.

Ah, the worthless inheritrix! I could have slain her on the spot. And Andine! oh, could I but claw her soul to shreds, send it screaming to perdition. Andine robbed us. She must have robbed us nineteen years ago, at the very birth of the new demoness. I curse her, and my curses fly shrieking around the spheres. Impotent. As impotent as Lilene. Lilene, my mortal, human, worthless daughter.

And now! All this time she has been forging her own secret path.

This, I was not shown. But then, I did not look for it. All this chaos in my realm was of her making.

But now there is one last use for her. The contract with Zairopo will be honoured. We will even aid him to entrap her. Darkness shall be served. She shall meet darkness face to face. Then she shall burn in the Draconhood's fire, to honour the darkness.

Now that she had him at last, she was terrified of losing him. She could scarcely bear him out of her sight. He left her tower only for the shortest possible times, by necessity having to oversee his company below, returning at a rush up the spiral, wild for her embrace. Every night he lay behind her, her body curved into his, his limbs tight around her, half-sleeping, time after time turning to her for them to weave their long intense passages of love. His life he peeled naked before her, and to her all his secrets were known.

Tallis came as near to dereliction of duty as he had ever done in his life, leaving Recansky in charge of the men, apart from infrequent, hurried and half-hearted appearances below.

Recansky, who had an eye on promotion, kept the men hard at work. Very soon they had restored the garden to its former order. They rebuilt the outer wall, making it more invulnerable, even lugging great stones up from the bay. They rebuilt the outbuildings and mended the windows. They fashioned a great new gate, cleared the wells and ponds and unblocked the streams. Tallis, looking remarkably pale and unseasonably younger, addressed them twice, once to applaud their efforts and once referring to his absences.

"As you know, the Princess Royal is in residence. I am standing as her personal guard during her time here."

None of the men dared even look at one another, for Lieutenant Recansky had very sharp eyes and a tongue to match. They merely straightened their faces to an unnatural sobriety, and went about their work, which was all but complete.

Barbel was very quiet. She cooked for the men, using the provision store left at the Abbey. She carried trays up to the door at the top of the spiral and left them outside at intervals. She found wine, the House of Brides vintage, and served it in flagons of precious metal to the lovers. She kept to herself. She talked a lot to Tallis's mare, saying things such as: "He's happy. We wanted him to be happy, didn't we?" And the mare, being wise in the manner of horseflesh, knew there was no answer and gave none.

Recansky came to him one morning, his face troubled.

"Captain, the abbess's grave; it's been desecrated. We've never seen the like—as if some big animal had savaged it. The poor old lady was dug up and lying outside on the grass."

"And no one saw anything?"

"No, nor heard a sound. The strangest part—the corpse wasn't decomposed at all, just looked asleep. Smiling too. And no rotten smell. Only a scent like a rose garden."

Tallis swore softly. He said: "Put everything to rights and mount a guard on the grave."

"It's done, Captain."

"And say nothing to the princess when you see her. It would only distress her."

He went unquietly to Lilene, his mind made up. She had braided her hair in thick gold serpents and bound it round her head. Her slender honey-coloured nape was exposed. Even now, her beauty was like a sublime shock to him. He said: "I think it's time, my love."

"Time, my Ricalpa?"

"To be moving from here. There's all kinds of danger abroad. I feel it in my bloodstream."

She was silent for a moment. "I'd planned to stay here. But I made no promise to the Matrix. I thought never to see you again. Oh, Ricalpa. If only we could stay here forever, like this."

"We can't," he said. "But I'll tell you now. I never had a marriage, or a honeymoon. This has been both for me. Every dream I ever wished for, and a thousand times more. You'll come with me now. We'll go due north along the coast. I want you to see as few of the terrible sights as possible. We'll head for Singstar Pass and . . ."

"What terrible sights?" she said sharply.

He told her in terse unembroidered language. She got up and went to the window, and he heard her begin to weep. "I didn't know," she said. "My poor little ones. My poor people. Why didn't they wait? Why, in the name of all kind gods, didn't they wait?"

He stared at her back. He thought: I've been blind, and deaf, and insane.

"Lilene," he began. She stopped him, without turning.

"Ricalpa," she said softly. "I'd like to be alone for a few moments. I want to pray for them." She burst out crying, and he left her, going down the spiral at a run, out into the courtyard, where the men were tidying up. Alpac was there, cleaning a sword, and the little boy Timbel, eating a piece of fruit given him by Barbel. Barbel was standing by, and gave Tallis a strange look, as if she had never seen him before.

"Alpac," said Tallis. "One question. Who led the rebellion? Whose idea was it?"

Alpac opened his mouth hesitantly, but the little boy dropped his apple and flew at him, shrieking: "You mustn't tell! You must never tell!"

"It's all right, Timbel," said Alpac sadly. "The news is out. Captain," he said in his rough coast dialect, "I trust you. Our blessed lady -" he pointed to the tower. "Her."

Tallis shouted for Recansky, in a voice that made everyone jump to attention. The lieutenant came running.

"Clear up all traces of our presence. Be ready to move out. Is there a carriage for the princess?"

"Only horses, Captain."

"Saddle the bay. She can ride." He turned and ran back up the tower. Lilene was sitting by the window, composed. Why, in the gods' name, didn't you tell me? he thought, as he flung open her clothes chest and began pulling out garments in a frenzy.

"You'll have to travel light, my darling," he said. "Where are the warm clothes—the wool, the fur. It'll be cold, going over the Tiranians."

"You're taking me to Taratamia?"

"Lilene. The Draconhood are on the road. I'm taking you home, with me, to safety."

"The Draconhood cannot touch me," she said quite proudly. "I am Karling. Their justice does not apply, whatever I may have done."

"It's a risk I'm not taking," he said grimly. "Lilene, make ready."

"Can't we stay here?" she whispered longingly. "Forever?"

"Gods," he said in despair. "Do I have to put you in chains? Take you over the border as my hostage? It would probably start the war off again with a bang. My love, hurry."

"Take me as your hostage," she said. "Or take me as your wife!"

He turned very white. "Oh, gods!" he said again. "If only I could! I'm just an army man. You're Lilene of Karling. No priest would marry us, in either of our countries. I'll love and serve you for as long as I live. But as for marriage—oh, don't speak of it. It's heartbreaking."

She looked at him very searchingly. Every facet of him so familiar, so beloved. If ever there was a time to tell him one of the two secrets she carried, one of them deadly, the other momentous, it was now. The implications of the second could alter much. They could change him. Lilene was not used to happiness, yet out of nowhere she found a kind of gambler's courage.

"Ricalpa," she said. "You are not just an army man."

"I am. I do my best. I'm proud of what I am."

"Ricalpa," she said, "your father was not Colonel Tallis. Your father is King Valm the Seventh. You are his love-child by the lady Carilene. And today you are heir to the Opal Throne."

It was a long time before he returned to her. He walked the garden for hours, away from the sight of the men. He stood by Andine's grave, remembering her affection which had mystified him. Remembering Queen Sarene's bitter looks, and the Karkian assassin undoubtedly hired by her.

He held Prince Ataret's letter to Andine; the crackling parchment felt like a rock in his clenched fist.

For some time he had not believed Lilene. Only the letter, one paragraph in particular, had convinced him.

"The end of the dynasty seems inevitable. I am greatly alarmed and inclined to favour the living heir, as, under the Second Tamic Law as laid down by the Old Kings, a monarch's natural son, if sound in body and mind, can and should inherit the throne of Capashenet. Captain Tallis has, by Queen Sarene's command, been kept so far in ignorance of his birthright. My dear great aunt you are aware that there was and is much bitter feeling on the part of the queen regarding the king's past liaison with Carilene. General Camlot was aware . . ."

Lilene had watched while he read it. She had not anticipated his almost crazed laughter.

He had rolled the letter and struck the table hard with it.

"It's a joke!" he shouted. "Me, the king's bastard! It's a tale like they tell children when they won't sleep. It's not true. Tallis was my beloved father. It's a damned lying fairy story. These things don't happen in real life. It's a bad joke!" And, crushing the letter in his hand, he had rushed from the room. She had sat waiting until dusk fell, rising to pack and unpack her baggage. When he finally returned she ran to him but was almost afraid to embrace him. He took her in his arms, and she shook with relief. In the lamplight she had kindled, his face was tired and drawn.

"I believe it," he said. "It is terrible." He looked at her very closely. "Have you any more revelations for me, Lilene? Or have you shocked me enough for one day?"

She shook her head. She would not send him to his death. But he lifted her face and gazed hard into her eyes. He said in the softest voice: "Lilene. If you are holding anything more back from me that I should know, I shall never forgive you. I shall always love you, with everything I have and am. But I shall never forgive you. Remember that."

He looked out at the dusk. "It's too late to start out now. Come to bed."

As always, he held her night-long, and she slept a little. He stared into the blackness, trying to adjust thirty-three years of living delusion to some kind of reality. One thought swirled to the top of the maelstrom in his mind. I may be the byblow of King Valm, but Colonel Tallis is the only father I knew and loved. My pledge remains unbroken, eternal. To avenge him.

Malkar the Subtle One, the Dream Fiend, the leech of souls. Maelikali the Voracious One, powered by the sea, older than the rocks. The fathomless darkness, a small black bat with white between its ears. Clinging head down at the casement, watching, just before dawn.

He was asleep at last. His arms round Lilene, his one hand covering her breast, his other arm firmly about her waist as if he feared she might slip away. A fur rug covered them both from the waist down.

She saw his spare, disciplined body. She saw the recent wound in his psyche. Even that had not weakened him. She would have liked to take him. If he survived, Malkar, the waiter on change and chance, would do so, would cast him down among the damned. He should not escape the dark design.

"Esteemed, revered, unutterably clever and very beloved father," said Mayla, Duchess of Mayt. It was the kind of language she hoped would alert the duke to the fact that the present world was continuing about him. He lived most of his days somewhere beyond the stars, where he was very at ease.

"Will you kindly give me your attention?" She clenched her fists, which were braceleted and ringed with dozens of silver ornaments. She had often felt like striking her father, and never more so than now. She looked down at her toes in silver sandals with ruby buckles, and saw them curling up in frustration.

"Dear Daddy," she said. The duke raised his head from the arcane manuscript he was studying. A large, high-browed head with a mass of grey tangled hair that fell below his shoulder-blades. Fronds of this luxuriance strayed round to meet a beard of immense length, in which small remnants of his frugal meals sometimes clung.

The duke was usually a person of deep contentedness. He vaguely remembered Mayla being born, and was aware she needed cherishing, but had left her upbringing to a phalanx of competent guardians and ministers. He had many years ago misplaced his wife, who, irate at his inattention, had run off with one of her young physicians, and was believed to have died in Karkis. At this moment, however, he was unhappy. He had been torn away from his philosophical and alchemical studies to spend a rare visit in the Royal Household at Tam. This was Mayla's doing. Persuading him to come had all but worn her out, but certain privy reasons had made her feel the stress was worth it.

"My dear," he said, aware enough to register her prettiness and the vibrations of her impatience. "What can I do for you, and when are we going home please?"

Oh father, she thought in despair. How I do need a father!

"I am a woman," she announced. He looked at her north and south, nodding towards her plump little breasts.

"Indeed you are, my child. You have all the appurtenances. Well done."

"And I am in love."

"Ah. Love." He furrowed his great noble brow. "An abstract concept. It takes on many guises."

"I am in love and don't know what to do," said Mayla.

"Love is thought to be a mixture of chemical reaction and emotional need," said the duke. "The procreative urge . . ."

"Father!" said Mayla very loudly.

"Sex breaks all barriers," said the duke. "An illustration of this has been my latest experiment—not, hrr, hrr, a total success, but enlightening."

As on cue, something leaped from the folds of his gown. As part of his alchemical studies, the duke had succeeded by various means in mating a cat with a toad. The result of this, covered in green fur with claws and whiskers, now sprang into a niche in the wall, emitting a kind of feline croaking.

"I was cheated of one husband," said Mayla. "I was almost raped, but not quite. Now I am ready for love and I want you to know how I feel. Please, Father. Be a father."

The duke woke up sharply. "Rape?" he cried. "You said nothing. The person shall be killed forthwith."

"It was some time ago and it doesn't matter now," said Mayla. "I am speaking of the present."

The duke smiled very sweetly. "Love, yes. Love should be known by all, except for those with higher aspirations, such as myself. Yes, child. Know love, and tell me how it feels to you. Whatever you do, you have my blessing." He frowned. "One thing—the man must be of noble birth."

"Oh Father," said Mayla happily. "He is."

Replete with approval, she went from him, leaving him staring into the cat-toad's bug eyes with perplexed pride. She passed through lines of bowing guard. Her women caught up with her and were dismissed, as she passed the apartments of Queen Sarene. These days Sarene seldom left her chamber. There came the doleful sound of chanting and prayers.

Her goal, a tall gilt-studded door, was slightly ajar. She tiptoed in. King Valm was waiting for her. He was very spruce, in white with golden trimmings. Any trace of grey in his hair had been dyed out. As she had matured, so had he grown younger. His eyes were so kind, paternal, with a spark in them not at all paternal. He held out to her a golden cage in which preened two white doves.

"Look!" he said softly. "They are in love!" And Mayla gave him a ravishing smile.

"It is so warm today," said Mayla, and carelessly unfastened the six silver clasps that held the top of her gown together. The pupils of King Valm's eyes grew large and black.

"Beloved sire," said Mayla, her smile like a bright flame in his eyes. "Shall I close the door?"

Valm nodded, and suddenly ceased a long and painful struggle. "Yes," he said. "And shoot the bolt!" He set the birdcage down and, murmuring "Adorable one!" sat as if pushed backwards on a voluminous couch.

As Mayla obeyed him there came the faint chanting of a requiem from Queen Sarene's apartments. With great determination she shut it out, turned, and went eagerly into the outstretched arms of the king.

The Taken had been selected from the palace guard; a new man, a descendant of a Despran enslaved after a long-ago skirmish. He had the nut-brown skin and tight-curled black hair of Despra, and had risen to his present position through his ability and physical strength. He was tall and muscled and proud, and he had been summoned to stand outside Malkar's chamber for the night.

He stayed faithfully awake, and at midnight heard the cry from the queen's chamber. He came to strict attention; the door was flung open and the queen appeared, darkly outlined against dim light, clad in her bedgown. She was distraught, and beckoned him with a shaking hand.

"There is an intruder," she whispered. She wrapped silk around her little body and looked up at him, her eyes wide with fright. The guard drew his sword and stepped forward.

"Permit me, majesty." He went through into the chamber and she followed him, closing the door. He saw her shadow shivering on the wall. For a second he glanced at it puzzled; it was a large, rather shapeless shadow for one so small, then his own merged with it as he strode about the room, poking behind the hangings with his sword.

"No one here, your majesty."

"He was in my bathing suite," she whispered. She was very frightened, for she held on to the sleeve of his tunic and he felt her warmth. He marched into the bathroom. It was lit by a solitary sconce of candles. Something dark and silent moved abruptly in the corner. He lunged forward, the movement evaporated, as, behind his back, Malkar dismissed the shade with a swift flick of her fingers.

"Come out!" roared the young man, and ran towards the source of the movement. Malkar was weeping. He could hear her sobs behind him. "Kill him, oh, I beg you," she cried.

He lit more candles, and the room became bright. The room was windowless; there was nothing. He turned to the queen.

"Your majesty, there's nothing to fear," he said. "It was a trick of the candles." But still she wept, and clutched him round the waist. Without a thought, his arms went round her. "There, your majesty," he said, and swallowed hard. She felt lovely, and her clothing was diaphanous, her perfume like an orange grove. Her gown had parted, she had nothing underneath. This is not right, he thought. Treason! and tried to let her go. It was impossible; he was bound to her like a beast in a thicket.

"Madam," he stammered.

"Stay with me," she breathed. "In case he comes back. I am frightened. You are so strong."

She was the strong one. Her arms were flowers of iron. His Despran blood uttered a tiny atavistic warning, but already she was leading him to her couch, extinguishing candles as she did so.

"I shall not fear the dark if you are with me," she whispered. She lay down, drawing him with her.

In minutes the fatal enchantment began.

She had doused the light for a purpose. There was now a slackening and mottling of her thighs which could not be repaired. But her flesh still had magic and her limbs were serpentine, coiling about the naked gasping body of the guard as he pressed her down upon the furs of the bed, and her mouth was a ravenous flower. Pulsing, she worked him swiftly to a climax, felt his strong heart on the verge of bursting, and reared to take him. But the last tiny vestige of Despran wisdom caught at him, and in the instant before his seed flowed, he withdrew from her body.

The darkness erupted in a titanic fury. A roar came from its belly, like seas in a cavern. The thing he lay upon was black snarling bone, slime and fangs and corruption. He caught one glimpse of the horror and his strength went from him; tentacles emerged from the darkness and netted the flying soul in an agonising grip. The young man's spine snapped; blood poured from all the openings of his body. In the arms of darkness he disintegrated, and joined the howling company of the damned.

She arose, renewed in form and vigour. She shivered with power. On the bed the guard's body was a shell, scarcely recognisable as human. The dwarf would dispose of it easily.

The sanctum was seething with excitement at the recent chase and conquest. The black mirror avidly received the pearl's image.

Show me the worthless one, the ordained sacrifice.

Zairopo is tardy. It is time she was taken from the House of Brides.

There they lie together, she and the Captain. She is exhaustedly asleep after passion. He cannot leave her alone. What power she could have had! He is in thrall to her. And she to him.

She is too happy even to dream. Through the essence of that young guard, we will send her a nightmare.

The only truth was the dream. Lilene sank and floundered in it. Strong-willed, she fought and surfaced to the sound of her own screaming, which emerged no louder than a whimper.

"It's all right, I'm here." Tallis said softly. He turned her over to face him. His voice was strong; he had not slept.

Sweat ran down between Lilene's breasts; her forehead was wet, and the palms of her hands.

"Don't be afraid," he said. "We'll soon be away, and safe."

"Light the lamp."

She was pale, hollow-eyed. "Honyia," she said. "My sister, Honyia. It was terrible. I saw her—she was very small, inside a great shell—the shell had two beating hearts and Honyia was being crushed between them, growing smaller and smaller, dying . . ."

"No, no," he said. "Only a dream. I have them a lot." All the same he felt a frisson down his back.

"She couldn't speak," said Lilene, sitting up. "But she was screaming for me. Ricalpa, I cannot leave Karenia knowing she is in danger." She rose and shivering, wrapped herself in a fur. "My mother hates her. If I leave Karenia without her permission, she will vent her rage on Honyia."

"But you are leaving." Tallis got up too and pulled on his breeches. "Malkar seems not to care what you do. And you're mine. You have no choice."

"She will care if I defect to Taratamia. I shall not leave without Honyia. I intend to go to Karlinkis and fetch her."

He looked at her in disbelief.

"No, and again no," he said. "You must be mad."

"The Draconhood cannot touch me. I am of the Royal House. There is no danger at Karlinkis. I can ride there and fetch Honyia out. No one would notice. I'm going, Ricalpa."

"You will not go, Lilene," he said. "I entirely forbid you. We leave for home today." And he remembered with a sinking heart how Pancora had defied him.

"I would never forgive myself," she said. "If I were happy with you, not knowing what had become of my poor little sister."

"Your half-sister," he said roughly. "And she's older than you anyway."

"She's out of her mind," said Lilene. She was dressing, rolling on her silk stockings. "Ricalpa, if you will not take me to Karlinkis, I shall ask Lieutenant Recansky."

"Recansky obeys my orders."

"Then," said Lilene, looking at him as a warrior might, "I shall go on my own."

They were still arguing when dawn broke. Lilene was adamant, while every instinct urged Tallis to go north without delay. Recansky came knocking at the door.

"Captain, sorry to disturb you. There's a whole lot of people at the gate, waiting to speak with her highness."

Tallis went outside and signalled to the sergeant on the gate. "Let them come in, just the leaders." Three men in soiled and ragged mantles rode through. They seemed nervous, and were armed with swords.

The first man said: "Captain, forgive our intrusion. We want to speak to our beloved leader."

"You're rebels?" said Tallis. "I thought you had all been rounded up."

Lilene had come from the house. She had her cloak on ready for her chosen journey, and heard what the man said.

"Not all of us," he said. "The tide is turning. We have reinforcements now. We are re-arming. Princess." He knelt and kissed the hem of Lilene's cloak.

"May the gods protect you then," said Lilene breathlessly.

"We came for your blessing. We shall soon be on the march. The road is quiet today."

"The road to Karlinkis?"

"Not a soul on it. The cursed Draconhood are holed up in Kalvaria."

"You see? You hear?" She turned to Tallis. "It will be easy. I can fetch Honyia and be with you in days." She addressed the ragged man. "Will you escort me to Karlinkis?"

He bowed very low. "It will be the honour of our life, princess."

There was a long stony silence. Tallis's men fidgeted in the background. Barbel, appearing from nowhere, stood behind Lilene, surveying the rebels with folded arms. Her inscrutable eyes moved to Tallis, then back to the man, on his knees now in homage to Lilene. Then Barbel turned and walked a little away.

"Lieutenant Recansky," said Lilene. "Will you saddle my horse?"

Recansky looked at Tallis, who gave the briefest nod, his face like thunder. He took Lilene aside. "For the last time, beloved."

She gave him a brilliant smile. "All will be well," she said. "We will meet you on the road. In the Forest of Rulen."

The rebel leader had come close. "Yes," he said. "We could bring her to you there, Captain. We'll take good care of her highness. We'll keep her well out of sight of Zairopo."

"The Grand Master?" said Tallis.

"Yes. Him. The old one with six fingers and a bad leg."

Tallis went completely rigid. Then his attention was caught by Lilene. A flush had started at her collar; it washed her neck and face, while her eyes became completely blank, with a kind of terrified dismay. She looked like a criminal tried and sentenced. His heart began painfully to pound. He took Lilene's wrist and drew her away out of the others' hearing. She turned her face away.

"You knew," he whispered. "You knew the man I sought. Don't deny it, don't lie. I see it in your face. You knew, Lilene"

"I knew," she said, in tears. "Long before you told me. You passed close to him in the Forest. I didn't tell you because I knew you would go after him and be killed. If you die, I shall die. You are the other half of my soul. Forgive me."

"You have betrayed me." His eyes were as she had first seen them, cold, almost pitiless. "You held the key. I cannot forgive you. I would never have known but for this rebel man. Now I know, and nothing in this world will stop me. I'm going to Kalvaria. To kill Zairopo."

He turned and left her. To the rebel leader he said: "Are you well armed? What is your strength?"

"I've a hundred men with swords outside the gate, Captain."

"Then I give the princess into your charge. Take every care of her, or answer to me. Return her to me in the Forest."

The man led Lilene's horse to her. "Mount up, princess." She sat astride the horse in her silken breeches and long cloak, her eyes full of tears. She looked at Tallis's back; he was moving towards the house.

"Farewell, Ricalpa," she said.

"The gods protect you," he answered. He did not turn. The men escorted Lilene through the gate, and soon the sound of their horses' hooves faded along the rough track.

He was burning with the excitement of forecasting Zairopo's death, shaking with blood-lust, with anger at Lilene, with the shock of the last few hours. *I am the king's son. I have found the man who killed my father. How could she have held these things from me for so long?*

"That was harsh, Tallis." He turned quickly. Barbel stood behind him, in her haphazard page's gear, accusing eyes peering out from under her cap.

"You never said farewell to her," said Barbel in a queer expressionless voice. "And she loves you. The gods only know why anyone loves you. But they do. What if she never returns?"

He made to walk past her. He was feeling the Lion sword under his hand. It was growing warm, his merciless intent heating it up.

"I saw your light last night."

"The princess had a dream." He drew the sword and slashed at a stray blackthorn impudently growing near the gate. The tough stem parted like butter.

"I had a dream too," Barbel said, "that the Stone Lion had come down and was drinking at the river. That's a bad omen for the Opal House, isn't it?"

"Some say." Tallis was experiencing a sharp pain over his heart. *We could have ridden with them,* he thought, *much of* the way before branching off towards Kalvaria. It's best to go north-west over Treaty Bridge, cut straight across and be in Kalvaria long before they start back towards the Forest. And yet . . .

"You never embraced her," said Barbel, leaving him.

He turned, ran fast to the stable, where his mare, who had been saddled for hours, waited patiently. He leaped aboard her, and set off at a gallop through the gate. He pushed the mare hard, sure-footed over the track where berries and wild rose-hips hung like drops of blood among the thorns, and the cypresses whispered warnings. The bay was an azure badge between the green cliffs to the east, tinged with gold where the sun crept upon it. Birds, disturbed by his swift ride, flew out of the bushes as the mare dashed by; a pair of finches, a magpie, a southern jewel-bird. Squirrels trapezed among the oaks.

They had ridden fast, but he was faster, and he caught them up a few miles along the road, where the carriageway was wider, cutting through meadowlands stacked with sheaves. She was riding in the middle of a close bunch of protecting horsemen, but he barged through the startled ranks and came up close to her. He leaned from his mare and embraced her.

"I love you," he said, breathless. "I forgive you. You're my life. We'll meet again soon."

"I love you, Ricalpa," she said, laughing and crying. "We'll meet at the Lobster."

He rode back slowly, formulating his plans. Returning to the House of Brides, he called Recansky and the others. "Straight to Kalvaria," he told them.

Recansky pursed his lips. "There's not many of us, Captain. Are we to ride into the city?"

"No," said Tallis. "I plan to lure that devil out." The Lion sword jumped in his hand.

There was no mistake. The pearl was losing a very little of its lustre now. It took its light from the belly that housed it, and around the belly's curve could now be seen a faint line like a scar. A line where muscle and tissue were succumbing to age.

Zairopo was slow in keeping his word regarding the release of those to be Taken. Malkar was hungry, and the pitiless deeps were clamouring through the black mirror, rapacious, questing.

The dwarf brought her a post-pubertal boy stolen from a line of the Draconhood's prisoners. The boy came terrified with all he had seen and the promises of torture, and fell into Malkar's arms, weeping with joy.

She took him quickly. His young soul cried and writhed like a snared rabbit, as she drew it out into the void.

The faint line remained.

The boy Timbel had been almost enjoying himself, jouncing on the saddle-bow of Sergeant Mollane, who held him, giving him a sense of safety. The death of his father he had managed to put from him for a while.

Sergeant Mollane was swearing at the pace of the journey. He feared for Tallis's sanity. Sweat was whitening the necks and flanks of the horses which the Captain usually nursed like children. All the men were sweating, filthy with dust. They had scarcely slept or eaten, as the Captain pushed them on. Forests streamed past, little hills fell behind. Only the spare horses, galloping alongside, were relatively unwearied. The cavalcade arrowed out of a copse of trees and on to the plain. There in the distance, a living mausoleum of blackened granite, stood Kalvaria.

Timbel, seeing it, began to weep.

Above the massive walls of the city, the sky hung low, palled with smoke. The standard of the Draconhood, a green shell on a white ground, flapped sluggishly. Even at a distance, there was a stench like roasting pork.

"Don't you cry, my lad," said Sergeant Mollane. "When all this is over, you're coming home with me."

Within sight of the city, Tallis held up his hand and the company jolted to a halt. His thoughts were terrible; the precise tortures he planned for Zairopo were images so gruesome that they seeped into his soul like acid.

Yes. Zairopo must die slowly, but he must know why, must be met face to face. He said to Recansky, "Walk on," and, to Sergeant Mollane, "Get the child away," and the sergeant answered: "One less sword for you, though, Captain." Tallis made a dismissive gesture and the sergeant wheeled his mount and rode westward.

"Captain." One of the men rode from the rear of the company. "I have to report we're missing someone. We must have ridden too fast for them. Young Barbel. And the Karenian fisherman."

Tallis frowned at him abstractedly, then said: "Just as well." He urged his mount forward. "Barbel will catch us up. She can take care of herself. And Alpac's a liability."

They proceeded at a leisurely pace towards the city gate, which was manned by two of the Draconhood's personal guard, in white and green livery and holding pikes. They looked curiously at the ruffianly company, saw their foreign colours, and challenged them.

Tallis dismounted. He saluted the guard as smartly and precisely as if presenting to a commander.

"State your business in Kalvaria." The guard was pale, frigid and lined of face, like all inhabitants of the city.

"We have an urgent message for Colonel Zairopo."

"Enter." The guardsmen lowered their pikes.

"Impossible," said Tallis firmly. "Under the terms of the truce agreement, armed forces are not to enter Kalvaria."

"I never heard that," said the guard grimly, "Who's the message from, anyway?"

"From King Vergon," said Tallis, and swallowed his breath.

The guard's face was not quite hostile. "But you're Tamian. Why should the king . . ."

"There's trouble in Karlinkis. The king wanted swift-messengers. We were available. Under the truce agreement Tamians can be used as couriers. Surely you know that."

Gods speed my lying tongue, and grant these men are as ignorant as they look. There was a very long and agonizing pause while the guard drew together and conferred, glancing towards Tallis's company. Finally the first guard came forward from the gate.

"You say your word is urgent?"

"Vital. And for the colonel's ears alone."

"Wait," said the guard, and disappeared inside the gate. Lieutenant Recansky stared after him, alarmed.

"Captain," he said dubiously, "What's the plan? He'll have Draconhood troops. How do you reckon on snatching him? We could all be cut down in a flash."

Tallis did not answer. He was at that moment, almost insane. The gods have sent this moment to me, he thought. The Lion will strengthen my right arm. I have not been brought to this time to fail my father now.

The guard was tramping past the Square of Burning, through the warrens of streets until he came to the House of Questions. There was a busy air, messengers were going in and out, mounting horses to ride from the city. The guard entered into the passage pervaded by the chill of the underground spring. He entered a large antechamber where Zairopo sat alone, reading through a large pile of depositions from the civil court; traitors, to be handed to his power. He had wine beside him. He no longer got drunk. The wine merely heated up his brain and fed his mania.

"What is it?" he said irritably and the guard relayed Tallis's message.

"I am too busy to talk with Taratamians," he said. "I am summoning a conclave of the Draconhood. All its familiars from the entire realm will be arriving for the questioning and execution of the Princess Royal. This is an important time for our Order."

He could think only of Lilene and the capitulation of her mother. He thought: the day of the Pearl is drawing to a close. All heretics, traitors, rebels and sorcerers will soon be gone from the land. Karenia will be squeezed by the iron fist of the Draconhood into absolute obedience, masses conforming totally to its laws, which will supersede all other laws.

"I cannot see these people," he said. "I have no business with Taratamia. Send them on a wild-boar hunt."

When the guard had gone, Zairopo raised his wine-cup and surveyed his own six-fingered hand. Some say it is the mark of an evil spirit, but no. It is the mark of the cleanser. Torture was going on below as always, at this moment. With absolute dispassion Zairopo thought of the hundreds and hundreds put to the question in his lifetime. And as ever, the wine worked its rancid perverted logic in his brain. I have no wife, no children, no mistress, no catamite. It is not pain that feeds and warms me. It is my closeness to the victim, man, woman and child. The only way I have ever come close, the suffocating ecstasy of closeness; sharing their death. They are my surrogates. Without feeling it, I feel a lifetime of pain in a few hours or days. Their screams are a triumph written on my core. For life is pain . . .

Tallis's mare, distressed by the proximity to Kalvaria, was whirling on the spot when the guard reappeared.

"Captain, Colonel Zairopo is not in the city. He has gone to Incana-on-the-Takk, to round up the last of the traitors who helped your country. You'll have to ride north."

He took up his mute stance again, pike at attention.

Tallis sat still, controlling the mare, his heart pounding. Rage, excitement and disappointment warred in him.

"What now, Captain?" asked Recansky doubtfully.

He thought for a moment, then said: "My plan is unaltered, but for this. We will ride north, after we have met the princess and her sister at the Lobster. I will go to Incana with a few men and kill Zairopo. You will take the women on over the border at Knife Pass. Is that clear, lieutenant?"

"Clear," said Recansky even more doubtfully.

"You will need to keep to the west coast—away from Incana."

"I just pray," said Recansky, "that we don't meet any Despran raiders on the way. It would be goodbye to the princesses."

"Recansky," said Tallis with a twisted smile, "we have more than Desprans to worry about."

He turned his horse and led the party, more slowly this time, towards the road leading to the Forest of Rulen, his rage and death-lust cooled a little; his soul-sickness diminished at the thought of being once more with Lilene.

Three things began to worry Lilene as the ride, equally as fast as Tallis's frantic journey had been, progressed along the Karlinkis road. The first thing was, oddly enough, the thighs of the men who rode around her. Those of the four men closest to her were plump and in one case, actually flabby with fat. The legs of Lilene's rebels were almost without exception, malnourished. Neither did they grip their horses so expertly. Maybe these have fed better of late, she told herself, and tried to be calm.

The second thing was the way the leaders laughed together. And the final doubt came when, a few miles after Treaty Bridge, the party veered towards a waiting barge on the river.

"Don't look so anxious, highness," soothed the ragged leader, as she hovered at the edge of the gangplank. "We stole this craft. All the oarsmen are fugitive slaves, like us."

The men at the oars grinned up at her mirthlessly.

She tried to quiz him as the barge was borne upstream. He answered her courteously enough, drawing his rags close as they stood on the choppy deck, for there was a breeze on the river.

"Do you know how my sister is?"

"Poorly, highness. Afraid, poor lady."

Lilene said: "When will you begin the new uprising? I told the first of your people to wait for better weapons. You know what happened to Solon?"

"Oh, he's alive and well, highness." The leader smiled at her with rotten teeth. "Ready to forge ahead again. Forge—smith—see?" And laughed merrily, and Lilene's heart turned cold at the lie.

She went to the side of the boat, wondering whether to throw herself into the river. There was no escape. She was trapped, overcome by a terror so craven she was ashamed.

And then the first pearly bridge came in sight, and the white towers of Karlinkis and the statues of marine life, among them the Crab of Malkar. She said, in a last desperate effort to change fate: "Should you not go back now? It is dangerous for rebels to enter the city . . ." and the leader smiled, a smile almost of pity. He threw off his rags, as did his companions, just as the barge bumped against the pilings of the royal watergate. They all wore green, and, hoisted suddenly by one of the men at the prow, flew the green and white standard of the Draconhood.

Alpac had been in the company of Barbel for some time. He had ridden beside her, and, since she seemed to have detached herself from Tallis, had conversations with her daily. They made a strange pair, he so nervous and intense, she brusque and unfathomable. He had thought he knew her—strange, cool, tough in her androgynous attire. What he had not expected was this sudden crazed impulse, and the overwhelming power of her will.

"He'll not miss us," she said somewhat bitterly, as they peeled off from the tail of the racing company. "He's on a quest. Ha!" She laughed, a peculiar laugh like a cross jaybird. She leaned in the saddle to grip Alpac's rein more securely. She's mad, he thought, powerless, as his mount bore him away beside her along the Karlinkis road, and the dust from Tallis's company quickly faded in the north-west.

"Stop!" Alpac yelled. Barbel hauled on her reins and both horses screamed and floundered to a halt. "Do you want to get us both killed? Where are we going?"

"Just follow me. Do as I say, Alpac." She turned and glared at him, no longer a grubby female youth, but a warrior, clear-headed, and Alpac's will disintegrated before her, for when he protested, she drew a knife with a small Lion engraved on the handle, and held it to his throat.

"You're with me in this, Alpac," she said. "Or I'll kill your horse and leave you wandering on the road. Then the Draconhood will get you. Have you forgotten you're a chief rebel? I need you with me. We're going to Karlinkis."

"For the gods' love, why?" he cried.

"The princess," said Barbel. Her lips drew back from her teeth in a kind of fury. "Did you see those men she went with? Did you know them?"

"Can't say I did, but I'm a coastdweller. I don't know all the rebel force."

"Did you see their hands?" He shook his head. "That's what warned me. I only thought of it after they'd gone. Their fingers had white bits. They'd worn rings all their lives, and taken them off. What rebel wears a costly ring? They're not real, Alpac. The lady's in trouble."

"I didn't think you cared what happened to her," said Alpac acutely.

"I don't, but he does. Without her he'll be done for. Damn her, and damn him and—oh, come on, Alpac! She's your goddess, isn't she?"

"Yes," he said, troubled. "She was our inspiration. Without her we should never have had the courage to rise."

"And a lot of you would still be alive," said Barbel under her breath, but Alpac cried: "No! it was worth it! Some died, but we'll rise again. And again, until liberation is ours. If she's in danger, I'll die for her. Yes!" And he kicked his horse into a gallop to match Barbel's as they resumed the road to Karlinkis.

They were both thin and light and the horses did not founder. Barbel found by chance a little used way to the city, fringed with thick copses of oak and sycamore, and there by night they slept, concealing their mounts in the trees. They stole fruit and begged bread. They drank from the streams that flowed from the River Braf. The chill nights they spent curled together under a saddle-blanket. Alpac was a dreadful sleeper; he tossed and moaned, and Barbel woke him, cross.

"Stop dreaming, Alpac. Why do folk dream so much?"

"You dream too."

"Not since the Stone Lion dream. That spells a warning for Capashenet."

He sat up under the cold stars and saw her face, ghostly, the whites of her eyes catching the gleam.

"How do you know the way, Barbel? What will you do when we get there?"

"I don't know how I know. Something pulls me. When we get there I shall know what to do." She sounded a little uncertain.

"I'm sorry my dream disturbed you."

"What do you dream? It must be terrible."

"It's not. It's a dream of longing. I dream I'm back in Despra with Gwldas. Ever since my time there, Gwldas has been with me. She dreams of me too. I know that as sure as I'm lying on this thorn. She's part of me."

"Love," said Barbel. "Oh, this love business!"

"Gwldas is black," he said softly. "With a skin like coal, but as if there were a lamp lit inside the coal. She has a sheen like a polished riverstone. She held me close. And more. I've had a pain in my side all my life, and she took it away. She showed me the coils and windings of the life that goes on forever. It's more than love, Barbel."

The next day they reached the south gate of Karlinkis and Alpac grew secretly afraid. Barbel merely jammed her cap over her hair, stuck the knife down the top of her boot, and led Alpac straight to a tavern in a small cobbled court near the city gate.

"The Sea Scorpion," said Barbel, looking up at the swinging sign. "Let's have some beer."

"Have you any money?"

"Tallis pays me a bit. I'm on the strength, remember?"

They entered the shabby tawdry place. A couple of off-duty palace guard sat in one corner over ale. Two crones rested their feet after market. Alone on a bench was a fat sullen youth. He wore the Oyster badge on his tunic, which had seen better days. Barbel sat down near him, nodded at him and put her feet up. Alpac gingerly took a place beside her. The landlord brought them beer. There was a dingy window opposite them, through which the river-light reflected the white towers of the palace. Barbel grinned at the fat youth.

"Will you take a drink?"

He looked surprised, then pushed his tankard for the landlord to fill. Barbel spun a quarter karin on the table.

"Your health," she said. The youth grunted and took a swig.

"You're not from these parts."

"Looking for work," said Barbel. "Me and my old brother here." She squinted at his badge. "You're from the palace. Anything going there, d'you reckon?"

"If you're willing to work for next to nothing. I'm under-under gardener at that madhouse. Things go on there. Folk vanish. Still, it's a living."

He juggled with his empty tankard. "Another?" said Barbel.

"That's civil. Yes. I don't know why I stay. Still, we've had a bit of excitement this past day or two."

"What's that then?" said Barbel carelessly.

"The Princess Royal. Being attainted for treason. The Draconhood will soon be taking her to Kalvaria. I take care to keep my nose clean, I can tell you. Madness, that rebellion. It could never have succeeded. I can't help feeling sorry for the wench, but she asked for it."

"In prison, is she?" said Barbel, yawning to crack her jaws.

"Oh, Malkar the Wise has charge of her until they come. If you look out," he craned towards the window, "you'll see her tower. Shut up there under guard, she is. Poor bitch."

Barbel got up and strolled to the window. The towers of the palace streamed into the heavens, pearly as a dawn sky, solid as rock. From the nearest bridge there was a tiny walkway rambling round the feet of the building. Gargoyles jutted their fierce snouts up the tower; sea-horses, crayfish, mermen. At the very top a single glass window reflected the sky.

"I have brought you here," said Malkar, "so that I may see for myself the nature of your unworthiness."

Lilene stood before her in the room at the top of the tower. Malkar was dressed in black, hung with tiny silver and glass bugles. She wore a thin veil. She was remote and mysterious. Lilene did not know her.

"I am concerned for my sister," she said. "Where and how is Honyia, your majesty?"

Malkar laughed, as if genuinely amused.

"Why, the Thing is as always. Mute. Fed. Playing her dreary music. She is of no account and never will be. As for you, Lilene. I fear that what is left of your life will not be comfortable."

She is waiting for me to plead with her, Lilene thought. She tried to look into Malkar's eyes. The veil made her a shadow.

"Oh, daughter," said Malkar. The veil quivered with the suspicion of a sigh. "That accursed, meddling Andine! What a legacy she deprived you of! You could have had the world's power between your thighs. The power of a thousand years. We are darkness, you and I. But light was let into your darkness. You are nothing. You have nothing. Only death."

"I have love," said Lilene.

"There is no such thing. Only lust, and power, and control. These are the imperatives. All the rest is illusion. You are the blood-price now. We shall not meet again. You will be ended. I shall remain."

Lilene said steadily: "Pride is part of the illusion, Malkar. You forget that one day you too must die."

Then Malkar lifted the veil, and Lilene saw how her beauty was diminished. Its radiance had lost its edge. The queen smiled.

"Oh, child," she said softly, "I have been dead many times. I have learned the secrets of the grave."

A shudder ran over Lilene's body. She stared at the queen. Malkar's outline changed. It became unstable, like a horizon under earthquake. It lost all semblance of humanity. Blackness stood there, shapeless, volatile, exhibiting a power as blind and primitive as the birth of planets from chaos. Then the veil was quickly dropped again, on the edges of something so terrible that it threatened sanity and life, and the small slender queen turned and left the room.

Lilene sat down, shaking, on the bed. Apart from the bed there was no furniture in the room. She had been there some days, and the room was familiar as a bad dream. She heard the guard changed outside the door. The voices were low and weary. Finally one guard was left alone.

Lilene went to the one window, gazing at the river far below, the huddle of houses on its further bank, the end of the bridge which led to freedom. She quelled the terror that threatened to destroy her, crushing the desire to tear at the stone walls, and pressed on the window. It opened on autumn mist, thickening as the sun went from the land. The mist enhanced her imprisonment. It began to cut off her life.

I regret nothing. From that first moment, out hunting in the forest, when I saw the landlord's bailiffs descend upon a family so poor they could hardly afford to eat, let alone pay their rent. I sat on my beautiful horse and watched while they whipped them out of doors. One of the women had a newborn crying in her arms, birth-blood fouling her shift. They pushed her down into the red mud, almost the colour of the blood. Then they fired the dwelling, took away the lean pig which was the family's prospective winter sustenance. And they laughed. They were enjoying it. The sights would not leave me. And when I learned of the treatment received by the slaves, my heart swelled with grief. I was ashamed, of my birthright, my indolence, the food in my belly. At first I acted to assuage my guilt, then I became one with them. I regret nothing, except, most bitterly, that the cause has failed.

And oh, Ricalpa. Gods keep you. May you be victorious over Zairopo, but how can you succeed against that malevolence? I wish I were fighting with you. I wish I could raise power.

I could try to raise the Crystal Lion, but my soul is too crazed. She closed her eyes, tried to work as Andine had shown her, building the Lion from the frail ether. Terror had built a wall against serenity. She opened her eyes, saw the mist drifting into the room, redolent of the river.

Alpac stood shivering in the mist. The chilly fog grew up from the river, blocking out the palace from the feet up. The two horses he held chewed their fog-damp bits. Condensation dripped from the sign of the Sea Scorpion. Alpac stared at Barbel, his eyes wide with disbelief.

"It's impossible," he said. "You'll be killed. Or you'll be caught. It can't be done."

"Oh yes, it can," she said. "Don't you tell me what to do. You're not Tallis."

"Since when have you ever obeyed Tallis?" said Alpac gloomily.

"Gods, this fog. What an ally! Alpac, stay here." She pointed to a long low building whence came the smell and sound of horses. "Take the nags in there and wait. You'll need a lantern. Steal one. Look out for who comes. It will either be me, or that love of his life. Anyway, Alpac old friend. I'm off."

"Gods keep you, Barbel," he said, shivering harder. "I'll go mad, waiting."

"When she comes, make all speed. If you let us down, I'll kill you. So be ready. Think of something to calm you."

"I'll think of Gwldas." Suddenly his shivering ceased. Gwldas stood before him, coming through the mist, ebony with a light beneath her skin and in her eyes. She vanished, smiling, nodding. Warmth flowed over him.

The fog embraced Barbel. Alpac and the horses disappeared from her sight. There was the ghostly outline of a Taratamian grain barge, moored on the wharf, her crew's voices sounding hollow in the fog.

She went steadily towards the palace, crossing the bridge, her scuffed boots making a quiet moist sound. She turned abruptly left and stepped on to the narrow walkway running alongside the river. She looked up at the tower; it seemed insubstantial in the murk. There were jutting stones at the base, almost in the form of a staircase. The guard's footsteps were going further away as he patrolled the perimeter. Barbel set her foot on the lowest stone projection.

There were handholds and Barbel went upwards like a fly, her feet finding niches and outcrops in the wall. She began to sing in a tiny voice, like the buzzing of a fly.

> *"My father was a mountain man,*
> *I can do it, yes I can,*
> *My dad he was a mountain man."*

She rose higher, and her head and shoulders began to emerge above the mist. To her left were the tips of spires and temples. She tried to go faster. Her foot slipped, and she hung on a ledge for seconds, her shin-bone grazed by the wall, her heart in her throat, before wriggling her toes into a crevice. She glanced over her right shoulder and saw houses and the inn, like the dwellings of dolls. Sweat dripped from her forehead; her palms grew treacherous with it. And now here was a dreadful hiatus in the foot-and-handholds. A blank space of wall, with a solitary projection high above her head.

Holding on to a shallow ledge with her left hand, she stretched up to the limit, standing on her toes on a round slippery jutting stone. She caught the projection in her fingers and, legs dangling, levered herself up. With her raw pounding chest scraping the wall, she pulled herself level. A gargoyle's worn stone eyes gazed into hers. It was a sea-horse, and she clung for moments to the bosses on its arched neck. She went on up, her foot slipping several times. She did not look about her. Sweat tracked the dirt on her face, her legs burned. The gargoyles were numerous now; she wound her hands round their stone ears and horns and noses. One moved under her hand, and she came near to falling in that instant. She was almost exhausted.

One thought came clear: the princess could never climb down this way. Even I couldn't. And then her head bumped against the underside of the windowsill.

Barbel heaved herself up over the sill and sat on it. Now she was conscious of the dreadful drop below over which her legs dangled. Her stomach heaved. She pulled at the half-open window so that it swung wide. Lilene had her back to the window, her hands raised as if in prayer. She turned, her mouth fell open. Then she rushed to pull Barbel into the room.

Barbel fell to the floor and was bruised. She glared up at Lilene, who whispered: "What—?" and no more. Barbel said firmly, rising: "I'm your saviour, princess. You're going to be grateful to me one day."

Lilene, horrified, looked out of the window and down, shaking her head.

"Yes, I climbed," said Barbel crossly. "In the fairy tales, it's always the handsome prince. This time it's me, the village idiot."

She tore off her big cap and her hair cascaded, a dirty gold. "Strip," she commanded.

"It's an old trick, but it may work. You're going to be a page, Lilene." It was the first time she had so addressed her, and it gave her pleasure. "I'm going to be the Princess Royal. You're going out of here as me."

"They'll show you no mercy," said Lilene.

"For the gods' love," said Barbel furiously. "Take off your clothes. Let me dirty your face," she said, as Lilene dressed in the shabby breeches and boots, the jerkin, the cap. Barbel smeared filth and cobwebs over Lilene's cheeks and forehead. Then she struggled into the princess's clothes, raked her fingers through her own hair and got into the bed. She arranged herself, face to the wall, her hair spread over the coverlet:

"Put on the belt," Barbel said, her voice muffled by the covers. "Mind the knife in it, it's sharp. If you have to kill anyone, go for the vein behind the ear. They die quiet that way."

"Oh, Barbel," said Lilene, almost in tears.

"Now you're off duty. Go straight to the Sea Scorpion, then ride north with Alpac. I'll make out you've gone back to Brides. Now shout for the guard." And she told her tersely, what to say.

Lilene rapped on the door.

"What is it, highness?"

"I wish to be alone. Release my servant."

"Didn't know you had one." He opened the door, saw the figure in the bed. The slovenly creature walked out past him.

Lilene went quietly down the stairs, her heartbeat choking her. She passed through the guard in silence, folding her arms about her as if cold. The guard ignored her but she thought she felt their curious aftergaze as she went down the lowest flight of steps to a postern beside the watergate. Someone called after her, and she quickened her steps.

High above, Barbel lay in the bed. She was cold, with the cold of the grave, but even while she trembled, she smiled a little into the pillow.

The Crystal Lion hovered on the edge of the world. It had surged at Lilene's summoning, then drawn back unbanished, fragmenting into a thousand potent entities scattered throughout the chaos of the time.

For some time it stayed around the palace, where it had had its current incarnation. It merged with and prolonged the heavy mist. Its crystalline atoms took on the colours of blue and pink and silver, invisible to all save those locked in deep trance. It swooped down to touch the grain-barge on the wharf. It lulled the guard outside the tower room into slumbrousness; it dulled the sight of those who brought food to the figure in the bed.

Vergon found himself maddened by unfathomable pinpricks of its power. He sat, his body crammed with noxious stimulants, his heart with old resentments against Malkar. Surrounded by meaningless glories, he muttered threats and strategies. I am the king.

The silvery threads sought out Honyia. Neglected, doggedly mastering the lyre and lute, she sat surrounded by a haze of crystal filaments, and saw a very little of their colours. Crystal invaded her forced tranquillity, crept beneath her tongue, stilled by water. And she opened her mouth and sang, one soft note, and like a swan in death, no more.

And there was enough power left in the Lion for it to go with Alpac and Lilene, skimming along with them on their wild ride north, blessing them with its vapours, giving them a sixth sense so that they hid themselves in a dense copse of spruce as the Draconhood came thundering by. Alpac had wept nearly all the way, primarily for the fate of Barbel. He tried to speak of it to Lilene.

"I can't bear to think of it, Alpac. May the Lion protect her."

Standing listening to the dying hoofbeats of the Draconhood, she said: "They are on their way to fetch me from the palace."

"No," said Alpac. "It is part of the chapter from the north. They are gathering at Kalvaria for—for your execution. I heard talk of it outside the tavern."

"They'll be disappointed, Alpac. Brave Alpac."

"Oh, princess. Are we nearly there?"

As he spoke, the face of Gwldas swam before him. Smiling, a little anxious, she vanished, becoming one with the black spruce-branches. I love you, he thought. In the last life, in this life, in the next. Protect us all.

It was one of the more sharp-witted guards who, looking into the princess's room, noted that all was not as it should be. Barbel had been hot, cloistered for so long under the bedcovers, and had stuck her feet outside to cool them. Her feet were filthy, calloused with marching, and they gave her away.

The guard rushed to sound an alarm which brought Malkar aloft. She was accompanied by the dwarf; he hopped and scrambled behind the queen. He ran to the bed and came eyeball to eyeball with Barbel, who laughed in terror at the sight of him.

The guard dragged Barbel out of bed. She stood barefoot before Malkar. She realised she was face to face with a legend. She did not show her fear. She saw the lids of Malkar fall over the bright eyes; two second smooth white eyes that saw everything.

"Tell me, creature," said Malkar in her childlike voice. "Where is the princess?"

"Standing before you," said Barbel. "That's a damned uncomfortable bed. Don't you know me, Mother?"

The dwarf was walking round Barbel. He twitched up her clothes to look at her legs. Barbel kicked him in the belly. He mewed crossly.

"How long has she been gone?" asked one of the guard.

"Years," said Barbel. "She'll be safe now, at the nunnery."

Malkar said nothing for a moment. Then, "It is of no importance. She is under sentence of death. She will find no safety anywhere." Her sparkling amber eyes, revealed again, fixed on Barbel. Malkar was puzzled by the sacrifice.

"What a heroine we have here," she murmured. "What do we do with it? The Draconhood? Treason's here, certainly, and yet . . ." She looked down at the dwarf.

"I have never rewarded you, Quarl," she said. "Would you like a plaything of your very own?"

The dwarf opened his mouth wide, showing a flailing blue tongue and a row of pointed teeth.

His appearance was enough to make stronger than Barbel quail. He flexed his long strong arms which almost trailed on the ground. She saw that his one eye grew halfway down his cheek like a suppurating red ruby. He began to chuckle and rub his satin crotch where an enormous bulge was growing. Drool oozed over his malformed lower lip and ran from his nose. Barbel took a step backwards.

"Yes," said Malkar. "Creature, I am going to give you to Quarl. He likes girls. He likes boys. He likes dogs. He likes anything with a hole in it."

The dwarf tittered. He stumped on his little legs towards Barbel, crooning. She could smell him, the miasma of stagnant ponds. She turned her head towards the window. Cold air was rushing in. The guard were standing back, in line with Malkar, as Quarl stalked his prey. And in the second before he reached her, Barbel moved. She took three running steps towards the open window with its mighty drop and went through it like a bird in flight. The fog rose to embrace her fall.

"Love," said Lieutenant Recansky out loud. "It's a terrible thing."

"Lieutenant sir?" said the sergeant.

"It addles a man," said Recansky wearily. "Makes him incautious. Unwary." He glanced up the dark stairs. "Get on with your dinner, sergeant."

Obediently the sergeant dug into his leathery beef stew. He called in vain for ale. The landlord was on the brink of collapse from the weight of harbouring the fugitive princess. There were no other guests in the Lobster; the long tavern-room was occupied by Tallis's small tired company. They ate unenthusiastically, or stood at the window looking out on to the starless and peaceful night.

The sergeant spat out gristle. "I wish we had our little cook back," he said to a companion.

They had not been told the full story. Their one desire was to leave the forests and plains of Karenia. Their uniforms were smirched, one or two of their horses were lamed. No longer did they look like a detachment of the smart Red Royals. Idly buffing his sword-hilt, Recansky said: "We'll be on the homeward road tomorrow. Back to civilisation." He looked up again to the upper chambers and frowned.

"Hold me, Ricalpa," said Lilene. "Hold me forever. Don't let me go."

He held her with all his strength. She stood in her filthy clothes, briars in her hair. He could not stop her trembling. She had the smell of Barbel about her, all the meals that Barbel had cooked, the smell of stables and horses and sweat.

"She gave me her life," she whispered.

"She gave me mine, for you are mine. Ah, don't weep, my sweet one. I've got you now."

"I've seen some dreadful things," said Lilene softly. "Something I could hardly believe. My mother . . ."

"Not now, Lilene. It will keep until we are home. Tomorrow we must put on all speed. Where are the Draconhood?"

"Converging on Kalvaria." She gave a shuddering laugh. "To watch me burn."

"Pray gods then that Zairopo is still at Incana, for there I shall face him and end him. Slowly." She could not see his cruel, implacable expression. "My darling. Be still."

"Poor Barbel," she whispered, and he answered: "I thank the Lion for Barbel. I curse myself for letting you out of my sight."

"Without you, I'm nothing. My life began with you."

Her eyes were calmer, though her face was sullied with dirt and tears. She said: "Ricalpa. I beg you. Do not go after Zairopo. One day, his wickedness will overtake him. Don't risk your life, not now."

"I have sworn," he said harshly. "Let it be, Lilene."

He lit the lamp. It illuminated his sword, propped at the wall. Lilene stretched out and touched it.

"It's warm!" she whispered.

"Yes. My anger warms it. It burns to find lodging in Zairopo."

"Barbel made me take her knife. I hid it." She turned to show him the back of her head. Within the great cluster of braids the knife was slotted, a mere flash of branzel in the gold.

"That's clever. Let me take it now, you may hurt your

head."

He began to unbraid her hair.

"I haven't even kissed you yet."

"Not yet. I'm too dirty. I stink."

"I don't care. My love."

"Let me bathe first."

He called down the stairs and presently the landlord's daughter came with a large tin bath, toiling up and down with jugs of water just off the fire.

Lilene stood naked in the water. He washed her face tenderly. He washed the amber stem of her neck, where the little gold lion lay, the nape where the thick sunny fall divided; he washed the straight square of her shoulders and with great delicacy her beautiful breasts; he laved her back and buttocks with vervain soap and soft water, and sponged her golden cleft. He washed her belly and legs, her feet and her strong fragile hands. Her apricot skin with its invisible down became a willowy lamplit amphora, the flood of long hair like living light. His washing of her was a priestly rite, the desire it evoked its true amen.

He dropped the cloth and pulled her against him, dripping, soaking his shirt and breeches. He lifted her from the tub and kissed her as he had never kissed her before, as if for the first or the last time. She closed her eyes; her head fell back. He seized a towel and dried her, hurrying, feeling desire chasing him to the point of madness. She clung round his neck, her feet leaving the floor as he took her to the bed. In less than a moment she felt his weight upon her.

This bed, she thought. Here, I lay nightlong, wanting him, like the pain of death. Here is the miraculous coming, the circle fully joined. Now. As he took her, penetrating her unfalteringly deep, she uttered a tumultuous, birdlike cry.

She was like a flame in his arms, burning up and down, crying out in concord with his rhythms, while he groaned incoherently into her neck and arched his body to take her lips, her throat, her breast into his mouth. He was not gentle; he drove at her womb until she rose against him in full flight, a searing celebration of the springing rush of his seed, a consummation that had death and near-death within it, remembering fear and doubt and longing.

They lay still together.

After a while she said: "I am your wife."

"You are my wife in truth, and more than that, we must marry at once. I accept now that I am Capashenet. I am fitted to marry you, my love, my Lilene. Prince Ataret will marry us. If I am the unlucky heir to the Taratamian throne, I can command it. Tomorrow, we must ride fast for Tamia."

He looked at her where she lay, her body marked and slick from passion.

"My darling," he said. "It's getting late. We must be ready to leave very soon. We must be away before the dawn."

A black nightingale sat outside the window. It had a white poll.

"My darling," he said again. He watched her eyes, blurred and distant as if, awake, she dreamed.

The bird opened its beak and sang very sweetly, almost a string of liquid mystical words. Its voice wafted over the bed. Lilene was filled by a hot darkness.

"It's time to go, my love," he said. "We mustn't delay. We should leave now."

"Not yet," she whispered, and reached for him. "Again, Ricalpa."

And her arms were round him and she began to kiss his body, her lips and tongue over his heart, his ribs, his belly; she worked her will on him, rose on him, slid over him with her rapt and glowing face and her rain of golden hair and he was lost.

Recansky, playing a half hearted game of bugle with a drowsy sergeant, looked up towards the stairs again and frowned.

"It's late."

The sergeant yawned. "How late is it?"

"It must lack only a couple of hours until dawn. Gods, this is a long night."

"I remember longer. Once, when we were holed up in ambush towards Kardespra and the enemy never showed . . ."

"Quiet," said Recansky. "I heard something."

The door creaked open.

The landlord's daughter, who was serving those awake with ale, almost jumped out of her shoes. The pale face of Alpac appeared round the doorframe.

"What are you creeping about in the dark for, fisherboy?" demanded the sergeant.

"It was cold in the stable," said Alpac, trembling. "Can I come by the fire?"

Alpac was still in his dirty travel clothes. His spirits were at their lowest ebb. He mourned for Barbel. He hated being in the forest. There he had seen again the bodies of his comrades, blackened now by weather, and ribboned by scavengers. Above all he thought with a passionate longing of Gwldas. He had stayed in the stable to weep alone.

The dawn showed as the faintest pink shadow on the dingy window. From far away came a soft thunder.

Dressed for the road, Tallis and Lilene descended the stairs.

"Time we were away," said the Captain. "All present, lieutenant?"

"All present and correct, sir."

"Pay the landlord," said Tallis, and Recansky took a fistful of karin and laid them on the table. One of them rolled to the floor and sped under the window. Alpac bent to retrieve it from a dark crevice which was suddenly illuminated by a blazing light, in thunder which was not thunder but the hooves of many horses, in a dawn that was no dawn but the light of a hundred blazing torches surrounding the inn.

"Sweet merciful gods, they've found us," said Recansky. Lilene let out one muted cry. They came, thick dozens armed with swords and sabres, breaking the door off its hinges. The fighting arm of the Draconhood, mailed beneath their green robes and hoods. They flooded the room.

Tallis's company went for their weapons. Disorganised, surprised, they were swiftly disarmed, backed up against the wall. Lieutenant Recansky sprang on a table and struck at the leader's head, but two others pulled him down.

Tallis moved back, pushing Lilene behind him on to the lowest stair. The Draconhood had formed ranks across the room. The pommel of the Lion sword grew hot in Tallis's hand. We're lost, he thought. All for the sake of one hour! What possessed us?

"Lay down your weapon, Captain. We're here for the princess. No harm will come to you or your men. We have no quarrel with Taratamia."

Tallis answered softly, but he was heard to the back of the room.

"Take her then, through my blade." He drew his sword, gleaming in the torchlight.

"Put up, Captain," said the leader. "We are on a mission for our Holy Order. Stand away."

Tallis's face was like a deathmask. He said: "Is Zairopo among you? Let him come forward now."

"The Grand Master is at Kalvaria. He waits to preside over the trial." He bowed to Lilene. "You have been indiscreet, madam. I was present the moment you announced your destination. This very inn." He took a step nearer.

Tallis raised his sword to eye level, and measured along it with a look. "One by one, come forward," he said softly. "You'll not lay a glove on her." And felt the sword grow and blossom like a live thing.

The Draconhood leader stepped forward, sword in hand, and Tallis moved to meet him, his weapon slanted obliquely to deflect the thrust, his gaze aimed at the man's heart.

The black nightingale tapped its beak on the window. It emitted a piercing intricate call, like some language from another world.

The Lion sword went cold as ancient embers in the Captain's hand. It iced the nerves in his fingers so that his grip ebbed to nothing. The sword dropped to the floor; he stared in disbelieving horror as the Dracon picked it up and handed it to a lieutenant.

"No more talk," said the Dracon. "Will you come with us fittingly, princess, or do we have to handle you?"

Tallis felt for Lilene's hand. He covered her with his body.

"Touch her and you'll regret it. She is my betrothed. She is Karling. She is royal."

"The Draconhood is not concerned with who she is. The Grand Master's aim is to clean this realm. And you will die, for thwarting us." He turned to those behind him. "Take her."

Lilene stepped out. "I'll come alone," she said. "Let these brave men here be." And she tugged her hand from Tallis's and walked into the midst of the Draconhood.

"No!" Tallis shouted. "I am coming with her. Where she goes, I go." The Dracon narrowed his eyes. "So be it," he said. "As her ally, the Grand Master will find you of significance. Arrest him."

They bound Tallis with ropes. Lilene they did not trouble to bind. Tallis went through the ranks behind her, seeing her head with its golden braids held high. He passed Recansky bleeding on the floor, who muttered: "I'm sorry Captain, gods speed . . ." and saw his men standing weaponless against the wall. He also saw the Draconhood had Alpac, in chains.

"This is the runaway rebel we lost, sir," said one, and the leader nodded.

The three of them, closely guarded within the green mesh of their captors, were taken out into the dawn, coming up peach and pearl. The Draconhood were in and out of the stable quickly, taking the horses belonging to Tallis's company, loading them with weapons belonging to Tallis's men. And they mounted the Captain, Lilene and Alpac on three horses roped to others, and thus turned south for Kalvaria, and the Place of Burning.

Tanzin, as was his habit, was working into the night, which was dark and overcast. He was a student, poor and self-taught, without prospects as such, for the universities at Karlinkis were the province of the aristocracy. He felt he owed himself to be learned in logic and philosophy. He was tall and thin, with long black hair.

The City Crier called midnight. Tanzin squinted down through candlelight at his third-hand dog-eared book. He had begun a thesis on occultism versus logic, and its ramifications made him yawn.

A shadow stole across the rooftops and poured itself through his window, landing softly at his feet. It jumped up on his table, startling him.

It was a magnificent black cat, well-fed, unlike the starving animals of Karlinkis, with a luxuriant pelt. It had a snow-white breast and a white bar between its ears. Its eyes were amber candles.

Tanzin admired it for a moment, then wrote: "Yet the result of the work of a witch, whether by the usage of herbals or incantations can be explained as the direct result of psychological threat. If a man for example is aware of a witch's influence upon his potency, he will be affected accordingly, not by her but by his own belief, and . . ."

A paw like a black puffball darted out and twitched the pen from his hand.

"Oho!" he said, into the steady golden gaze. "So you want to play." He shuffled his papers into a pile. "It's bedtime, anyway."

He was not displeased when the cat leaped on to his little bed. It arranged itself to maximum comfort in the angle of his hip, and began to purr. Its purr resonated throughout the room, dark and mysterious, like a sea-shanty of long ago.

"You can stay" he told it sleepily. "It's nice to have your company. But I can't feed you."

He blew out the candle and began to dream of witches. The Draconhood were burning one. It was not a pleasant dream, with screaming and heat. The heat broke through his dream and he felt the weight and pressure of the cat, now with him beneath the blanket. Half awake he turned to it for comfort. Its fur was gone, replaced by soft flesh smooth as paper. Little feet curved about his ankles, damp perfumed breath invaded his mouth. His heartbeat crashed against his ribs and his whole being rose to embrace what lay with him. The purring continued, translated into low-voiced endearments.

Cats can see in the dark. The thing that was Malkar reserved that privilege. As Tanzin stormed within her, she enjoyed his slenderness and black hair. Had he some Tamian blood? At the moment when she trapped the bewildered soul, her thoughts were of another. The Draconhood had *him*.

In this particular matter, Malkar had been cheated, and a moment's anger made her vicious with the soul.

The Taken was sentient of its agony and howled as it was sucked into Malkar, into the pearl, its shredded remains whirling down, down into the maelstrom of the damned. As darkness claimed it, a fragment of logic remained. Yes, there are witches. And they are angels . . . compared to this . . . the soul plummeted into a black eternity.

The cat surveyed him: a little bloody froth lay on his lips where he had fought her. This Taking had been pleasurable. How much more so it would have been, with Zairopo's captive.

Filled with the cream of power, the cat leaped elegantly through the window and streaked across the rooftops. The dawn shuddered at its passing.

Zairopo had been drinking all day and all the previous night and the day before that. Wine kept the dark gate at the base of his brain open, whence were transmitted the grandiose notions of pain and power. Zairopo had not ridden out from Kalvaria since his interview with Malkar. As he called admittance to Goloram, his second-in-command, he arranged his green sleeve carefully over his deformed fingers. Goloram came in slightly harassed.

"What is your report, Brother Dracon?"

"A courier from the Eastern lodge. The Brothers there are a few days away and ride towards us. Then the conclave is complete."

Zairopo said: "I do not want to start the proceedings until all are gathered. This is a momentous time for us, Goloram."

"I think we should be congratulated, Grand Master, you especially, for the capture of the princess."

He waited in vain for a personal accolade. Zairopo merely said: "Her execution, Goloram. Do you realise that this is the first step in our supremacy over the House of Karling? How long have our prisoners been with us?"

"Three days, colonel"

"And no questioning has begun without my sanction?"

"The princess has been lightly interviewed. Certain mental coercion is being applied. She betrays nothing and no one."

"She will before she dies. What of the rebel fisherman? I understand he was one of the prime movers, one of the first to rise."

"He has been tortured, but only to the first degree. He is silent. This Captain Tallis, on the other hand, vows to lose his life for the pleasure of seeing you dead, Grand Master."

"He's just another terrorist," said Zairopo, but his eyes became thoughtful. He refilled his wine-cup.

"Continue," he said. "Apply the mental pressures to fill in the gaps in our knowledge. Where the arms came from, where was the first pocket of resistance. And issue a proclamation to all townspeople and those in the environs. They are to come when summoned to the Place of Burning. I want everyone to witness that not even the greatest in the realm is proof against our Holy Order. I want the burning cage suspended in the centre of the square. Slow timber is to be used. This must be an unforgettable spectacle."

"And the rebel fisherman?"

"Drowning would be appropriate. He is a small fish." Zairopo laughed at his own wit.

"And the Captain?"

"He was certainly involved. He shall also be burned. Let him witness her end first. Go now. We should not have long to wait for the Eastern lodge to arrive. Then all our chapters will be complete."

A dark unease hung over the Palace at Karlinkis. It touched all within the walls. In Malkar's bower, the tall mirrors had been draped with veiling. Below, the dark chamber boiled with chaos.

The dwarf, bitterly disappointed, went down to the riverside in hopes of finding Barbel's body to play with, but the autumn tides were gathering and the current was strong. He found a bewildered boy and brought him to Malkar, setting him down beside her in the dark chamber, on the bed covered with the skins of men.

Although only one of the spire-shell lanterns burned, there was enough light for the boy to see that Malkar was not quite what she once was. He showed a little reluctance to surrender, and for that the darkness punished him.

She kissed him into agony; she caressed him with torments. In her arms he saw the deeps and the damned while she held him on the razor edge of fulfilment and death. She tore him asunder with her terrible love, and he wept and bled. Demons sucked at his phallus, demonic forces squeezed his testes of the last drops of his soul; he died crying, pleading, "I love you!" to the thing of bone and decay that held him, and the pearl was fuelled into a glow.

Show me the prison, darkness.

Here is the worthless one, grown thin from a jail-fast. She fears the fire, most dreadfully.

Here is my Captain, half out of his mind with despair.

Here is my servant, Zairopo, drinking and waiting, while the Truth Doctor sharpens his tools.

Show me the king, the wastrel, Vergon. He is of little use. He burns with resentment. He has no idea what his mother is. He is a grain of dust. He has no part in our future, no more than his doomed sister.

Show me the Thing, Honyia. Mute, keeping to her quarters. She has mastered her music and can play a tune. Lord Ing's son, Dogmar, is with her. He is handsome! He loves music and passing her chamber, hears her chords and arpeggios. He has the sense to come on days when no one is about. He thinks it a pity she is witless. One day she shall serve us as the dwarf serves us, but lower than the dwarf. When our Great Change comes again. When shall that be?

Ah. Kalvaria. My Captain is being beaten! Men are sent into his cell. They beat him senseless. His ribs break. He revives, bleeding and half-naked. "You should take lessons from Brother Sundew, boys." He grins at them through his pain. How strong his soul is! it whets the appetite anew. How rapturously we would have fed upon it! Now, when he dies, that soul will live on, in the Far Lands; that soul! it should have been ours by right.

There are little marks under Malkar's eyes, and a faint crease running from below the cherry mouth.

The Great Change draws near, Maelikali.

After many days, Gwldas found herself alone with the High King. She had saved her moment until her dance was right; she came before him trying hard to quell her urgency. The High King's heart ran slow and judicial, and was not stirred by incontinent petitioners.

It was important that he should be alone when she drifted, shadowy, into the meadhall. The queens were not jealous, but no one could dance like Gwldas, and they might have wanted, vainly competitive, to join in. The only other person present was Kwm, the blind musician. His harp was ivory with gold strings and on its high prow perched a sleek pitch-black raven, the same colour as Gwldas. Every time Kwm's fingers drew forth a high note, the raven preened and mantled its feathers in a static dance of its own.

Brwcwch sat easily on his throne, brown-eyed, faun--eyed, in the great framing of antlers. He had a dish of ripe plums to hand; as he watched Gwldas dance he bit into a fat bronze jewel and its juice washed his fingers. The harpist played rhythmically, with a heavy accented lilt that led the steps of Gwldas as she danced before the throne. She was bare but for an emerald cincture and a short fringe of embroidery at her loins. She had anointed her hands and feet with red aromatics and in her navel was a star.

Gwldas danced, a piece of shining night invading the bright morning. Sea wind washed through the window arch, bearing the cry of gulls. Gwldas used her body as a storyteller. Her body was gleaming obsidian, lit cinnabar from within as the fires in a volcano. She swung and lifted her taut round belly and hips, fetched glories and sorrows from the air with her long fingers and arms. Her feet leaped and landed without sound. Her eyes, black within the long brilliant whites, never left the king. She took him into dreams of far lands and near lands, the hot country of the body, and strewed before him the blossoms of her soul. She weaved back and forth the spirals and circles of life after life. She gathered up death, knitting it into the coils of eternity. She cast off her small garment and as she danced opened her sex with her fingers to show the king her holy power. Finally she fell soundless and prone before him, her black head raised like a cobra, her eyes fixed on his.

"Erun blesses your dance, sweet Gwldas," he said. The harpist took up a little drum and tapped it like a heart beat, token that he covered a private audience.

"My dance was for you, beloved," said Gwldas. She did not need to tell him what was in her heart, but she could not read his answer.

"Closer," said Brwcwch, and she rose and came to his arms, lifting herself astride his lap as he indicated. He stroked her shaven head, admiring its beautiful shape. Beneath her vulva she felt the stir of his awesome potency.

"Love," she said softly, "I am full of love."

She looked deep into his nut-brown eyes with their eternal spark of war. She felt the risen serpent beneath her begin to slide into her body, a swooning touch. For all his prodigious dimensions Brwcwch never hurt his women; he was Erun, the antlered god, protector and cherisher even in his mating. Gwldas let her body rejoice, keeping her mind clear.

"So. Love," he breathed. He did not move within her. He took a ripe plum and bit it, letting the juice run like blood between her breasts. He bent and licked the juice away, a stag at a pool.

"Love is everywhere," he said. "You do not need to look for it, black flower, in Karenia."

"I have been talking with Mervhu," she said. "He sent spies lately through Karkis to the border. He learned . . ."

"I know all this." He stirred faintly inside her. He broke another plum and let the juice run down her face, licking it from her eyes. "Mervhu told me of the Draconhood's latest coup."

"They have my lover," said Gwldas. "They will kill him."

"Yes, the little Alpac," said Brwcwch softly. He closed his eyes, pressed far upwards into her, and she caught her breath, pulsing upon him with tiny movements. "Everyone must die, Gwldas, die to live. And you are young. There will be many more lovers, as we are lovers in this moment."

His breath was quickening. She bit her lips, leaned back her head, said faintly, "It is more. He was with me before, where I came from."

"And where did you come from, my Gwldas?" He laughed softly, moving faster inside her. "Ruva? You told me once, Ruva. It is uninhabited."

"Before that," and she gasped. "Alpac was with me when I was cutting cane, in a hot land. He was my baby, six months old. I left my machete on the ground and he fell upon it. He was wounded in the side and died in my arms. When he came to me again, the baby's wound still hurt the man. I healed him. I owe him a life."

The king thrust upwards and Gwldas cried out, but not in pain. The seed of Brwcwch splashed her womb and ran down, sticky as the juice of the plum. Gwldas looked at his smiling lips. There were tears in her eyes. She dismounted from his lap very slowly.

"Is your answer no, beloved?" she whispered. The harpist stopped tapping his little drum. The raven clattered away into the rafters of the meadhall.

"It is no time for us to interfere," said Brwcwch, drawing his robe together. "Sweet Gwldas. The time will soon come when we will take Karenia and heal all her evils. What must be will be. My thanks for the pleasure, for the dance. Erun bless you, black jewel."

She turned from him quickly so he should not see her tears, for they would hurt him. She was not finished. She left the hall and went straight to Mervhu's dwelling, the largest in the city, carved stags round the wattle door, fine horses at the palisade. She donned a cloak before entering, fastening the great round brooch at her throat. She passed through the round outer chamber, where Mervhu's pregnant wife sprawled disconsolately on a couch. Two tiny greyhounds frisked about her. She groaned softly as one landed on her belly.

"Do you well, lady?" Gwldas asked respectfully, for Mervhu had great standing in the community.

"Passable. Sick every morning."

"I will bring you something. Is your lord at large?"

A languid hand was waved towards the inner chamber, and Gwldas went in. Mervhu, his boots off, was playing a game with Shan, the king's heir, rolling oakapples on a squared board. He raised his brows at Gwldas.

"Again, so soon, healer woman? How you love my company."

He stroked his great moustaches and bared his white teeth. "My lord, I think I hear your father calling," he said to Shan, who ran out immediately.

"I am not here for that, Mervhu." Gwldas was feeling tired; already she had lain with Mervhu that day. She went and knelt by his chair. He shook his head, pleased.

"Don't kneel," he said. "We are friends. What now?"

"Mervhu," said Gwldas. "I am indeed your friend. My body is yours, to your wishes. While your woman is sick . . ."

"Ah, my woman," he said fondly. "She grows big with the two. But she is not beautiful. This gives her pain. Children should be beautiful. Hers will be like frogs. So she is melancholy. I do not like her melancholy."

"Mervhu," said Gwldas urgently, "There is not much time. Speak to the High King. I could not move him. He says that fate is fixed. Mervhu. Anything I have. I have many jewels, a chest full. Take them. Go back to Karenia. Speak to the king."

"If you could not move him, then neither can I."

"You could, you could. You go where you please. Through the rat run of Karkis, to the border and beyond. I have jewels to bribe the Karkian frontier guard, more than they have ever been paid . . ."

"How you do love this little fisherman," said Mervhu, no longer smiling.

"I beg you, Mervhu, in great Erun's name. In love's name. In life's name. I entreat you."

He lowered his great hairy brows until they met his lids. He said: "I hate the bloody Draconhood. One day . . .but I have only just returned from a reconnaissance. I need a rest." He got up. "I will now go and hunt boar."

Gwldas burst into tears. "They will kill my man," she said. "What can I do?"

He turned and grinned at her wolfishly. "You'll think of something."

He left her and she wept. Then she passed through again to where the wife lay with her great melancholy, and here the healer's nature surfaced, even through her own misery. She went and placed her slender ebony hand on the woman's swollen belly. High above, a shadow of crystal began to form.

"My poor lady," she said softly. "How can I help you?"

Vergon stood before Malkar's throne, his brain confused and treacherous from a concentrate of substances: narcotics, stimulants, aphrodisiacs, some so dangerous they would have killed anyone not inured as he was. They focussed his obsession; he was righteous and unafraid.

"Madam." He did not kneel or bow. He kissed her hand, ascending the dais to stand by her, his hand resting on the arm of the throne. He drew his glittering robe about him; he had grown thin from the constant abuse of his body, and his lips were stained.

"I thought you were at your villa."

She was veiled; he could only dimly see her eyes, and they seemed distant.

"I came, madam, to discuss the future."

"Ah. The future."

"Yes, madam. My future as ruler of this realm. I think it is more than time for my coronation to take place. I also intend to seek a wife. I have in mind one of the young Karkian princesses. It is time my dynasty was assured."

She made no reply. It was almost as if she were asleep. He peered at the veil with a little anger.

"Well, madam?" he said sharply.

She said in a lazy voice, "You need not trouble yourself about the dynasty. Its future is secure for a thousand years of power, through agencies which are beyond your understanding."

Impatience grew to match his anger. Why, she talks nonsense, he thought. It was hard to remember he had once been afraid of her, had let her rule and manipulate him. He gripped the throne more firmly, as if threatening to dislodge her.

"I do not understand you," he said. "I know only that I am the King of Karenia, and it is time my sovereignty was recognised." The veil annoyed him. He could not meet her face to face; it was as if he spoke his challenge to a wall.

"Why do you cling to power, madam?" he demanded harshly. "The power is mine by right. I am your son."

"You are Enial's son," said the lazy voice. "You are none of mine. Any more than is your sister."

"Ah, my benighted sister! I understand you have rid yourself of her. Well, madam, I am a different proposition. Not all your spells and potions can make me budge from my intent."

There, I've said it, he thought. They whisper of her witchhood. No doubt she dabbles. What of it? Then he heard her laugh behind the gauze.

"Ah, so you have guessed my little secrets, Vergon. How percipient you are. I have nothing further to say to you. Leave me now."

"Indeed I will not leave," said Vergon in a quiet rage. "I demand my right. And I would prefer to see your face while we discuss the matter."

"By all means," she said, and raised the veil.

"Why, Mother, you are growing old!"

She let the veil fall gently. "Yes. We are very old, Vergon." The voice behind the veil sounded different, darker, deeper, almost male.

"But . . ." he stammered. "Not so long ago, you were . . ."

"Young? Fair? Ah yes. An illusion, an instrument . . ." Then she laughed. "Perhaps, Vergon, I mixed the wrong potion!"

He became fearless, curious and insolent.

"So, madam! And where does all this alchemy take place, I beg to know? I have never seen you crouched over a cauldron. I think all this is merely time, come on you in a rush."

"So," she said softly. "You wish to know my secrets? You wish to see alchemy? I have nothing against that. Go down now to my sanctum."

"That black door below? It is a false door, a blind door. There is no handle. I have never seen any pass through it."

"The dwarf will show you." She clapped her hands. Quarl appeared from behind the throne. He glanced at Vergon, then began to hobble on his little legs across the room, beckoning with one long arm. Vergon stared at Malkar, who appeared to have lapsed again into sleepy silence.

"Very well," he said mockingly. "But don't think this will divert me. I shall come back with my ministers. I will summon the privy council. I have adherents ready to swear to my supremacy."

He followed the dwarf down through badly lit ways into the labyrinth where Vergon had once or twice uninterestedly strayed. They came to the black door.

"Touch the tongue," said the dwarf. "I am too short."

Vergon looked at the leering merman's head, then back down at the dwarf, whose repellent face swam up at him in the torchlight. Madam's loathsome familiar, he thought. Here's something to show I am no longer in awe of her. And he drew a knife from his belt and stabbed the dwarf through the heart.

Stepping over the body, he touched the merman's tongue. The door came open and he entered.

The landfish had been in there for days. They had devoured the black bed's covers, made from the skins of men. They crouched in a corner. One of the spire-shell lamps glowed green, otherwise there was darkness.

Vergon was immediately sucked into a howling black vortex. The roaring energy of seas bound and blinded him. An immense voice spoke, a judgement like the booming of tides in a cave.

"This soul is poisoned. Let it go."

An awesome stillness fell on the chamber. The ravenous landfish crept out of their lair.

He had come to the end of his life, much sooner than he had expected. Even in battle there had been odds, and a chance. Now every second, full of pain and fear as it was, was precious and rushing on, far too fast, to that moment of death.

He could hear the drone of many voices from the Hall of Interrogation and Testimony. It was situated below ground level like the cells and was reached from outside by a door and a flight of steps. His captors led Tallis out into the passage, and death moved a few moments nearer.

It would be a bad death. Not a clean sweep on a churned field, but slow, public, humiliating, filled with unbelievable agony. Worse: Lilene would suffer it too. His own soul-sickness diminished. He was in that moment consumed by utter selflessness, as he thought: that must not be allowed to happen. Beside her fate, mine is dust in the wind.

They took him along the passage, unfettering him, for he must stand entire before judgement. Another thought came forcibly to him. Lilene has led me to this. Absolutely without resentment, he thought: it was almost worth it. This is the price I pay. But I never dreamed that Spring day when Narzet and I rode over Singstar Pass, that my journey would end like this.

He looked in anguish at the door of her cell. Although she had come to him in a kind of dream, telling him she was unharmed, he could hardly bear to watch as she emerged. Very thin, pale, her gown soiled, but perfect still. They had not tortured her; they had lied to him to bring him down, as they had to her, for a smile of desperate relief lit her face as she saw him. She flung herself into his arms and he held her, caring nothing for the pain in his ribs. They were put apart and taken along the corridor to where the voices sounded, loud as a swarm, and entered the great room, lit by a hundred flaring torches.

Every member of the Most Holy Order of the Draconhood had come from all corners of the kingdom to witness the disgrace of the princess. Some were quite young, others were ancients, hoary with cruelty and fanaticism. They sat in tiers around the room, like a bank of poisonous grass in their green gowns and hoods. The centre of the hall was occupied by two figures: the Truth Doctor, standing by a table crowded with his instruments at the side of which fire burned in a brazier. Close to him, enthroned, sat Zairopo. His head was bare, and for once his hands were exposed, lying lightly in his lap.

Tallis stared at him. His racing heart pounded harder. His terror was replaced by rage that brought the blood into his eyes, together with a look so venomous that something in Zairopo felt it. His eyes moved almost lazily to Tallis, were held there by hatred, then fixed on Lilene.

Oh, gods! that I could only kill you before I die, thought Tallis. He glanced towards the only exit, heavily guarded at the top of a flight of stairs. There was no escape. Then Zairopo began to speak, in a wine-rough drawl.

"Lilene of Karling. You have been tried and found guilty in your absence. That you did conspire to bring about anarchy and rebellion in the Kingdom of Karenia, inciting the commons to riot, to murder their masters and to effect chaos in the land. That you did procure armaments to prosecute said anarchy, and did feloniously abstract treasure to finance rebellion. That you did by countless spells, sorcery and witchcraft, instil the common people with the will to rise. Your crimes have been attested to by witnesses.

You are not judged by any royal or civil jurisdiction, but by the powers of the Most Ancient and Holy Order of the Draconhood, sworn to purify the kingdom of all sorcerers and malcontents, until perfect obedience to the Order is maintained by every living soul. Lilene of Karling, what say you?"

Lilene was trembling as if a strong gale blew her. She answered Zairopo in a calm clear voice.

"I am no witch. I did as I did to uphold the right. And I regret nothing."

A thunderous murmur arose from the ranked Draconhood. There was a slight commotion from the direction of the cells. They were bringing in Alpac, half-carrying him. His hands and feet were black with blood and bruising where the nails had been torn out. Lilene did not turn. She was trembling not only with terror but with effort. She was trying to raise the Crystal Lion.

Come to me, oh, come to me. Andine, save us. Exhort the Lion you gave me, from your high place in the Far Lands. She looked above Zairopo's head, while the Truth Doctor's fire flamed in the corner of her eye, looked for that subtle shimmer of the ether. There was nothing. Zairopo was speaking again.

"You are sentenced to death. You will be taken hence and burned over slow fires in an iron cage in the public square. The same sentence to be carried out on your disciple in treason, Captain Tallis of Taratamia, who stands accused with you and has been found guilty in his absence. The rebel Alpac is to suffer death by drowning."

Lilene said: "Captain Tallis is the heir to the Taratamian throne. You have no jurisdiction over the royal House of Capashenet."

"He has wrought treason in our country through his alliance with you," said Zairopo. "We will hear no more of him. Come forward, Lilene of Karling."

They pushed Lilene near to the throne. Tallis tried to follow her but was restrained. He saw her slim body, her dirty dress, her hair braided in a great mass of pristine gold about her head. There was an ornament in it at the back, almost concealed. He stared. It was no ornament. It was the branzel Lion-knife. Gods, he thought. She was armed all the time!

But what could she have done with it? one small knife against a hive of murderers. He heard Zairopo's next words with horror.

"Lilene of Karling, before you die, you are commanded to disclose the names of those rebels first consorting with you in the beginning, so that they may be apprehended. You will also disclose the source of the weapons supplied in this rebellion. Answer."

"I will disclose nothing," said Lilene softly. Zairopo answered: "You will regret it."

"I brought the weapons," said Tallis loudly. To his dismay he found his eyes were filling with tears. "The princess was only a pawn. She is innocent."

It was as if he had not spoken. Lilene bowed her head on her breast as if defeated. Zairopo turned to the Truth Doctor.

"The princess has refused to answer the most Holy Order of the Draconhood. Put out both her eyes."

Tallis's shout startled both himself and the nearby Draconhood.

"Zairopo! Stop! I demand that you hear me!"

Zairopo raised his hand, and the guard pushing Lilene towards the Truth Doctor, halted.

"Come forward, Captain," he said. "Where I can see you."

Tallis went forward. He was so close to Zairopo now that he could see the madness in his eyes, the grey in his odd-coloured hair. And he was also very close to Lilene.

"What have you to say to me, Captain, before you burn?" said Zairopo pleasantly.

"Two things," said Tallis as calmly as he was able. "First, I accuse you, Zairopo, of the murder of a man I loved, many years ago."

"What man?" said Zairopo lazily. "I have killed many men in the service of the Order."

"You were not a Dracon then," said Tallis. "This was done out of your drunken evil. You tortured a noble warrior to death. Do you remember my foster-father, Colonel Tallis? Do you remember the Plain of Tirkar? I owe you a death, Zairopo. Would to all the living gods I could give it to you. Instead, I lay my curse on you, Zairopo, forever."

Zairopo said: "Yes. Now I remember the name. And the second thing?"

"A request," said Tallis with difficulty. "As our death is so near, I ask you to allow me to embrace the princess once more before we part."

Zairopo smiled like a deathshead. He leaned forward on his throne.

"The Most Holy Order is all-powerful. Through that power your request is granted."

Lilene was looking at Tallis, startled. She was as white as a corpse. He took her by the waist. He put one hand behind her head and kissed her lips. When he withdrew he had the knife palmed in his hand, the handle in his sleeve. It felt sweet. One swift lunge forward, and Zairopo would be dead on his throne. A sick exaltation rose in him. My last wish granted, after all the years.

And then he looked in Lilene's blue, blue eyes. And knew his terrible choice. There was only one blow in this knife. To fulfil his ancient vengeance, or to spare Lilene agony. He looked at her breast, saw her heart beating like a bird against the stuff of her dress. He took the knife firmly in his hand. Zairopo saw it, and jerked forward. Tallis said softly to Lilene: "Love of my life" and drew back the knife to plunge it into her. And in that instant the world blew up.

The end of the world! It has been prophesied for years. The end, when the gods come to weigh our faults. The gods are noisy. His head rang from the first deafening roar. His closed eyes still held a flash of the fireball seen shooting down the stairs, letting in a glare from the door above, blasting the bodies of the guards. The noise went on: more thunder, cracking explosions, screams of agony, bellowing from the gods. The world shuddered.

He was lying on the floor; it was hot and wet. There was a thick acrid stench. He managed to open his eyes. A forest surged about him. The gods were trees, their branches held high, fire in their hands. More explosions, screams, a stentorian voice shouting. He closed his eyes again. Wetness rippled around him. Blood, he thought, but there was no pain.

He sought blindly about for Lilene with his hands and found her; her hip, waist, shoulder. She was calling his name. His opened his eyes fully at last. She was lying near, her dress in tatters, her face and hair black as soot. He rolled his head the other way, and saw Zairopo.

The Grand Master lay half under his throne. His legs had been blown off at the groin. Blood pumped from the stumps in rich gouts. His eyes moved wildly. An awful howling was coming from the Truth Doctor, impaled on one of the struts of his brazier, with live coals falling on his head.

Tallis managed to sit up carefully. He hauled Lilene to a sitting position. His voice was a croak, as was hers when she answered, over the continuous tumult.

"Are you hurt, Ricalpa?"

Painfully he shook his head. Looking carefully about, he absorbed the astounding scene.

The hall was teeming with Desprans. There must have been eight hundred of them, in full war gear, wearing the antlers of Erun on their heads and chain mail over their jerkins. Some wore voluminous green robes, which tossed on the air as they leaped about armed with swords, sabres, long killing-knives and clubs. Nearly all were armed, more lethally, with the turineko. They had the loading and firing to a fine art, working in pairs.

The Draconhood were no longer in ranks, but lay in contorted postures, heads and limbs blown away, some hanging head down from the tiers of seats. The hall was like an abattoir. Only a few of the Draconhood were still whole, and these Mervhu, the author of the great bellow, was herding against the wall where a turineko squad was dispatching them. By now Lilene and Tallis lay in several inches of water, pumping from the underground spring through a fractured seam in the floor. The fireball had been precisely aimed through the door, down the steps to smite Zairopo's throne. The blast had blown Lilene and Tallis away from the throne, while the missile had bounded on to decimate those Dracon sitting directly opposite Zairopo.

The noises took on a new note. There was only the occasional bang. The shouting had formed into a rhythm. "Erun! Erun! Hail, Turinek! Turinek!" Tallis felt his head, a little sticky with blood, then examined Lilene. Black, unscathed save for a deep cut on her foot. Tallis stared at Zairopo. The blood still spasmed from the rents in his body. His eyes emptily returned Tallis's stare.

A large antlered shape leaned down close. Huge white teeth under a thick fall of moustache plaited like ropes. Mervhu laid a bloody hand on Tallis's shoulder.

"Tallis-Cap! You here, huh?"

"Mervhu," said Tallis weakly. "You are the gods." Mervhu roared. He was drunk with blood and triumph. His command of the Taratamian language was suffering.

"Gods no send. Come we for fisherboy of Gwldas. Why you here are, Tallis-Cap?"

"You didn't know, Mervhu?"

Mervhu shrugged. "Pleased you live. One day we have scrap. Not today. Get fisherboy." His eyes roved. "Who woman she?"

"The Princess Royal."

"Ah so. The Lilene. All get up. Soon drown." He hauled them to their feet. A little way off a massive Despran was holding Alpac in his arms like a baby.

"Mervhu, you prince," said Tallis. "My thanks forever." He looked about him astonished at the unbelievable carnage.

"We blow up bloody Draconhood today," said Mervhu. He jerked his head at Zairopo. "Say prayers, big chief. Me finish."

"No, Mervhu," Tallis found he could stand unsteadily alone. "He's mine."

Mervhu, holding Lilene enthusiastically against his chest, nodded in approval. He unsheathed a thin curved knife and handed it to Tallis. Tallis walked over to Zairopo. He knelt and looked deep into his eyes.

There was nothing. No madness, no sentience, no memory.

Death was eating his years. Tallis set the knifepoint under Zairopo's ear where the artery pulsed weakly. And then a thought so omnipotent, so undeniable, entered Tallis like the voice of truth.

Never have I killed a helpless man.

He picked up Zairopo's limp hand, and with one slash severed the sixth finger. He tossed the finger into the embers of the Truth Doctor's fire, and stood up. He gave the knife back to Mervhu, who bent and cut the throat slowly, with unscrupulous growls of satisfaction.

"Why you spare him?" he asked Tallis.

"Because it would have made me as he was."

Mervhu grunted. The Desprans were busy, looting items of silverware from the alcoves and walls, tearing down standards, piling furniture in the centre of the hall.

"We blow up house proper now," said Mervhu. "Burn bloody Draconhood town. Drink some. Find women. Then homego."

"Homego," said Lilene, and looked lovingly up at Mervhu with her blue eyes.

"I would rather not, Father." The boy hung back as they entered the darkest precinct of Sluts' Wharf.

The father's large face crimsoned in annoyance. His bulk bullied his son along. The boy was not right. No son of mine, thought the big coarse man. At his age, I'd sampled everything. He stopped in a dark alcove and turned the boy to face him, looking disgustedly at the girlish face under the curly blond hair.

"I suppose you'd rather be at home. Playing with your rabbits and puppies, you lily."

The boy hung his head, thinking sadly of his little menagerie, their trusting, undemanding sweetness. If this awful thing were to happen, he felt he could never face them again.

"You'll go through with this," said the father violently, "or you'll find all your creatures in the cookpot."

"All right, Father," whispered the defeated boy.

A hag sat on the steps of a filthy house. The father greeted her genially.

"Is Clamel free?" he asked, and the crone shook her head.

"Where've you been, master? Clamel's dead of the rubet pox this moonspan. This your lad?"

"Damn," muttered the father.

"Her house stands empty," said the hag. "I could fetch you Madlyn, or Quella, if you see me right."

"They're too young. He clings to his mother. We need someone older. Make him feel at home."

"Can't help you then," said the old woman.

"I can," said a soft voice. The house door was suddenly open. A figure stood silhouetted in candleshine. "I am Karmal," the voice said.

The man squinted at her. Shadowy slenderness, sleek black hair. There was a white streak. Ideal. This one was old enough.

"Are you clean?"

The woman laughed. "None cleaner. And I am free to virgins."

The father pushed his son forward. A free ride was better than he had hoped for. "Go to it," he said severely, "and don't disgrace yourself, or me!"

He stumped off down the alley, where there was another kind of darkness—two of the Karenian poor, starving, armed with razors; they left him throat-cut and purseless, dying in his blood . . ..

The boy was drawn upstairs. The walls dripped damp, but there was a pleasant perfume in the upper room where flames burned in conch shells. There was a narrow bed with pristine white sheets, and silver bowls in which black tulips grew. A low table bore an assortment of whips and restraints. The shuddering boy was fascinated despite his fear.

He surveyed the woman. She wore tight silver breeches and high boots. She had a wide silver chain about her white throat. She was not young, but admirable, and her small hands on him were like velvet.

"Now my little love," she said.

"No," he said, and turned from her.

"But yes."

There was a singing in his ears, like the sound that whales make from the depths of the ocean.

How it happened he never knew, but he was flat on the bed, his wrists manacled to the posts above his head. He was also nude. She bound his ankles with silver cords, and stripped off her boots and breeches. His eyes were drawn to her black bush; it looked soft, like one of his pet kittens. Still he fought his bonds, knowing that defloration would change and spoil what he was forever.

Her lips came to his; they tasted of honey and spice. They moved over his chin and chest and shrinking belly. She stroked his thighs, and placed one leg across him. She touched him where none had ventured. He began to weep with shame.

"Don't cry, my pet," she said, and then her mouth was there, her tongue gliding under his small slack member, drawing it against her palate where it was sucked like a fruit. His flesh changed under her law. It was a wicked pleasure and nothing to do with him, and he said brokenly, "Oh, Karmal."

"Come, my lovely boy," she whispered, her mouth releasing him. He stared down in amazement at the burgeoning tower. Only for an instant, for she was on him, light and gentle, and the tower was being fed into the black bush, where it was laved by honey.

"Come!" she said urgently. Convulsions of excitement roared through him; his lower body felt invaded by hot wires. She hung above him, sweet, maternal yet purposeful, and as her belly touched his he felt a flame glowing at her centre. The black bush was a dear little animal, it sucked at him lovingly, he would take it home to play with the others . . .

The orgasm hit him like a galloping horse. He shuddered upwards, trying to reach her face, and saw that it was animal indeed, the cruel face of an animal dead for centuries, and the horror of it killed him instantly.

His soul went crying down into darkness. The tragic hands of the damned reached up for it and dragged it into the deeps. Its agony was infinite; it screamed and wailed, for itself and for the lost generations.

The pearl had taken on the light of a full moon. It swelled with soul-seed. A black rat with a white-speckled head sat with it on a rickety worm-eaten bed in a stinking chamber. A tarnished mirror reflected the pearl.

What power there is in purity, Maelikali!

Oh yes. Pure power.

But so very young. The soul was never tempted.

And now we observe the Forest of Rulen. *He* is free. Ah, there are riches there. I crave that soul. More and more, for it has shown great nobility. It was willing to sacrifice its most fervent aims.

Yes. And all for integrity.

Oh, how Maelikali lusts for that great soul!

The black rat scurried. It whipped through a hole and down the stairs and out into the street, running over the foot of the ancient procuress, who was dozing, never now to wake.

"It was the Crystal Lion," she said. "I am ashamed. I had lost my faith. That shining, still with us. Ricalpa, are you in pain?"

The Lobster's landlord had bolted for the forest when the horde of noisy Despran warriors arrived. They found the cellar. They found a herd of pigs. They slaughtered and cooked and caroused. Their tents were dotted all over the orchard.

"I owe Mervhu a monstrous favour now." Tallis sat in the bathtub in the upper room, his side black from beatings, while Lilene washed blood from his head. Alpac lay on the bed. His hands and feet had been tended by the Despran healer-surgeon, who had sent salve and strapping for the wounds of Tallis and Lilene. Lilene wore the landlord's daughter's dress, which hung on her.

"It is Gwldas we owe," said Alpac softly. "My mother, my lover, my wife. This was her doing."

"Gods bless Gwldas then," said Tallis, dressing in borrowed breeches. He had never felt so weak or so tired. He felt twenty years older and in the past days his hair had whitened at the temples. He thought: Mervhu has given me back my life. He owns me. The times I've met the Desprans in battle. The gwgli was fierce beyond belief. He thought: if they ever attack Tamia with those weapons they will conquer in a very short time indeed. Until we find the secret birthplace of the magic powder, gods grant they attend martially on Karenia. Today I can't care too much.

"I can smell the smoke even now," said Lilene.

They had watched it all before leaving the environs of Kalvaria. The Desprans had laid further mines under the walls of the House of Questions. Posing as Draconhood with green robes and fine horses, they had already set mines to explode at the moment of invasion. The fireball which had dashed down the steps was an innovation.

"Gwch he make," said Mervhu proudly. "Twenty times more gwgli in big shell. Big big turineko. Long string, quick fire. Aim straight, aim good. Make bigger next time."

The Desprans had evacuated Kalvaria. Men, women and children had been herded from the city, which had then been fired and mined. Black smoke and the occasional fireball could be seen for miles. Soon there would be nothing left but a smear of black history on a lonely plain, standing within broken walls, where none would ever come again.

"And that was only a fraction of their army," said Tallis. "Do you know, Alpac, if they intend to take Karlinkis? Malkar would have to harry her generals into action." He looked at Lilene and grinned. "Even your brother might have to put on armour."

"Didn't you know, Captain?" said Alpac quickly. "King Vergon's dead. Mervhu sent spies south. Some animal killed him in the palace."

Mervhu clumped up the stairs and burst in, hung with the Draconhood's silver and gold, and holding a wineskin.

"Through window see, Tallis-Cap," he shouted. "More friends come."

Below was Recansky, with the dilapidated escort. And Sergeant Mollane and the boy Timbel. But no Barbel.

"Poor Barbel," he said as if to himself. "Poor, good, loyal Barbel."

Mervhu unsheathed a shining ray and offered it to Tallis. "We find in Dracon store. Lionsword. Yours, Tallis-Cap."

The pommel was cool with the end of trouble. "My thanks again, Mervhu. Now I have all my precious possessions back. All but one."

"Your mare outside," said Mervhu. "All your fine horses. All Dracon horses too. And nice Kalvaria women. They come back Despra with me. Mate with Despran boys. Breed warriors."

"I was speaking of Barbel."

"You never saw her as precious," said Lilene. "But she was."

"Whatsa Barbel?" asked Mervhu. "Woman? Oh, women very powerful. That Gwldas! I tell her I no go Karenia. But she see my woman. Do miracle. My woman in pig -" he told Lilene. "Ugly woman. All misery. Afraid children come out ugly like her. Gwldas fix."

"Gwldas can do anything," said Alpac.

"Gwldas lay hand on belly," said Mervhu. "Big light come from belly of woman. Two faces in cloud. Babies, lovely as stars. My woman angry with me then. Say I owe Gwldas. Make us come, blow ballocks off Draconhood."

He poured a jet of wine down his gullet. "We leave here tomorrow. Alpac come home Despra to Gwldas. Tallis-Cap homego to Tamia. The Lilene come to bed of High King."

"Oh no, Mervhu," said Tallis quickly. "The princess is my woman now. She stays with me."

"No, Tallis-Cap. The Lilene is for High King's bed. I take. All arrange."

Tallis felt as if he had been hit in the belly. He stared at Mervhu. He said: "Mervhu, I shall never raise sword against you again, unless I am provoked beyond reason. You've restored my life, but half my life is this woman. You shall not take her. King Brwcwch will have to do without."

"He want her," said Mervhu. His face was terrible, a Despran with one toe on the warpath. "Long time he want her. You give up. I take her from you now, I think."

"Then I must kill you," said Tallis sadly, and raised the Lion sword. It stayed cool, no anger in its grip.

"Oh, Tallis-Cap!" said Mervhu. Alpac raised himself from the bed and was looking anxiously at them both. "We friends. Woman no reason to scrap. I kill you now, though. You got women in Tamia. Women easy come. Why you die now?"

A tingling surge travelled up the sword into Tallis's hand, a tremor not of intent, but of inspiration. And he remembered the most sacred of all things to a Despran. He said: "She is my woman, Mervhu. She is with child by me."

He heard Lilene draw a little quick breath. Mervhu's hand dropped from his swordhilt. His face relaxed, became thoughtful, reverential. "Is this truth?" he asked. "You swear?"

"I swear on the Lion." Tallis raised and kissed the sword. "She carries my child. She is mine."

I've perjured myself, he thought. Now the Lion may turn against me. It's worth the risk.

"I tell the High King," said Mervhu softly. "You keep woman. Lovely child come. Be it so."

He crashed out of the room, nodding and muttering. Tallis sat down heavily on the bed.

"Holy gods," he said. "Just when I thought our troubles were over."

"They are over, Ricalpa," said Lilene. "The Draconhood are no more."

Alpac stirred uneasily.

"But there is Maelikali," he whispered. "The Voracious One."

They were embracing, and did not hear him.

The Crystal Lion was still abroad, empowered by its invisible raising at Kalvaria, where it slid in and out of the smokes, until the atmosphere became too impure for its comfort and it swirled again, an invisible shining, south again to Karlinkis. It was frailer than the youngest spiderweb, more evanescent than a soap-bubble. Mostly it resembled the mist-mirror of a rainbow, and its colours were in the rainbow's image.

The Court was in mourning for Vergon, whose remains had been interred in the royal mausoleum. The Crystal Lion skipped ethereally through the false ambience of sorrow and roosted, as customary in Honyia's apartments.

She was playing a small ancient Despran harp and singing, always the song's final note, clear and true. Dogmar sat lovingly at her feet. The crystal filaments wove the little dark girl into beauty, and she smiled at Dogmar with her brown eyes. More and more Dogmar reminded her of Jonakin. Every day he begged her to leave her harp and dance with him, for they needed no music. Meanwhile the Crystal Lion, invisibly spinning light about them, remained, a provocation and a challenge to darkness.

On either side the ascent of Knife Pass was a towering riot of bronze and cinnabar; leaves twirled soundlessly to earth, and the horses tramped through a carpet crisp as corn.

The Pass was safe; Mervhu had pledged they would go unmolested and the mountain bandits were hiding away perhaps to dream of a new revolution. As the party came up through the sharp defile, the breeze already bore the distant ache of snow, though the sun limned the Tiranians with hard yellow. Birds flew south, and a pair of eagles hunted overhead. This was the season called Lateglow by the Tamians, slotted between autumn and winter, perhaps the most magical of all.

The guards on the Karenian frontier were in mourning for King Vergon. They waved the company through with barely a customs check or a peep into Lilene's litter. She had no papers, and Tallis had added her as "wife" on his own documents.

In pain, he had shared Lilene's litter for the last fifty miles. She had stroked his hurts, wrapping him in her white furs, but with the frontier's approach he took horse again and led the party through. Taratamia, he thought, and could have kissed the earth.

"I shall have to see Pancora."

"She will be angry."

"That's likely. I'll get it over right away."

He sent a rider ahead to arrange for a suite of rooms for Lilene. Pancora would have to be asked to leave his house. I shall have to maintain her, he thought, some kind of pension. He smiled to himself. I shall be keeping two women! Lilene had brought only the barest necessities, a handful of jewels. It could not matter less.

At the frontier a young man erupted out of the customs house, a stranger to Tallis.

"Captain, welcome back. There was talk of sending a search party for you. Anything to declare? Wine, pearls, silks?"

Another appeared, bowing low. Glaring at the youth, he muttered: "Show respect! Your highness," he said to Tallis, "Welcome home."

Tallis's lightheartedness faded. Oh gods! I had hoped that wretched business had gone underground.

"Jankel," he said. "Stop this nonsense. Let's go inside for a minute."

Inside, Jankel said: "The word is, Captain, that I address you as Prince. It's all over the city. I'm taking no chances. Everyone's been asking for you; your high commander, and Prince Ataret. They're saying you'll be our next ruler, sire."

Tallis swore luridly. Jankel went to the door and looked out at the waiting company. "It that the princess?" he asked.

"I'm going to marry her," said Tallis shortly. "And that's no rumour."

"Pass on, my lord," said Jankel humbly. He bowed again, while the Captain glared. He's out of his mind, thought Jankel. I wish someone would offer me the Opal Throne. From the customs house he watched the company out of sight.

Here were the tall clean houses of Tam, the river, the taverns, the small green parks, the principal bridge over which they clattered, and, high above, the Lion of Stone perpetually on watch over the city. And the spires and domes of the palace, commanding, beckoning.

He gave Lilene over to Recansky's care to see her safe in the inn. Then he took the old road home, to his house, which looked small and sleepy, as if he had been away for a hundred years. No one about to greet him. Only the great heart of Palbo in its shaggy ancient frame, ambling shakily towards him, trembling with joy. You old rat, you old fool, said Tallis, are you pleased to see me? And Palbo, leaning his head against Tallis's thigh: oh, you are back, you are safe. I dreamed of you, my legs ache, my jaws ache, from defending you in my dreams.

He greeted his servants briefly, then, steeling himself, went straight to where Pancora was.

She stood before a log fire, modest in dark blue satin with a lace collar. She made no move, though she smiled a little. She was taller and broader than he remembered. He went forward and kissed her politely on both cheeks.

"How are you, Pan?"

"I'm well, Ricalpa. I hear you are to be our next king. Is it true?"

He said: "Shall we sit down?" and they sat one on either side of the fire.

"Many strange things have happened, Pancora. I have barely escaped with my life. There is talk of my being the heir, yes. I have to see Prince Ataret, to try to clear it up."

He studied her. She seemed uneasy, glancing now and again over her shoulder.

"I'm glad you came to no harm, Ricalpa. It's good to see you again. Are you hurt?"

"Minor injuries. I shall heal. Thank you." He looked at her more closely. He remembered early years of love, over and done with. Five years with this woman, swept away by a few weeks of deathly, limitless passion. Pancora said softly: "Would you like me to welcome you home, Ricalpa? Do you want to take me to bed?"

And he said: "No, Pancora. Not now, or ever again. I'm sorry." She glanced over her shoulder again. She said: "If you are king, shall I not be your queen?"

"Is that what you wanted?"

"Once, yes. I would have wanted it. Not now. I have all that I want."

He stared, hardly believing his own suspicions.

"You've found someone else."

And she nodded, smiling quite ravishingly. "Yes, Ricalpa, and we're to be married. He's quite well-born, though not of the blood royal, as they say you are . . . we plan a big family. In fact," she said hesitatingly, "he's here now. May I bring him in?"

"Of course." Tallis could hardly keep his face straight.

The man was younger than Pancora, very beautiful, and extremely apprehensive. Pancora planted him before Tallis, who recognised him. A young commissioned officer not long out of cadet school; his father was a friend of Narzet Senior. Tallis shook his hand; the young man winced and smiled. "Congratulations, lieutenant. You are a fortunate man. Gods send you every happiness."

The young man looked down at his mirror-bright boots, and blushed. Pancora came to Tallis and embraced him. "Thank you, Ricalpa," she whispered. "For all the good times. And for being so understanding."

She had been ready for this moment. Her gowns and music and lapdogs were all packed. They chatted amiably while the wagons were loaded, and he told her a little of his escapades. Lilene he did not mention; there was no necessity. It was only when Pancora asked: "How is little Barbel?" that he suddenly became choked and could not answer.

He watched the new lovers leave his house and thought: the gods are with us all. There goes proof of it. The gods have finished their games.

The thing that was Malkar sat sole on her oyster throne. Round the glass walls the fish swam, the sea-predators hopped and pounced, but many had died and lay half-eaten or as bones, gently moving from the tides of those still alive.

A boy entered the Hall of the Sea. Malkar was so quiet and still he thought he was alone. He had brought a tank in which swam creatures to replenish the aquaria. He unloaded a small turtle into a tank. It observed its surroundings, decided it disliked them, and withdrew its antique head into the mosaic of its shell. The boy advanced, plopping fish into their new habitation, looked up and saw Malkar. The fish-boy was about fifteen, with pale Karenian hair. He looked vague, slovenly.

"Come here," said Malkar softly. The boy laid down the tank and approached the dais. He bobbed a nervous bow, and plaited his fingers.

Malkar drew up her gown, revealing veined, mottled legs. "Come," she said. "Lie with me. Make love, boy."

The boy, his heart banging with terror, slunk closer. "Touch me," she said, and he laid a hand on her knee. Her flesh was so cold it was like a burn. "Lie with me," she whispered, and leaned back in the throne.

"I can't," he muttered. A desperate lie leaped to save him. "I have the rubet disease. My parts are rotten. Forgive me, greatness."

And he was off like a hare through the hall, tripping, spilling the contents of his tank. Dying fish flapped round the throne.

She sat thoughtfully for a few moments. Then rose and without haste, descended to the sanctum. She removed the pearl from her belly and placed it where it would shine through the mirror. The pearl was half the size it once was, yet it burned feverishly, like the last renewal of vigour sometimes seen in the dying, and the darkness spoke through it, and Malkar to the darkness. Through the medium of the pearl the darkness had a keen incisive voice, like a needle in the brain, and rose from fathoms deep.

Malkar, your daughter lives. See, she is in Taratamia.

It is of no importance.

Speak to us, Malkar.

Malkar is hungry. Voracious.

But Malkar, Maelikali, the present form is outworn. We have worked it to the limit. The Great Change is coming. Do you not desire the Great Change?

More than anything. But I desire to finish what was begun. The throne of Karenia, of Taratamia, the rule from north to south, from the Far Lands to Ruva. Supremacy for a thousand years.

This will all come to pass. It is written, in sand, in pebbles, in sunsets, in thunder. It is written in salt.

But to rule without the beauty? They will not know me on my throne.

They will be too terrified not to acknowledge you. You will be more terrible than oceans, than flames or shipwreck. In your cells will swim the dreadful power of the damned. You will have their kingdoms within you, to bring you strength. No eyes will ever dare light on your countenance. Armies will fall dead at your name, blood turn to acid and swords rust.

I am content. Only—

Malkar, Maelikali, what do you still desire?

One more soul, darkness. One more soul for my crown. I name him.

And the pearl said: "So be it," flared up, and turned to ashes.

She walked ways along which she seldom came, down broad stairs leading to an apartment near the gardens, the door to which lay open. She heard music. Little teasing jewels strung on the threadwork of the lyre. It flirted with a minor key then changed to the major with the ultimate phrase, which was echoed by a strange, birdlike sound. A man's voice said clearly: "Beautiful, beloved. Now let us perform what you promised."

There followed not quite a silence, with little rushing tapping sounds. Malkar nudged the door ajar. Honyia was dancing with handsome Dogmar, who adored her with his eyes.

Malkar entered. The dancers froze. Handsome Dogmar went down on one knee. Honyia stood, her skirt swinging from the dance.

Malkar took Honyia by the wrist. The years rolled back for them both, to Jonakin, the other dance and its sequel. Time flowed forward and the pattern began to repeat itself. Dogmar stood back, alarmed, unsure. Honyia was drawn past him, dragged through the open door, out into the garden on to the lawn at the edge of which lay the great lake with its abundant stream leading eventually to the sea. Honyia saw it and began to struggle uselessly. With her free hand Malkar took her by the hair. She dragged her until they stood by the lakeshore. The lake was full, lapping greedily against its surround of loose rocks. The water was clear but the bottom was invisible.

Dogmar had followed quietly and stood a few yards behind them. He heard Malkar say, in a voice not her own:

"We warned you before, Thing. Young men are not for you. We send you now, to serve darkness."

Dogmar watched in desperation, trying to decide whether to intervene. Malkar had Honyia on her knees, pushing her down into the water, and as he looked at her, a kind of migrainous shimmer passed over his eyes, like the crystal filaments of a web. Then Honyia spoke.

He never knew what she said, in a voice that was rusty from years of unuse, but firm and loud. It caused Malkar to step away a pace, releasing Honyia's hair. Honyia rose lithely, in her hand one of the rocks from the lakeside. She raised her hand and struck Malkar a great blow on the temple. Malkar pitched sideways, and then she was in the lake, leaving one of her slippers behind on the grass.

Dogmar ran forward, trying to brush away the shimmer from his eyes. It hung about Honyia and faded as he reached her side.

The queen's head appeared above the water a few yards out, as if she had been swimming. The black hair with the white streak showed a little smear of blood. The amber eyes were fiery, stained red like glass. Darkness suffused the face; it became black as the hair. The eyes glared, then the head sank beneath the water, gently, as if coaxed below. And a sound arose, so awful that Dogmar and Honyia caught at one another in fright. A groaning yell, a multitude of voices as one, like a nation lamenting a holocaust. Like a thousand damned souls, or the cries of a million unborn children.

There was absolute silence. Honyia let out a deep sigh. Dogmar saw she was smiling, a faint smile that grew.

"The queen has drowned, Dogmar my love," she said in her rusty voice. "The queen is dead. Long live—"

"You spoke!" he said breathlessly.

And then, far out in the lake, the water erupted. Something rose from the depths and continued to rise, a gigantic form with a massive head and shoulders, human yet not human, coal-black and plated with scales. It rose until its huge head measured the height of the treetops, its clawed hands upraised and dripping. Its long hair was shining black weed. Its back was to the watchers, but the power of its structure proclaimed it to be male. For a long moment it stood poised on the water's skin, immobile save for a weaving from side to side of its great head as it surveyed its surroundings. Then slowly it began to sink back into the water, which closed on it without a ripple.

Dogmar and Honyia stood holding one another for an hour. They watched the absolute stillness. Then a line of moorhens drove placidly across the lake. On the far side the stream flowed on its inexorable way to the sea.

The principal temple was so thick with incense that Tallis could scarcely see across it. At every one of the opal-decked shrines of the Lion, priests and acolytes were on their knees. He was ushered into Ataret's sanctum. Although it was high daylight outside, there were many candles burning, reflecting the jewel-starred altars and hangings.

Ataret, the Lion tattoos dark on his shaven head, came forward to meet him.

"Your Holiness," said Tallis, and prepared to kneel.

"Your highness," replied Ataret. Tallis winced.

"I suppose I am now to call you brother, Ataret?"

Ataret held out his hand, which Tallis took in silence. "We have always been brothers, Ricalpa. I can welcome you now to the House of Capashenet, in truth and faith."

"So you always knew, Ataret?" He tried to keep the anger out of his voice.

"Yes. I knew. Rost and Lepo did not. You were not to have been told, unless such a contingency as this arose. The Abbess Andine kept the secret. Likewise General Camlot. The king, our father . . ."

"Yes," said Tallis softly and violently, "what of the king? He never troubled to acknowledge me. How useful I have become all of a sudden."

"Do not be bitter," said Ataret. "It would not have made for harmony. The queen, my mother . . ."

"She tried to have me murdered."

"Yes. Probably. My mother hated your mother. Gods help her, she said once she'd rather the dynasty died out than that you should inherit. Now she's changed. She submerges herself in prayer and is more at peace."

Ataret sat down. "The king did his best for you, Ricalpa. He had you and your mother given over to his most beloved warrior. He saw you were not in want. Did you never wonder how you lived so well? Your house was bought for your foster-father to bequeath to you."

"I wasn't asking for the king's charity. I am independent. I have my captain's salary. I have a lot of back pay coming too," he said inconsequentially.

"You have more than that coming eventually. The homage of the nation."

Tallis started to walk nervously about. "It's the most ridiculous situation I ever heard. I am not shaped to rule. I can only just rule my own household. I know nothing but the army. I love the Red Royals. I have all that I need, especially now."

"And," said Ataret quietly, "do you not love Taratamia?"

Tallis stopped pacing and looked Ataret in the eyes. "With all my heart. I have fought and nearly died for her on many an occasion."

"Then isn't it time you put away selfishness? Do you want to see Taratamia given over to whatever country fancies taking her? Do you want the noble name of Capashenet to vanish forever? You are being offered the Opal Throne as your inheritance."

Tallis felt something like cold panic. "I could not do it," he said. "I've had no training. I know nothing of protocol. I'm scarcely interested in politics. Did the king sire no other bastards? Are there no far-flung cousins?"

"None other in the direct line, Ricalpa. You have King Valm's blood. And no, there are no other natural offspring. The king loved your mother, and grieved when she died."

Tallis was silent. Then he said: "Ataret, I can't do it. I'm not fitted. I have no right to it. I decline the inheritance."

"Ricalpa. Under the Second Tamic Law you are the natural and only heir. You are not at liberty to refuse. As for protocol and politics, you would have aides and advisors to guide you. The Council would be behind you. You are personable, with a record of bravery—you would be popular. And you could provide an heir, to preserve the dynasty."

Tallis began to shake with anger. "And there's another thing," he said aggressively. "Do not, any of you, king, councillors, priests, even think of marrying me off to some Karkian Princess or Maytian noblewoman. I intend to marry Lilene of Karling. You can call me heir, but one thing you cannot do is yoke me to any other woman. In this I am adamant."

Ataret smiled gently. "Remain calm, Ricalpa. Your attachment to the princess has not gone unnoticed. It would not be an undesirable marriage. It is a union similar to that of King Enial and the Princess Doro in reverse. It would stabilise relations between the two countries. The truce could finally be ratified. All this of course," he added, "would depend on the acquiescence of Queen Malkar." And he swallowed hard, as if to clear his mouth of a foul taste.

Emotion, and the many candles, had made the chamber stifling. "Let's go up on the roof," Tallis said.

The temple was on the hill from which the Lion of Stone surveyed the city high above. Below were lesser temples of white marble, the big bridge, and the river, flushed with autumn rains. A horseman was coming over the bridge, riding fast from the south, foam spraying from his mount's neck. He charged through a knot of gossips, and dashed up the street leading to the palace.

"Courier," said Tallis, watching him over the parapet.

"Now, Ricalpa," said Ataret, "are we any nearer, do you think?"

"If I can have Lilene as my consort . . . but no, Ataret. I am an army man. Gods! what should I do without the army? I don't mind being a prince. They have some freedom—when I remember how Lepo, gods rest him, used to go on . . . but to king me is to cage me. I'm Captain Tallis of the Red Royals."

"You'd be high Commander in Chief. You'd review the troops on feast days."

"Bah!" said Tallis. From far below came the voice of the City Newscrier, bawling something they were too high up to hear, and ringing his bell. The courier suddenly appeared again at full gallop, and rode east along the rivercourse.

"That horse will founder if he pushes it like that," said Tallis.

"Think of the reforms you could order," said Ataret cunningly.

"I'd make ill-treating a horse a flogging offence."

"Exactly."

"And," Ataret murmured, "you'd own the Royal Stud in time, and all the racers. The finest breeding stock there is."

"You devil, Ataret," said Tallis rudely to the High Priest.

"I think you have agreed," said Ataret softly. Tallis sighed. He stretched his arms above his head. Massive, the Lion of Stone surveyed him from above.

"What do I have to do?"

"You have to swear acknowledgement that you are next in line to the throne under the Second Tamic Law which legitimizes you from bastardy. That you will hold yourself ready to ascend the throne on the king's death, unless extraordinary circumstances should unseat you from that privilege."

"And I sign in my blood, I suppose."

"As a matter of fact, you do."

"I don't want my life to change yet. I want to continue to live in my house, with Lilene."

"And why not? Princes, as you say, have some freedom."

"Thank the gods. Tell me, Ataret. Is our father in good health?"

"Extremely. You see, Ricalpa, you need not be so unhappy."

"I am unhappy. May the king live forever."

"Gods grant it."

"And you will marry us, Ataret? very soon? Don't refuse, or I shall get some hedge-priest to do it, and that will be a fine disgrace for Prince Ricalpa."

"I will. I shall send a courier today to Queen Malkar. Come below now, and take the oath."

He went from Ataret strangely light of heart. *The king is hale, Ataret admitted it. He could even outlive us all. And princes can do as they like.* He rode fast towards the Palace Inn. *Now to fix our wedding. Cursed Malkar will raise no objections. Lilene is marrying the heir to Tamia. That should please the malignant witch.*

He threw his reins to a groom and went into the inn. He was guarding Lilene's reputation and therefore had not installed her in his house as he longed to do. His craving for her chafed him unbearably.

"The princess is in her chamber."

He found her door bolted from the inside. He knocked several times until, very slowly, she drew the bolt and he entered.

She had been crying so much that her eyes were swollen almost closed. The breast of her gown was soaked with tears. She stood tearing a square of lace to pieces, and when he went, disturbed, to embrace her, stepped back a pace.

"In the gods' name, what is it? Are you ill? Tell me!" She said: "Oh, Ricalpa," then burst out crying.

"Tell me, calmly."

"A courier has come from Karenia. Oh, Ricalpa! My mother is dead."

Deep within him, an explosion of laughter threatened. Controlling it, he said: "I can't believe what I see. You say Malkar is dead."

"Yes. Drowned in the lake at Karlinkis. An accident. Lord Ing's son witnessed it."

"And you're weeping—for her?"

She turned away, unable to speak. He said roughly: "My beloved Lilene. Have you forgotten? Gods! She handed you over to the Draconhood!"

She turned back to face him. With great difficulty she said: "I am not weeping for her death. I am weeping because you and I must part."

Speechless, he sat down on the bed. Tears continued to pour from her eyes.

"You don't realise what this means, Ricalpa. It means I must leave you, perhaps forever. I must go back to Karenia."

He thought: she is deranged. She has been through much danger and misery and now it takes its toll. He said quietly: "Lilene, my heart. You're talking nonsense. You can't leave me. I shall soon be your husband. Besides," he said, laughing to try to make her laugh, "I am now the heir to Taratamia."

"Yes," she said. Her tears stopped flowing, as if defeated. "And I am now the sole heir to Karenia."

"What?"

"Yes. It's in the new Statutes. A woman can rule. Vergon is dead, Malkar is dead. I have to go back and take the throne. Karenia is without a ruler."

He grew instantly angry and confused. "So," he said. "Let the damned dynasty die out. They're all rotten to the core, except you. Stop this. We're getting married. I've seen Ataret about it already."

"No, Ricalpa." A dead voice, dry of tears. "It is not for the dynasty. It is for the people of Karenia, who suffered so much at my instigation. The Draconhood may be destroyed, but there are still secret cells within the parliament and the priesthood, men who would seize power within a day if given a chance. Chaos will return to Karenia, worse than ever. I must stop this happening. I owe it to the people, the poor people. Oh, Ricalpa! this has broken my heart!"

Quietly he said, because he was so angry, "What do you think it has done to mine?"

She started to cry again. "Yes, weep," he said violently. "Weep for me! You've done what sword or knife or even the Draconhood couldn't do. You've killed me, Lilene."

He sprang up and caught her by the shoulders. "Did it mean so little to you? Have you forgotten? How we faced death together? How we've lain together as one body, one soul? You are my soul. You are my life. You can't do this. Not for a country, not for a people. Gods! Lilene! Have you forgotten?"

"How could I ever forget?" she whispered. Her face was milk-white, aged by grief.

He said harshly, "I would have died for you a thousand times. I loved you more than I suspect you ever knew. You can't leave me."

"I must leave you," she said. "And I feel that I shall die from it."

He walked away, and with his back to her, said: "I don't believe you ever loved me. You took all that I had, and now you're destroying it. At one time I believed you were a witch, for witches use their power to destroy. I wonder now if I was right."

"These are terrible things to say to me," she whispered.

"You are Malkar's daughter. And even now, Malkar is parting us by her death."

He felt her come up close. She leaned against his shoulder, and he felt her pain run through him like a blade.

"There is an answer," she said softly. "Come with me to Karenia, as my consort."

He swung round in a frenzy. "I can't!" he yelled. He thrust his hand, where blood was drying, under her eyes. "I signed the oath of inheritance not an hour ago! They've trapped us. Oh, Lilene . . ." and took her at last in his arms, where they wept together.

"So this is the end," he said into her hair. "I once had the notion it was too good to last. Death wouldn't have parted us. But the people of Karenia, that cursed country, are more powerful than death. They're taking the love that was mine."

"No!" she cried, standing away from him. "I love you forever. I never knew such love. I never knew such pain. It's not love for my country that's parting us."

"What is it then?" he said dully. His body hurt, as if all the words exchanged had been daggers.

"It is my duty," she said, and suddenly she seemed remote, as if they were already apart by miles.

They stared at one another, silent. A doom, a judgement, hung over them, composed of one word. Duty. He knew himself beaten, finished. All joy went from his heart, leaving him dry, like an ancient well.

He could not touch or kiss her. All that remained was to bid her farewell and this he could not do. He looked hard at her, imprinting her for the lost future. Two awful words tolled in his mind, and he gave them a voice.

He said: "Never again."

And hearing this she turned from him and threw herself face down on the bed in a storm of weeping, while he went from her and from the inn like a ghost.

It had been raining most of the day. Wet shone on the red roofs and white walls of the city. Rain dripped from the eaves of the temples and shone darkly on the pavements. It gleamed on the Lion of Stone, turning its granite the colour of onyx. The Lion suffered its drenching majestically, thinking its stone thoughts of centuries.

Tallis sat in the cave between the outstretched paws of the Lion, protected from the weather by its massive chest and neck. If he stretched his hand high enough he could touch its imperious stone beard, hanging below the great muzzle out of his sight above.

He scarcely remembered climbing the three hundred steps, until the roof of Ataret's temple diminished to a square and people in the streets below turned into insect life. Had he been told he had been there for twelve hours, he would have been surprised. He was trying desperately not to feel or to think, which was impossible, although the sanctuary of the Lion's paws seemed to contain the thoughts within the bounds of madness. Occasionally he found himself thirsty, and caught the rainwater which ran down the Lion's nose. The water tasted of granite, but it was holy. The cave where he sat was carpeted with a little sparse grass, and was a favourite summer trysting place for lovers. Many a child had been conceived up here; it was supposed to bring luck. There were various discreet scratches on the underside of the Lion's breast; pledges of love, a rough prayer set there by someone in despair. And there was a more formal legend deeply incised over the Lion's heart. It had been put there long ago by priests: the Lion's own stern motto. FAIZ A'N BALT. I make and I break.

No one could see him weep up here. That was over now; the piercing anguish had changed, had become like the onset of a slowly killing sickness. His loss brought back earlier losses: his own mother, Carilene, Colonel Tallis, General Camlot, Lepo, Andine, Barbel. They seemed to be all around him, whispering.

I MAKE AND I BREAK. He traced the legend with a finger, as dusk came down. He began to rage against the cruel caprices of life which offered rescue, hope and joy then snatched it back. Why? And the answer came clear. I perjured myself in the name of the Lion, and the Lion has turned against me.

He had a pain in his ribs and chest, and coughed at it. Perhaps I shall take a fever and die. No, that would be too easy. My fate is a life without Lilene. A life eventually spent in the court, where I can order all destinies other than my own. They will have married her to some facile prince and he will give her the children that should have been mine; and he bit his lip, opening the old scar, which bled out of the past into the future.

Lilene. Every scratch and mark on the Lion's body her name. He saw her—laughing, troubled, in fear of her life. He saw her face, contorted in ecstasy at the climax of love. The peasants in the forest, worshipping her. Her people, whom she would not desert. And the first faintest flicker of admiration for her began. *She loves me, as I love her. And her sacrifice is of such magnitude it can hardly be measured. She is right in her decision. But it has given me death in life.*

The rain stopped, the sky cleared to black. Under the Lion's jowl a bright low star gleamed. The faint city-noises below diminished. He fell into a comfortless sleep, when he dreamed of her.

He was awakened by a tumult of bells. He thought drearily that some festival must be afoot, but could not think of one. People were out in the streets early, and among them he thought he could distinguish the figure of the Newscrier who had told of Malkar's death. He sat on through the hours, oblivious. During the day further bells rang, from temple and palace. He wondered vaguely whether war had broken out again. Then, *everyone will be wondering where I am, especially the garrison. I have not made my report to the commander.* It seemed unimportant.

He moved to the front of the recess and sat beneath the Lion's nose. From here he could see couriers who came and went in haste. A large procession came from the direction of the palace. It bore the standard of Queen Sarene, the Crow of Karkis quartered with the Lion. The procession passed over the bridge and took the road south. *Holy Sarene,* he thought, *going off on pilgrimage somewhere. Pray for me, Sarene. As if you would.*

Below, there was more street life than he had seen for years. Knots of people were talking, breaking off to form other groups. He came from the cave and stood up, stiff with damp and immobility, shattered by a sudden renewal of grief. Yes, he thought. Her motives were heroic, but how could she do this to me? And thought with certainty: I shall never get over this.

He turned away from the city and walked round the Lion. He stared into the distance where, in a jagged haze of whiteness, the Towers of Kite met the clouds. Beyond lay the Far Lands. We were in the Far Lands once, she and I, here on earth. Never again. After a long while he turned and walked back. And saw suddenly, the figure reaching the top of the steps.

Small, fragile, shawled by hair of glittering sunlight, she came to him, weary from her climb, but smiling. He felt his heart stop, then race. She came to him running, and cast herself into his arms.

He clutched her to him and wept, telling himself: this is a dream. My longing invented her.

"Oh, sweet merciful gods," he whispered. "Lilene, my Lilene, my love, my darling."

She looked into his face. She was pale, her eyes were radiant, moist with past tears.

"I couldn't do it," she said. "I couldn't leave you. Not for anything. Not for the world. I love you too much. My darling. Oh, don't weep."

She raised her lovely, full, rose-pink mouth to his. He kissed her passionately, and his tears fell on her face.

She was crying too, stroking his hair, crying, "I'm sorry. I'm so sorry. Forgive me, darling."

"Oh, Lilene," he said, and tried to laugh. "Don't ever do this to me again. What you've put me through. Thank the gods my company can't see me now. Respect would be a thing of the past."

"No, no, my love," she said. She was holding him close, her soft face against his unshaven one. "You'll always have that. You're their Captain. My darling Captain."

He drew her body into his, feeling her supple warmth, saying "I've got you now. Don't ever think of leaving me again."

"I'll never leave you. I'm here forever. Yours forever. Oh, kiss me, kiss me."

When they finally drew apart, he said: "Lilene, my love, we must marry at once. We should go now and see Ataret. I think I can just walk down the steps. I feel as if I've been through a battle."

"Oh, darling, rest a little," she said, frowning in concern. "Sit with me. Hold me. I want this moment to go on. I thought it would never come again."

"I was in despair," he said, and sat with her on the stretch of grass. She slid her arms round him, and rested her head on his shoulder. "I love you," she whispered. He felt her trembling. "I couldn't live without you, without this, oh love, forgive me for hurting you. Love me now, to show you forgive me." And she lay down in his arms, her rose-and-cream breast and throat exposed, her lips parted as he bent to kiss them.

He began to tremble. He said, against her breast, "I can't wait to love you. Come below. Come to my house, my bed. I've always wanted you there . . . come, where we can be private . . ."

She pressed herself against him. "No, no," she whispered. "Now. Here." She drew him after her, away from the Lion of Stone. "We mustn't shock him, he's holy," she said, laughing a little, and Tallis, fully aroused by now, said: "Don't worry, my love, he's seen it all before . . . oh, my Lilene . . ." while she pulled him on top of her. He was ready and she said, closing her eyes in rapture, "Oh, my Captain, my darling Captain," in a sobbing voice.

She's never called me Captain before, he thought deliriously, as he opened her gown to bare her body. It seems to excite her . . . his head was a little higher than hers, his face close to her hair. And suddenly he saw a paleness at the crown, a snow-white streak like a livid scar among the gold.

The instant warning shrilled like a battle trumpet. Knowledge from somewhere outside himself came by a lightning instinct. Her arms were round his neck; he broke their hold with two swift blows from the hard edge of his hands, and she screamed. He tore himself from her. Her eyes opened wide, they were blazing, enormous. She rose up and caught at his thighs, crying piteously, and he saw in a second that the gold Lion was gone from her neck.

He came to his feet in one spring, and turning away from her beauty, kicked her hard in the side. She screamed again, this time more of a snarl, and one hand gripped his boot, while the other shot out and grasped the flap of his breeches. She was immensely strong. Throwing herself backwards she hauled him off balance and he fell on her, smothered by her hair. She locked her arms and legs around him and rammed her naked groin against his. A purr growled deep in her throat. She seized his hair and forced his mouth to hers, devouring him with her lips and tongue, while he freed one hand and clawed at her face. He caught her head and banged it on the ground, and she laughed into his face, chanting softly, "Come, my beloved, my Captain, come!" The voice was as seductive as her lascivious movements beneath him, and he knew then that he was fighting for far more than his life.

She writhed under him, gripping his thighs with hers, tearing at his clothing to bare his loins. He wrenched an arm free and struck the lovely face a terrible blow, struck the beautiful breasts to a scarlet print, and she laughed again, and crooned, while he felt her wet sex rubbing and rising to enfold him. And, horribly, even while he raged and fought her, his body remained tumescent, eager.

He turned violently on his side, breaking the contact. He found his dagger and struck her again and again in breast and throat, and where the blade entered a bloodless gash appeared and closed immediately. And the rose-mouth of the false Lilene closed over his again, and his strength ebbed and he thought: I am lost.

A mighty wind began to whirl around them where they lay, as she inched herself over his groin. There were sea-waves and darkness in the rushing wind, and voices screaming—one of them unmistakably that of Andine crying: "Avaunt, Maelikali! Back, Malkar!" so that the deathly embrace slackened a fraction and the creature's head turned momentarily to listen, and all beauty fled from the face, that was now no longer human.

A black beast with a luxuriant pelt and taloned paws held him. A white streak on its skull, a fanged mouth emitting gusts of carnivorous breath. It wound him round with the long muscle of its tail and wrapped its hind legs about his back. It was female and as mad to mate as the demoness; its hot vulva, rancid with musk, rubbed at his body. He tore at its yellow eyes, rolling over and over with it, his body's weakness fighting with his mind and spirit, fighting to stay in the world of souls, fighting for his immortality.

The panther-thing was gone and he was in the grip of a great black swan with wings like oak branches and a trail of fiery white crowning its poll. It had him down, covering him under a pall of steely feathers. It hissed and pecked him with cruel kisses. And he struggled under it, rolling away, free for an instant, rolling towards the impassive, dreaming form of the Lion of Stone. A weight leaped on his back. He lurched forward under its charge and it plunged over his shoulders—a female ape, coal-coloured, with the white line on its brow. Its strong black hands grabbed for him and he found strength to strike it in its womb. It howled terribly, its form dissolved and he was caught in the coils of a great black and silver serpent.

The rushing wind and the tumult of voices began again. The serpent's coils were hot, but he was cool and steady now, the unnatural lust gone, still battling, weak but undefeated. The serpent crushed him in her embrace and he feigned death. After a moment the pressure eased a little. He lay with closed eyes, his heart bursting, then rolled a little to the right and the snake coiled along with him. They lay at the edge of the shadow cast by the Lion of Stone. The serpent toiled amorously about him. He shot out an arm and gripped its scaly throat as it lay above him. He strangled it, and it faded beneath his fingers. The scales shivered away, and under his hand was a throat soft as a rose. He opened his eyes, and looked into the glowing amber eyes of Malkar.

Light and slim and naked, she lay above him, more beautiful, more desirable than she had ever been. She smiled, and spoke, running her fingers tenderly across his face.

"Oh, Captain, my sweet. What a brave soul you have. I always knew it. Now at last we are together. I am so looking forward to our love. You are good at love. I have watched you. This will be the best. The last, the best."

And she bent and kissed him with a kiss of sublime enchantment, so that his body swelled and hardened and his life began to rush eagerly forward towards her, like a lemming to the sea. But his soul became suddenly raging, adamant, and mastered his body with one surge of indefatigable power. He took Malkar's throat and choked her, and her face blackened and changed to that which none could witness without losing their sanity.

He fought it with closed eyes. The body was clinging slime over an armature strong as iron, the long skull of black bone bore a living vein of white The arms were dripping lianas, and bound him fast. The power was oceanic, elemental. He fought on, losing, no longer silent, but gasping curses and prayers into the unbearable face with tight-shut eyes, rocking from side to side and rolling, under the roaring tumult of the astral wind, into the embrace of dissolution and eternal damnation.

And into the great shadow of the Lion.

Anger had been building in the Lion since the Bay of Moons tragedy. Unlike its Crystal counterpart it had kept aloof, but the struggle proceeding beneath it spurred it into fury. Below its head, in immortal danger, lay Capashenet. Only a sprig of the ancient House but none the less deserving of protection.

The Lion stirred. It raised a gigantic granite paw and, like the first teasing blow a cat deals a captive mouse, flicked its stone talons down and across. A claw the length of a scimitar raked the head of darkness where the white streak bisected it. It tore into the formless brain, gouged out the cataclysm of centuries, split darkness to the core. A lightning flash like the bursting of a million suns accompanied the Lion's strike, followed by one immense thunderclap which shook the city below to its foundations.

FAIZ A'N BALT. I make and I break.

The Lion had not made darkness, but darkness was broken by it. Darkness lost its form; it flattened and liquefied, spreading outwards in a black river, thinning to ink, beginning to drip down the flight of steps, mutable, soundless, spent. Even so, it was a pollution, and the Lion roared more thunder. The clouds burst open, and a torrent washed darkness away.

The Lion surveyed Capashenet's senseless form. With a leaf-light touch of its giant paw it rolled him into the cave beneath its chest, out of the deluge. Then it settled once more into its immoveable, eternal vigilance.

The lovely ethereal sound of the evening chant coaxed him from a rich sleep. He opened his eyes. He was in the temple, lying on cushions near to the altar. It was early dusk and all around candles bloomed like flowers. He sat up, vaguely anticipating pain, but feeling strong, his body smooth as if he had been bathed. Ataret stood before him, in full priests' regalia, candlelight moving on the tattoos on his shaven head.

"What am I doing here, Ataret?" He tried to get up, but it seemed too much of an effort at the moment. "How long have I been here?"

"Long enough, Ricalpa. How do you feel?"

"Well. I feel well." Bowls of incense were burning all round him, pungent, intoxicating clouds.

"What do you remember?"

"I remember the rain. There was a storm, wasn't there?"

"Oh yes." Ataret smiled faintly. "There was a storm. Tam has not seen its like for centuries. One of my acolytes remembered seeing you climbing the mountain. He omitted to tell me for some time. We found you stark naked. Your clothes were shredded and black. Perhaps from the lightning." He raised his brows.

"I was struck by lightning?"

"If you say so." Ataret was no longer smiling. "You remember nothing else?"

"Only the rain." He looked down at himself. "Why am I wearing my uniform?"

"We sent to your house for clothing. The uniform was the handiest. Can you rise?"

"Yes." He got up and stood, resting his hand on the altar.

"I had been looking for you for hours," said Ataret. "I have something to tell you. First, my healers had to work on you very intensely."

Tallis shook his head and frowned.

"We have only just put the temple to rights," said Ataret. "It was full of the Crystal Lion's energy. So much so that many objects were smashed, several of my priests were rendered unconscious . . ."

Tallis's expression changed, became sombre. "I remember now why I went up there. For refuge from despair."

"Malkar is dead," said Ataret very softly.

"Yes, I know, and I have lost Lilene. A pity the lightning didn't finish me off."

"That is ungrateful," said Ataret severely. "Do you not want to hear my news?"

"I doubt anything could interest me, Ataret."

"Ah, but this will, Ricalpa. Astonishing, sudden news. The city's on fire with it. Listen to me. I gathered the other day you did not relish the idea of being heir to the throne."

"As if my wishes mattered. It's settled."

"Well, you are no longer the heir," said Ataret with a little triumph. "You can rest easy. Go back to the Red Royals. You're still a prince, but you're not the heir apparent. There's a better claimant coming."

Tallis stared at him.

"Didn't you hear the bells? They announce the marriage of King Valm to Mayla, Duchess of Mayt. And it will be soon, for the duchess is with child by him. The duchess's old father, who we all thought so eccentric, has scried into her, and sees a boy for certain. You're free of the future you didn't want. Your oath has been rescinded. I don't think your services will be required now. Mayla is the delight of the physicians; they've never seen a lustier young woman."

"Mayla," said Tallis in wonder.

"The king is besotted. She's been his mistress for some time. I think the queen knew. Did you see her departure?"

"She's abdicated in favour of Mayla?"

"Under the first Tamic Law, Mayla is now the principal wife. My mother the queen has expressed a desire to become the new abbess at the House of Brides. It is a solution sent by the gods. Praise the Lion!" And Ataret kissed the altar.

"Praise him," said Tallis soberly.

"You can go where you want now, Ricalpa."

"I could go to Karenia."

"It would not be my choice. But yes, my brother, you could."

"Ataret," said Tallis suddenly. "I want you to hear my confession."

"O Lion, be with us."

Tallis knelt. He made his brief confession and waited. Ataret frowned. "You have broken a sacred law, my son. Maybe the Lion will punish you."

"He has done so."

"If you think you have sinned, you must make restitution. Give up something dear."

"It is done."

"Then go in peace. Ricalpa. Go home!"

Tallis kissed the altar, and bowed to Ataret. He walked steadily from the temple into the clear evening.

Ataret turned to his chief priest.

"He remembers nothing. His mind has been wiped clean. He need never know that his soul was half out of his body. The Lion is merciful. Let us now give thanks that we are liberated from darkness."

Tallis found his mare, tethered outside the temple, and mounted her. He took his homeward road. He was thinking deeply.

I can still have her. I can live with her in Karenia, if it is not already too late. It will mean leaving the Red Royals, my house, my city, my country. Beloved, glorious Taratamia. To live in Karenia, with its long history of ill-doing and sorcery and blood, my country's old enemy, where my father—where Colonel Tallis died. Lilene will initiate her reforms, certainly, she will work to the bone for them if I know her at all. But a Tamian consort on the Oyster Throne will not please the nation. Blood-soaked Karenia was always ill-luck to me.

Yet Karenia led me to Lilene.

Glorious Taratamia! whose anthem warms my blood with pride. My roots are deep. My life is pledged to defend Taratamia. Can I give her up for love?

It would wash me clean of my false oath. And I love Lilene more than anything in the universe. I should not even be hesitating.

He felt tired now, his ribs hurt, but his mind was steady. *I must find her. It will be a hard road to ride.* He went through the city. The river had burst its banks for the second time in a year. People were going to bed, lamps were being extinguished as dusk intensified. He rode past the east gate, where a burst of raucous laughter came from the Crescent Moon, and he thought of the times spent there with Lepo. *Time and change,* he thought. *There's one thing that never changes. How I want my girl.*

The new Queen of Karenia was preparing to hold her first audience prior to coronation. She sat in the antechamber of the Hall of the Sea, almost invisible among the throng jostling to serve her. They had come from all over the Court, officials, servants, waiting-women, in an unquestioning homage not far removed from joy. As yet uncrowned but breathtaking in her magnificence, she sat quietly while the finishing touches were put to her splendour.

She seemed to those around her to have grown taller. Her eyes were very bright. Her shining hair was looped and garlanded with pearls, hanging low on her pale forehead.

Her velvet gown was brocaded with ten thousand pearls, and on her fingers were more pearls, amethysts, sea-emeralds. A great ruby lay on her breast, partially obscuring the tiny gold Lion on its chain. Later, the Lion would supersede all other jewels, but that time was to come. Later she would dismantle the Oyster throne and replace it with a subtle frieze of lions. The Lion-power was in her. Those about her recognized it only as a force-field which tingled their hands as they touched her in reverence. Its shining was invisible to them and so would remain during the long days of her power.

Power poured from her. It was definite and limitless. She had wasted no time in the preparation of its exercise. She had, through the visions of her renewed spirit, searched the hearts of councillors and ministers. She knew whom she could trust, and those whom she would presently cast down. Her mind was crystalline, unerring in its judgement. It mapped out guidelines which had lain waiting for her most of her life, invisible counsellors, silent until now, lay in her heart and under her tongue. The reforms she would command were ranked like soldiers of the future. There was personal reward too. Soon she would marry, bear sons into this reformation. And soon, Karenia would throw off its grim history and begin to smile, as she now smiled her regal smile.

Music, imperial, soft, came to her from the Hall of the Sea. Slowly she rose and the courtiers fell back before her.

"It is time," she said.

"All await your Serene Majesty."

It was a new, apt title, for serenity was the key to her. An unfamiliar, awesome serenity. A crystal army defending her. They were calling for her; her name rebounded from the walls like shards of crystal. To a young man she said:—

"Then we will receive their homage. Wait:—"

"Majesty?"

"You have made certain my little sister has been informed? I believe she has suffered much."

"You need have no fear on that score, majesty. A relay of fast couriers was sent, the moment your majesty set her hand upon the throne."

She smiled at him sweetly. "Then all's well. Come, Lord Dogmar, you shall bear my train."

They flung open the doors. The crying of her name was the breaking of a wave.

Music. Then: "May the gods bless Queen Honyia! Hail to Queen Honyia!"

He came to his house and rode up the path, which was slightly overgrown with weeds. The mare's hooves made no sound. No one was expecting him. No grooms came from the back of the house. He dismounted and let the mare eat grass in the dim dusk. He set his hand on the front door. This would have been our house, hers and mine. I shall need to dismiss my servants. Some of them have been with me for years. In the morning I must make ready to leave for Karenia. Tonight I must rest. He pushed the door and went in.

Palbo greeted him, whining softly. He seemed to want to be outside, so Tallis opened the door for him and he crawled away to lie on the path. The house seemed deserted, though a very faint murmur came from the servants' quarters. He let them be; he wanted to talk to no one tonight. It was almost totally dark in the hall, but faint light came from above. He went to the foot of the stairs and looked up. At the bend in the staircase someone had placed a lantern.

Then he saw the rose silk cloak flung over the newel post at the stairfoot.

He went up the stairs in the space of three heartbeats. Outside the door to his bedchamber lay another token, a pair of rose silk slippers neatly side by side as if left by someone approaching a temple.

Trembling, he entered the very masculine chamber where even Pancora had never been; a chamber hung with swords and flags, furnished with a large oak bed. Lilene was in his bed.

Her hair drew all the gold light from nearby candles. Her bare arm was flung up on the pillow. She was deeply asleep.

All strength went out of him. He sat down as gently as possible on the bottom of the bed, and leaned his back against one of its lower posts. He sat and watched her sleeping, with a look of such unutterable tenderness that it lit him from within, like the candlelight.

He saw that something lay under her hand. Her fingers were spread out over it, holding it firmly down as something precious. It was a letter, the parchment sealed with the Royal Arms of Karenia. He let her sleep on, until the vibration of his loving look awakened her, and she opened her eyes, opened her arms to him, and she was warm, like a gentle flame bathing every one of his wounds, the old and the new.

They did not speak for a long time; there was no need, nor were they able. Then she whispered: "I waited so long. I thought you'd never come."

"I'm here, you're here. My love, my only love."

"In our house."

"Yes, in our house. Oh, my Lilene. The Lion has forgiven me."

"Forgiven you? For what?"

And he told her about it. She began to laugh, softly then merrily, clasping him, kissing him, her eyes shining.

"It's no laughing matter, my love."

"But you spoke the truth. There was no blasphemy. I was with child by you. I am with child by you. I wasn't sure, but now I am. I'm so happy, Ricalpa."

Much later, he said: "Then why did the Lion put us through all this pain?" He was lying beside her, holding her so close that she could only answer against his lips:

"The Lion was testing us, Ricalpa. And we have passed the test."

Before they slept, entwined, he rose and took a lantern and set it in the window.

"For protection, Ricalpa? There is nothing more to fear."
"No, my darling. To honour the Lion of Night."

Epilogue

Palbo had lain on the path outside the house for hours. He knew there was a rug and supper waiting for him in the stable. He also knew he had to wait, and that the waiting was almost over. He raised his long head from his sore old paws. His nose, the most efficient part of his ancient body, caught scent, and his tail thumped on the path.

Slowly, through the first glimmers of dawn, came a strange figure approaching with utmost weariness in tattered boots patched from inside with clumps of grass. The remnants of its silk breeches clung to its dirty knees; its cloak was a grain sack. Its hanging hair was a mixture of gold and mud. The figure sank down to Palbo's level. Arms went round him, and a voice he knew and liked much spoke in his ear.

"Dear old Palbo," said Barbel. "I feel as old as you, today."

Palbo raised his rheumy eyes making sure of her in the gloom.

"You want to hear about it?" said Barbel wearily. "About the river—how I went down, down until I thought I'd never come up? And do you know I would be drowned but there were a lot of skellingtons underneath and they all floated up and pushed me to the top—wasn't that nice? and there was a grain barge I clung to that was going to Tamia—wasn't that lucky

Palbo? and they were nice, very nice. But they only took me to the Bay of Moons, and it was slow, and I had to walk the rest of the way. And I'm tired. Oh, Palbo—is everyone all right?"

Palbo beat his tail enthusiastically on the path. He stood up and Barbel, clinging to his fur from tiredness, rose too. She looked up at the Captain's house. She smiled.

"There's a light in the window," said Barbel. "We've all come home."

ABOUT THE AUTHOR

Rosemary Hawley Jarman was born in Worcester, England and came to fame in 1971 with her novel *We Speak No Treason*. Reprinted many times, the book's hero is the much maligned King Richard III. It sold 30,000 copies in its first week of publication, and gained her the prestigious Author's Club Silver Quill for best first novel, while in the U.S.A. she was nominated as a Daughter of Mark Twain. Further equally successful novels followed, also an illustrated account of the Battle of Agincourt. She lives in an antique stone cottage between sea and mountain in West Wales. *The Captain's Witch* is her first fantasy novel, and she is now working on a sequel.

Her website is: www.rosemaryhawleyjarman.com